STATE of FEAR

Also by Michael Crichton

Fiction

The Andromeda Strain
The Terminal Man
The Great Train Robbery
Eaters of the Dead
Congo
Sphere
Jurassic Park
Rising Sun
Disclosure
The Lost World
Airframe
Timeline
Prey

Non-fiction

Five Patients
Jasper Johns
Electronic Life
Travels

MICHAEL CRICHTON

STATE OF FEAR

HarperCollins*Publishers*

HarperCollins*Publishers*
77–85 Fulham Palace Road,
Hammersmith, London W6 8JB

www.harpercollins.co.uk

Published by HarperCollins*Publishers* 2004
1

A catalogue record for this book
is available from the British Library

ISBN 0 00 718159 0
ISBN 0 00 718161 2 (trade paperback)

Printed and bound in Great Britain by
Clays Limited, St Ives plc

This is a work of fiction. Characters, corporations, institutions, and organizations in this novel are the product of the author's imagination, or, if real, are used fictitiously without any intent to describe their actual conduct. However, references to real people, institutions, and organizations that are documented in footnotes are accurate. Footnotes are real.

There is something fascinating about science. One gets such wholesale returns of conjecture out of such a trifling investment of fact.

— MARK TWAIN

Within any important issue, there are always aspects no one wishes to discuss.

— GEORGE ORWELL

INTRODUCTION

In late 2003, at the Sustainable Earth Summit conference in Johannesburg, the Pacific island nation of Vanutu announced that it was preparing a lawsuit against the Environmental Protection Agency of the United States over global warming. Vanutu stood only a few feet above sea level, and the island's eight thousand inhabitants were in danger of having to evacuate their country because of rising sea levels caused by global warming. The United States, the largest economy in the world, was also the largest emitter of carbon dioxide and therefore the largest contributor to global warming.

The National Environmental Resource Fund, an American activist group, announced that it would join forces with Vanutu in the lawsuit, which was expected to be filed in the summer of 2004. It was rumored that wealthy philanthropist George Morton, who frequently backed environmental causes, would personally finance the suit, expected to cost more than $8 million. Since the suit would ultimately be heard by the sympathetic Ninth Circuit in San Francisco, the litigation was awaited with some anticipation.

But the lawsuit was never filed.

No official explanation for the failure to file has ever been given either by Vanutu or NERF. Even after the sudden disappearance of George Morton, an inexplicable lack of interest by the media has left the circumstances surrounding this lawsuit unexamined. Not until the end of 2004 did several former NERF board members begin to speak publicly about what had happened within that organization. Further revelations by Morton's staff, as well as by former members of the Los Angeles law firm of Hassle and Black, have added further detail to the story.

Thus it is now clear what happened to the progress of the Vanutu litigation between May and October of 2004, and why so many people died in remote parts of the world as a result.

MC
Los Angeles, 2004

STATE OF FEAR

From the Internal Report to the National Security Council (NSC) from the AASBC (Classified). Redacted portions from AASBC. Obtained FOIA 03/04/04.

In retrospect the ▓▓▓▓▓▓▓ conspiracy was extremely well-planned. Preparations were under way for more than a year before the events themselves took place. There were preliminary ▓▓▓▓▓ as early as March ▓▓ 2003, and reports to the British ▓▓▓▓ ▓▓▓▓ and the German ▓▓ ▓▓▓▓.

The first incident took place in Paris, in May of 2004. It is ▓▓ ▓▓▓▓ ▓▓▓▓ that the authorities ▓▓▓▓▓▓ But there now can be no doubt that what happened in Paris ▓▓▓▓▓, and the serious consequences that followed.

1

AKAMAI

In the darkness, he touched her arm and said, "Stay here." She did not move, just waited. The smell of salt water was strong. She heard the faint gurgle of water.

Then the lights came on, reflecting off the surface of a large open tank, perhaps fifty meters long and twenty meters wide. It might have been an indoor swimming pool, except for all the electronic equipment that surrounded it.

And the very strange device at the far end of the pool.

Jonathan Marshall came back to her, grinning like an idiot. "*Qu'est-ce que tu penses?*" he said, though he knew his pronunciation was terrible. "What do you think?"

"It is magnificent," the girl said. When she spoke English, her accent sounded exotic. In fact, everything about her was exotic, Jonathan thought. With her dark skin, high cheekbones, and black hair, she might have been a model. And she strutted like a model in her short skirt and spike heels. She was half Vietnamese, and her name was Marisa. "But no one else is here?" she said, looking around.

"No, no," he said. "It's Sunday. No one is coming."

Jonathan Marshall was twenty-four, a graduate student in physics from London, working for the summer at the ultra-modern Laboratoire Ondulatoire—the wave mechanics laboratory—of the French Marine

Institute in Vissy, just north of Paris. But the suburb was mostly the residence of young families, and it had been a lonely summer for Marshall. Which was why he could not believe his good fortune at meeting this girl. This extraordinarily beautiful and sexy girl.

"Show me what it does, this machine," Marisa said. Her eyes were shining. "Show me what it is you do."

"My pleasure," Marshall said. He moved to the large control panel and began to switch on the pumps and sensors. The thirty panels of the wave machine at the far end of the tank clicked, one after another.

He glanced back at her, and she smiled at him. "It is so complicated," she said. She came and stood beside him at the control panel. "Your research is recorded on cameras?"

"Yes, we have cameras in the ceiling, and on the sides of the tank. They make a visual record of the waves that are generated. We also have pressure sensors in the tanks that record pressure parameters of the passing wave."

"These cameras are on now?"

"No, no," he said. "We don't need them; we're not doing an experiment."

"Perhaps we are," she said, resting her hand on his shoulder. Her fingers were long and delicate. She had beautiful fingers.

She watched for a minute, then said, "This room, everything is so expensive. You must have great security, no?"

"Not really," he said. "Just cards to get in. And only one security camera." He gestured over his shoulder. "That one back in the corner."

She turned to look. "And that is turned on?" she said.

"Oh yes," he said. "That's always on."

She slid her hand to caress his neck lightly. "So is someone watching us now?"

"Afraid so."

"Then we should behave."

"Probably. Anyway, what about your boyfriend?"

"Him." She gave a derisive snort. "I have had enough of him."

• • •

Earlier that day, Marshall had gone from his small apartment to the café on rue Montaigne, the café he went to every morning, taking a journal article with him to read as usual. Then this girl had sat down at the next table, with her boyfriend. The couple had promptly fallen into an argument.

In truth, Marshall felt that Marisa and the boyfriend didn't seem to belong together. He was American, a beefy, red-faced fellow built like a footballer, with longish hair and wire-frame glasses that did not suit his thick features. He looked like a pig trying to appear scholarly.

His name was Jim, and he was angry with Marisa, apparently because she had spent the previous night away from him. "I don't know why you won't tell me where you were," he kept repeating.

"It is none of your business, that's why."

"But I thought we were going to have dinner together."

"Jimmy, I told you we were not."

"No, you told me you were. And I was waiting at the hotel for you. All night."

"So? No one made you. You could go out. Enjoy yourself."

"But I was waiting for you."

"Jimmy, you do not own me." She was exasperated by him, sighing, throwing up her hands, or slapping her bare knees. Her legs were crossed, and the short skirt rode up high. "I do as I please."

"That's clear."

"Yes," she said, and at that moment she turned to Marshall and said, "What is that you are reading? It looks very complicated."

At first Marshall was alarmed. She was clearly talking to him to taunt the boyfriend. He did not want to be drawn into the couple's dispute.

"It's physics," he said briefly, and turned slightly away. He tried to ignore her beauty.

"What kind of physics?" she persisted.

"Wave mechanics. Ocean waves."

"So, you are a student?"

"Graduate student."

"Ah. And clearly intelligent. You are English? Why are you in France?"

And before he knew it, he was talking to her, and she introduced the boyfriend, who gave Marshall a smirk and a limp handshake. It was still very uncomfortable, but the girl behaved as if it were not.

"So you work around here? What sort of work? A tank with a machine? Really, I can't imagine what you say. Will you show me?"

And now they were here, in the wave mechanics laboratory. And Jimmy, the boyfriend, was sulking in the parking lot outside, smoking a cigarette.

"What shall we do about Jimmy?" she said, standing beside Marshall while he worked at the control panel.

"He can't smoke in here."

"I will see that he does not. But I don't want to make him more angry. Can I let him in, do you think?"

Marshall felt disappointment flood through him. "Sure. I guess."

Then she squeezed his shoulder. "Don't worry, he is busy later with other business of his."

She went and opened the door at the back of the lab, and Jimmy came in. Marshall glanced back and saw him hanging back, hands in his pockets. Marisa came up to stand beside Marshall again, at the control panel.

"He's all right," she said. "Now show me."

The electric motors at the far end of the tank whirred, and the wave paddles generated the first wave. It was a small wave, and it rippled smoothly down the length of the tank, to splash on a slanted panel at the near end.

"So, this is a tidal wave?" she said.

"It is a simulation of a tsunami, yes," Marshall said, his fingers tapping the keyboard. On the control panel, displays showed temperature and pressure, generated false-color images of the wave.

"A simulation," she said. "Meaning what?"

"We can make waves up to one meter high in this tank," Marshall said. "But the real tsunamis are four, eight, ten meters high. Occasionally even more."

"A wave in the ocean that is ten meters?" Her eyes widened. "Really?" She was looking toward the ceiling, trying to imagine it.

Marshall nodded. That would be over thirty feet high, the height of a three-story building. And it would be moving at eight hundred kilometers an hour, roaring up to the shore.

"And when it comes to the shore?" she said. "Is that the slope at this end? It looks like a pebble texture on it. Is that the shore?"

"That's right," Marshall said. "How high the wave goes up the shore is a function of the angle of the slope. We can adjust the slope to any angle."

The boyfriend came forward, moving closer to the tank, but still he hung back. He never said a word.

Marisa was excited. "You can adjust it? How?"

"It is motorized."

"To any angle?" She giggled. "Show me *vingt-sept* degrees. Twenty-seven."

"Coming up." Marshall typed at the keyboard. With a slight grinding sound, the slope of the shore angled higher.

The American boyfriend went closer to the tank to look, drawn by the activity. It *was* fascinating, Marshall thought. Anybody would be interested. But the guy never spoke. He just stood and watched the pebbled surface tilt. Soon it stopped.

"So that is the slope?" she said.

"Yes," Marshall said. "Although in point of fact, twenty-seven degrees is fairly steep, more than the average shoreline in the real world. Maybe I should set it to—"

Her dark hand closed over his. "No, no," she said. Her skin was soft. "Leave it. Show me a wave. I want to see a wave."

Small waves were being generated every thirty seconds. They rippled along the length of the tank, with a slight whoosh. "Well, I first have to know the shape of the shoreline. Right now, it's flat beach, but if it was an inlet of some kind . . ."

"Will it change to make an inlet?"

"Of course."

"Really? Show me."

"What kind of inlet do you want? A harbor, a river, a bay . . ."

"Oh," she said, shrugging, "make a bay."

He smiled. "Fine. How big?"

With the whir of electric motors, the shoreline began to sink into a curve, the slope indenting into a bowl.

"Fantastic," she said. "Come on, Jonathan, show me the wave."

"Not yet. How big is the bay?"

"Oh . . ." She gestured in the air. "One mile. A bay of one mile. Now will you show me?" She leaned toward him. "I do not like to wait. You should know this."

He smelled her perfume. He typed quickly. "Here it comes," he said. "A big wave, coming into a one-mile bay, with a twenty-seven-degree slope."

There was a much louder whoosh as the next wave was generated at the far end of the tank, and then it rippled smoothly toward them, a raised line of water about six inches high.

"Oh!" Marisa pouted. "You promised me it would be *big*."

"Just wait," he said.

"It will grow?" she said, giggling. She put her hand on his shoulder again. Then the American glanced back, and gave her a dirty look. She jerked her chin in the air, defiant. But when he looked back at the tank, she took her hand away.

Marshall felt despondent again. She was just using him, he was a pawn in this game between them.

"You said it will grow?" she said.

"Yes," Marshall said, "the wave will grow as it comes to the shore. In deep water a tsunami is small, but in shallow water it builds. And the inlet will concentrate its power, so it goes higher."

The wave rose higher, and then smashed against the curved shore at the near end. It foamed white, and sloshed up the sides of the shore. It came up about five feet, he guessed.

"So it comes high," she said. "In the real world?"

"That's about forty, fifty feet," he said. "Fifteen meters."

"Ooh la la," she said, pursing her lips. "So a person cannot run away from this."

"Oh no," Marshall said. "You can't outrun a tidal wave. There was a wave in Hilo, Hawaii, in 1957, came right down the streets of the town, tall as the buildings, people ran from it but—"

"So that's it?" the American said. "That's all it does?" His voice was growly, like he needed to clear his throat.

"Don't mind him," she said quietly.

"Yes, that's what we do here," Marshall said. "We generate waves—"

"Jesus fucking A," the American said. "I could do that in my bathtub when I was six months old."

"Well," Marshall said, gesturing to the control panel, and the monitors displaying data, "we generate a lot of databases for researchers around the world who are—"

"Yeah, yeah. That's enough. Boring as whale shit. I'm leaving. You coming, Marisa, or not?" He stood and glared at her.

Marshall heard her suck in her breath.

"No," she said. "I am not."

The American turned and walked off, slamming the door loudly as he left.

Her apartment was just across the river from Notre Dame, and from the balcony in the bedroom he had a beautiful view of the cathedral, which was lighted at night. It was ten o'clock, but there was still a deep blue in the sky. He looked down at the street below, the lights of the cafés, the crowds walking on the streets. It was a busy and glamorous scene.

"Don't worry," she said, behind him. "If you're looking for Jimmy, he won't come here."

Actually, the thought hadn't occurred to him, until she mentioned it. "No?"

"No," she said. "He will go elsewhere. Jimmy has many women." She took a sip of red wine, then set the glass down on the bedside table. Unceremoniously, she pulled her top over her head and dropped her skirt. She was wearing nothing beneath.

Still in her high heels, she walked toward him. He must have seemed surprised, because she said, "I told you: I do not like to wait," and threw her arms around him and kissed him hard, fiercely, almost angrily. The next moments were awkward, trying to kiss while she tore off his clothes. She was breathing hard, almost panting. She never spoke. She was so passionate she seemed almost angry, and her beauty, the physical perfection of her dark body, intimidated him, but not for long.

Afterward she lay against him, her skin soft but her body taut beneath the surface. The bedroom ceiling had a soft glow from the church façade opposite. He was relaxed, but she seemed, if anything, to be energized, restless after making love. He wondered if she had really come, despite her moans and her final cries. And then abruptly, she got up.

"Anything wrong?"

She took a sip of wine. "To the toilet," she said, and turned away, passing through a door. She had left her wineglass. He sat up and took a sip, seeing the delicate pattern of her lipstick on the rim.

He looked at the bed and saw the dark streaks on the sheets from her heels. She had not taken them off until midway through their love-making. Now the heels were tossed away, coming to a stop beneath the window. Signs of their passion. He still felt, even now, as if he were in a dream. He had never been with a woman like this. Beautiful like this, living in a place like this. He wondered how much this apartment cost, the wood paneling, the perfect location . . .

He took another sip of wine. He could get used to this, he thought.

He heard water running in the bathroom. A humming sound, a tuneless song.

With a *bang!* the front door slammed open and three men burst into the bedroom. They were wearing dark raincoats and hats. Terrified, Marshall set the wineglass on the table—it fell—and dived for his clothes beside the bed to cover himself, but in an instant the men were on him, grabbing him with gloved hands. He yelled in alarm and panic as they threw him over, shoving him facedown on the bed. He was still yelling as they pushed his face into a pillow. He thought they were going to suffocate him, but they didn't. One man hissed, "Be quiet. Nothing will happen if you are quiet."

He didn't believe him, so he struggled, calling out again. Where was Marisa? What was she doing? It was happening so fast. One man was sitting on his back, knees digging into his spine, his cold shoes on Marshall's bare buttocks. He felt the man's hand on his neck, shoving him into the bed.

"Be quiet!" the man hissed again.

The other men had each taken one of his wrists, and they were pulling his arms wide, spread-eagling him on the bed. *They were getting ready to do something to him.* He felt terrified and vulnerable. He moaned, and somebody hit him on the back of the head. "Quiet!"

Everything was happening quickly, it was all impressionistic. Where was Marisa? Probably hiding in the bathroom, and he couldn't blame her. He heard a sloshing sound and saw a plastic baggie and something white in it, like a golf ball. They were placing the baggie under his armpit, on the fleshy part of his arm.

What the hell were they doing? He felt the water cold against his underarm, and he struggled but they held him tight, and then inside the water, something soft pressed against the arm, and he had a *sticky* sensation, like sticky chewing gum, something sticky and tugging against the flesh of his arm, and then he felt a little pinch. Nothing, hardly noticeable, a momentary sting.

The men were moving quickly, the baggie was removed, and at that

moment he heard two surprisingly loud gunshots and Marisa was screaming in rapid French—*"Salaud! Salopard! Bouge-toi le cul!"*—and the third
man had tumbled off Marshall's back and fallen to the ground, then scrambled up, and Marisa was still screaming, there were more shots, and he
could smell powder in the air, and the men fled. The door slammed, and
she came back, stark naked, babbling in French he could not understand,
something about *vacherie*, which he thought was a cow but he wasn't thinking straight. He was starting to tremble on the bed.

She came over and threw her arms around him. The barrel of the gun
was hot and he yelled, and she set it aside. "Oh Jonathan, I am so sorry,
so sorry." She cradled his head against her shoulder. "Please, you must
forgive me, it is all right now, I promise you."

Gradually his trembling stopped, and she looked at him. "Did they
hurt you?"

He shook his head, no.

"Good. I did not think so. Idiots! Friends of Jimmy, they think they
make a joke, to scare you. And me I am sure. But you are not hurt?"

He shook his head again. He coughed. "Perhaps," he said, finding his
voice at last. "Perhaps I should be going."

"Oh, no," she said. "No, no, you cannot do this to me."

"I don't feel—"

"Absolutely no," she said. She pushed closer to him, so her body was
touching his. "You must stay a while."

"Should we call the police?"

"*Mais non.* The police will do nothing. A quarrel of lovers. In France
we do not do this, call the police."

"But they broke in . . ."

"They are gone now," she said, whispering in his ear. He felt her
breath. "There is only us, now. Only us, Jonathan." Her dark body slid
down his chest.

It was after midnight when he was finally dressed and standing at the
window, looking out at Notre Dame. The streets were still crowded.

"Why will you not stay?" she said, pouting prettily. "I want you to stay. Don't you want to please me?"

"I'm sorry," he said. "I have to go. I don't feel very well."

"I will make you feel better."

He shook his head. In truth, he really did not feel well. He was experiencing waves of dizziness, and his legs felt oddly weak. His hands were trembling as he gripped the balcony.

"I'm sorry," he said again. "I have to leave."

"All right, then I will drive you."

Her car, he knew, was parked on the other side of the Seine. It seemed far to walk. But he just nodded numbly. "All right," he said.

She was in no rush. They strolled arm in arm, like lovers, along the embankment. They passed the houseboat restaurants tied up to the side, brightly lit, still busy with guests. Above them, on the other side of the river, rose Notre Dame, brilliantly lit. For a while, this slow walk, with her head on his shoulder, the soft words she spoke to him, made him feel better.

But soon he stumbled, feeling a kind of clumsy weakness coursing through his body. His mouth was very dry. His jaw felt stiff. It was difficult to speak.

She did not seem to notice. They had moved past the bright lights now, under one of the bridges, and he stumbled again. This time he fell on the stone embankment.

"My darling," she said, worried and solicitous, and helped him to his feet.

He said, "I think . . . I think . . ."

"Darling, are you all right?" She helped him to a bench, away from the river. "Here, just sit here for a moment. You will feel better in a moment."

But he did not feel better. He tried to protest, but he could not speak. In horror he realized he could not even shake his head. *Something was very wrong.* His whole body was growing weak, swiftly and astonishingly weak, and he tried to push up from the bench, but he could not move his limbs, he could not move his head. He looked at her, sitting beside him.

"Jonathan, what is wrong? Do you need a doctor?"

Yes, I need a doctor, he thought.

"Jonathan, this is not right . . ."

His chest was heavy. He was having trouble breathing. He looked away, staring straight ahead. He thought in horror: *I am paralyzed.*

"Jonathan?"

He tried to look at her. But now he could not even move his eyes. He could only look straight forward. His breathing was shallow.

"Jonathan?"

I need a doctor.

"Jonathan, can you look at me? Can you? No? You cannot turn your head?"

Somehow, her voice did not sound concerned. She sounded detached, clinical. Perhaps his hearing was affected. There was a rushing sound in his ears. It was harder and harder to breathe.

"All right, Jonathan, let's get you away from here."

She ducked her head under his arm and with surprising strength got him to his feet. His body was loose and floppy, sagging around her. He could not control where he looked. He heard the clicking of footsteps approaching and thought, *Thank God.* He heard a man's voice say in French, "Mademoiselle, do you need help?"

"Thank you, but no," she said. "Just too much to drink."

"Are you sure?"

"He does this all the time."

"Yes?"

"I can manage."

"Ah. Then I wish you *bonne nuit.*"

"*Bonne nuit,*" she said.

She continued on her way, carrying him. The footsteps became fainter. Then she paused, turned to look in all directions. And now . . . *she was moving him toward the river.*

"You are heavier than I thought," she said, in a conversational tone.

He felt a deep and profound terror. He was completely paralyzed. He could do nothing. His own feet were scraping over the stone.

Toward the river.

"I am sorry," she said, and she dropped him into the water.

It was a short fall, and a stunning sense of cold. He plunged beneath the surface, surrounded by bubbles and green, then black. He could not move, even in the water. He could not believe this was happening to him, he could not believe that he was dying this way.

Then slowly, he felt his body rise. Green water again, and then he broke the surface, on his back, turning slowly.

He could see the bridge, and the black sky, and Marisa, standing on the embankment. She lit a cigarette and stared at him. She had one hand on her hip, one leg thrust forward, a model's pose. She exhaled, smoke rising in the night.

Then he sank beneath the surface again, and he felt the cold and the blackness close in around him.

At three o'clock in the morning the lights snapped on in the Laboratoire Ondulatoire of the French Marine Institute, in Vissy. The control panel came to life. The wave machine began to generate waves that rolled down the tank, one after another, and crashed against the artificial shore. The control screens flashed three-dimensional images, scrolled columns of data. The data was transmitted to an unknown location somewhere in France.

At four o'clock, the control panel went dark, and the lights went out, and the hard drives erased any record of what had been done.

The twisting jungle road lay in shadow beneath the canopy of the Malay rain forest. The paved road was very narrow, and the Land Cruiser careened around the corners, tires squealing. In the passenger seat, a bearded man of forty glanced at his watch. "How much farther?"

"Just a few minutes," the driver said, not slowing. "We're almost there."

The driver was Chinese but he spoke with a British accent. His name was Charles Ling and he had flown over from Hong Kong to Kuala Lumpur the night before. He had met his passenger at the airport that morning, and they had been driving at breakneck speed ever since.

The passenger had given Ling a card that read "Allan Peterson, Seismic Services, Calgary." Ling didn't believe it. He knew perfectly well that there was a company in Alberta, ELS Engineering, that sold this equipment. It wasn't necessary to come all the way to Malaysia to see it.

Not only that, but Ling had checked the passenger manifest on the incoming flight, and there was no Allan Peterson listed. So this guy had come in on a different name.

Furthermore, he told Ling he was a field geologist doing independent consulting for energy companies in Canada, mostly evaluating potential oil sites. But Ling didn't believe that, either. You could spot those petroleum engineers a mile off. This guy wasn't one.

So Ling didn't know who the guy was. It didn't bother him. Mr. Peterson's credit was good; the rest was none of Ling's business. He had only one interest today, and that was to sell cavitation machines. And this looked like a big sale: Peterson was talking about three units, more than a million dollars in total.

He turned off the road abruptly, onto a muddy rut. They bounced through the jungle beneath huge trees, and suddenly came out into sunlight and a large opening. There was a huge semicircular gash in the ground, exposing a cliff of gray earth. A green lake lay below.

"What's this?" Peterson said, wincing.

"It was open-face mine, abandoned now. Kaolin."

"Which is . . . ?"

Ling thought, this is no geologist. He explained that kaolin was a mineral in clay. "It's used in paper and ceramics. Lot of industrial ceramics now. They make ceramic knives, incredibly sharp. They'll make ceramic auto engines soon. But the quality here was too low. It was abandoned four years ago."

Peterson nodded. "And where is the cavitator?"

Ling pointed toward a large truck parked at the edge of the cliff. "There." He drove toward it.

"Russians make it?"

"The vehicle and the carbon-matrix frame are Russian made. The electronics come from Taiwan. We assemble ourselves, in Kuala Lumpur."

"And is this your biggest model?"

"No, this is the intermediate. We don't have the largest one to show you."

They pulled alongside the truck. It was the size of a large earthmover; the cab of the Land Cruiser barely reached above the huge tires. In the center, hanging above the ground, was a large rectangular cavitation generator, looking like an oversize diesel generator, a boxy mass of pipes and wires. The curved cavitation plate was slung underneath, a few feet above the ground.

They climbed out of the car into sweltering heat. Ling's eyeglasses clouded over. He wiped them on his shirt. Peterson walked around the truck. "Can I get the unit without the truck?"

"Yes, we make transportable units. Seagoing containers. But usually clients want them mounted on vehicles eventually."

"I just want the units," Peterson said. "Are you going to demonstrate?"

"Right away," Ling said. He gestured to the operator, high up in the cab. "Perhaps we should step away."

"Wait a minute," Peterson said, suddenly alarmed. "I thought we were going to be alone. Who is that?"

"That's my brother," Ling said smoothly. "He's very trustworthy."

"Well . . ."

"Let's step away," Ling said. "We can see better from a distance."

The cavitation generator fired up, chugging loudly. Soon the noise blended with another sound, a deep humming that Ling always seemed to feel in his chest, in his bones.

Peterson must have felt it, too, because he moved back hastily.

"These cavitation generators are hypersonic," Ling explained, "producing a radially symmetric cavitation field that can be adjusted for focal point, rather like an optical lens, except we are using sound. In other words, we can focus the sound beam, and control how deep the cavitation will occur."

He waved to the operator, who nodded. The cavitation plate came down, until it was just above the ground. The sound changed, becoming deeper and much quieter. The earth vibrated slightly where they were standing.

"Jesus," Peterson said, stepping back.

"Not to worry," Ling said. "This is just low-grade reflection. The main energy vector is orthogonal, directed straight down."

About forty feet below the truck, the walls of the canyon suddenly seemed to blur, to become indistinct. Small clouds of gray smoke obscured the surface for a moment, and then a whole section of cliff gave way, and rumbled down into the lake below, like a gray avalanche. The whole area filled with smoke and dust.

As it began to clear, Ling said, "Now we will show how the beam is focused." The rumbling began again, and this time the cliff blurred much farther down, two hundred feet or more. Once again the gray sand gave way, this time sliding rather quietly into the lake.

"And it can focus laterally as well?" Peterson said.

Ling said it could. A hundred yards north of the truck, the cliff was shaken free, and again tumbled down.

"We can aim it in any direction, and any depth."

"Any depth?"

"Our big unit will focus at a thousand meters. Although no client has any use for such depths."

"No, no," Peterson said. "We don't need anything like that. But we want beam power." He wiped his hands on his trousers. "I've seen enough."

"Really? We have quite a few other techniques to demon—"

"I'm ready to go back." Behind his sunglasses, his eyes were unreadable.

"Very well," Ling said. "If you are sure—"

"I'm sure."

Driving back, Peterson said, "You ship from KL or Hong Kong?"

"From KL."

"With what restrictions?"

Ling said, "How do you mean?"

"Hypersonic cavitation technology in the US is restricted. It can't be exported without a license."

"As I said, we use Taiwanese electronics."

"Is it as reliable as the US technology?"

Ling said, "Virtually identical." If Peterson knew his business, he would know that the US had long ago lost the capacity to manufacture such advanced chipsets. The US cavitation chipsets were manufactured in Taiwan. "Why do you ask? Are you planning to export to the US?"

"No."

"Then there is no difficulty."

"What's your lead time?" Peterson said.

"We need seven months."

"I was thinking of five."

"It can be done. There will be a premium. For how many units?"

"Three," Peterson said.

Ling wondered why anyone would need three cavitation units. No geological survey company in the world owned more than one.

"I can fill that order," Ling said, "upon receipt of your deposit."

"You will have it wired to you tomorrow."

"And we are shipping where? Canada?"

"You will receive shipping instructions," Peterson said, "in five months."

Directly ahead, the curved spans of the ultra-modern airport designed by Kurokawa rose into the sky. Peterson had lapsed into silence. Driving up the ramp, Ling said, "I hope we are in time for your flight."

"What? Oh yes. We're fine."

"You're heading back to Canada?"

"Yes."

Ling pulled up at the international terminal, got out, and shook Peterson's hand. Peterson shouldered his day bag. It was his only luggage. "Well," Peterson said. "I'd better go."

"Safe flight."

"Thank you. You, too. Back to Hong Kong?"

"No," Ling said. "I have to go to the factory, and get them started."

"It's nearby?"

"Yes, in Pudu Raya. Just a few kilometers."

"All right, then." Peterson disappeared inside the terminal, giving a final wave. Ling got back in the car and drove away. But as he was heading down the ramp, he saw that Peterson had left behind his cell phone on the car seat. He pulled over to the curb, glancing back over his shoulder. But Peterson was gone. And the cell phone in his hand was lightweight, made of cheap plastic. It was one of those prepaid-card phones, the disposable ones. It couldn't be Peterson's main phone.

It occurred to Ling that he had a friend who might be able to trace the phone and the card inside it. Find out more about the purchaser. And Ling would like to know more. So he slipped the phone into his pocket and drove north, to the factory.

Richard Mallory looked up from his desk and said, "Yes?"

The man standing in the doorway was pale-complected, slender, and American-looking, with a blond crew cut. His manner was casual, his dress nondescript: dirty Adidas running shoes and a faded navy tracksuit. He looked as if he might be out for a jog and had stopped by the office for a moment.

And since this was Design/Quest, a hot graphics shop located on Butler's Wharf, a refurbished warehouse district below London's Tower Bridge, most of the employees in the office were casually dressed. Mallory was the exception. Since he was the boss, he wore slacks and a white shirt. And wingtip shoes that hurt his feet. But they were hip.

Mallory said, "Can I help you?"

"I've come for the package," the American said.

"I'm sorry. What package?" Mallory said. "If it's a DHL pickup, the secretary has it up front."

The American looked annoyed. "Don't you think you're overdoing it?" he said. "Just give me the fucking package."

"Okay, fine," Mallory said, getting up from behind the desk.

Apparently the American felt he had been too harsh, because in a quieter tone he said, "Nice posters," and pointed to the wall behind Mallory. "You do 'em?"

"We did," Mallory said. "Our firm."

There were two posters, side by side on the wall, both stark black with a hanging globe of the Earth in space, differing only in the tag line. One said "Save the Earth" and beneath it, "It's the Only Home We Have." The other said "Save the Earth" and beneath that, "There's Nowhere Else to Go."

Then off to one side was a framed photograph of a blond model in a T-shirt: "Save the Earth" and the copy line was "And Look Good Doing It."

"That was our 'Save the Earth' campaign," Mallory said. "But they didn't buy it."

"Who didn't?"

"International Conservation Fund."

He went past the American and headed down the back stairs to the garage. The American followed.

"Why not? They didn't like it?"

"No, they liked it," Mallory said. "But they got Leo as a spokesman, and used him instead. Campaign went to video spots."

At the bottom of the stairs, he swiped his card, and the door unlocked with a click. They stepped into the small garage beneath the building. It was dark except for the glare of daylight from the ramp leading to the street. Mallory noticed with annoyance that a van partly blocked the ramp. They always had trouble with delivery vans parking there.

He turned to the American. "You have a car?"

"Yes. A van." He pointed.

"Oh good, so that's yours. And somebody to help you?"

"No. Just me. Why?"

"It's bloody heavy," Mallory said. "It may just be wire, but it's half a million feet of it. Weighs seven hundred pounds, mate."

"I can handle it."

Mallory went to his Rover and unlocked the boot. The American whistled, and the van rumbled down the ramp. It was driven by a tough-looking woman with spiked hair, dark makeup.

Mallory said, "I thought you were alone."

"She doesn't know anything," the American said. "Forget her. She brought the van. She just drives."

Mallory turned to the open boot. There were stacked white boxes marked "Ethernet Cable (Unshielded)." And printed specifications.

"Let's see one," the American said.

Mallory opened a box. Inside was a jumble of fist-sized coils of very thin wire, each in shrink-wrap plastic. "As you see," he said, "it's guide wire. For anti-tank missiles."

"Is it?"

"That's what they told me. That's why it's wrapped that way. One coil of wire for each missile."

"I wouldn't know," the American said. "I'm just the delivery man." He went and opened the back of his van. Then he began to transfer the boxes, one at a time. Mallory helped.

The American said, "This guy tell you anything else?"

"Actually, he did," Mallory said. "He said somebody bought five hundred surplus Warsaw Pact rockets. Called Hotfire or Hotwire or something. No warheads or anything. Just the rocket bodies. The story is they were sold with defective guide wire."

"I haven't heard that."

"That's what he said. Missiles were bought in Sweden. Gothenburg, I think. Shipped out from there."

"Sounds like you're worried."

"I'm not worried," Mallory said.

"Like you're afraid you're mixed up in something."

"Not me."

"Sure about that?" the American said.

"Yes, of course I'm sure."

Most of the boxes were transferred to the van. Mallory started to sweat. The American seemed to be glancing at him out of the corner of his eye. Openly skeptical. He said, "So, tell me. What'd he look like, this guy?"

Mallory knew better than to answer that. He shrugged. "Just a guy."

"American?"

"I don't know."

"You don't know whether he was American or not?"

"I couldn't be sure of his accent."

"Why is that?" the American said.

"He might have been Canadian."

"Alone?"

"Yeah."

"Because I hear talk about some gorgeous woman. Sexy woman in high heels, tight skirt."

"I would have noticed a woman like that," Mallory said.

"You wouldn't be . . . leaving her out?" Another skeptical glance. "Keeping her to yourself?" Mallory noticed a bulge on the American's hip. Was it a gun? It might be.

"No. He was alone."

"Whoever the guy was."

"Yes."

"You ask me," the American said, "I'd be wondering why anybody needed half a million feet of wire for anti-tank missiles in the first place. I mean, for what?"

Mallory said, "He didn't say."

"And you just said, 'Right, mate, half a million feet of wire, leave it to me,' with never a question?"

"Seems like you're asking all the questions," Mallory said. Still sweating.

"And I have a reason," the American said. His tone turned ominous. "I got to tell you, pal. I don't like what I am hearing."

The last of the boxes were stacked in the van. Mallory stepped back. The American slammed the first door shut, then the second. As the second door closed, Mallory saw the driver standing there. The woman. She had been standing behind the door.

"I don't like it either," she said. She was wearing fatigues, army surplus stuff. Baggy trousers and high-laced boots. A bulky green jacket. Heavy gloves. Dark glasses.

"Now wait a minute," the American said.

"Give me your cell phone," she said. Holding out her hand for it. Her other hand was behind her back. As if she had a gun.

"Why?"

"Give it to me."

"Why?"

"I want to look at it, that's why."

"There's nothing unusual—"

"Give it to me."

The American pulled the cell phone out of his pocket and handed it to her. Instead of taking it, she grabbed his wrist and pulled him toward her. The cell phone clattered to the ground. She brought her other hand from around her back and quickly gripped the side of his neck with her gloved hand. She held him with both hands around his neck, as if she were strangling him.

For a moment he was stunned; then he began to struggle. "What the fuck are you doing?" he said. "What are you—hey!" He knocked her hands away and jumped back as if he had been burned. "What was that? What did you *do?*"

He touched his neck. A tiny trickle of blood ran down, just a few drops. There was red on his fingertips. Almost nothing.

"What did you do?" he said.

"Nothing." She was stripping off her gloves. Mallory could see she was doing it carefully. As if something were in the glove. Something she did not want to touch.

"Nothing?" the American said. "*Nothing?* Son of a bitch!" Abruptly, he turned and began to run up the ramp toward the street outside.

Calmly, she watched him go. She bent over, picked up the cell phone, and put it in her pocket. Then she turned to Mallory. "Go back to work."

He hesitated.

"You did a good job. I never saw you. You never saw me. Now go."

Mallory turned and walked to the back-stairs door. Behind him, he heard the woman slam the van door, and when he glanced back, he saw the van racing up the ramp into the glare of the street. The van turned right, and was gone.

• • •

Back in his office, his assistant, Elizabeth, came in with a mockup for the new ultralight computer ads for Toshiba. The shoot was tomorrow. These were the finals to go over. He shuffled through the boards quickly; Mallory had trouble concentrating.

Elizabeth said, "You don't like them?"

"No, no, they're fine."

"You look a little pale."

"I just, um . . . my stomach."

"Ginger tea," she said. "That's best. Shall I make some?"

He nodded, to get her out of the office. He looked out the window. Mallory's office had a spectacular view of the Thames, and the Tower Bridge off to the left. The bridge had been repainted baby blue and white (was that traditional or just a bad idea?), but to see it always made him feel good. Secure somehow.

He walked closer to the window, and stood looking at the bridge. He was thinking that when his best friend had asked if he would lend a hand in a radical environmental cause, it had sounded like something fun. A bit of secrecy, a bit of dash and derring-do. He had been promised that it would not involve anything violent. Mallory had never imagined he would be frightened.

But he was frightened now. His hands were shaking. He stuck them in his pockets as he stared out the window. Five hundred rockets? he thought. *Five hundred rockets.* What had he gotten himself into? Then, slowly, he realized that he was hearing sirens, and there were red lights flashing on the bridge railings.

There had been an accident on the bridge. And judging from the number of police and rescue vehicles, it was a serious accident.

One in which someone had died.

He couldn't help himself. Feeling a sense of panic, he left the office, went outside to the quay, and with his heart in his throat, hurried toward the bridge.

• • •

From the upper level of the red double-decker bus, the tourists were staring down, covering their mouths in horror. Mallory pushed through the crowd clustered near the front of the bus. He got close enough to see a half-dozen paramedics and police crouched around a body lying in the street. Above them stood the burly bus driver, in tears. He was saying that there was nothing he could have done, the man had stepped in front of the bus at the last moment. He must have been drunk, the driver said, because he was wobbling. It was almost as if he fell off the curb.

Mallory could not see the body; the policemen blocked his view. The crowd was nearly silent, just watching. Then one of the policemen stood, holding a red passport in his hands—a German passport. Thank God, Mallory thought, feeling a flood of relief that lasted until a moment later, when one of the paramedics stepped away and Mallory saw one leg of the victim—a faded black tracksuit and a dirty Adidas running shoe, now soaked with blood.

He felt a wave of nausea, and turned away, pushing back through the crowd. The faces stared past him, impassive or annoyed. But nobody even glanced at him. They were all looking at the body.

Except for one man, dressed like an executive in a dark suit and tie. He was looking directly at Mallory. Mallory met his eyes. The man nodded slightly. Mallory made no response. He just pushed through the last of the crowd and fled, hurrying back down the stairs to his office, and realizing that somehow, in some way that he did not understand, his life had changed forever.

IDEC, the International Data Environmental Consortium, was located in a small brick building adjacent to the campus of Keio Mita University. To the casual observer, IDEC was part of the university, and even showed the coat of arms (*"Calamus Gladio Fortior"*), but in fact it was independent. The center of the building consisted of a small conference room with a podium and two rows of five chairs facing a screen at the front.

At ten in the morning, IDEC director Akira Hitomi stood at the podium and watched as the American came in and took a seat. The American was a large man, not so tall but thick in the shoulders and chest, like an athlete. For such a large man he moved easily, quietly. The Nepali officer entered right behind him, dark-skinned and watchful. He took a seat behind the American and off to one side. At the podium, Hitomi nodded to them and said nothing.

The wood-paneled room darkened slowly, to allow eyes to adjust. On all sides, the wood panels slid silently away, exposing huge flat-panel screens. Some of the screens moved smoothly out from the walls.

At last, the main door closed and locked with a click. Only then did Hitomi speak.

"Good morning, Kenner-san." On the main screen it said "Hitomi Akira" in English and Japanese. "And good morning, Thapa-san."

Hitomi flipped open a very small, very thin silver laptop. "Today I will present data from the last twenty-one days, correct up to twenty minutes ago. These will be findings from our joint project, Akamai Tree."

The two visitors nodded. Kenner smiled in anticipation. As well he should, Hitomi thought. Nowhere else in the world could he see such a presentation, for Hitomi's agency was the world leader in the accumulation and manipulation of electronic data. Now images on the screens came up, glowing one after another. They showed what appeared to be a corporate logo: a green tree on a white background, and the lettering AKAMAI TREE DIGITAL NETWORK SOLUTIONS.

This name and image had been chosen for their similarity to actual Internet companies and their logos. For the last two years, Akamai Tree's network of servers actually consisted of carefully designed traps. They incorporated multilevel quad-check honeynets established in both business and academic domains. This enabled them to track backward from servers to user with an 87 percent success rate. They had baited the net starting last year, first with ordinary feed and then with increasingly juicy morsels.

"Our sites mirrored established geology, applied physics, ecology, civil engineering, and biogeography sites," Hitomi said. "To attract deep divers, typical data included information on the use of explosives in seismic recordings, the tests of the stability of structures to vibration and earthquake damage, and in our oceanographic sites, data on hurricanes, rogue waves, tsunamis, and so forth. All this is familiar to you."

Kenner nodded.

Hitomi continued: "We knew we had a disseminated enemy, and a clever one. Users often operate behind netnanny firewalls, or used AOL accounts with teen ratings, to imply they are juvenile pranksters or kiddie scripters. But they are nothing of the sort. They are well organized, patient, and unrelenting. In recent weeks, we have begun to understand more."

The screen changed, showing a list.

"Out of a mix of sites and discussion groups, our sys progs found the deep divers clustered on the following category topics:

Aarhus, Denmark
Argon/Oxygen Drives
Australian Military History
Caisson Seawalls
Cavitation (Solid)
Cellular Encryption
Controlled Demolition
Flood Mitigation
High-Voltage Insulators
Hilo, Hawaii
Mid-Ocean Relay Network (MORN)
Missionary Diaries of the Pacific
National Earthquake Information Center (NEIC)
National Environmental Resource Fund (NERF)
Network Data Encryption
Potassium Hydroxide
Prescott, Arizona
Rain Forest Disease Foundation (RFDF)
Seismic Signatures, Geological
Shaped Explosives (Timed)
Shinkai 2000
Solid Rocket Propellant Mixtures
Toxins and Neurotoxins
Wire-guided Projectiles

"An impressive, if mysterious list," Hitomi said. "However, we have filters to identify smees and high-performance clients. These are individuals attacking firewalls, setting trojans, wild spiders, and so forth. Many of them are looking for credit card lists. But not all." He tapped his little computer, and the images changed.

"We added each of these topics into the honeynet with increasing stickiness, finally including hints of forthcoming research data, which we exposed as e-mail exchanges among scientists in Australia, Germany, Canada, and Russia. We drew a crowd and watched the traffic. We eventually sorted a complex nodal North America—Toronto, Chicago, Ann Arbor, Montreal—with spines to both American coasts, as well as England, France, and Germany. This is a serious Alpha extremist group.

They may already have killed a researcher in Paris. We're awaiting data. But the French authorities can be . . . slow."

Kenner spoke for the first time. "And what's the current delta cellular?"

"Cellular traffic is accelerating. E-mail is heavily encrypted. STF rate is up. It is clear there is a project under way—global in scope, immensely complicated, extremely expensive."

"But we don't know what it is."

"Not yet."

"Then you'd better follow the money."

"We are doing it. Everywhere." Hitomi smiled grimly. "It is only a matter of time before one of these fishes takes the hook."

VANCOUVER
TUESDAY, JUNE 8
4:55 P.M.

Nat Damon signed the paper with a flourish. "I've never been asked to sign a nondisclosure agreement before."

"I'm surprised," the man in the shiny suit said, taking the paper back. "I would have thought it was standard procedure. We don't want our proprietary information to be disclosed." He was a lawyer accompanying his client, a bearded man with glasses, wearing jeans and a work shirt. This bearded man said he was a petroleum geologist, and Damon believed him. He certainly looked like the other petroleum geologists he had dealt with.

Damon's company was called Canada Marine RS Technologies; from a tiny, cramped office outside Vancouver, Damon leased research submarines and remote submersibles to clients around the world. Damon didn't own these subs; he just leased them. The subs were located all over the world—in Yokohama, Dubai, Melbourne, San Diego. They ranged from fully operational fifty-foot submersibles with crews of six, capable of traveling around the globe, to tiny one-man diving machines and even smaller remote robotic vehicles that operated from a tender ship on the surface.

Damon's clients were energy and mining companies who used the subs for undersea prospecting or to check the condition of offshore rigs and platforms. His was a specialized business, and his little office at the back of a boat repair yard did not receive many visitors.

Yet these two men had come through his door just before closing time. The lawyer had done all of the talking; the client merely gave Damon a business card that said Seismic Services, with a Calgary address. That made sense; Calgary was a big city for hydrocarbon companies. Petro-Canada, Shell, and Suncor were all there, and many more. And dozens of small private consulting firms had sprung up there to do prospecting and research.

Damon took a small model down from the shelf behind him. It was a tiny white snub-nosed submarine with a bubble top. He set it on the table in front of the men.

"This is the vehicle I would recommend for your needs," he said. "The RS Scorpion, built in England just four years ago. Two-man crew. Diesel and electric power with closed cycle argon drive. Submerged, it runs on twenty percent oxygen, eighty percent argon. Solid, proven technology: potassium hydroxide scrubber, two-hundred-volt electrical, operational depth of two thousand feet, and 3.8 hours dive time. It's the equivalent of the Japanese Shinkai 2000, if you know that one, or the DownStar 80, of which there are four in the world, but they're all on long leases. The Scorpion is an excellent submarine."

The men nodded, and looked at each other. "And what kind of external manipulators are there?" the bearded man said.

"That's depth dependent," Damon said. "At lesser depths—"

"Let's say at two thousand feet. What external manipulators are there?"

"You want to collect samples at two thousand feet?"

"Actually, we're placing monitoring devices on the bottom."

"I see. Like radio devices? Sending data to the surface?"

"Something like that."

"How large are these devices?"

The bearded man held his hands two feet apart. "About so big."

"And they weigh what?"

"Oh, I don't know exactly. Maybe two hundred pounds."

Damon concealed his surprise. Usually petroleum geologists knew precisely what they were going to place. Exact dimensions, exact weight, exact specific gravity, all that. This guy was vague. But perhaps Damon was just being paranoid. He continued. "And these sensors are for geological work?"

"Ultimately. First we need information on ocean currents, flow rates, bottom temperatures. That kind of thing."

Damon thought: *For what?* Why did they need to know about currents? Of course, they might be sinking a tower, but nobody would do that in two thousand feet of water.

What were these guys intending to do?

"Well," he said, "if you want to place external devices, you have to secure them to the exterior of the hull prior to the dive. There are lateral shelves on each side—" he pointed to the model "—for that purpose. Once you're at depth, you have a choice of two remote arms to place the devices. How many devices are you talking about?"

"Quite a few."

"More than eight?"

"Oh yes. Probably."

"Well, then you're talking about multiple dives. You can only take eight, maybe ten external devices on any given dive." He talked on for a while, scanning their faces, trying to understand what lay behind the bland looks. They wanted to lease the sub for four months, starting in August of that year. They wanted the sub and the tender ship transported to Port Moresby, New Guinea. They would pick it up there.

"Depending on where you go, there are some required marine licenses—"

"We'll worry about that later," the lawyer said.

"Now, the crew—"

"We'll worry about that later, too."

"It's part of the contract."

"Then just write it in. However you do it."

"You'll return the tender to Moresby at the end of the lease period?"

"Yes."

Damon sat down in front of the desktop computer and began to fill in the estimate forms. There were, all in all, forty-three categories (not including insurance) that had to be filled out. At last he had the final number. "Five hundred and eighty three thousand dollars," he said.

The men didn't blink. They just nodded.

"Half in advance."

They nodded again.

"Second half in escrow account prior to your taking delivery in Port Moresby." He never required that with his regular customers. But for some reason, these two made him uneasy.

"That will be fine," the lawyer said.

"Plus twenty percent contingency, payable in advance."

That was simply unnecessary. But now he was trying to make these guys go away. It didn't work.

"That will be fine."

"Okay," Damon said. "Now, if you need to talk to your contracting company before you sign—"

"No. We're prepared to proceed now."

And then one of them pulled out an envelope and handed it to Damon.

"Tell me if this is satisfactory."

It was a check for $250,000. From Seismic Services, payable to Canada Marine. Damon nodded, and said it was. He put the check and the envelope on his desk, next to the submarine model.

Then one of the men said, "Do you mind if I make a couple of notes?" and picked up the envelope and scribbled on it. And it was only after they were gone that Damon realized they had given him the check and taken back the envelope. So there would be no fingerprints.

Or was he just being paranoid? The following morning, he was inclined to think so. When he went to Scotiabank to deposit the check, he stopped by to see John Kim, the bank manager, and asked him to find out if there were sufficient funds in the Seismic Services account to cover the check.

John Kim said he would check right away.

Christ, it was cold, George Morton thought, climbing out of the Land Cruiser. The millionaire philanthropist stamped his feet and pulled on gloves, trying to warm himself. It was three o'clock in the morning, and the sky glowed red, with streaks of yellow from the still-visible sun. A bitter wind blew across the *Sprengisandur*, the rugged, dark plain in the interior of Iceland. Flat gray clouds hung low over the lava that stretched away for miles. The Icelanders loved this place. Morton couldn't see why.

In any case, they had reached their destination: directly ahead lay a huge, crumpled wall of dirt-covered snow and rock, stretching up to the mountains behind. This was Snorrajökul, one tongue of the huge Vatnajökull glacier, the largest ice cap in Europe.

The driver, a graduate student, climbed out and clapped his hands with delight. "Not bad at all! Quite warm! You are lucky, it's a pleasant August night." He was wearing a T-shirt, hiking shorts, and a light vest. Morton was wearing a down vest, a quilted windbreaker, and heavy pants. And he was still cold.

He looked back as the others got out of the backseat. Nicholas Drake, thin and frowning, wearing a shirt and tie and a tweed sport coat beneath his windbreaker, winced as the cold air hit him. With his thinning hair, wire-frame glasses, and pinched, disapproving manner, Drake conveyed a scholarly quality that in fact he cultivated. He did not want to be taken for what he was, a highly successful litigator who had retired to become the director of the National Environmental Resource Fund, a major American activist group. He had held the job at NERF for the last ten years.

Next, young Peter Evans bounced out of the car. Evans was the youngest of Morton's attorneys, and the one he liked best. Evans was twenty-eight and a junior associate of the Los Angeles firm of Hassle and Black. Now, even late at night, he remained cheerful and enthusiastic. He pulled on a Patagonia fleece and stuck his hands in his pockets, but otherwise gave no sign that the weather bothered him.

Morton had flown all of them in from Los Angeles on his Gulfstream G5 jet, arriving in Keflavík airport at nine yesterday morning. None of them had slept, but nobody was tired. Not even Morton, and he was sixty-five years old. He didn't feel the slightest sense of fatigue.

Just cold.

Morton zipped up his jacket and followed the graduate student down the rocky hill from the car. "The light at night gives you energy," the kid said. "Dr. Einarsson never sleeps more than four hours a night in the summer. None of us does."

"And where is Dr. Einarsson?" Morton asked.

"Down there." The kid pointed off to the left.

At first, Morton could see nothing at all. Finally he saw a red dot, and realized it was a vehicle. That was when he grasped the enormous size of the glacier.

Drake fell into step with Morton as they went down the hill. "George," he said, "you and Evans should feel free to go on a tour of the site, and let me talk to Per Einarsson alone."

"Why?"

"I expect Einarsson would be more comfortable if there weren't a lot of people standing around."

"But isn't the point that I'm the one who funds his research?"

"Of course," Drake said, "but I don't want to hammer that fact too hard. I don't want Per to feel compromised."

"I don't see how you can avoid it."

"I'll just point out the stakes," Drake said. "Help him to see the big picture."

"Frankly, I was looking forward to hearing this discussion," Morton said.

"I know," Drake said. "But it's delicate."

As they came closer to the glacier, Morton felt a distinct chill in the wind. The temperature dropped several degrees. They could see now the series of four large, tan tents arranged near the red Land Cruiser. From a distance, the tents had blended into the plain.

From one of the tents a very tall, blond man appeared. Per Einarsson threw up his hands and shouted, "Nicholas!"

"Per!" Drake raced forward.

Morton continued down the hill, feeling distinctly grouchy about being dismissed by Drake. Evans came up to walk alongside him. "I don't want to take any damn tour," Morton said.

"Oh, I don't know," Evans said, looking ahead. "It might be more interesting than we think." Coming out of one of the other tents were three young women in khakis, all blond and beautiful. They waved to the newcomers.

"Maybe you're right," Morton said.

Peter Evans knew that his client George Morton, despite his intense interest in all things environmental, had an even more intense interest in pretty women. And indeed, after a quick introduction to Einarsson, Morton happily allowed himself to be led away by Eva Jónsdóttir, who was tall and athletic, with short-cropped white blond hair and a radiant smile. She was Morton's type, Evans thought. She looked rather like Morton's beautiful assistant, Sarah Jones. He heard Morton say, "I had no idea so many women were interested in geology," and Morton and Eva drifted away, heading toward the glacier.

Evans knew he should accompany Morton. But perhaps Morton

wanted to take this tour alone. And more important, Evans's firm also represented Nicholas Drake, and Evans had a nagging concern about what Drake was up to. Not that it was illegal or unethical, exactly. But Drake could be imperious, and what he was going to do might cause embarrassment later on. So for a moment Evans stood there, wondering which way to go, which man to follow.

It was Drake who made the decision for him, giving Evans a slight, dismissive wave of his hand as he disappeared into the big tent with Einarsson. Evans took the hint, and ambled off toward Morton and the girl. Eva was chattering on about how 12 percent of Iceland was covered in glaciers, and how some of the glaciers had active volcanoes poking out from the ice.

This particular glacier, she said, pointing upward, was of the type called a surge glacier, because it had a history of rapid advances and retreats. At the moment, she said, the glacier was pushing forward at the rate of one hundred meters a day—the length of a football field, every twenty-four hours. Sometimes, when the wind died, you could actually hear it grinding forward. This glacier had surged more than ten kilometers in the last few years.

Soon they were joined by Ásdís Sveinsdóttir, who could have been Eva's younger sister. She paid flattering attention to Evans, asking him how his trip over had been, how he liked Iceland, how long he was staying in the country. Eventually, she mentioned that she usually worked in the office at Reykjavík, and had only come out for the day. Evans realized then that she was here doing her job. The sponsors were visiting Einarsson, and Einarsson had arranged for the visit to be memorable.

Eva was explaining that although surge-type glaciers were very common—there were several hundred of them in Alaska—the mechanism of the surges was not known. Nor was the mechanism behind the periodic advances and retreats, which differed for each glacier. "There is still so much to study, to learn," she said, smiling at Morton.

That was when they heard shouts coming from the big tent, and considerable swearing. Evans excused himself, and headed back to the tent. Somewhat reluctantly, Morton trailed after him.

Per Einarsson was shaking with anger. He raised his fists. "I tell you, no!" he yelled, and pounded the table.

Standing opposite him, Drake was very red in the face, clenching his teeth. "Per," he said, "I am asking you to consider the realities."

"You are not!" Einarsson said, pounding the table again. "The reality is what you do *not* want me to publish!"

"Now, Per—"

"The *reality*," he said, "is that in Iceland the first half of the twentieth century was warmer than the second half, as in Greenland.* The *reality* is that in Iceland, most glaciers lost mass after 1930 because summers warmed by .6 degrees Celsius, but since then the climate has become colder. The *reality* is that since 1970 these glaciers have been steadily advancing. They have regained half the ground that was lost earlier. Right now, eleven are surging. That is *the reality*, Nicholas! And I will not lie about it."

"No one has suggested you do," Drake said, lowering his voice and glancing at his newly arrived audience. "I am merely discussing how you word your paper, Per."

Einarsson raised a sheet of paper. "Yes, and you have *suggested* some wording—"

"Merely a suggestion—"

"That twists truth!"

"Per, with due respect, I feel you are exaggerating—"

"Am I?" Einarsson turned to the others and began to read. "This is what he wants me to say: 'The threat of global warming has melted glaciers throughout the world, and in Iceland as well. Many glaciers are shrinking dramatically, although paradoxically others are growing. How-

---

* P. Chylek, et al. 2004, "Global warming and the Greenland ice sheet," *Climatic Change* 63, 201–21. "Since 1940 . . . data have undergone predominantly a cooling trend. . . . The Greenland ice sheet and coastal regions are not following the current global warming trend."

ever, in all cases recent extremes in climate variability seem to be the cause . . . blah . . . blah . . . blah . . . *og svo framvegis.*' " He threw the paper down. "That is simply not true."

"It's just the opening paragraph. The rest of your paper will amplify."

"The opening paragraph is not true."

"Of course it is. It refers to 'extremes in climate variability.' No one can object to such vague wording."

"*Recent* extremes. But in Iceland these effects are not recent."

"Then take out 'recent.' "

"That is not adequate," Einarsson said, "because the implication of this paragraph is that we are observing the effects of global warming from greenhouse gases. Whereas in fact we are observing local climate patterns that are rather specific to Iceland and are unlikely to be related to any global pattern."

"And you can say so in your conclusion."

"But this opening paragraph will be a big joke among Arctic researchers. You think Motoyama or Sigurosson will not see through this paragraph? Or Hicks? Watanabe? Ísaksson? They will laugh and call me compromised. They will say I did it for grants."

"But there are other considerations," Drake said soothingly. "We must all be aware there are disinformation groups funded by industry—petroleum, automotive—who will seize on the report that some glaciers are growing, and use it to argue against global warming. That is what they always do. They snatch at anything to paint a false picture."

"How the information is used is not my concern. My concern is to report the truth as best I can."

"Very noble," Drake said. "Perhaps not so practical."

"I see. And you have brought the source of funding right here, in the form of Mr. Morton, so I do not miss the point?"

"No, no, Per," Drake said hastily. "Please, don't misunderstand—"

"I understand only too well. What is he doing here?" Einarsson was furious. "Mr. Morton? Do you approve of what I am being asked to do by Mr. Drake?"

It was at that point that Morton's cell phone rang, and with ill-concealed relief, he flipped it open. "Morton. Yes? Yes, John. Where are you? Vancouver? What time is it there?" He put his hand over the mouthpiece. "John Kim, in Vancouver. Scotiabank."

Evans nodded, though he had no idea who that was. Morton's financial operations were complex; he knew bankers all over the world. Morton turned and walked to the far side of the tent.

An awkward silence fell over the others as they waited. Einarsson stared at the floor, sucking in his breath, still furious. The blond women pretended to work, giving great attention to the papers they shuffled through. Drake stuck his hands in his pockets, looked at the roof of the tent.

Meanwhile, Morton was laughing. "Really? I hadn't heard that one," he said, chuckling. He glanced back at the others, and turned away again.

Drake said, "Look, Per, I feel we have gotten off on the wrong foot."

"Not at all," Einarsson said coldly. "We understand each other only too well. If you withdraw your support, you withdraw your support."

"Nobody is talking about withdrawing support . . ."

"Time will tell," he said.

And then Morton said, "*What? They did what? Deposited to what? How much money are we—? Jesus Christ, John. This is unbelievable!*" And still talking, he turned and walked out of the tent.

Evans hurried after him.

It was brighter, the sun now higher in the sky, trying to break through low clouds. Morton was scrambling up the slope, still talking on the phone. He was shouting, but his words were lost in the wind as Evans followed him.

They came to the Land Cruiser. Morton ducked down, using it as a shield against the wind. "Christ, John, do I have legal liability there? I mean—no, I didn't know a thing about it. What was the organization? Friends of the Planet Fund?"

Morton looked questioningly at Evans. Evans shook his head. He'd never heard of Friends of the Planet. And he knew most of the environmental organizations.

"Based where?" Morton was saying. "San Jose? California? Oh. Jesus.

What the hell is based in Costa Rica?" He cupped his hand over the phone. "Friends of the Planet Fund, San José, Costa Rica."

Evans shook his head.

"I never heard of them," Morton said, "and neither has my lawyer. And I don't remember—no, Ed, if it was a quarter of a million dollars, I'd remember. The check was issued where? I see. And my name was where? I see. Okay, thanks. Yeah. I will. Bye." He flipped the phone shut.

He turned to Evans.

"Peter," he said. "Get a pad and make notes."

Morton spoke quickly. Evans scribbled, trying to keep up. It was a complicated story that he took down as best he could.

John Kim, the manager of Scotiabank, Vancouver, had been called by a customer named Nat Damon, a local marine operator. Damon had deposited a check from a company called Seismic Services, in Calgary, and the check had bounced. It was for $300,000. Damon was nervous about whoever had written the check, and asked Kim to look into it.

John Kim could not legally make inquiries in the US, but the issuing bank was in Calgary, and he had a friend who worked there. He learned that Seismic Services was an account with a postal box for an address. The account was modestly active, receiving deposits every few weeks from only one source: The Friends of the Planet Foundation, based in San José, Costa Rica.

Kim placed a call down there. Then, about that time, it came up on his screen that the check had cleared. Kim called Damon and asked him if he wanted to drop the inquiry. Damon said no, check it out.

Kim had a brief conversation with Miguel Chavez at the Banco Credito Agricola in San José. Chavez said he had gotten an electronic deposit from the Moriah Wind Power Associates via Ansbach (Cayman) Ltd., a private bank on Grand Cayman island. That was all he knew.

Chavez called Kim back ten minutes later to say he had made inquiries at Ansbach and had obtained a record of a wire transfer that was paid into the Moriah account by the International Wilderness Preservation Society three days before that. And the IWPS transfer noted in the comment field, "G. Morton Research Fund."

John Kim called his Vancouver client, Nat Damon, to ask what the check was for. Damon said it was for the lease of a small two-man research submarine.

Kim thought that was pretty interesting, so he telephoned his friend George Morton to kid him a bit, and ask why he was leasing a submarine. And to his surprise, Morton knew absolutely nothing about it.

Evans finished taking down notes on the pad. He said, "This is what some bank manager in Vancouver told you?"

"Yes. A good friend of mine. Why are you looking at me that way?"

"Because it's a lot of information," Evans said. He didn't know the banking rules in Canada, to say nothing of Costa Rica, but he knew it was unlikely that any banks would freely exchange information in the way Morton had described. If the Vancouver manager's story was true, there was more to it that he wasn't telling. Evans made a note to check into it. "And do you know the International Wilderness Preservation Society, which has your check for a quarter of a million dollars?"

Morton shook his head. "Never heard of them."

"So you never gave them two hundred and fifty thousand dollars?"

Morton shook his head. "I'll tell you what I did do, in the last week," he said. "I gave two hundred and fifty grand to Nicholas Drake to cover a monthly operating shortfall. He told me he had some problem about a big contributor from Seattle not coming through for a week. Drake's asked me to help him out before like that, once or twice."

"You think that money ended up in Vancouver?"

Morton nodded.

"You better ask Drake about it," Evans said.

"I have no idea at all," Drake said, looking mystified. "Costa Rica? International Wilderness Preservation? My goodness, I can't imagine."

Evans said, "You know the International Wilderness Preservation Society?"

"Very well," Drake said. "They're excellent. We've worked closely with them on any number of projects around the world—the Everglades, Tiger Tops in Nepal, the Lake Toba preserve in Sumatra. The only thing I can think is that somehow George's check was mistakenly deposited in the wrong account. Or . . . I just don't know. I have to call the office. But it's late in California. It'll have to wait until morning."

Morton was staring at Drake, not speaking.

"George," Drake said, turning to him. "I'm sure this must make you feel very strange. Even if it's an honest mistake—as I am almost certain it is—it's still a lot of money to be mishandled. I feel terrible. But mistakes happen, especially if you use a lot of unpaid volunteers, as we do. But you and I have been friends for a long time. I want you to know that I will get to the bottom of this. And of course I will see that the money is recovered at once. You have my word, George."

"Thank you," Morton said.

They all climbed into the Land Cruiser.

The vehicle bounced over the barren plain. "Damn, those Icelanders are stubborn," Drake said, staring out the window. "They may be the most stubborn researchers in the world."

"He never saw your point?" Evans said.

"No," Drake said, "I couldn't make him understand. Scientists can't adopt that lofty attitude anymore. They can't say, 'I do the research, and I don't care how it is used.' That's out of date. It's irresponsible. Even in a seemingly obscure field like glacier geology. Because, like it or not, we're in the middle of a war—a global war of information versus disinformation. The war is fought on many battlegrounds. Newspaper op-eds. Television reports. Scientific journals. Websites, conferences, classrooms—and courtrooms, too, if it comes to that." Drake shook his head. "We have truth on our side, but we're outnumbered and outfunded. Today, the environmental movement is David battling Goliath. And Goliath is Aventis and Alcatel, Humana and GE, BP and Bayer, Shell and Glaxo-Wellcome—huge, global, corporate. These people are the implacable enemies of our planet, and Per Einarsson, out there on his glacier, is irresponsible to pretend it isn't happening."

Sitting beside Drake, Peter Evans nodded sympathetically, though in fact he took everything Drake was saying with a large grain of salt. The head of NERF was famously melodramatic. And Drake was pointedly ignoring the fact that several of the corporations he had named made substantial contributions to NERF every year, and three executives from those companies actually sat on Drake's board of advisors. That was true of many environmental organizations these days, although the reasons behind corporate involvement were much debated.

"Well," Morton said, "maybe Per will reconsider later on."

"I doubt it," Drake said gloomily. "He was angry. We've lost this battle, I'm sorry to say. But we do what we always do. Soldier on. Fight the good fight."

It was silent in the car for a while.

"The girls were damn good looking," Morton said. "Weren't they, Peter?"

"Yes," Evans said. "They were."

Evans knew that Morton was trying to lighten the mood in the car. But Drake would have none of it. The head of NERF stared morosely at the barren landscape, and shook his head mournfully at the snow-covered mountains in the distance.

Evans had traveled many times with Drake and Morton in the last couple of years. Usually, Morton could cheer everybody around him, even Drake, who was glum and fretful.

But lately Drake had become even more pessimistic than usual. Evans had first noticed it a few weeks ago, and had wondered at the time if there was illness in the family, or something else that was bothering him. But it seemed there was nothing amiss. At least, nothing that anyone would talk about. NERF was a beehive of activity; they had moved into a wonderful new building in Beverly Hills; fund-raising was at an all-time high; they were planning spectacular new events and conferences, including the Abrupt Climate Change Conference that would begin in two months. Yet despite these successes—or because of them?—Drake seemed more miserable than ever.

Morton noticed it, too, but he shrugged it off. "He's a lawyer," he said. "What do you expect? Forget about it."

By the time they reached Reykjavík, the sunny day had turned wet and chilly. It was sleeting at Keflavík airport, obliging them to wait while the wings of the white Gulfstream jet were de-iced. Evans slipped away to a corner of the hangar and, since it was still the middle of the night in the US, placed a call to a friend in banking in Hong Kong. He asked about the Vancouver story.

"Absolutely impossible," was the immediate answer. "No bank would divulge such information, even to another bank. There's an STR in the chain somewhere."

"An STR?"

"Suspicious transfer report. If it looks like money for drug trafficking or terrorism, the account gets tagged. And from then on, it's tracked. There are ways to track electronic transfers, even with strong encryption. But none of that tracking is ever going to wind up on the desk of a bank manager."

"No?"

"Not a chance. You'd need international law-enforcement credentials to see that tracking report."

"So this bank manager didn't do all this himself?"

"I doubt it. There is somebody else involved in this story. A policeman of some kind. Somebody you're not being told about."

"Like a customs guy, or Interpol?"

"Or something."

"Why would my client be contacted at all?"

"I don't know. But it's not an accident. Does your client have any radical tendencies?"

Thinking of Morton, Evans wanted to laugh. "Absolutely not."

"You quite sure, Peter?"

"Well, yes . . ."

"Because sometimes these wealthy donors amuse themselves, or justify themselves, by supporting terrorist groups. That's what happened with the IRA. Rich Americans in Boston supported them for decades. But times have changed. No one is amused any longer. Your client should be careful. And if you're his attorney, you should be careful, too. Hate to visit you in prison, Peter."

And he hung up.

The flight attendant poured Morton's vodka into a cut-glass tumbler. "No more ice, sweetie," Morton said, raising his hand. They were flying west, over Greenland, a vast expanse of ice and cloud in pale sun beneath them.

Morton sat with Drake, who talked about how the Greenland ice cap was melting. And the rate at which the Arctic ice was melting. And Canadian glaciers were receding. Morton sipped his vodka and nodded. "So Iceland is an anomaly?"

"Oh yes," Drake said. "An anomaly. Everywhere else, glaciers are melting at an unprecedented rate."

"It's good we have you, Nick," Morton said, putting his hand on Drake's shoulder.

Drake smiled. "And it's good we have *you*, George," he said. "We wouldn't be able to accomplish anything without your generous support. You've made the Vanutu lawsuit possible—and that's extremely important for the publicity it will generate. And as for your other grants, well . . . words fail me."

"Words never fail you," Morton said, slapping him on the back.

Sitting across from them, Evans thought they really were the odd couple. Morton, big and hearty, dressed casually in jeans and a workshirt, always seeming to burst from his clothes. And Nicholas Drake, tall and painfully thin, wearing a coat and tie, with his scrawny neck rising from the collar of a shirt that never seemed to fit.

In their manner, too, they were complete opposites. Morton loved to be around as many people as possible, loved to eat, and laugh. He had a penchant for pretty girls, vintage sports cars, Asian art, and practical jokes. His parties drew most of Hollywood to his Holmby Hills mansion; his charity functions were always special, always written up the next day.

Of course, Drake attended those functions, but invariably left early, sometimes before dinner. Often he pleaded illness—his own or a friend's. In fact, Drake was a solitary, ascetic man, who detested parties and noise. Even when he stood at a podium giving a speech, he conveyed an air of isolation, as if he were alone in the room. And, being Drake, he made it work for him. He managed to suggest that he was a lone messenger in the wilderness, delivering the truth the audience needed to hear.

Despite their differences in temperament, the two men had built a durable friendship that had lasted the better part of a decade. Morton, the heir to a forklift fortune, had the congenital uneasiness of inherited wealth. Drake had a good use for that money, and in return provided Morton with a passion, and a cause, that informed and guided Morton's life. Morton's name appeared on the board of advisors of the Audubon Society, the Wilderness Society, the World Wildlife Fund, and the Sierra Club. He was a major contributor to Greenpeace and the Environmental Action League.

All this culminated in two enormous gifts by Morton to NERF. The first was a grant of $1 million, to finance the Vanutu lawsuit. The second was a grant of $9 million to NERF itself, to finance future research and litigation on behalf of the environment. Not surprisingly, the NERF board had voted Morton their Concerned Citizen of the Year. A banquet in his honor was scheduled for later that fall, in San Francisco.

Evans sat across from the two men, idly thumbing through a magazine. But he had been shaken by the Hong Kong call, and found himself observing Morton with some care.

Morton still had his hand on Drake's shoulder, and was telling him a joke—as usual, trying to get Drake to laugh—but it seemed to Evans that he detected a certain distance on Morton's part. Morton had withdrawn, but didn't want Drake to notice.

This suspicion was confirmed when Morton stood up abruptly and headed for the cockpit. "I want to know about this damn electronic thing," he said. Since takeoff, they had been experiencing the effects of a major solar flare that rendered satellite telephones erratic or unusable. The pilots said the effect was heightened near the poles, and would soon diminish as they headed south.

And Morton seemed eager to make some calls. Evans wondered to whom. It was now four A.M. in New York, one A.M. in Los Angeles. Who was Morton calling? But of course it could concern any of his ongoing environmental projects—water purification in Cambodia, reforestation in Guinea, habitat preservation in Madagascar, medicinal plants in Peru. To say nothing of the German expedition to measure the thickness of the ice in Antarctica. Morton was personally involved in all these projects. He knew them in detail, knew the scientists involved, had visited the locations himself.

So it could be anything.

But somehow, Evans felt, it wasn't just anything.

Morton came back. "Pilots say it's okay now." He sat by himself in the front of the plane, reached for his headset, and pulled the sliding door shut for privacy.

Evans turned back to his magazine.

Drake said, "You think he's drinking more than usual?"

"Not really," Evans said.

"I worry."

"I wouldn't," Evans said.

"You realize," Drake said, "we are just five weeks from the banquet in his honor, in San Francisco. That's our biggest fund-raising event of the year. It will generate considerable publicity, and it'll help us launch the conference on Abrupt Climate Change."

"Uh-huh," Evans said.

"I'd like to ensure that the publicity focuses on environmental issues, and not anything else. Of a personal nature, if you know what I mean."

Evans said, "Isn't this a conversation you should be having with George?"

"Oh, I have. I only mention it to you because you spend so much time with him."

"I don't, really."

"You know he likes you, Peter," Drake said. "You're the son he never had or—hell, I don't know. But he *does* like you. And I'm just asking you to help us, if you can."

"I don't think he'll embarrass you, Nick."

"Just . . . keep an eye on him."

"Okay. Sure."

At the front of the plane, the sliding door opened. Morton said, "Mr. Evans? If you please."

Peter got up and went forward.

He slid the door shut behind him.

"I have been on the phone to Sarah," Morton said. Sarah Jones was his assistant in LA.

"Isn't it late?"

"It's her job. She's well paid. Sit down." Evans sat in the chair opposite. "Have you ever heard of the NSIA?"

"No."

"The National Security Intelligence Agency?"

Evans shook his head. "No. But there are twenty security agencies."

"Ever heard of John Kenner?"

"No . . ."

"Apparently he's a professor at MIT."

"No," Evans said. "Sorry. Does he have something to do with the environment?"

"He may. See what you can find out."

Evans turned to the laptop by his seat, and flipped open the screen. It was connected to the Internet by satellite. He started to type.

In a few moments he was looking at a picture of a fit-looking man with prematurely gray hair and heavy horn-rim glasses. The attached biography was brief. Evans read it aloud. "Richard John Kenner, William T. Harding Professor of Geoenvironmental Engineering."

"Whatever that means," Morton said.

"He is thirty-nine. Doctorate in civil engineering from Caltech at age twenty. Did his thesis on soil erosion in Nepal. Barely missed qualifying for the Olympic ski team. A JD from Harvard Law School. Spent the next four years in government. Department of the Interior, Office of Policy Analysis. Scientific advisor to the Intergovernmental Negotiating Committee. Hobby is mountain climbing; he was reported dead on Naya Khanga peak in Nepal, but he wasn't. Tried to climb K2, driven back by weather."

"K2," Morton said. "Isn't that the most dangerous peak?"

"I think so. Looks like he's a serious climber. Anyway, he then went to MIT, where I'd say his rise has been spectacular. Associate professor in '93. Director of the MIT Center for Risk Analysis in '95. William T. Harding Professor in '96. Consultant to the EPA, the Department of the Interior, the Department of Defense, the government of Nepal, God knows who else. Looks like a lot of corporations. And since 2002, on faculty leave."

"Meaning what?"

"It just says he's on leave."

"For the last two years?" Morton came and looked over Evans's shoulder. "I don't like it. The guy burns up the track at MIT, goes on leave, and never comes back. You think he got into trouble?"

"I don't know. But . . ." Evans was calculating the dates. "Professor Kenner got a doctorate from Caltech at twenty. Got his law degree from

Harvard in two years instead of three. Professor at MIT when he's twenty-eight . . ."

"Okay, okay, so he's smart," Morton said. "I still want to know why he's on leave. And why he's in Vancouver."

Evans said, "He's in Vancouver?"

"He's been calling Sarah from Vancouver."

"Why?"

"He wants to meet with me."

"Well," Evans said, "I guess you'd better meet with him."

"I will," Morton said. "But what do you think he wants?"

"I have no idea. Funding? A project?"

"Sarah says he wants the meeting to be confidential. He doesn't want anybody to be told."

"Well, that's not hard. You're on an airplane."

"No," Morton said, jerking his thumb. "He specifically doesn't want Drake to be told."

"Maybe I'd better attend this meeting," Evans said.

"Yes," Morton said. "Maybe you should."

The iron gates swung open, and the car drove up the shaded driveway to the house that slowly came into view. This was Holmby Hills, the wealthiest area of Beverly Hills. The billionaires lived here, in residences hidden from the street by high gates and dense foliage. In this part of town, security cameras were all painted green, and tucked back unobtrusively.

The house came into view. It was a Mediterranean-style villa, cream colored, and large enough for a family of ten. Evans, who had been speaking to his office, flipped his cell phone shut and got out as the car came to a stop.

Birds chirped in the ficus trees. The air smelled of the gardenia and jasmine that bordered the driveway. A hummingbird hung near the purple bougainvillea at the garage. It was, Evans thought, a typical California moment. Evans had been raised in Connecticut and schooled in Boston; even after five years in California, the place still seemed exotic to him.

He saw that another car was parked in front of the house: a dark gray sedan. It had government license plates.

From out of the front door came Morton's assistant, Sarah Jones, a tall blond woman of thirty, as glamorous as any movie star. Sarah was dressed in a white tennis skirt and pink top, her hair pulled back in a pony tail. Morton kissed her lightly on the cheek. "You playing today?"

"I was. My boss came back early." She shook Evans's hand and turned back to Morton. "Good trip?"

"Fine. Drake is morose. And he won't drink. It gets tiresome."

As Morton started toward the door, Sarah said, "I think I ought to tell you, they're here right now."

"Who is?"

"Professor Kenner. And another guy with him. Foreign guy."

"Really? But didn't you tell them they had to—"

"Make an appointment? Yes, I did. They seem to think that doesn't apply to them. They just sat down and said they'd wait."

"You should have called me—"

"They got here five minutes ago."

"Huh. Okay." He turned to Evans. "Let's go, Peter."

They went inside. Morton's living room looked out on the garden in back of the house. The room was decorated with Asian antiques, including a large stone head from Cambodia. Sitting erectly on the couch were two men. One was an American of middle height, with short gray hair and glasses. The other was very dark, compact, and very handsome despite the thin scar that ran down the left side of his face in front of his ear. They were dressed in cotton slacks and lightweight sport coats. Both men sat on the edge of the couch, very alert, as if they might spring up at any moment.

"Look military, don't they?" Morton muttered, as they went into the room.

The two men stood. "Mr. Morton, I'm John Kenner from MIT, and this is my colleague, Sanjong Thapa. A graduate student from Mustang. In Nepal."

Morton said, "And this is *my* colleague, Peter Evans."

They shook hands all around. Kenner's grip was firm. Sanjong Thapa gave a very slight bow as he shook hands. He spoke softly, with a British accent. "How do you do."

"I didn't expect you," Morton said, "so soon."

"We work quickly."

"So I see. What's this about?"

"I'm afraid we need your help, Mr. Morton." Kenner smiled pleasantly at Evans and Sarah. "And unfortunately, our discussion is confidential."

"Mr. Evans is my attorney," Morton said, "and I have no secrets from my assistant—"

"I'm sure," Kenner said. "You may take them into your confidence whenever you choose. But we must speak to you alone."

Evans said, "If you don't mind, I'd like to see some identification."

"Of course," Kenner said. Both men reached for wallets. Evans was shown Massachusetts driver's licenses, MIT faculty cards, and passports. Then they handed out business cards.

> John Kenner, PhD
> Center for Risk Analysis
> Massachusetts Institute of Technology
> 454 Massachusetts Avenue
> Cambridge, MA 02138

> Sanjong Thapa, PhD
> Research Associate
> Department of Geoenvironmental Engineering
> Building 4-C 323
> Massachusetts Institute of Technology
> Cambridge, MA 02138

There were telephone numbers, fax, e-mail. Evans turned the cards over. It all looked straightforward.

Kenner said, "Now, if you and Miss Jones will excuse us . . ."

They were outside, in the hallway, looking into the living room through the large glass doors. Morton was sitting on one couch. Kenner and San-jong were on the other. The discussion was quiet. In fact, it looked to Evans just like one more of the endless investment meetings that Morton endured.

Evans picked up the hall phone and dialed a number. "Center for Risk Analysis," a woman said.

"Professor Kenner's office, please."

"One moment." Clicking. Another voice. "Center for Risk Analysis, Professor Kenner's office."

"Good afternoon," Evans said. "My name is Peter Evans, and I'm calling for Professor Kenner."

"I'm sorry, he is not in the office."

"Do you know where he is?"

"Professor Kenner is on extended leave."

"It is important that I reach him," Evans said. "Do you know how I could do that?"

"Well, it shouldn't be hard, since you are in Los Angeles and so is he."

So she had seen the caller ID, Evans thought. He would have imagined Morton had a blocked ID. But evidently not. Or perhaps the secretary in Massachusetts had a way to unblock it.

"Well," Evans said, "can you tell me—"

"I'm sorry, Mr. Evans," she said, "but I'm not able to help you further."

Click.

Sarah said, "What was that about?"

Before Evans could answer, a cell phone rang in the living room. He saw Kenner reach into his pocket, and answer briefly. Then he turned, looked at Evans, and waved.

Sarah said, "His office called him?"

"Looks like it."

"So I guess that's Professor Kenner."

"I guess it is," Evans said. "And we're dismissed."

"Come on," Sarah said. "I'll give you a ride home."

They walked past the open garage, the row of Ferraris glinting in the sun. Morton owned nine vintage Ferraris, which he kept in various garages. These included a 1947 Spyder Corsa, a 1956 Testa Rossa, and a 1959 California Spyder, each worth more than a million dollars. Evans knew this because he reviewed the insurance every time Morton bought another one. At the far end of the line was Sarah's black Porsche convertible. She backed it out, and he climbed in beside her.

Even by Los Angeles standards, Sarah Jones was an extremely beautiful woman. She was tall, with a honey-colored tan, shoulder-length blond hair, blue eyes, perfect features, very white teeth. She was athletic in the casual way that California people were athletic, generally showing up for work in a jogging suit or short tennis skirt. She played golf and tennis, scuba dived, mountain biked, skied, snowboarded, and God knew what else. Evans felt tired whenever he thought about it.

But he also knew that she had "issues," to use the California word. Sarah was the youngest child of a wealthy San Francisco family; her father was a powerful attorney who had held political office; her mother was a former high fashion model. Sarah's older brothers and sisters were all happily married, all successful, and all waiting for her to follow in their footsteps. She found her family's collective success a burden.

Evans had always wondered why she chose to work for Morton, another powerful and wealthy man. Or why she had come to Los Angeles at all, since her family regarded any address south of the Bay Bridge to be hopelessly tawdry. But she was good at her job, and devoted to Morton. And as George often said, her presence was aesthetically pleasing. And the actors and celebrities who attended Morton's parties agreed; she had dated several of them. Which further displeased her family.

Sometimes Evans wondered if everything she did was rebellion. Like her driving—she drove quickly, almost recklessly, shooting down Benedict Canyon, heading into Beverly Hills. "Do you want to go to the office, or your apartment?"

"My apartment," he said. "I have to pick up my car."

She nodded, swerved around a slow-moving Mercedes, then cut left down a side street. Evans took a deep breath.

"Listen," she said. "Do you know what netwar is?"

"What?" He wasn't sure he had heard her over the sound of the wind. "Netwar."

"No," he said. "Why?"

"I heard them talking about it, before you showed up. Kenner and that Sanjong guy."

Evans shook his head. "Doesn't ring a bell. You sure it wasn't net*ware?*"

"Might have been." She sped across Sunset, running a yellow light, and then downshifted as she came to Beverly. "You still on Roxbury?"

He said he was. He looked at her long legs, protruding from the short white skirt. "Who were you going to play tennis with?"

"I don't think you know him."

"It's not, uh . . ."

"No. That's over."

"I see."

"I'm serious, it's *over*."

"Okay, Sarah. I hear you."

"You lawyers are all so suspicious."

"So, it's a lawyer you're playing with?"

"No, it is not a lawyer. I don't play with lawyers."

"What do you do with them?"

"As little as possible. Like everybody else."

"I'm sorry to hear that."

"Except you, of course," she said, giving him a dazzling smile.

She accelerated hard, making the engine scream.

Peter Evans lived in one of the older apartment buildings on Roxbury Drive in the flats of Beverly Hills. There were four units in his building, across the street from Roxbury Park. It was a nice park, a big green expanse, always busy. He saw Hispanic nannies chatting in groups while they minded the children of rich people, and several oldsters sitting in the sun. Off in a corner, a working mother in a business suit had taken off lunch to be with the kids.

The car screeched to a stop. "Here you are."

"Thanks," he said, getting out.

"Isn't it time to move? You've been here five years."

"I'm too busy to move," he said.

"Got your keys?"

"Yeah. But there's always one under the doormat." He reached in his pocket, jingled metal. "All set."

"See you." And she raced off, squealed around the corner, and was gone.

Evans walked through the little sunlit courtyard, and went up to his apartment, on the second floor. As always, he had found Sarah slightly distressing. She was so beautiful, and so flirtatious. He always had the feeling that she kept men at a distance by keeping them off balance. At least, she kept *him* off balance. He could never tell if she wanted him to ask her out or not. But considering his relationship with Morton, it was a bad idea. He would never do it.

As soon as he walked in the door, the phone began to ring. It was his assistant, Heather. She was going home early because she felt sick. Heather frequently felt sick toward the afternoon, in time to beat rush hour traffic. She tended to call in sick on Fridays or Mondays. Yet the firm showed a surprising reluctance to fire her; she had been there for years.

Some said she had had a relationship with Bruce Black, the founding partner, and that, ever since, Bruce lived in constant dread that his wife would find out, since she had all the money. Others claimed Heather was seeing another of the firm's partners, always unspecified. A third story was that she had been on the scene when the firm moved offices from one Century City skyscraper to another, in the course of which she stumbled on some incriminating documents, and copied them.

Evans suspected the truth was more mundane: that she was a clever woman who had worked in the firm long enough to know everything about wrongful termination suits, and now carefully gauged her repeated infractions against the cost and aggravation of their firing her. And in this way worked about thirty weeks a year.

Heather was invariably assigned to the best junior associate in the firm, on the assumption that a really good attorney wouldn't be hampered by her inconstancy. Evans had tried for years to get rid of her. He was promised a new assistant next year. He saw it as a promotion.

"I'm sorry you don't feel well," he told Heather dutifully. One had to go along with her pretense.

"It's just my stomach," she said. "I have to see the doctor."

"Are you going today?"

"Well, I'm trying to get an appointment . . ."

"All right, then."

"But I wanted to tell you they just set a big meeting for the day after tomorrow. Nine o'clock in the big conference room."

"Oh?"

"Mr. Morton just called it. Apparently ten or twelve people are called."

"You know who?"

"No. They didn't say."

Evans thought: Useless. "Okay," he said.

"And don't forget you have the arraignment for Morton's daughter next week. This time it's Pasadena, not downtown. And Margo Lane's calling about her Mercedes lawsuit. And that BMW dealer still wants to go forward."

"He still wants to sue the church?"

"He calls every other day."

"Okay. Is that it?"

"No, there's about ten others. I'll try to leave the list on your desk if I feel well enough . . ."

That meant she wouldn't. "Okay," he said.

"Are you coming in?"

"No, it's too late. I need to get some sleep."

"Then I'll see you tomorrow."

He realized he was very hungry. There was nothing to eat in the refrigerator except a container of yogurt of indeterminate age, some wilted celery, and a half-finished bottle of wine left over from his last date, about two weeks earlier. He had been seeing a girl named Carol who did product liability at another firm. They'd picked each other up in the gym and had begun a desultory, intermittent affair. They were both busy, and not especially interested in each other, to tell the truth. They met once or twice a week, had passionate sex, and then one of them would plead a breakfast appointment the next day and go home early. Sometimes they went to dinner as well, but not usually. Neither of them wanted to take the time.

He went into the living room to check his answering machine. There was no message from Carol, but there was a message from Janis, another girl he sometimes saw.

Janis was a trainer in the gym, the possessor of one of those LA bodies, perfectly proportioned and rock hard. Sex for Janis was an athletic event, involving multiple rooms, couches, and chairs, and it always left Evans feeling vaguely inadequate, as if his body fat weren't low enough for her. But he continued to see her, feeling vaguely proud that he could have a girl who looked so astonishing, even if the sex wasn't that good. And she was often available on short notice. Janis had a boyfriend who was older, a producer for a cable news station. He was out of town a lot, and she was restless.

Janis had left a message the night before. Evans didn't bother to call her back. With Janis it was always that night, or forget it.

Before Janis and Carol, there had been other women, more or less the same. Evans told himself he should find a more satisfying relationship. Something more serious, more adult. More suited to his age and station in life. But he was busy, and just took things as they came.

Meanwhile he was hungry.

He went back down to his car and drove to the nearest drive-in, a hamburger joint on Pico. They knew him there. He had a double cheeseburger and a strawberry shake.

He went home, intending to go to bed. Then he remembered that he owed Morton a call.

"I'm glad you called," Morton said, "I've just been going over some things with—going over some things. Where are we now on my donations to NERF? The Vanutu lawsuit, all that?"

"I don't know," Evans said. "The papers are drawn and signed, but I don't think anything's been paid yet."

"Good. I want you to hold off payments."

"Sure, no problem."

"Just for a while."

"Okay."

"There's no need to say anything to NERF."

"No, no. Of course not."

"Good."

Evans hung up. He went into the bedroom to get undressed. The phone rang again.

It was Janis. The exercise instructor.

"Hey," she said. "I was thinking about you, and I wondered what you were doing."

"As a matter of fact, I was going to go to bed."

"Oh. Pretty early for that."

"I just got in from Iceland."

"So you must be tired."

"Well," he said. "Not that tired."

"Want company?"

"Sure."

She giggled and hung up.

Evans awoke to the sound of rhythmic gasping. He flung his hand across the bed, but Janis wasn't there. Her side of the bed was still warm. He raised his head slightly, yawning. In the warm morning light he saw one slender, perfectly formed leg rise above the foot of the bed, to be joined by the other leg. Then both legs slowly descended. Gasping. Then legs up again.

"Janis," he said, "what are you doing?"

"I have to warm up." She stood, smiling, naked and at ease, confident of her appearance, every muscle outlined. "I have a class at seven."

"What time is it?"

"Six."

He groaned, and buried his head in the pillow.

"You really should get up now," she said. "It shortens your lifespan to sleep in."

He groaned again. Janis was full of health information; it was her job. "How can it possibly shorten my life to sleep?"

"They did studies on rats. They didn't let them sleep, and you know what? They lived longer."

"Uh-huh. Would you mind turning on the coffee?"

"Okay," she said, "but you really should give up coffee . . ." She drifted out of the room.

He swung his feet onto the floor and said, "Haven't you heard? Coffee prevents strokes."

"It does not," she said, from the kitchen. "Coffee has nine hundred twenty-three different chemicals in it, and it is *not* good for you."

"New study," he said. It was true, too.

"Besides, it causes cancer."

"That's never been shown."

"And miscarriages."

"Not a concern for me."

"And nervous tension."

"Janis, please."

She came back, crossing her arms across her perfect breasts as she leaned against the doorjamb. He could see the veins in her lower abdomen, running down to her groin. "Well, you *are* nervous, Peter. You have to admit it."

"Only when I look at your body."

She pouted. "You don't take me seriously." She turned back into the kitchen, showing him her perfect, high glutes. He heard her open the refrigerator. "There's no milk."

"Black is fine."

He stood, and headed for the shower.

"Did you have any damage?" she said.

"From what?"

"From the earthquake. We had a little one, while you were gone. About 4.3."

"Not that I know."

"Well, it sure moved your TV."

He stopped in mid-stride. "What?"

"It moved your TV. Look for yourself."

The morning sunlight that slanted through the window clearly showed the faint outline where the base of the television had compressed the carpet. The TV had been moved about three inches from its former position. It was an old thirty-two-inch monitor, and damned heavy. It didn't move easily. Looking at it now gave Evans a chill.

"You're lucky," she said. "You have all those glass things on your mantel. They break all the time, even in a small quake. Do you have an insurance policy?"

He didn't answer. He was bent over, looking behind the television at the connections. Everything looked normal. But he hadn't looked behind his TV for about a year. He wouldn't really know.

"By the way," she said, "this is not organic coffee. You should at least drink organic. Are you listening to me?"

"Just a minute." He had crouched down in front of the television, looking for anything unusual beneath the set. He could see nothing out of the ordinary.

"And what is *this?*" she said.

He looked over. She was holding a donut in her hand. "Peter," Janis said severely, "do you know how much fat's in these things? You might as well just eat a stick of butter."

"I know . . . I should give them up."

"Well, you should. Unless you want to develop diabetes later in life. Why are you on the floor?"

"I was checking the TV."

"Why? Is it broken?"

"I don't think so." He got to his feet.

"The water is running in your shower," she said. "That's not environmentally conscious." She poured coffee, handed it to him. "Go and take your shower. I've got to get to my class."

When he came out of the shower, she was gone. He pulled the covers up over the bed (as close as he ever came to making it) and went into the closet to dress for the day.

CENTURY CITY
TUESDAY, AUGUST 24
8:45 A.M.

The law firm of Hassle and Black occupied five floors of an office building in Century City. They were a forward-looking, socially aware firm.
They represented many Hollywood celebrities and wealthy activists who
were committed to environmental concerns. The fact that they also represented three of the biggest land developers in Orange County was less
often publicized. But as the partners said, it kept the firm balanced.

Evans had joined the firm because of its many environmentally active
clients, particularly George Morton. He was one of four attorneys who
worked almost full-time for Morton, and for Morton's pet charity, the
National Environmental Resource Fund, NERF.

Nevertheless, he was still a junior associate, and his office was small,
with a window that looked directly at the flat glass wall of the skyscraper
across the street.

Evans looked over the papers on his desk. It was the usual stuff that
came to junior attorneys. There was a residential sublet, an employment
agreement, written interrogatories for a bankruptcy, a form for the Fran-
chise Tax Board, and two drafted letters threatening lawsuits on behalf
of his clients—one for an artist against a gallery refusing to return his
unsold paintings, and one for George Morton's mistress, who claimed
that the parking attendant at Sushi Roku had scratched her Mercedes
convertible while parking it.

The mistress, Margaret Lane, was an ex-actress with a bad temper and a propensity for litigation. Whenever George neglected her—which, in recent months, was increasingly often—she would find a reason to sue somebody. And the suit would inevitably land on Evans's desk. He made a note to call Margo; he didn't think she should proceed with this suit, but she would take convincing.

The next item was a spreadsheet from a Beverly Hills BMW dealer who claimed that the "What Would Jesus Drive?" campaign had hurt his business because it denigrated luxury cars. Apparently his dealership was a block from a church, and some parishioners had come around after services and harangued his sales staff. The dealer didn't like that, but it looked to Evans as if his sales figures were higher this year than last. Evans made a note to call him, too.

Then he checked his e-mails, sorting through twenty offers to enlarge his penis, ten offers for tranquilizers, and another ten to get a new mortgage now before rates started to rise. There were only a half-dozen e-mails of importance, the first from Herb Lowenstein, asking to see him. Lowenstein was the senior partner on Morton's account; he did mostly estate management, but handled other aspects of investments as well. For Morton, estate management was a full-time job.

Evans wandered down the hall to Herb's office.

Lisa, Herb Lowenstein's assistant, was listening on the phone. She hung up and looked guilty when Evans entered. "He's talking to Jack Nicholson."

"How is Jack?"

"He's good. Finishing a picture with Meryl. There were some problems."

Lisa Ray was a bright-eyed twenty-seven-year-old, and a dedicated gossip. Evans had long ago come to rely on her for office information of all sorts.

"What's Herb want me for?"

"Something about Nick Drake."

"What's this meeting about tomorrow at nine?"

"I don't *know*," she said, sounding amazed. "I can't find out a *thing*.
"Who called it?"

"Morton's accountants." She looked at the phone on her desk. "Oh, he's hung up. You can go right in."

Herb Lowenstein stood and shook Evans's hand perfunctorily. He was a pleasant-faced balding man, mild-mannered and slightly nerdy. His office was decorated with dozens of pictures of his family, stacked three and four deep on his desk. He got on well with Evans, if only because these days, whenever Morton's thirty-year-old daughter got arrested for cocaine possession, it was Evans who went downtown at midnight to post her bail. Lowenstein had done it for many years, and now was glad to sleep through the night.

"So," he said, "how was Iceland?"

"Good. Cold."

"Is everything okay?"

"Sure."

"I mean, between George and Nick. Everything okay there?"

"I think so. Why?"

"Nick is worried. He called me twice in the last hour."

"About what?"

"Where are we on George's NERF donation?"

"Nick's asking that?"

"Is there a problem about it?"

"George wants to hold off for a while."

"Why?"

"He didn't say."

"Is it this Kenner guy?"

"George didn't say. He just said, hold off." Evans wondered how Lowenstein knew about Kenner.

"What do I tell Nick?"

"Tell him it's in the works and we don't have a date for him yet."

"But there's not a problem with it, is there?"

"Not that I've been told," Evans said.

"Okay," Lowenstein said. "In this room. Tell me: Is there a problem?"

"There might be." Evans was thinking that George rarely held up charitable donations. And there had been a certain tension in the brief talk he had with him the night before.

"What's this meeting about tomorrow morning?" Lowenstein said. "The big conference room."

"Beats me."

"George didn't tell you?"

"No."

"Nick is very upset."

"Well, that's not unusual for Nick."

"Nick has heard of this Kenner guy. He thinks he's a troublemaker. Some kind of anti-environmental guy."

"I doubt that. He's a professor at MIT. In some environmental science."

"Nick thinks he's a troublemaker."

"I couldn't say."

"He overheard you and Morton talking about Kenner on the airplane."

"Nick should stop listening at keyholes."

"He's worried about his standing with George."

"Not surprising," Evans said. "Nick screwed up on a big check. Got deposited in the wrong account."

"I heard about that. It was an error by a volunteer. You can't blame Nick for that."

"It doesn't build confidence."

"It was deposited to the International Wilderness Preservation Society. A great organization. And the money is being transferred back, even as we speak."

"That's fine."

"Where are you in this?"

"Nowhere. I just do what the client says."

"But you advise him."

"If he asks me. He hasn't asked."

"It sounds like you've lost confidence yourself."

Evans shook his head. "Herb," he said. "I'm not aware of any problem. I'm aware of a delay. That's all."

"Okay," Lowenstein said, reaching for the phone. "I'll calm Nick down."

Evans went back to his office. His phone was ringing. He answered it. "What are you doing today?" Morton said.

"Not much. Paperwork."

"That can wait. I want you to go over and see how that Vanutu lawsuit is coming."

"Jeez, George, it's still pretty preliminary. I think the filing is several months away."

"Pay them a visit," Morton said.

"Okay, they're in Culver City, I'll call over there and—"

"No. Don't call. Just go."

"But if they're not expecting—"

"That's right. That's what I want. Let me know what you find out, Peter."

And he hung up.

The Vanutu litigation team had taken over an old warehouse south of Culver City. It was an industrial area, with potholes in the streets. There was nothing to see from the curb: just a plain brick wall, and a door with the street number in battered metal numerals. Evans pushed the buzzer and was admitted to a small walled-off reception area. He could hear the low murmur of voices from the other side of the wall, but he could see nothing at all.

Two armed guards stood on either side of the far door, leading into the warehouse itself. A receptionist sat at a small desk. She gave him an unfriendly look.

"And you are?"

"Peter Evans, Hassle and Black."

"To see?"

"Mr. Balder."

"You have an appointment?"

"No."

The receptionist looked disbelieving. "I will buzz his assistant."

"Thank you."

The receptionist talked on the phone in a low voice. He heard her mention the name of the law firm. Evans looked at the two guards. They were from a private security firm. They stared back at him, their faces blank, unsmiling.

The receptionist hung up and said, "Ms. Haynes will be out in a moment." She nodded to the guards.

One of them came over and said to Evans, "Just a formality, sir. May I see some identification?"

Evans gave him his driver's license.

"Do you have any cameras or recording equipment on your person?"

"No," Evans said.

"Any disks, drives, flash cards, or other computer equipment?"

"No."

"Are you armed, sir?"

"No."

"Would you mind raising your arms for a moment?" When Evans gave him a strange look, the guard said, "Just think of it like airport security," and he patted him down. But he was also clearly feeling for wires. He ran his fingers over the collar of Evans's shirt, felt the stitching in his jacket, ran his finger around his waistband, and then asked him to take off his shoes. Finally he passed an electronic wand over him.

"You guys are serious," Evans said.

"Yes we are. Thank you, sir."

The guard stepped away, resuming his place at the wall. There was no place to sit, so Evans just stood there and waited. It was probably two minutes before the door opened. An attractive but tough-looking woman in her late twenties, with short dark hair and blue eyes, wearing jeans and a white shirt, said, "Mr. Evans? I'm Jennifer Haynes." Her handshake was firm. "I work with John Balder. Come this way."

They went inside.

They were in a narrow corridor, with a locked door at the far end. Evans realized it was a security lock—two doors to get inside.

"What was that all about?" he said, indicating the guards.

"We've had a little trouble."

"What kind of trouble?"

"People want to know what's going on here."

"Uh-huh . . ."

"We've learned to be careful."

She held her card against the door, and it buzzed open.

They entered an old warehouse—a vast, high-ceilinged space, separated into large rooms by glass partitions. Immediately to his left, behind glass, Evans saw a room filled with computer terminals, each manned by a young person with a stack of documents beside their keyboard. In big lettering on the glass it said, "DATA-RAW."

To his right, there was a matching conference room labeled "SATELLITES/RADIOSONDE." Evans saw four people inside that room, busily discussing huge blowups of a graph on the wall, jagged lines on a grid.

Farther along there was another room marked "GENERAL CIRCULATION MODELS (GCMS)." Here the walls were plastered with large maps of the world, graphical representations in many colors.

"Wow," Evans said. "Big operation."

"Big lawsuit," Jennifer Haynes replied. "These are all our issue teams. They're mostly graduate students in climate science, not attorneys. Each team is researching a different issue for us." She pointed around the warehouse. "The first group does raw data, meaning processed data from the Goddard Institute for Space Studies at Columbia University, in New York, from the USHCN at Oak Ridge, Tennessee, and from Hadley Center in East Anglia, England. Those are the major sources of temperature data from around the world."

"I see," Evans said.

"Then the group over there works on satellite data. Orbiting satellites have recorded temperatures of the upper atmosphere since 1979, so there is more than a twenty-year record. We're trying to figure out what to do about it."

"What to do about it?"

"The satellite data's a problem," she said.

"Why?"

As though she hadn't heard him, she pointed to the next room. "The team there is doing comparative analyses of GCMs—meaning the computer-generated climate models—from the 1970s to the present. As you know, these models are immensely complex, manipulating a million variables or more at once. They are by far the most complex computer models ever created by man. We're dealing with American, British, and German models, primarily."

"I see . . ." Evans was starting to feel overwhelmed.

"And the team down there is doing sea-level issues. Around the corner is paleoclimate. Those're proxy studies, of course. And the final team is dealing with solar irradiance and aerosols. Then we have an off-site team at UCLA that is doing atmospheric feedback mechanisms, primarily focusing on cloud cover as it varies with temperature change. And that's about all of it." She paused, seeing the confusion on Evans's face. "I'm sorry. Since you work with George Morton, I assumed you were familiar with all this stuff."

"Who said I work with George Morton?"

She smiled. "We know our job, Mr. Evans."

They passed a final glass-walled room that had no label. It was filled with charts and huge photographs, and three-dimensional models of the earth set inside plastic cubes. "What's this?" he said.

"Our AV team. They prepare visuals for the jury. Some of the data is extremely complex, and we're trying to find the simplest and most forceful way to present it."

They walked on. Evans said, "Is it really that complicated?"

"That's correct," she said. "The island nation of Vanutu is actually four coral atolls in the southern Pacific, which have a maximum elevation of twenty feet above sea level. The eight thousand inhabitants of those islands are at risk of being flooded out by rising sea levels caused by global warming."

"Yes," Evans said. "I understand that. But why do you have so many people working on the science?"

She looked at him oddly. "Because we're trying to win the case."

"Yes . . ."

"And it's not an easy case to win."

"What do you mean?" Evans said. "This is global warming. Everybody knows that global warming is—"

A voice boomed from the other end of the warehouse. "Is *what?*"

A bald, bespectacled man came toward them. He had an ungainly gait, and looked like his nickname: the Bald Eagle. As always, John Balder was dressed all in blue: a blue suit, a blue shirt, and a blue tie. His manner was intense, his eyes narrowed as he looked at Evans. In spite of himself, Evans was intimidated to meet the famous litigator.

Evans extended his hand. "Peter Evans, Hassle and Black."

"And you work with George Morton?"

"Yes sir, I do."

"We are indebted to Mr. Morton's generosity. We strive to be worthy of his support."

"I'll tell him that, sir."

"I'm sure you will. You were speaking of global warming, Mr. Evans. Is it a subject that interests you?"

"Yes, sir, it does. And every concerned citizen of the planet."

"I certainly agree. But tell me. What *is* global warming, as you understand it?"

Evans tried to conceal his surprise. He hadn't expected to be quizzed. "Why do you ask?"

"We ask everybody who comes here. We're trying to get a feel for the general state of knowledge. What's global warming?"

"Global warming is the heating up of the earth from burning fossil fuels."

"Actually, that is not correct."

"It's not?"

"Not even close. Perhaps you'd try again."

Evans paused. It was obvious he was being interrogated by a fussy and precise legal mind. He knew the type only too well, from law school. He thought for a moment, choosing his words carefully. "Global warming is, uh, the heating up of the surface of the earth from the excess of carbon dioxide in the atmosphere that is produced by burning fossil fuels."

"Again, not correct."

"Why not?"

"Several reasons. At a minimum, I count four errors in the statement you just made."

"I don't understand," Evans said. "My statement—that's what global warming is."

"In fact, it is not." Balder's tone was crisp, authoritative. "Global warming is the *theory*—"

"—hardly a theory, anymore—"

"No, it is a *theory*," Balder said. "Believe me, I wish it were otherwise. But in fact, global warming is the *theory* that increased levels of carbon dioxide and certain other gases *are causing* an increase in the *average temperature* of the earth's *atmosphere* because of the so-called 'greenhouse effect.'"

"Well, okay," Evans said. "That's a more exact definition, but . . ."

"Mr. Evans, you yourself believe in global warming, I take it?"

"Of course."

"Believe in it strongly?"

"Sure. Everybody does."

"When you have a strongly held belief, don't you think it's important to express that belief accurately?"

Evans was starting to sweat. He really felt like he was back in law school. "Well, sir, I guess . . . not really, in this case. Because when you refer to global warming, everybody knows what you are talking about."

"Do they? I suspect that even you don't know what you are talking about."

Evans felt a burst of hot anger. Before he could check himself, he had blurted, "Look, just because I may not be expressing the fine details of the science—"

"I'm not concerned about *details*, Mr. Evans. I'm concerned about the *core* of your strongly held beliefs. I suspect you have no basis for those beliefs."

"With all due respect, that's ridiculous." He caught his breath. "Sir."

"You mean you do have such a basis?"

"Of course I do."

Balder looked at him thoughtfully. He seemed pleased with himself. "In that case, you can be a great help to this lawsuit. Would you mind giving us an hour of your time?"

"Uh . . . I guess so."

"Would you mind if we videotaped you?"

"No, but . . . why?"

Balder turned to Jennifer Haynes, who said, "We're trying to establish a baseline for what a well-informed person such as yourself knows about global warming. To help us refine our jury presentation."

"Sort of a mock jury of one?"

"Exactly. We've interviewed several people already."

"Okay," Evans said. "I guess I could schedule that at some point."

"*Now* is a good time," Balder said. He turned to Jennifer. "Get your team together in room four."

"Of course I'd like to help," Evans said, "but I came here to get an overview—"

"Because you've heard there are problems with the lawsuit? There aren't. But there are significant challenges," Balder said. He glanced at his watch. "I'm about to go into a meeting," he said. "You spend some time with Ms. Haynes, and when you're done, we'll talk about the litigation as I see it. Is that all right with you?"

There was nothing Evans could do but agree.

They put him in a conference room at the end of a long table, and aimed the video camera at him from the far end. Just like a deposition, he thought.

Five young people drifted into the room and took seats at the table. All were casually dressed, in jeans and T-shirts. Jennifer Haynes introduced them so quickly that Evans didn't catch their names. She explained that they were all graduate students in different scientific disciplines.

While they were setting up, Jennifer slipped into a chair beside his and said, "I'm sorry John was so rough on you. He's frustrated and under a lot of pressure."

"From the case?"

"Yes."

"What kind of pressure?"

"This session may give you some idea what we're dealing with." She turned to the others. "Are we ready?"

Heads nodded, notebooks flipped open. The camera light came on. Jennifer said, "Interview with Peter Evans, of Hassle and Black, on Tuesday, August twenty-fourth. Mr. Evans, we'd like to go over your views about the evidence that supports global warming. This isn't a test; we'd just like to clarify how you think about the issue."

"Okay," Evans said.

"Let's begin informally. Tell us what you know about the evidence for global warming."

"Well," Evans said, "I know that temperatures around the globe have risen dramatically in the last twenty or thirty years as a result of increases in carbon dioxide that is released by industry when fossil fuels are burned."

"Okay. And by a dramatic rise in temperature, you mean how much?"

"I think about a degree."

"Fahrenheit or Celsius?"

"Fahrenheit."

"And this rise has occurred over twenty years?"

"Twenty or thirty, yes."

"And earlier in the twentieth century?"

"Temperatures went up then, too, but not as fast."

"Okay," she said. "Now I am going to show you a graph . . ." She pulled out a graph* on foam core backing:

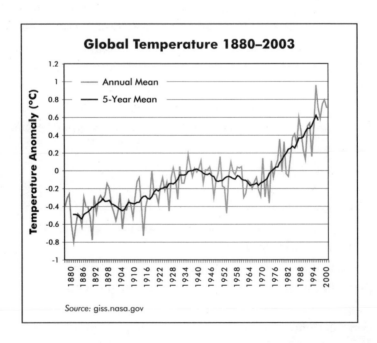

* All graphs are generated using tabular data from the following standard data sets: GISS (Columbia); CRU (East Anglia); GHCN and USHCN (Oak Ridge). See Appendix II for a full discussion.

"Does this look familiar to you?" she asked.

"I've seen it before," Evans said.

"It's taken from the NASA–Goddard data set used by the UN and other organizations. Do you consider the UN a trustworthy source?"

"Yes."

"So we can regard this graph as accurate? Unbiased? No monkey business?"

"Yes."

"Good. Do you know what this graph represents?"

Evans could read that much. He said, "It's the mean global temperature from all the weather stations around the world for the last hundred years or so."

"That's right," she said. "And how do you interpret this graph?"

"Well," he said, "it shows what I was describing." He pointed to the red line. "World temperatures have been rising since about 1890, but they start to go up steeply around 1970, when industrialization is most intense, which is the real proof of global warming."

"Okay," she said. "So the rapid increase in temperature since 1970 was caused by what?"

"Rising carbon dioxide levels from industrialization."

"Good. In other words, as the carbon dioxide goes up, the temperature goes up."

"Yes."

"All right. Now you mentioned the temperature started to rise from 1890, up to about 1940. And we see here that it did. What caused that rise? Carbon dioxide?"

"Um . . . I'm not sure."

"Because there was much less industrialization back in 1890, and yet look how temperatures go up. Was carbon dioxide rising in 1890?"

"I'm not sure."

"Actually, it was. Here is a graph showing carbon dioxide levels and temperature."

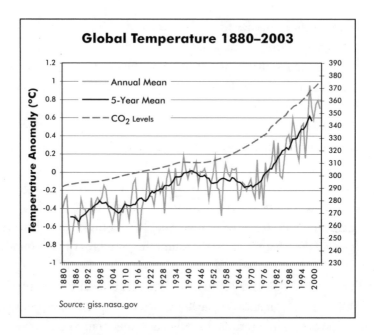

"Okay," Evans said. "Just what you would expect. Carbon dioxide goes up, and makes temperatures go up."

"Good," she said. "Now I want to direct your attention to the period from 1940 to 1970. As you see, during that period the global temperature actually went down. You see that?"

"Yes . . ."

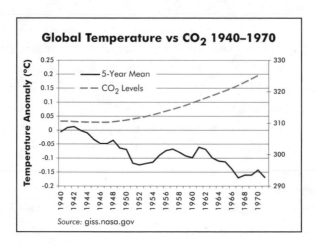

STATE OF FEAR ▶ 87

"Let me show you a closeup of that period." She took out another chart.

"This is a thirty-year period. One third of a century during which temperatures declined. Crops were damaged by frost in summer, glaciers in Europe advanced. What caused the decline?"

"I don't know."

"Was carbon dioxide rising during that period?"

"Yes."

"So, if rising carbon dioxide is the cause of rising temperatures, why didn't it cause temperatures to rise from 1940 to 1970?"

"I don't know," Evans said. "There must have been another factor. Or it could be an anomaly. There are anomalies within broad secular trends. Just look at the stock market."

"Does the stock market have anomalies that last thirty years?"

He shrugged. "Or it could have been soot. Or particulate matter in the air. There were a lot of particulates back then, before environmental laws took effect. Or maybe some other factor."

"These graphs show that carbon dioxide rose continuously, but temperature did not. It rose, then fell, then rose again. Even so, I take it you remain convinced that carbon dioxide has caused the most recent temperature rise?"

"Yes. Everybody knows that's the cause."

"Does this graph trouble you at all?"

"No," Evans said. "I admit it raises some questions, but then not everything is known about the climate. So, no. The graph doesn't trouble me."

"Okay, good. I'm glad to hear it. Let's move on. You said this graph was the average of weather stations around the world. How reliable is that weather data, do you think?"

"I have no idea."

"Well, for example, in the late nineteenth century, the data were generated by people going out to a little box and writing down the temperature twice a day. Maybe they forgot for a few days. Maybe somebody in their family was sick. They had to fill it in later."

"That was back then."

"Right. But how accurate do you think weather records are from Poland in the 1930s? Or Russian provinces since 1990?"

"Not very good, I would guess."

"And I would agree. So over the last hundred years, a fair number of reporting stations around the world may not have provided high-quality, reliable data."

"That could be," Evans said.

"Over the years, which country do you imagine has the best-maintained network of weather stations over a large area?"

"The US?"

"Right. I think there is no dispute about that. Here is another graph."

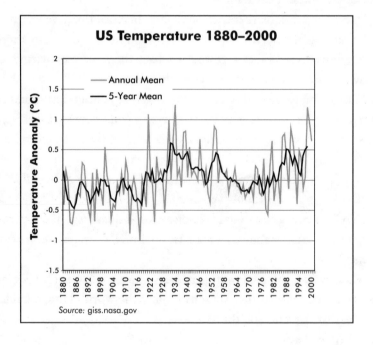

"Does this graph look like the first one we saw of world temperatures?"

"Not exactly."

"What is the change in temperature since 1880?"

"Looks like, uh, a third of a degree."

A third of a degree Celsius in a hundred and twenty years. Not very dramatic." She pointed to the graph. "And what was the warmest year of the last century?"

"Looks like 1934."

"Does this graph indicate to you that global warming is occurring?"

"Well. The temperature *is* going up."

"For the last thirty years, yes. But it went *down* for the previous thirty years. And current temperatures in the US are roughly the same as they were in the 1930s. So: Does this graph argue for global warming?"

"Yes," Evans said. "It's just not as dramatic in the US as it is in the rest of the world, but it's still happening."

"Does it trouble you that the most accurate temperature record shows the least warming?"

"No. Because global warming is a global phenomenon. It's not just the US."

"If you had to defend these graphs in a court of law, do you think you could persuade a jury of your position? Or would a jury look at the graph and say, this global warming stuff is nothing serious?"

"Leading the witness," he said, laughing.

In fact, Evans was feeling slightly uneasy. But only slightly. He'd heard such claims before, at environmental conferences. Industry hacks could slap together data that they had massaged and twisted, and give a convincing, well-prepared speech, and before Evans knew it, he'd start to doubt what he knew.

As if she were reading his mind, Jennifer said, "These graphs show solid data, Peter. Temperature records from Goddard Institute for Space Studies at Columbia University. Carbon dioxide levels from Mauna Loa and the Law Dome ice cores in Antarctica.* All generated by researchers who believe firmly in global warming."

"Yes," he said. "Because the overwhelming consensus of scientists

---

* D. M. Etheridge, et al., 1996, "Natural and anthropogenic changes in atmospheric CO_2 over the last 1,000 years from air in Antarctic ice and firn," *Journal of Geophysical Research* 101 (1996): 4115–28.

around the world is that global warming *is* happening and it *is* a major worldwide threat."

"Okay, good," she said smoothly. "I'm glad that none of this changes your views. Let's turn to some other questions of interest. David?"

One of the graduate students leaned forward. "Mr. Evans, I'd like to talk to you about land use, the urban heat island effect, and satellite data on the temperature of the troposphere."

Evans thought, *Oh Jesus*. But he just nodded. "Okay . . ."

"One of the issues we're trying to address concerns how surface temperatures change with land use. Are you familiar with that issue?"

"Not really, no." He looked at his watch. "Frankly, you people are working at a level of detail that is beyond me. I just listen to what the scientists say—"

"And we're preparing a lawsuit," Jennifer said, "based on what scientists say. This level of detail is where the suit will be fought."

"Fought?" Evans shrugged. "Who's going to fight it? Nobody with any stature. There isn't a reputable scientist in the world who doesn't believe in global warming."

"On that point, you are wrong," she said. "The defense will call full professors from MIT, Harvard, Columbia, Duke, Virginia, Colorado, UC Berkeley, and other prestigious schools. They will call the former president of the National Academy of Sciences. They may also call some Nobel Prize winners. They will bring in professors from England, from the Max Planck Institute in Germany, from Stockholm University in Sweden. These professors will argue that global warming is at best unproven, and at worst pure fantasy."

"Their research paid for by industry, no doubt."

"A few. Not all."

"Arch-conservatives. *Neocons*."

"The focus in litigation," she said, "will be on the data."

Evans looked at them and saw the concern on their faces. And he thought, *They really believe they might lose this thing.*

"But this is ridiculous," Evans said. "All you have to do is read the newspapers, or watch television—"

"Newspapers and television are susceptible to carefully orchestrated media campaigns. Lawsuits are not."

"Then forget mass media," Evans said, "and just read the scientific journals—"

"We do. They're not necessarily helpful to our side. Mr. Evans, we have a lot to go over. If you'd hold your protestations, we can get on with the issues."

It was at that moment that the phone buzzed, and Balder delivered him from his torment. "Send the guy from Hassle and Black into my office," he said. "I have ten minutes for him."

Balder was ensconced in a glass-walled office, with his feet up on a glass desk, working his way through a stack of briefs and research papers. He didn't take his feet down as Evans came in.

"You find it interesting?" he said. He meant the interrogation.

"In a way," Evans said. "But if you'll pardon my saying so, I get the sense they're worried they might lose."

"I have no doubt that we will win this case," Balder said. "No doubt whatsoever. But I don't want my people thinking that way! I want them worried as hell. I want my team running scared before any trial. And especially this one. We are bringing this suit against the EPA, and in anticipation of that, the agency has retained outside counsel in the person of Barry Beckman."

"Whew," Evans said. "Big guns."

Barry Beckman was the most famous litigator of his generation. A professor at Stanford Law School at twenty-eight, he left the university in his early thirties to go into private practice. He had already represented Microsoft, Toyota, Phillips, and a host of other multinationals. Beckman had an incredibly agile mind, a charming manner, a quick sense of humor, and a photographic memory. Everyone knew that when he argued before the Supreme Court (as he had done three times already) he cited document page numbers as he answered the Justices' questions. "Your honor, I believe you will find that in footnote 17 on the bottom of page 237." Like that.

"Barry has his faults," Balder said. "He has so much information at his fingertips that he can easily slip into irrelevance. He likes to hear himself talk. His arguments drift. I have beaten him once. And lost to him, once. But one thing is sure: We can expect an *extremely* well-prepared opposition."

"Isn't it a little unusual to hire an attorney before you've even filed?"

"It's a tactic," Balder said. "The current administration doesn't want to defend this lawsuit. They believe they will win, but they don't want the negative publicity that will accompany their brief against global warming. So they hope to intimidate us into dropping the case. And of course we never would. Especially now that we are fully funded, thanks to Mr. Morton."

"That's good," Evans said.

"At the same time, the challenges are significant. Barry will argue that there is insufficient evidence for global warming. He will argue that the supporting science is weak. He will argue that the predictions from ten and fifteen years ago have already been shown to be wrong. And he will argue that even leading proponents of global warming have publicly expressed doubts about whether it can be predicted, whether it is a serious problem—and indeed, whether it's occurring at all."

"Leading proponents have said that?"

Balder sighed. "They have. In journals."

"I've never read anything of that sort."

"The statements exist. Barry will dig them out." He shook his head. "Some experts have expressed different views at different times. Some have said rising carbon dioxide isn't a big problem; now they say it is. So far, we don't have a single expert witness that can't be turned. Or made to look very foolish on cross."

Evans nodded sympathetically. He was familiar with this circumstance. One of the first things you learned in law school was that the law was not about truth. It was about dispute resolution. In the course of resolving a dispute, the truth might or might not emerge. Often it did not. Prosecutors might know a criminal was guilty, and still be unable to convict him. It happened all the time.

"That's why," Balder said, "this case is going to hinge on the sea-level records in the Pacific. We are collecting all available data records now."

"Why does the case hinge on that?"

"Because I believe," Balder said, "that this is a case we should bait and switch. The case is about global warming, but that's not where the emotional impact is for a jury. Juries aren't comfortable reading graphs. And all this talk about tenths of a degree Celsius goes right over their heads. It's technical detail; it's the quibbles of experts; and it's incredibly boring for normal people.

"No, the jury will see this as a case about helpless, victimized, impoverished people being flooded out of their ancestral homelands. A case about the terror of sea levels rising precipitously—and inexplicably—with no conceivable cause *unless you accept that something extraordinary and unprecedented has affected the entire world* in recent years. Something that is causing the sea levels to rise and to threaten the lives of innocent men, women, and children."

"And that something is global warming."

Balder nodded. "The jury will have to draw their own conclusions. If we can show them a convincing record of rising sea levels, we will be on very strong ground. When juries see that damage has been done, they are inclined to blame *somebody*."

"Okay." Evans saw where Balder was going. "So the sea-level data is important."

"Yes, but it needs to be solid, irrefutable."

"Is that so hard to obtain?"

Balder cocked an eyebrow. "Mr. Evans, do you know anything about the study of sea levels?"

"No. I just know that sea levels are rising around the world."

"Unfortunately, that claim is in considerable dispute."

"You're joking."

"It is well known," Balder said, "that I have no sense of humor."

"But sea level can't be disputed," Evans said. "It's too simple. You put a mark on a dock at high tide, measure it year after year, watch it go up . . . I mean, how difficult can it be?"

Balder sighed. "You think sea level is simple? Trust me, it's not. Have you ever heard of the geoid? No? The geoid is the equipotential surface of the earth's gravitational field that approximates the mean sea surface. That help you?"

Evans shook his head.

"Well, it is a core concept in the measurement of sea levels." Balder flipped through the stack of papers in front of him. "How about glacio-hydro-isostatic modeling? Eustatic and tectonic effects on shoreline dynamics? Holocene sedimentary sequences? Intertidal foraminifera distributions? Carbon analysis of coastal paleoenviron-ments? Aminostratigraphy? No? Not ringing a bell? Let me assure you, sea level is a fiercely debated specialty." He tossed the last of the papers aside. "That's what I'm working through now. But the disputes within the field give added importance to finding an unimpeachable set of data."

"And you are obtaining this data?"

"Waiting for them to arrive, yes. The Australians have several sets. The French have at least one in Moorea and perhaps another in Papeete. There is a set that was funded by the V. Allen Willy Foundation, but it may be of too short a duration. And other sets as well. We will have to see."

The intercom buzzed. The assistant said, "Mr. Balder, it's Mr. Drake on the line, from NERF."

"All right." Balder turned to Evans, extended a hand. "Nice talking with you, Mr. Evans. Again, our thanks to George. Tell him any time he wants to have a look around, he can drop by. We are always hard at work here. Good luck to you. Close the door on your way out."

Balder turned away, picking up the phone. Evans heard him say,

"Well, Nick, what the fuck is going on at NERF? Are you going to fix this for me, or not?"

Evans closed the door.

He walked out of Balder's office with a sense of nagging unease. Balder was one of the most persuasive men on the planet. He had known Evans was there on behalf of George Morton. He knew Morton was on the verge of making a huge contribution to the lawsuit. Balder should have been totally upbeat, radiating confidence. And he had, indeed, begun that way.

I have no doubt we will win this lawsuit.

But then, Evans had heard:

The challenges are significant.

I do not have a single expert witness who can't be turned.

This is a case we should bait and switch.

This case will hinge on sea-level records.

Sea level is a fiercely debated specialty.

We will have to see.

It certainly wasn't a conversation calculated to raise Evans's level of confidence. Neither, for that matter, was the video session he'd had with Jennifer Haynes, discussing the scientific problems the lawsuit would face.

But then, as he considered it, he decided that these expressions of doubt were actually a sign of confidence on the part of the legal team. Evans was an attorney himself; he had come to learn the issues sur-rounding the trial, and they had been forthright with him. It was a case they would win, even though it would not be easy, because of the complexity of the data and the short attention span of the jury.

So: would he recommend that Morton continue?

Of course he would.

Jennifer was waiting for him outside Balder's office. She said, "They're ready for you back in the conference room."

Evans said, "I'm really sorry, I can't. My schedule . . ."

"I understand," she said, "we'll do it another time. I was wondering if your schedule was really tight, or whether there was time for you and me to have lunch."

"Oh," Evans said, without missing a beat, "my schedule isn't that tight."

"Good," she said.

They had lunch in a Mexican restaurant in Culver City. It was quiet. There were a handful of film editors in the corner, from nearby Sony Studios. A couple of high school kids necking. A group of older women in sunhats.

They sat in a corner booth and both ordered the special. Evans said, "Balder seems to think the sea-level data is key."

"That's what Balder thinks. Frankly, I'm not so sure."

"Why is that?"

"Nobody's seen all the data. But even if it's high quality, it needs to show a substantial sea-level rise to impress a jury. It may not."

"How could it not?" Evans said. "With glaciers melting, and breaking off Antarctica—"

"Even so, it may not," she said. "You know the Maldive Islands in the Indian Ocean? They were concerned about flooding, so a team of Scandinavian researchers came in to study sea levels. The scientists found no rise in several centuries—and a fall in the last twenty years."

"A fall? Was that published?"

"Last year," she said. The food came; Jennifer gave a dismissive wave of her hand: enough shop talk for now. She ate her burrito with gusto, wiping her chin with the back of her hand. He saw a jagged white scar running from her palm down the underside of her forearm. She said, "God, I love this food. You can't get decent Mexican food in DC."

"Is that where you're from?"

She nodded. "I came out to help John."

"He asked you?"

"I couldn't turn him down." She shrugged. "So I see my boyfriend on alternate weekends. He comes out here, or I go back there. But if this trial goes forward, it will be a year, maybe two years. I don't think our relationship will make it."

"What does he do? Your boyfriend."

"Attorney."

Evans smiled. "Sometimes I think everyone's an attorney."

"Everyone is. He does securities law. Not my thing."

"What's your thing?"

"Witness prep and jury selection. Psychological analysis of the pool. That's why I'm in charge of the focus groups."

"I see."

"We know that most people we might put on the jury will have heard of global warming, and most will probably be inclined to think it is real."

"Jesus, I'd *hope* so," Evans said. "I mean, it's been an established fact for the last fifteen years."

"But we need to determine what people will believe in the face of contrary evidence."

"Such as?"

"Such as the graphs I showed you today. Or the satellite data. You know about the satellite data?"

Evans shook his head.

"The theory of global warming predicts that the upper atmosphere will warm from trapped heat, just like a greenhouse. The surface of the Earth warms later. But since 1979 we've had orbiting satellites that can continuously measure the atmosphere five miles up. They show that the upper atmosphere is warming much less than the ground is."

"Maybe there's a problem with the data—"

"Trust me, the satellite data have been re-analyzed dozens of times," she said. "They're probably the most intensely scrutinized data in the world. But the data from weather balloons agree with the satellites. They show much less warming than expected by the theory." She shrugged. "Another problem for us. We're working on it."

"How?"

"We think it'll prove too complex for a jury. The details of MSUs—microwave-sounding units, cross-track scanners with four-channel radiance analysis—and the questions about whether channel 2 has been corrected for diurnal drifts and inter-satellite offsets, time-varying non-linear instrumental responses . . . We hope it will make them throw up their hands. Anyway. Enough of all that." She wiped her face with her napkin and again he saw the white scar that ran down the underside of her arm.

"How'd you get that?" he said.

She shrugged. "In law school."

"And I thought my school was tough."

"I taught an inner-city karate class," she said. "Sometimes it went late. You want any more of these chips?"

"No," he said.

"Shall we get the check?"

"Tell me," he said.

"There's not a lot to tell. One night, I got in my car to drive home, and a kid jumped in the passenger seat and pulled a gun. Told me to start driving."

"Kid from your class?"

"No. An older kid. Late twenties."

"What'd you do?"

"I told him to get out. He told me to drive. So I started the car, and as I put it in gear I asked him where he wanted me to go. And he was stupid enough to point, so I hit him in the windpipe. I didn't hit him hard enough, and he got off a round, blew out the windshield. Then I hit him again with my elbow. Couple, three times."

"What happened to him?" he said.

"He died."

"Jesus," Evans said.

"Some people make bad decisions," she said. "What're you staring at me like that for? He was six-two and two-ten and had a record from here to Nebraska. Armed robbery, assault with a deadly weapon, attempted rape—you name it. You think I should feel sorry for him?"

"No," Evans said quickly.

"You do, I can see it in your eyes. A lot of people do. They go, He was just a kid, how could you do that? Let me tell you, people don't know what the hell they're talking about. One of us was going to get killed that night. I'm glad it wasn't me. But of course, it still bothers me."

"I'll bet."

"Sometimes I wake up in a cold sweat. Seeing the gunshot blow the windshield in front of my face. Realizing how close I came to dying. I was stupid. I should have killed him the first time."

Evans paused. He didn't know what to say.

"You ever had a gun at your head?" she said.

"No . . ."

"Then you have no idea how it feels, do you?"

"Was there trouble about it?" he said.

"You bet your ass there was trouble. For a while I thought I wasn't going to be able to practice law. They claimed I led him on. Do you believe that shit? I never saw the guy in my life. But then a very good attorney came to my rescue."

"Balder?"

She nodded. "That's why I'm here."

"And what about your arm?"

"Ah hell," she said, "the car crashed and I cut it on the broken glass." She signaled to the waitress. "What do you say we get the check?"

"I'll do that."

Minutes later they were back outside. Evans blinked in the milky midday light. They walked down the street. "So," Evans said. "I guess you're pretty good at karate."

"Good enough."

They came to the warehouse. He shook her hand.

"I'd really like to have lunch again some time," she said. She was so direct about it, he wondered whether it was personal, or whether she wanted him to know how the lawsuit was going. Because like Balder, much of what she had said was not encouraging.

"Lunch sounds great," he said.

"Not too long?"

"Deal."

"Will you call me?"

"Count on it," he said.

BEVERLY HILLS
TUESDAY, AUGUST 24
5:04 P.M.

It was almost dark when he went home to his apartment and parked
in the garage facing the alley. He was going up the back stairs when the
landlady poked her head out the window. "You just missed them," she
said.

"Who?"

"The cable repair people. They just left."

"I didn't call any cable repair people," he said. "Did you let them in?"

"Of course not. They said they would wait for you. They just left."

Evans had never heard of cable repair people waiting for anyone.
"How long did they wait?"

"Not long. Maybe ten minutes."

"Okay."

He got up to the second-floor landing. A tag was hooked on his doorknob. "Sorry We Missed You." There was a check box to "Call again to
reschedule service."

Then he saw the problem. The address was listed as 2119 Roxbury.
His address was 2129 Roxbury. But the address was on the front door,
not the back door. They'd just made a mistake. He lifted his doormat to
check on the key he kept there. It was right where he'd left it. It hadn't
been moved. There was even a ring of dust around it.

He unlocked the door and went inside. He went to the refrigerator, and saw the old container of yogurt. He needed to go to the supermarket but he was too tired. He checked the messages to see if Janis or Carol had called. They hadn't. Now of course there was the prospect of Jennifer Haynes, but she had a boyfriend, she lived in DC, and . . . he knew it would never work.

He thought of calling Janis, but decided not to. He took a shower, and was considering calling for pizza delivery. He lay down on the bed to relax for a minute before he called. And he fell immediately asleep.

The meeting was held in the big conference room on the fourteenth floor. Morton's four accountants were there; his assistant Sarah Jones; Herb Lowenstein, who did estate planning; a guy named Marty Bren, who did tax work for NERF, and Evans. Morton, who hated all financial meetings, paced restlessly.

"Let's get to it," he said. "I am supposedly giving ten million dollars to NERF, and we have signed papers, is that right?"

"Right," Lowenstein said.

"But now they want to attach a rider to the agreement?"

"Right," Marty Bren said. "It's pretty standard boilerplate for them." He shuffled through his papers. "Any charity wants to have full use of the money they receive, even when it is earmarked for a particular purpose. Maybe that purpose costs more or less than predicted, or it is delayed, or mired in litigation, or set aside for some other reason. In this case, the money has been earmarked for the Vanutu lawsuit, and the relevant phrase NERF wants to add is "said moneys to be used to defray the cost of the Vanutu litigation, including fees, filing, and copying costs . . . blah blah . . . or for other legal purposes, or for such other purposes as NERF shall see fit in its capacity as an environmental organization."

Morton said, "That's the phrase they want?"

"Boilerplate, as I said," Bren said.

"It's been in my previous donation agreements?"

"I don't recall offhand."

"Because," Morton said, "it sounds to me like they want to be able to pull the plug on this lawsuit, and spend the money elsewhere."

"Oh, I doubt that," Herb said.

"Why?" Morton said. "Why else would they want this boilerplate? Look, we had a signed deal. Now they want a change. Why?"

"It's not really a change," Bren said.

"It sure as hell is, Marty."

"If you look at the original agreement," Bren said calmly, "it says that any money not spent on the lawsuit goes to NERF for other purposes."

"But that's only if there's money left after the lawsuit ends," Morton said. "They can't spend it on anything else until the suit is decided."

"I think they imagine there may be long delays here."

"Why should there be delays?" Morton turned to Evans. "Peter? What is going on over there in Culver City?"

"It looks like the suit is going forward," Evans said. "They have a large operation. There must be forty people working on that one case. I don't think they plan to give it up."

"And are there problems with the suit?"

"There are certainly challenges," Evans said. "It's complicated litigation. They face strong opposing counsel. They're working hard."

"Why am I not convinced here?" Morton said. "Six months ago Nick Drake told me this damn lawsuit was a slam dunk and a great publicity opportunity, and now they want a bail-out clause."

"Maybe we should ask Nick."

"I got a better idea. Let's audit NERF."

Murmurs in the room. "I don't think you have that right, George."

"Make it part of the agreement."

"I'm not sure you can do that."

"They want a rider. I want a rider. What's the difference?"

"I'm not sure you can audit their entire operation—"

"George," Herb Lowenstein said. "You and Nick are friends of long standing. You're their Concerned Citizen of the Year. Auditing them seems a little out of character for your relationship."

"You mean it looks like I don't trust them?"

"Put bluntly, yes."

"I don't." Morton leaned on the table and looked at everyone sitting there. "You know what I think? They want to blow off the litigation and spend all the money on this conference on abrupt climate change that Nick is so excited about."

"They don't need ten million for a conference."

"I don't know what they need. He already misplaced two hundred and fifty thousand of my money. It ended up in fucking Vancouver. I don't know what he is doing anymore."

"Well, then you should withdraw your contribution."

"Ah ah," Marty Bren said. "Not so fast. I think they've already made financial commitments based on the reasonable expectation that the money was coming."

"Then give them some amount, and forget the rest."

"No," Morton said. "I'm not going to withdraw the grant. Peter Evans here says the litigation is going forward, and I believe him. Nick says that the two hundred and fifty grand was a mistake, and I believe him. I want you to ask for an audit and I want to know what happens. I will be out of town for the next three weeks."

"You will? Where?"

"I'm taking a trip."

"But we'll have to be able to reach you, George."

"I may be unreachable. Call Sarah. Or have Peter here get in touch with me."

"But George—"

"That's it, guys. Talk to Nick, see what he says. We'll be in contact soon."

And he walked out of the room, with Sarah hurrying after him.

Lowenstein turned to the others. "What the hell was that all about?"

VANCOUVER
THURSDAY, AUGUST 26
12:44 P.M.

Thunder rumbled ominously. Looking out the front windows of his office, Nat Damon sighed. He had always known that that submarine lease would mean trouble. After the check bounced, he had canceled the order, hoping that that would be the end of it. But it wasn't.

For weeks and weeks he had heard nothing, but then one of the men, the lawyer in the shiny suit, had come back unexpectedly to poke a finger in his face and tell him that he had signed a nondisclosure agreement and could not discuss any aspect of the submarine lease with anybody, or risk a lawsuit. "Maybe we'll win, and maybe we'll lose," the lawyer said. "But either way, you're out of business, friend. Your house is mortgaged. You're in debt for the rest of your life. So, think it over. And keep your mouth shut."

All during this, Damon's heart was pounding. Because the fact was, Damon had already been contacted by some sort of revenue service guy. A man named Kenner, who was coming to Damon's office that very afternoon. To ask a few questions, he had said.

Damon had been afraid that this Kenner would show up while the lawyer was still in his office, but now the lawyer was driving away. His car, a nondescript Buick sedan with Ontario plates, drove through the boatyard, and was gone.

Damon started to clean up the office, getting ready to go home. He was toying with the idea of leaving before Kenner arrived. Kenner was some revenue agent. Damon had done nothing wrong. He didn't have to meet any revenue agent. And if he did, what would he do, say he couldn't answer questions?

The next thing, he'd be subpoenaed or something. Dragged into court.

Damon decided to leave. There was more thunder, and the crack of distant lightning. A big storm was moving in.

As he was closing up, he saw that the lawyer had left his cell phone on the counter. He looked out to see if the lawyer was coming back for it. Not yet, but surely he would realize he had left it, and come back. Damon decided to leave before he showed up.

Hastily, he slipped the cell phone in his pocket, turned out the lights, and locked the office. The first drops of rain were spattering the pavement as he went to his car, parked right in front. He opened the door and was climbing into the car when the cell phone rang. He hesitated, not sure what to do. The phone rang insistently.

A jagged bolt of lightning crashed down, striking the mast of one of the ships in the boatyard. In the next instant there was a burst of light by the car, a blast of furious heat that knocked him to the ground. Dazed, he tried to get up.

He was thinking that his car had exploded, but it hadn't; the car was intact, the door blackened. Then he saw that his trousers were on fire. He stared stupidly at his own legs, not moving. He heard the rumble of thunder and realized that *he had been struck by lightning.*

My God, he thought. I was hit by lightning. He sat up and slapped at his trousers, trying to put out the fire. It wasn't working, and his legs were beginning to feel pain. He had a fire extinguisher inside the office.

Staggering to his feet, he moved unsteadily to his office. He was unlocking the door, his fingers fumbling, when there was another explosion. He felt a sharp pain in his ears, reached up, touched blood. He looked at his bloody fingertips, fell over, and died.

Under normal circumstances, Peter Evans spoke to George Morton every day. Sometimes twice a day. So after a week went by without hearing from him, Evans called his house. He spoke to Sarah.

"I have no idea what is going on," she said. "Two days ago he was in North Dakota. North Dakota! The day before that he was in Chicago. I think he might be in Wyoming today. He's made noises about going to Boulder, Colorado, but I don't know."

"What's in Boulder?" Evans said.

"I haven't a clue. Too early for snow."

"Has he got a new girlfriend?" Sometimes Morton disappeared when he was involved with a new woman.

"Not that I know," Sarah said.

"What's he doing?"

"I have no idea. It sounds like he has a shopping list."

"A shopping list?"

"Well," she said, "sort of. He wanted me to buy some kind of special GPS unit. You know, for locating position? Then he wanted some special video camera using CCD or CCF or something. Had to be rush-ordered from Hong Kong. And yesterday he told me to buy a new Ferrari from a guy in Monterey, and have it shipped to San Francisco."

"Another Ferrari?"

"I know," she said. "How many Ferraris can one man use? And this one doesn't seem up to his usual standards. From the e-mail pictures it looks kind of beat up."

"Maybe he's going to have it restored."

"If he was, he'd send it to Reno. That's where his car restorer is."

He detected a note of concern in her voice. "Is everything okay, Sarah?"

"Between you and me, I don't know," she said. "The Ferrari he bought is a 1972 365 GTS Daytona Spyder."

"So?"

"He already has one, Peter. It's like he doesn't know. And he sounds weird when you talk to him."

"Weird in what way?"

"Just . . . weird. Not his usual self at all."

"Who's traveling with him?"

"As far as I know, nobody."

Evans frowned. That was very odd. Morton hated being alone. Evans's immediate inclination was to disbelieve it.

"What about that guy Kenner and his Nepali friend?"

"Last I heard, they were going to Vancouver, and on to Japan. So they're not with him."

"Uh huh."

"When I hear from him, I'll let him know you called."

Evans hung up, feeling dissatisfied. On an impulse, he dialed Morton's cell phone. But he got the voice mail. "This is George. At the beep." And the quick beep.

"George, this is Peter Evans. Just checking in, to see if there's anything you need. Call me at the office if I can help."

He hung up, and stared out the window. Then he dialed again.

"Center for Risk Analysis."

"Professor Kenner's office, please."

In a moment he got the secretary. "This is Peter Evans, I'm looking for Professor Kenner."

"Oh yes, Mr. Evans. Dr. Kenner said you might call."

"He did?"

"Yes. Are you trying to reach Dr. Kenner?"

"Yes, I am."

"He's in Tokyo at the moment. Would you like his cell phone?"

"Please."

She gave him the number, and he wrote it down on his yellow pad. He was about to call when his assistant, Heather, came in to say that something at lunch had disagreed with her, and she was going home for the afternoon.

"Feel better," he said, sighing.

With her gone, he was obliged to answer his own phone, and the next call was from Margo Lane, George's mistress, asking where the hell George was. Evans was on the phone with her for the better part of half an hour.

And then Nicholas Drake walked into his office.

"I am very concerned," Drake said. He stood at the window, hands clasped behind his back, staring at the office building opposite.

"About what?"

"This Kenner person that George is spending so much time with."

"I don't know that they're spending time together."

"Of course they are. You don't seriously believe George is *alone*, do you?"

Evans said nothing.

"George is never alone. We both know that. Peter, I don't like this situation at all. Not at all. George is a good man—I don't have to tell you that—but he is susceptible to influence. Including the wrong influence."

"You think a professor at MIT is the wrong influence?"

"I've looked into Professor Kenner," Drake said, "and there are a few mysteries about him."

"Oh?"

"His résumé says he spent a number of years in government. Department of the Interior, Intergovernmental Negotiating Committee, and so on."

"Yes?"

"The Department of the Interior has no record of his working there."

Evans shrugged. "It was more than ten years ago. Government records being what they are . . ."

"Possibly," Drake said. "But there is more. Professor Kenner comes back to MIT, works there for eight years, very successfully. Consultant to the EPA, consultant to Department of Defense, God knows what else—and then he suddenly goes on extended leave, and no one seems to know what happened to him since. He just fell off the radar."

"I don't know," Evans said. "His card says he is Director of Risk Analysis."

"But he's on leave. I don't know what the hell he is doing these days. I don't know who supports him. I take it you've met him?"

"Briefly."

"And now he and George are great pals?"

"I don't know, Nick. I haven't seen or spoken to George in more than a week."

"He's off with Kenner."

"I don't know that."

"But you know that he and Kenner went to Vancouver."

"Actually, I didn't know."

"Let me lay it out for you plainly," Drake said. "I have it on good authority that John Kenner has unsavory connections. The Center for Risk Analysis is wholly funded by industry groups. I needn't say more. In addition, Mr. Kenner spent a number of years advising the Pentagon and in fact was so involved with them that he even underwent some sort of training for a period of time."

"You mean military training?"

"Yes. Fort Bragg and Harvey Point, in North Carolina," Drake said. "There is no question the man has military connections as well as industry connections. And I am told he is hostile toward mainstream environmental organizations. I hate to think of a man like that working on poor George."

"I wouldn't worry about George. He can see through propaganda."

"I hope so. But frankly I do not share your confidence. This military man shows up, and the next thing we know, George is trying to audit us. I mean, my God, why would he want to do that? Doesn't George realize what a waste of resources that involves? Time, money, everything? It would be a *tremendous* drag on my time."

"I wasn't aware an audit was going forward."

"It's being discussed. Of course, we have nothing to hide, and we can be audited at any time. I have always said so. But this is an especially busy time, with the Vanutu lawsuit starting up, and the conference on Abrupt Climate Change to be planned for. All that's in the next few weeks. I wish I could speak to George."

Evans shrugged. "Call his cell."

"I have. Have you?"

"Yes."

"He call you back?"

"No," Evans said.

Drake shook his head. "That man," he said, "is my Concerned Citizen of the Year, and I can't even get him on the phone."

Morton sat at a sidewalk table outside a café on Beverly Drive at eight in the morning, waiting for Sarah to show up. His assistant was ordinarily punctual, and her apartment was not far away. Unless she had taken up with that actor again. Young people had so much time to waste on bad relationships.

He sipped his coffee, glancing at the *Wall Street Journal* without much interest. He had even less interest after an unusual couple sat down at the next table.

The woman was petite and strikingly beautiful, with dark hair and an exotic look. She might have been Moroccan; it was hard to judge from her accent. Her clothing was chic and out of place in casual Los Angeles—tight-fitting skirt, spike heels, Chanel jacket.

The man who accompanied her could not have been more different. He was a red-faced, beefy American, with slightly piggish features, wearing a sweater, baggy khakis, and running shoes. He was as big as a football player. He slumped at the table and said, "I'll have a latte, sweetheart. Nonfat. Grande."

She said, "I thought you would get one for me, like a gentleman."

"I'm not a gentleman," he said. "And you're no fucking lady. Not after you didn't come home last night. So we can forget about ladies and gentlemen, okay?"

She pouted. "*Chéri*, do not make a scene."

"Hey. I asked you to get a fucking latte. Who's making a scene?"

"But *chéri*—"

"You going to get it, or not?" He glared at her. "I've really had it with you, Marisa, you know that?"

"You don't own me," she said. "I do as I please."

"You've made that obvious."

During this conversation, Morton's paper had been slowly drifting downward. Now he folded it flat, set it on his knee, and pretended to read. But in fact he could not take his eyes off this woman. She was extremely beautiful, he decided, although not very young. She was probably thirty-five. Her maturity somehow made her more overtly sexual. He was captivated.

She said to the football player, "William, you are tiresome."

"You want me to leave?"

"Perhaps it is best."

"Oh, fuck you," he said, and slapped her.

Morton could not restrain himself. "Hey," he said, "take it easy there."

The woman gave him a smile. The beefy man stood up, fists bunched. "Mind your own fucking business!"

"You don't hit the lady, pal."

"How about just you and me?" he said, shaking his fist.

At that moment, a Beverly Hills cruiser drove by. Morton looked at it, and waved. The cruiser came over to the curb. "Everything all right?" one of the cops said.

"Just fine, officer," Morton said.

"Fuck this noise," the football player said, and turned away. He stalked off up the street.

The dark woman smiled at Morton. "Thank you for that."

"No problem. Did I hear you say you wanted a latte?"

She smiled again. She crossed her legs, exposing brown knees. "If you would be so kind."

Morton was standing to get it when Sarah called to him, "Hey,

George! Sorry to be late." She came jogging up in a tracksuit. As always, she looked very beautiful.

Anger flashed across the dark woman's features. It was fleeting, but Morton caught it and he thought, *Something is wrong here.* He didn't know this woman. She had no reason to be angry. Probably, he decided, she had wanted to teach the boyfriend a lesson. Even now the guy was hanging around at the end of the block, pretending to look in a shop window. But at this early hour, all the shops were closed.

"Ready to go?" Sarah said.

Morton made brief apologies to the woman, who made little gestures of indifference. He had the feeling now that she was French.

"Perhaps we will meet again," he said.

"Yes," she said, "but I doubt it. I am sorry. *Ça va.*"

"Have a nice day."

As they walked off, Sarah said, "Who was that?"

"I don't know. She sat down at the next table."

"Spicy little number."

He shrugged.

"Did I interrupt something? No? That's good." She handed Morton three manila folders. "This one's your contributions to NERF to date. This one is the agreement for the last contribution, so you have the language. And this one is the cashier's check you wanted. Be careful with that. It's a big number."

"Okay. It's not a problem. I'm leaving in an hour."

"You want to tell me where?"

Morton shook his head. "It's better you don't know."

Evans had heard nothing from Morton for almost two weeks. He could not remember ever having gone so long without contact with his client. He had lunch with Sarah, who was visibly anxious. "Do you hear from him at all?" he said.

"Not a word."

"What do the pilots say?"

"They're in Van Nuys. He's rented a different plane. I don't know where he is."

"And he's coming back . . ."

She shrugged. "Who knows?"

And so it was with considerable surprise that he received Sarah's call that day. "You better get going," she said. "George wants to see you right away."

"Where?"

"At NERF. In Beverly Hills."

"He's back?"

"I'll say."

It was a ten-minute drive from his offices in Century City to the NERF building. Of course the National Environmental Resource Fund was headquartered in Washington, DC, but they had recently opened a west coast office, in Beverly Hills. Cynics claimed that NERF had done it to be closer to the Hollywood celebrities who were so essential to their fund-raising. But that was just gossip.

Evans half expected to find Morton pacing outside, but he was nowhere in sight. Evans went into the reception area and was told that Morton was in the third-floor conference room. He walked up to the third floor.

The conference room was glass-walled on two sides. The interior was furnished with a large, boardroom-style table and eighteen chairs. There was an audiovisual unit in the corner for presentations.

Evans saw three people in the conference room, and an argument in progress. Morton stood at the front of the room, red-faced, gesticulating. Drake was also standing, pacing back and forth, pointing an angry finger at Morton, and shouting back at him. Evans also saw John Henley, the saturnine head of PR for NERF. He was bent over, making notes on a yellow legal pad. It was clearly an argument between Morton and Drake.

Evans was not sure what to do, so he stood there. After a moment, Morton saw him and made a quick jabbing motion, indicating that Evans should sit down outside. He did. And watched the argument through the glass.

It turned out there was a fourth person in the room as well. Evans hadn't seen him at first because he was hunched down behind the podium, but when that person stood, Evans saw a workman in clean, neatly pressed overalls carrying a briefcase-style toolbox and with a couple of electronic meters clipped to his belt. On his chest pocket a logo read AV NETWORK SYSTEMS.

The workman looked confused. Apparently Drake didn't want the workman in the room during the argument, whereas Morton seemed to like an audience. Drake wanted the guy to go; Morton insisted he stay. Caught in the middle, the workman looked uncomfortable, and ducked down out of sight again. But soon after, Drake prevailed, and the workman left.

As the workman walked past him, Evans said, "Rough day?"

The workman shrugged. "They got a lot of network problems in this building," he said. "Myself, I think it's bad Ethernet cable, or the routers are overheating . . ." And he walked on.

Back inside, the argument raged, fiercer than ever. It continued for another five minutes. The glass was almost entirely soundproof, but from time to time, when they shouted, Evans could hear a phrase. He heard Morton yell, "God damn it, I want to win!" and he heard Drake reply, "It's just too risky." Which made Morton even angrier.

And later Morton said, "Don't we have to fight for the most important issue facing our planet?" And Drake answered something about being practical, or facing reality. And Morton said, "Fuck reality!"

At which point the PR guy, Henley, glanced up and said, "My sentiments exactly." Or something like that.

Evans had the distinct impression that this argument concerned the Vanutu lawsuit, but it seemed to range over a number of other subjects as well.

And then, quite abruptly, Morton came out, slamming the door so hard that the glass walls shook. "Fuck those guys!"

Evans fell into step with his client. Through the glass, he saw the other two men huddle, whispering together.

"Fuck 'em!" George said loudly. He paused and looked back. "If we have right on our side, shouldn't we be telling the truth?"

Inside, Drake just shook his head sorrowfully.

"Fuck 'em," Morton said again, walking off.

Evans said, "You wanted me here?"

"Yes." Morton pointed. "You know who that other guy was?"

"Yes," he said. "John Henley."

"Correct. Those two guys *are* NERF," George said. "I don't care how many celebrity trustees they have on their letterhead. Or how many lawyers they keep on staff. Those two run the show, and everyone else rubberstamps. None of the trustees really knows anything about what is going on. Otherwise they wouldn't be a part of this. And let me tell you, I'm not going to be a part of this. Not anymore."

They started walking down the stairs.

"Meaning what?" Evans said to him.

"Meaning," Morton said, "I'm not giving them that ten-million-dollar grant for the lawsuit."

"You told them that?"

"No," he said, "I did not tell them that. And you will not tell them that either. I think I'll let it be a surprise, for later." He smiled grimly. "But draw up the papers now."

"Are you sure about this, George?"

"Don't piss me off, kid."

"I'm just asking—"

"And I said draw up the papers. So do it."

Evans said he would.

"*Today.*"

Evans said he would do it at once.

Evans waited until they got to the parking garage before he spoke again. He walked Morton to his waiting town car. His driver, Harry, opened the door for him. Evans said, "George, you have that NERF banquet honoring you next week. Is that still going ahead?"

"Absolutely," Morton said. "I wouldn't miss it for the world."

He got in the car, and Harry closed the door.

"Good day, sir," Harry said to Evans.

And the car drove off into the morning sunlight.

He called from his car: "Sarah."

"I know, I know."

"What is going on?"

"He won't tell me. But he's really angry, Peter. *Really* angry."

"I got that impression."

"And he just left again."

"What?"

"He left. Said he would be back in a week. In time to fly everybody up to San Francisco for the banquet."

Drake called Evans's cell phone. "What is going on, Peter?"

"I have no idea, Nick."

"The man's demented. The things he was saying . . . could you hear him?"

"No, actually."

"He's demented. I really am worried about him. I mean as a friend. To say nothing of our banquet next week. I mean, is he going to be all right?"

"I think so. He's taking a planeload of friends up there."

"Are you sure?"

"That's what Sarah says."

"Can I talk to George? Can you set something up?"

"My understanding," Evans said, "is that he just went out of town again."

"It's that damn Kenner. He's behind all this."

"I don't know what's going on with George, Nick. All I know is, he's coming to the banquet."

"I want you to promise me you'll deliver him."

"Nick," Evans said. "George does what he wants."

"That's what I'm afraid of."

TO SAN FRANCISCO
MONDAY, OCTOBER 4
1:38 P.M.

Flying up on his Gulfstream, Morton brought several of the most prominent celebrity supporters of NERF. These included two rock stars, the wife of a comedian, an actor who played the president on a television series, a writer who had recently run for governor, and two environmental lawyers from other firms. Over white wine and smoked salmon canapés, the discussion became quite lively, focusing on what the United States, as the world's leading economy, should be doing to promote environmental sanity.

Uncharacteristically, Morton did not join in. Instead, he slumped in the back of the plane, looking irritable and gloomy. Evans sat beside him, keeping him company. Morton was drinking straight vodka. He was already on his second.

"I brought the papers cancelling your grant," Evans said, taking them out of his briefcase. "If you still want to do this."

"I do." Morton scribbled his signature, hardly looking at the documents. He said, "Keep those safe until tomorrow." He looked back at his guests, who were now trading statistics on species loss as the rain forests of the world were cut down. Off to one side, Ted Bradley, the actor who played the president, was talking about how he preferred his electric car—which, he pointed out, he had owned for many years now—to the new hybrids that were so popular. "There's no comparison," he was saying. "The hybrids are nice, but they're not the real thing."

At the center table, Ann Garner, who sat on the boards of environmental organizations, was arguing that Los Angeles needed to build more public transportation so that people could get out of their cars. Americans, she said, belched out more carbon dioxide than any other people on the planet, and it was disgraceful. Ann was the beautiful wife of a famous attorney, and always intense, especially on environmental issues.

Morton sighed. He turned to Evans. "Do you know how much pollution we're creating right this minute? We'll burn four hundred fifty gallons of aviation fuel to take twelve people to San Francisco. Just by making this trip, they're generating more pollution per capita than most people on the planet will generate in a year."

He finished his vodka, and rattled the ice in the glass irritably. He handed the glass to Evans, who dutifully signaled for more.

"If there's anything worse than a limousine liberal," Morton said, "it's a Gulfstream environmentalist."

"But George," Evans said. "You're a Gulfstream environmentalist."

"I know it," Morton said. "And I wish it bothered me more. But you know what? It doesn't. I *like* flying around in my own airplane."

Evans said, "I heard you were in North Dakota and Chicago."

"I was. Yes."

"What'd you do there?"

"I spent money. A lot of money. A *lot*."

Evans said, "You bought some art?"

"No. I bought something far more expensive than art. I bought integrity."

"You've always had integrity," Evans said.

"Oh, not my integrity," Morton said. "I bought somebody else's."

Evans didn't know what to say to that. For a minute he thought Morton was joking.

"I was going to tell you about it," Morton continued. "I got a list of numbers, kid, and I want you to get it to Kenner. It is very much—for later. Hello, Ann!"

Ann Garner was coming toward them. "So, George, are you back for a while? Because we need you here now. The Vanutu lawsuit, which thank God you are backing, and the climate change conference that Nick has scheduled, and it's so important—my God, George. This is crunch time."

Evans started to stand to let Ann take his seat, but Morton pushed him back down again.

"Ann," he said, "I must say you look more lovely than ever, but Peter and I are having a small business discussion."

She glanced at the papers, and Evans's open briefcase. "Oh. I didn't know I was interrupting."

"No, no, if you'd just give us a minute."

"Of course. I'm sorry." But she lingered. "This is so unlike you, George, doing business on the plane."

"I know," Morton said, "but, if you must know, I am feeling quite unlike myself these days."

That made her blink. She didn't know how to take it, so she smiled, nodded, and moved away. Morton said, "She looks wonderful. I wonder who did her work."

"Her work?"

"She's had more, in the last few months. I think eyes. Maybe chin. Anyway," he said, waving his hand, "about the list of numbers. You are to tell this to no one, Peter. *No one.* Not anyone in the law firm. And especially not anyone at—"

"George, damn it, why are you hiding back there?" Evans looked over his shoulder and saw Ted Bradley coming toward them. Ted was already drinking heavily, though it was only noon. "It hasn't been the same without you, George. My God, the world without Bradley is a boring world. Oops! I mean, without George Morton, is a boring world. Come on, George. Get up out of there. That man is a lawyer. Come and have a drink."

Morton allowed himself to be led away. He glanced over his shoulder at Evans. "Later," he said.

The Grand Ballroom of the Mark Hopkins Hotel was darkened for the after-dinner speeches. The audience was elegant, the men in tuxedos, the women in ball gowns. Beneath the ornate chandeliers, the voice of Nicholas Drake boomed from the podium.

"Ladies and gentlemen, it is no exaggeration to say that we face an environmental crisis of unprecedented proportions. Our forests are disappearing. Our lakes and rivers are polluted. The plants and animals that make up our biosphere are vanishing at unprecedented rates. Forty thousand species become extinct every year. That's fifty species every single day. At present rates, we will lose half of all species on our planet in the next few decades. It is the greatest extinction in the history of earth.

"And what is the texture of our own lives? Our food is contaminated with lethal pesticides. Our crops are failing from global warming. Our weather is growing worse, and more severe. Flooding, droughts, hurricanes, tornadoes. All around the globe. Our sea levels are rising—twenty-five feet in the next century, and possibly more. And most fearsome of all, new scientific evidence points to the specter of abrupt climate change, as a result of our destructive behavior. In short, ladies and gentlemen, we are confronted by a genuine global catastrophe for our planet."

Sitting at the center table, Peter Evans looked around at the audience. They were staring down at their plates, yawning, leaning over and talking to one another. Drake wasn't getting a lot of attention.

"They've heard it before," Morton growled. He shifted his heavy frame and gave a soft belch. He had been drinking steadily through the evening, and was now quite drunk.

". . . Loss of biodiversity, shrinking of habitat, destruction of the ozone layer . . ."

Nicholas Drake appeared tall and ungainly, his tuxedo ill-fitting. The collar of his shirt was bunched up around his scrawny neck. As always, he gave the impression of an impoverished but dedicated academic, a latter-day Ichabod Crane. Evans thought no one would ever guess that Drake was paid a third of a million dollars a year to head the Fund, plus another hundred thousand in expenses. Or that he had no science background at all. Nick Drake was a trial attorney, one of five who had started NERF many years before. And like all trial attorneys, he knew the importance of not dressing too well.

". . . the erosion of bio-reservoirs, the rise of ever more exotic and lethal diseases . . ."

"I wish he'd hurry up," Morton said. He drummed his fingers on the table. Evans said nothing. He had attended enough of these functions to know that Morton was always tense if he had to speak.

At the podium, Drake was saying ". . . glimmers of hope, faint rays of positive energy, and none more positive and hopeful than the man whose lifelong dedication we are here to honor tonight . . ."

"Can I get another drink?" Morton said, finishing the last of his martini. It was his sixth. He set the glass on the table with a thud. Evans turned to look for the waiter, raising his hand. He was hoping the waiter wouldn't come over in time. George had had enough.

". . . for three decades has dedicated his considerable resources and energy to making our world a better, healthier, saner place. Ladies and gentlemen, the National Environmental Resource Fund is proud . . ."

"Ah screw, never mind," Morton said. He tensed his body, ready to push back from the table. "I hate making a fool of myself, even for a good cause."

"Why should you make a fool of—" Evans began.

". . . my good friend and colleague and this year's concerned citizen . . . Mr. *George Morton!*"

The room filled with applause, and a spotlight hit Morton as he stood and headed toward the podium, a hunched bear of a man, physically powerful, solemn, head down. Evans was alarmed when Morton stumbled on the first step, and for a moment he feared his boss would fall backward, but Morton regained his balance, and as he stepped to the stage he seemed all right. He shook hands with Drake and moved to the podium, gripping it on both sides with his large hands. Morton looked out at the room, turning his head from side to side, surveying the audience. He did not speak.

He just stood there, and said nothing.

Ann Garner, sitting beside Evans, gave him a nudge. "Is he all right?"

"Oh yes. Absolutely," Evans said, nodding. But in truth, he wasn't sure.

Finally George Morton began to speak. "I'd like to thank Nicholas Drake and the National Environmental Resource Fund for this award, but I don't feel I deserve it. Not with all the work that remains to be done. Do you know, my friends, that we know more about the moon than we do about the Earth's oceans? That's a real environmental problem. We don't know enough about the planet we depend on for our very lives. But as Montaigne said three hundred years ago, 'Nothing is so firmly believed as that which is least known.'"

Evans thought: Montaigne? George Morton quoting Montaigne?

In the glare of the spotlight, Morton was distinctly weaving back and forth. He was gripping the podium for balance. The room was absolutely silent. People were not moving at all. Even the waiters had stopped moving between the tables. Evans held his breath.

"All of us in the environmental movement," Morton said, "have seen many wonderful victories over the years. We have witnessed the creation of the EPA. We have seen the air and water made cleaner, sewage treatment improved, toxic dumps cleaned up, and we have regulated common poisons like lead for the safety of all. These are real victories, my friends. We take justifiable pride in them. And we know more needs to be done."

The audience was relaxing. Morton was moving onto familiar ground.

"But will the work get done? I am not sure. I know my mood has been dark, since the death of my beloved wife, Dorothy."

Evans sat bolt upright in his chair. At the next table, Herb Lowenstein looked shocked, his mouth open. George Morton had no wife. Or rather, he had six ex-wives—none named Dorothy.

"Dorothy urged me to spend my money wisely. I always thought I did. Now I am less sure. I said before that we don't know enough. But I fear that today, the watchword of NERF has become, We don't sue enough."

You could hear breath sucked in sharply all around the room.

"NERF is a law firm. I don't know if you realize that. It was started by lawyers and it is run by lawyers. But I now believe money is better spent on research than litigation. And that is why I am withdrawing my funding for NERF, and why I am—"

For the next few moments Morton could not be heard above the excited jabber of the crowd. Everyone was talking loudly. There were scattered boos; some guests got up to leave. Morton continued to talk, seemingly oblivious to the effect he was having. Evans caught a few phrases: ". . . one environmental charity is under FBI investigation . . . complete lack of oversight . . ."

Ann Garner leaned over and hissed, *"Get him off there."*

"What do you want me to do?" Evans whispered.

"Go and get him. He's obviously drunk."

"That may be, but I can't—"

"You have to stop this."

But on the stage, Drake was already moving forward, saying "All right, thank you, George—"

"Because to tell the truth right now—"

"Thank you, George," Drake said again, moving closer. He was actually pushing against Morton's bulk, trying to shove him away from the podium.

"Okay, okay," Morton said, clinging to the podium. "I said what I did for Dorothy. My dear dead wife—"

"Thank you, George." Drake was applauding now, holding his hands up at head height, nodding to the audience to join with him. "Thank you."

". . . who I miss desperately . . ."

"Ladies and gentlemen, please join me in thanking—"

"Yeah, okay, I'm leaving."

To muted applause, Morton shambled off the stage. Drake immediately stepped up to the podium and signaled the band. They started into a rousing rendition of Billy Joel's "You May Be Right," which someone had told them was Morton's favorite song. It was, but it seemed a poor choice under the circumstances.

Herb Lowenstein leaned over from the next table and grabbed Evans by the shoulder, pulling him close. "Listen," he whispered fiercely. "*Get him out of here.*"

"I will," Evans said. "Don't worry."

"Did you know this was going to happen?"

"No, I swear to God."

Lowenstein released Evans just as George Morton returned to the table. The assembled group was stunned. But Morton was singing cheerfully with the music, "You may be right, I may be crazy . . ."

"Come on, George," Evans said, standing up. "Let's get out of here."

Morton ignored him. ". . . But it just may be a loo-natic you're looking for . . ."

"George? What do you say?" Evans took him by the arm. "Let's go."

". . . Turn out the light, don't try to save me . . ."

"I'm not trying to save you," Evans said.

"Then how about another damn martini?" Morton said, no longer singing. His eyes were cold, a little resentful. "I think I fucking earned it."

"Harry will have one for you in the car," Evans said, steering Morton away from the table. "If you stay here, you'll have to wait for it. And you don't want to wait for a drink right now . . ." Evans continued talking, and Morton allowed himself to be led out of the room.

". . . too late to fight," he sang, "too late to change me . . ."

Before they could get out of the room, there was a TV camera with lights shining in their faces, and two reporters shoving small tape recorders in front of Morton. Everybody was yelling questions. Evans put his head down and said, "Excuse us, sorry, coming through, excuse us . . ."

Morton never stopped singing. They made their way through the hotel lobby. The reporters were running in front of them, trying to get some distance ahead, so they could film them walking forward. Evans gripped Morton firmly by the elbow as Morton sang:

"I was only having fun, wasn't hurting anyone, and we all enjoyed the weekend for a change . . ."

"This way," Evans said, heading for the door.

"I was stranded in the combat zone . . ."

And then at last they were through the swinging doors, and outside in the night. Morton stopped singing abruptly when the cold air hit him. They waited for his limousine to pull around. Sarah came out, and stood beside Morton. She didn't say anything, she just put her hand on his arm.

Then the reporters came out, and the lights came on again. And then Drake burst through the doors, saying "God damn it, George—"

He broke off when he saw the cameras. He glared at Morton, turned, and went back inside. The cameras remained on, but the three of them just stood there. It was awkward, just waiting. After what seemed like an eternity, the limousine pulled up. Harry came around, and opened the door for George.

"Okay, George," Evans said.

"No, not tonight."

"Harry's waiting, George."

"I said, *not tonight*."

There was a deep-throated growl in the darkness, and a silver Ferrari convertible pulled up alongside the limousine.

"My car," Morton said. He started down the stairs, lurching a bit.

Sarah said, "George, I don't think—"

But he was singing again: "And you told me not to drive, but I made it home alive, so you said that only proves that I'm in-sayyy-nnne."

One of the reporters muttered, "He's insane, all right."

Evans followed Morton, very concerned. Morton gave the parking attendant a hundred dollar bill, saying "A twenty for you, my good man." He fumbled with the Ferrari door. "These crummy Italian imports." Then he got behind the wheel of the convertible, gunned the engine, and smiled. "Ah, a manly sound."

Evans leaned over the car. "George, let Harry drive you. Besides," he added, "don't we need to talk about something?"

"We do not."

"But I thought—"

"Kid, get out of my way." The camera lights were still on them. But Morton moved so that he was in the shadow cast by Evans's body. "You know, the Buddhists have a saying."

"What saying?"

"Remember it, kid. Goes like this: 'All that matters is not remote from where the Buddha sits.'"

"George, I really think you should not be driving."

"Will you remember what I just said to you?"

"Yes."

"Wisdom of the ages. Good-bye, kid."

And he accelerated, roaring out of the parking lot as Evans jumped back. The Ferrari squealed around the corner, ignoring a stop sign, and was gone.

"Peter, come on."

Evans turned, and saw Sarah standing by the limousine. Harry was getting in behind the wheel. Evans got in the back seat with Sarah, and they drove off after Morton.

• • •

The Ferrari turned left at the bottom of the hill, disappearing around the corner. Harry accelerated, handling the huge limousine with skill.

Evans said, "Do you know where he's going?"

"No idea," she said.

"Who wrote his speech?"

"He did."

"Really?"

"He was working in the house all day yesterday, and he wouldn't let me see what he was doing . . ."

"Jesus," Evans said. "Montaigne?"

"He had a book of quotations out."

"Where'd he come up with Dorothy?"

She shook her head. "I have no idea."

They passed Golden Gate Park. Traffic was light; the Ferrari was moving fast, weaving among the cars. Ahead was the Golden Gate Bridge, brightly lit in the night. Morton accelerated. The Ferrari was going almost ninety miles an hour.

"He's going to Marin," Sarah said.

Evans's cell phone rang. It was Drake. "Will you tell me what the hell that was all about?"

"I'm sorry, Nick. I don't know."

"Was he serious? About withdrawing his support?"

"I think he was."

"That's unbelievable. He's obviously suffered a nervous breakdown."

"I couldn't say."

"I was afraid of this," Drake said. "I was afraid something like this might happen. You remember, on the plane coming back from Iceland? I said it to you, and you told me I shouldn't worry. Is that your opinion now? That I shouldn't worry?"

"I don't know what you're asking, Nick."

"Ann Garner said he signed some papers on the plane."

"That's right. He did."

"Are they related to this sudden and inexplicable withdrawal of support for the organization that he loved and cherished?"

"He seems to have changed his mind about that," Evans said.

"And why didn't you tell me?"

"He instructed me not to."

"Fuck you, Evans."

"I'm sorry," Evans said.

"Not as sorry as you will be."

The phone went dead. Drake had hung up. Evans flipped the phone shut.

Sarah said, "Drake is mad?"

"Furious."

Off the bridge, Morton headed west, away from the lights of the freeway, onto a dark road skirting the cliffs. He was driving faster than ever.

Evans said to Harry, "Do you know where we are?"

"I believe we're in a state park."

Harry was trying to keep up, but on this narrow, twisting road, the limousine was no match for the Ferrari. It moved farther and farther ahead. Soon they could see only the taillights, disappearing around curves a quarter mile ahead.

"We're going to lose him," Evans said.

"I doubt it, sir."

But the limousine fell steadily behind. After Harry took one turn too fast—the big rear end lost traction and swung wide toward a cliff's edge—they were obliged to slow down even more. They were in a desolate area now. The night was dark and the cliffs deserted. A rising moon put a streak of silver on the black water far below.

Up ahead, they no longer saw any taillights. It seemed they were alone on the dark road.

They came around a curve, and saw the next curve a hundred yards ahead—obscured by billowing gray smoke.

"Oh no," Sarah said, putting her hand to her mouth.

. . .

The Ferrari had spun out, struck a tree, and flipped over. It now lay upside down, a crumpled and smoking mass. It had very nearly gone off the cliff itself. The nose of the car was hanging over the edge.

Evans and Sarah ran forward. Evans got down on his hands and knees and crawled along the cliff's edge, trying to see into the driver's compartment. It was hard to see much of anything—the front windshield was flattened, and the Ferrari lay almost flush to the pavement. Harry came over with a flashlight, and Evans used it to peer inside.

The compartment was empty. Morton's black bow tie was dangling from the doorknob, but otherwise he was gone.

"He must have been thrown."

Evans shone the light down the cliff. It was crumbling yellow rock, descending steeply for eighty feet to the ocean below. He saw no sign of Morton.

Sarah was crying softly. Harry had gone back to get a fire extinguisher from the limousine. Evans swung his light back and forth over the rock face. He did not see George's body. In fact, he did not see any sign of George at all. No disturbance, no path, no bits of clothing. Nothing.

Behind him he heard the whoosh of the fire extinguisher. He crawled away from the cliff's edge.

"Did you see him, sir?" Harry said, his face full of pain.

"No. I didn't see anything."

"Perhaps . . . over there." Harry pointed toward the tree. And he was right; if Morton had been thrown from the car by the initial impact, he might be twenty yards back, on the road.

Evans walked back, and shone his flashlight down the cliff again. The battery was running down, the beam was weakening. But almost immediately, he saw a glint of light off a man's patent leather slipper, wedged among the rocks at the edge of the water.

He sat down in the road and put his head in his hands. And cried.

POINT MOODY
TUESDAY, OCTOBER 5
3:10 A.M.

By the time the police were finished talking with them, and a rescue team had rappelled down the cliff to recover the shoe, it was three o'clock in the morning. They found no other sign of the body, and the cops, talking among themselves, agreed that the prevailing currents would probably carry the body up the coast to Pismo Beach. "We'll find him," one said, "in about a week or so. Or at least, what's left by the great whites."

Now the wreck was being cleared away, and loaded onto a flatbed truck. Evans wanted to leave, but the highway patrolman who had taken Evans's statement kept coming back to ask for more details. He was a kid, in his early twenties. It seemed he had not filled out many of these forms before.

The first time he came back to Evans, he said, "How soon after the accident would you say you arrived on the scene?"

Evans said, "I'm not sure. The Ferrari was about half a mile ahead of us, maybe more. We were probably going forty miles an hour, so . . . maybe a minute later?"

The kid looked alarmed. "You were going forty in that limo? On this road?"

"Well. Don't hold me to it."

Then he came back and said, "You said you were the first on the scene. You told me you crawled around at the edge of the road?"

"That's right."

"So you would have stepped on broken glass, on the road?"

"Yes. The windshield was shattered. I had it on my hands, too, when I crouched down."

"So that explains why the glass was disturbed."

"Yes."

"Lucky you didn't cut your hands."

"Yes."

The third time he came back, he said, "In your estimation, what time did the accident occur?"

"What time?" Evans looked at his watch. "I have no idea. But let me see . . ." He tried to work backward. The speech must have started about eight-thirty. Morton would have left the hotel at nine. Through San Francisco, then over the bridge . . . "Maybe nine-forty-five, or ten at night."

"So, five hours ago? Roughly?"

"Yes."

The kid said, "Huh." As if he were surprised.

Evans looked over at the flatbed truck, which now held the crumpled remains of the Ferrari. One cop was standing on the flatbed, beside the car. Three other cops were on the street, talking with some animation. There was another man there, wearing a tuxedo. He was talking to the cops. When the man turned, Evans was surprised to see that it was John Kenner.

"What's going on?" Evans asked the kid.

"I don't know. They just asked me to check on the time of the accident."

Then the driver got into the flatbed truck, and started the engine. One of the cops yelled to the kid, "Forget it, Eddie!"

"Never mind, then," the kid said to Evans. "I guess everything's okay."

Evans looked over at Sarah, to see if she had noticed Kenner. She was leaning on the limousine, talking on the phone. Evans looked back in time to see Kenner get into a dark sedan driven by the Nepali guy, and drive off.

The cops were leaving. The flatbed turned around and headed up the road, toward the bridge.

Harry said, "Looks like it's time to go."

Evans got into the limousine. They drove back toward the lights of San Francisco.

Morton's jet flew back to Los Angeles at noon. The mood was somber. All the same people were on board, and a few more, but they sat quietly, saying little. The late-edition papers had printed the story that millionaire philanthropist George Morton, depressed by the death of his beloved wife, Dorothy, had given a disjointed speech (termed "rambling and illogical" by the *San Francisco Chronicle*) and a few hours later had died in a tragic automobile crash while test-driving his new Ferrari.

In the third paragraph, the reporter mentioned that single-car fatalities were frequently caused by undiagnosed depression and were often disguised suicides. And this, according to a quoted psychiatrist, was the likely explanation for Morton's death.

About ten minutes into the flight, the actor Ted Bradley said, "I think we should drink a toast in memory of George, and observe a minute of silence." And to a chorus of "Hear, hear," glasses of champagne were passed all around.

"To George Morton," Ted said. "A great American, a great friend, and a great supporter of the environment. We, and the planet, will miss him."

For the next ten minutes, the celebrities on board remained relatively subdued, but slowly the conversation picked up, and finally they began to talk and argue as usual. Evans was sitting in the back, in the same seat he had occupied when they flew up. He watched the action at the table in the center, where Bradley was now explaining that the US got only 2 percent of its energy from sustainable sources and that we needed a crash program to build thousands of offshore wind farms, like England and Denmark were doing. The talk moved on to fuel cells, hydrogen cars, and photovoltaic households running off the grid. Some talked about how much they loved their hybrid cars, which they had bought for their staff to drive.

Evans felt his spirits improve as he listened to them. Despite the loss of George Morton, there were still lots of people like these—famous, high-profile people committed to change—who would lead the next generation to a more enlightened future.

He was starting to drift off to sleep when Nicholas Drake dropped into the seat beside his. Drake leaned across the aisle. "Listen," he said. "I owe you an apology for last night."

"That's all right," Evans said.

"I was way out of line. And I want you to know I'm sorry for how I behaved. I was upset, and very worried. You know George has been acting weird as hell the last couple of weeks. Talking strangely, picking fights. I guess in retrospect he was beginning to have a nervous breakdown. But I didn't know. Did you?"

"I am not sure it was a nervous breakdown."

"It must have been," Drake said. "What else could it have been? My God, the man disowns his life's work, and then goes out and kills himself. By the way, you can forget about any documents that he signed yesterday. Under the circumstances, he obviously was not in his right mind. And I know," he added, "that you wouldn't argue the point differently. You're already conflicted enough, doing work both for him and for us. You really should have recused yourself and seen to it that any papers were drawn up by a neutral attorney. I'm not going to accuse you of malpractice, but you've shown highly questionable judgment."

Evans said nothing. The threat was plain enough.

"Well, anyway," Drake said, resting his hand on Evans's knee, "I just wanted to apologize. I know you did your best with a difficult situation, Peter. And . . . I think we're going to come out of this all right."

The plane landed in Van Nuys. A dozen black SUV limos, the latest fashion, were lined up on the runway, waiting for the passengers. All the celebrities hugged, kissed air, and departed.

Evans was the last to leave. He didn't rate a car and driver. He climbed into his little Prius hybrid, which he'd parked there the day before, and drove through the gates and onto the freeway. He thought he should go to the office, but unexpected tears came to his eyes as he negotiated the midday traffic. He wiped them away and decided he was too damned tired to go to the office. Instead, he would go back to his apartment to get some sleep.

He was almost home when his cell phone rang. It was Jennifer Haynes, at the Vanutu litigation team. "I'm sorry about George," she said. "It's just terrible. Everybody here is very upset, as you can imagine. He pulled the funding, didn't he?"

"Yes, but Nick will fight it. You'll get your funding."

"We need to have lunch," she said.

"Well, I think—"

"Today?"

Something in her voice made him say, "I'll try."

"Phone me when you're here."

He hung up. The phone rang again almost immediately. It was Margo Lane, Morton's mistress. She was angry. "What the fuck is going on?"

"How do you mean?" Evans said.

"Was anybody going to fucking call me?"

"I'm sorry, Margo—"

"I just saw it on TV. Missing in San Francisco and presumed dead. They had pictures of the car."

"I was going to call you," Evans said, "when I got to my office." The truth was, she had completely slipped his mind.

"And when would that have been, next week? You're as bad as that sick assistant of yours. You're his lawyer, Peter. Do your fucking job. Because, you know, let's face it, this is not a surprise. I knew this was going to happen. We all did. I want you to come over here."

"I have a busy day."

"Just for a minute."

"All right," he said. "Just for a minute."

Margo Lane lived on the fifteenth floor of a high-rise apartment building in the Wilshire Corridor. The doorman had to call up before Evans was allowed in the elevator. Margo knew he was coming up, but she still answered the door wrapped in a towel. "Oh! I didn't realize you'd be here so soon. Come in, I just got out of the shower." She frequently did something like this, flaunting her body. Evans came into the apartment and sat on the couch. She sat opposite him. The towel barely covered her torso.

"So," she said, "what's all this about George?"

"I'm sorry," Evans said, "but George crashed his Ferrari at very high speed and was thrown from the car. He fell down a cliff—they found a shoe at the bottom—and into the water. His body hasn't been recovered but they expect it to turn up in a week or so."

With her love of drama, he was sure Margo would start to cry, but she didn't. She just stared at him. "That's bullshit," she said.

"Why do you say that, Margo?"

"Because. He's hiding or something. You know it."

"Hiding? From what?"

"Probably nothing. He'd become completely paranoid. You know that."

As she said it, she crossed her legs. Evans was careful to keep his eyes on her face.

"Paranoid?" he asked.

"Don't act like you didn't know, Peter. It was obvious."

Evans shook his head. "Not to me."

"The last time he came here was a couple of days ago," she said. "He went right to the window and stood back behind the curtain, looking down onto the street. He was convinced he was being followed."

"Had he done that before?"

"I don't know. I hadn't seen him much lately; he was traveling. But whenever I called him and asked when he was coming over, he said it wasn't safe to come here."

Evans got up and walked to the window. He stood to one side and looked down at the street below.

"Are you being followed, too?" she said.

"I don't think so."

Traffic on Wilshire Boulevard was heavy, the start of afternoon rush hour. Three lanes of cars moving fast in each direction. He could hear the roar of the traffic, even up there. But there was no place to park, to pull out from the traffic. A blue Prius hybrid had pulled to the curb across the street, and traffic was backing up behind it, honking. After a moment, the Prius started up again.

No place to stop.

"Do you see anything suspicious?" she asked.

"No."

"I never did either. But George did—or thought he did."

"Did he say who was following him?"

"No." She shifted again. "I thought he should have medication. I told him."

"And what did he say to that?"

"He said I was in danger, too. He told me I should leave town for a while. Go visit my sister in Oregon. But I won't."

Her towel was coming loose. Margo tightened it, lowering it across her firm, enhanced breasts. "So I'm telling you, George went into hiding," she said. "And I think you better find him fast, because the man needs help."

"I see," Evans said. "But I suppose it's possible he isn't in hiding, that he really crashed his car. . . . In which case, there are things you need to do now, Margo."

He explained to her that if George remained missing, his assets could be ordered frozen. Which meant that she ought to withdraw everything from the bank account into which he put money for her every month. So she would be sure to have money to live on.

"But that's silly," she protested. "I know he'll be back in a few days."

"Just in case," Evans said.

She frowned. "Do you know something you're not telling me?"

"No," Evans said. "I'm just saying, it could be a while before this thing gets cleared up."

"Look," she said. "He's sick. You're supposed to be his friend. Find him."

Evans said that he would try. When he left, Margo was flouncing off to the bedroom to get dressed before going to the bank.

Outside, in the milky afternoon sunlight, fatigue overwhelmed him. All he wanted to do was go home and go to sleep. He got in his car and started driving. He was within sight of his apartment when his phone rang again.

It was Jennifer, asking where he was.

"I'm sorry," he said. "I can't come today."

"It's important, Peter. Really."

He said he was sorry, and would call her later.

Then Lisa, Herb Lowenstein's secretary, called to say that Nicholas Drake had been trying to reach him all afternoon. "He really wants to talk to you."

"Okay," Evans said, "I'll call."

"He sounds pissed."

"Okay."

"But you better call Sarah first."

"Why?"

His phone went dead. It always did in the back alley of his apartment; it was a dead spot in the cellular net. He slipped the phone into his shirt pocket; he'd call in a few minutes. He drove down the alley, and pulled into his garage space.

He walked up the back stairs to his apartment and unlocked the door. And stared.

The apartment was a mess. Furniture torn apart, cushions slashed open, papers all over the place, books tumbled out of the bookshelves and lying scattered on the floor.

He stood in the entrance, stunned. After a moment he walked into the room, straightened one of the toppled chairs and sat down in it. It occurred to him that he had to call the police. He got up, found the phone on the floor, and dialed them. But almost immediately the cell phone in his pocket began to ring. He hung up on the police and answered the cell phone. "Yes."

It was Lisa. "We got cut off," she said. "You better call Sarah right away."

"Why?"

"She's over at Morton's house. There was a robbery there."

"*What?*"

"I know. You better call her," she said. "She sounded upset."

Evans flipped the phone shut. He stood and walked into the kitchen. Everything was a mess there, too. He glanced into the bedroom. Everything was a mess. All he could think was the maid wasn't coming until next Tuesday. How could he ever clean this up?

He dialed his phone.

"Sarah?"

"Is that you, Peter?"

"Yes. What happened?"

"Not on the phone. Have you gone home yet?"

• • •

"Just got here."

"So . . . did it happen to you too?"

"Yes. Me too."

"Can you come here?"

"Yes."

"How soon?" She sounded frightened.

"Ten minutes."

"Okay. See you." She hung up.

Evans turned the ignition of his Prius and it hummed to life. He was pleased to have the hybrid; the waiting list in Los Angeles to get one was now more than six months. He'd had to take a light gray one, which wasn't his preferred color, but he loved the car. And he took a quiet satisfaction in noticing how many of them there were on the streets these days.

He drove down the alley to Olympic. Across the street he saw a blue Prius, just like the one he had seen below Margo's apartment. It was electric blue, a garish color. He thought he liked his gray better. He turned right, and then left again, heading north through Beverly Hills. He knew there would be rush hour traffic starting at this time of day and he should get up to Sunset, where traffic moved a little better.

When he got to the traffic light at Wilshire, he saw another blue Prius behind him. That same ugly color. Two guys in the car, not young. When he made his way to the light at Sunset, the same car was still behind him. Two cars back.

He turned left, toward Holmby Hills.

The Prius turned left, too. Following him.

Evans pulled up to Morton's gate and pressed the buzzer. The security camera above the box blinked on. "Can I help you?"

"It's Peter Evans for Sarah Jones."

A momentary pause, and then a buzz. The gates swung open slowly, revealing a curving roadway. The house was still hidden from view.

While he waited, Evans glanced down the road to his left. A block away, he saw the blue Prius coming up the road toward him. It passed him without slowing down, and disappeared around a curve.

So. Perhaps he was not being followed after all.

He took a deep breath, and let it out slowly.

The gates swung wide, and he drove inside.

It was almost four o'clock as Evans drove up the driveway to Morton's house. The property was crawling with security men. There were several searching among the trees near the front gate, and more in the driveway, clustered around several vans marked ANDERSON SECURITY SERVICE.

Evans parked next to Sarah's Porsche. He went to the front door. A security man opened it. "Ms. Jones is in the living room."

He walked through the large entryway and past the staircase that curved up to the second floor. He looked into the living room, prepared to see the same disarray that he'd witnessed at his own apartment, but here everything seemed to be in its place. The room appeared exactly as Evans remembered it.

Morton's living room was arranged to display his extensive collection of Asian antiquities. Above the fireplace was a large Chinese screen with shimmering gilded clouds; a large stone head from the Angkor region of Cambodia, with thick lips and a half-smile, was mounted on a pedestal near the couch; against one wall stood a seventeenth-century Japanese *tansu*, its rich wood glowing. Extremely rare, two hundred-year-old wood-cuts by Hiroshige hung on the back wall. A standing Burmese Buddha, carved in faded wood, stood at the entrance to the media room, next door.

In the middle of the room, surrounded by these antiquities, Sarah sat slumped on the couch, staring blankly out the window. She looked over as Evans came in. "They got your apartment?"

"Yes. It's a mess."

"This house was broken into, too. It must have happened last night. All the security people here are trying to figure out how it could have happened. Look here."

She got up and pushed the pedestal that held the Cambodian head. Considering the weight of the head, the pedestal moved surprisingly easily, revealing a safe sunk in the floor. The safe door stood open. Evans saw neatly stacked manila folders inside.

"What was taken?" he said.

"As far as I can tell, nothing," she said. "Seems like everything is still in its place. But I don't know exactly what George had in these safes. They were his safes. I rarely went into them."

She moved to the *tansu*, sliding open a center panel, and then a false back panel, to expose a safe in the wall behind. It, too, was open. "There are six safes in the house," she said. "Three down here, one in the second-floor study, one in the basement, and one up in his bedroom closet. They opened every one."

"Cracked?"

"No. Someone knew the combinations."

Evans said, "Did you report this to the police?"

"No."

"Why not?"

"I wanted to talk to you first."

Her head was close to his. Evans could smell a faint perfume. He said, "Why?"

"Because," she said. "Someone knew the combinations, Peter."

"You mean it was an inside job."

"It had to be."

"Who stays in the house at night?"

"Two housekeepers sleep in the far wing. But last night was their night off, so they weren't here."

"So nobody was in the house?"

STATE OF FEAR ▶ 151

"That's right."

"What about the alarm?"

"I armed it myself, before I went to San Francisco yesterday."

"The alarm didn't go off?"

She shook her head.

"So somebody knew the code," Evans said. "Or knew how to bypass it. What about the security cameras?"

"They're all over the property," she said, "inside the house and out. They record onto a hard drive in the basement."

"You've played it back?"

She nodded. "Nothing but static. It was scrubbed. The security people are trying to recover something, but . . ." She shrugged. "I don't think they'll get anywhere."

It would take pretty sophisticated burglars to know how to wipe a hard drive. "Who has the alarm codes and safe combinations?"

"As far as I know, just George and me. But obviously somebody else does, too."

"I think you should call the police," he said.

"They're looking for something," she said. "Something that George had. Something they think one of us has now. They think George gave it to one of us."

Evans frowned. "But if that's true," he said, "why are they being so obvious? They smashed my place so I couldn't help notice. And even here, they left the safes wide open, to be sure you'd know you'd been robbed . . ."

"Exactly," she said. "They want us to know what they're doing." She bit her lip. "They want us to panic, and rush off to retrieve this thing, whatever it is. Then they'll follow us, and take it."

Evans thought it over. "Do you have any idea what it could be?"

"No," she said. "Do you?"

Evans was thinking of the list George had mentioned to him, on the airplane. The list he never got around to explaining, before he died. But certainly the implication was that Morton had paid a lot of money for some sort of list. But something made Evans hesitate to mention it now.

"No," he said.

"Did George give you anything?"

"No," he said.

"Me neither." She bit her lip again. "I think we should leave."

"Leave?"

"Get out of town for a while."

"It's natural to feel that way after a robbery," he said. "But I think the proper thing to do right now is to call the police."

"George wouldn't like it."

"George is no longer with us, Sarah."

"George hated the Beverly Hills police."

"Sarah . . ."

"He never called them. He always used private security."

"That may be, but . . ."

"They won't do anything but file a report."

"Perhaps, but . . ."

"Did you call the police, about your place?"

"Not yet. But I will."

"Okay, well you call them. See how it goes. It's a waste of time."

His phone beeped. There was a text message. He looked at the screen. It said: N. DRAKE COME TO OFFICE IMMED. URGENT.

"Listen," he said. "I have to go see Nick for a bit."

"I'll be fine."

"I'll come back," he said, "as soon as I can."

"I'll be fine," she repeated.

He stood, and she stood, too. On a sudden impulse he gave her a hug. She was so tall they were almost shoulder to shoulder. "It's going to be okay," he said. "Don't worry. It'll be okay."

She returned the hug, but when he released her, she said, "Don't ever do that again, Peter. I'm not hysterical. I'll see you when you get back."

He left hastily, feeling foolish. At the door, she said, "By the way, Peter: Do you have a gun?"

"No," he said. "Do you?"

"Just a 9-millimeter Beretta, but it's better than nothing."

"Oh, okay." As he went out the front door, he thought, so much for manly reassurances for the modern woman.

He got in the car, and drove to Drake's office.

It was not until he had parked his car and was walking in the front door to the office that he noticed the blue Prius parked at the end of the block, with two men sitting inside it.

Watching him.

"No, no, *no!*" Nicholas Drake stood in the NERF media room, surrounded by a half-dozen stunned-looking graphic designers. On the walls and tables were posters, banners, flyers, coffee mugs, and stacks of press releases, and media kits. All were emblazoned with a banner that went from green to red, with the superimposed words: "Abrupt Climate Change: The Dangers Ahead."

"I hate it," Drake said. "I just fucking *hate* it."

"Why?"

"Because it's *boring*. It sounds like a damn PBS special. We need some punch here, some pizzazz."

"Well, sir," one of the designers said, "if you remember, you originally wanted to avoid anything that looked like overstatement."

"I did? No, I didn't. Henley wanted to avoid overstatement. Henley thought it should be made to look exactly like a normal academic conference. But if we do that, the media will tune us out. I mean, shit, do you know how many climate change conferences there are every year? All around the world?"

"No sir, how many?"

"Well, um, forty-seven. Anyway, that's not the point." Drake rapped the banner with his knuckles. "I mean look at this, 'Dangers.' It's so vague; it could refer to anything."

STATE OF FEAR ▶ 155

"I thought that's what you wanted—that it could refer to anything."

"No, I want 'Crisis' or 'Catastrophe.' 'The Crisis Ahead.' 'The Catastrophe Ahead.' That's better. 'Catastrophe' is much better."

"You used 'Catastrophe' for the last conference, the one on species extinction."

"I don't care. We use it because it works. This conference must point to a catastrophe."

"Uh, sir," one said, "with all due respect, is it really accurate that abrupt climate change will lead to catastrophe? Because the background materials we were given—"

"Yes, God damn it," Drake snapped, "it'll lead to a catastrophe. Believe me, it will! Now make the damn changes!"

The graphic artists surveyed the assembled materials on the table. "Mr. Drake, the conference starts in four days."

"You think I don't know it?" Drake said. "You think I fucking don't know it?"

"I'm not sure how much we can accomplish—"

"Catastrophe! Lose 'Danger,' add 'Catastrophe'! That's all I'm asking for. How difficult can it be?"

"Mr. Drake, we can redo the visual materials and the banners for the media kits, but the coffee mugs are a problem."

"Why are they a problem?"

"They're made for us in China, and—"

"*Made in China?* Land of pollution? Whose idea was that?"

"We always have the coffee mugs made in China for—"

"Well, we definitely can't use them. This is NERF, for Christ's sake. How many cups do we have?"

"Three hundred. They're given to the media in attendance, along with the press kit."

"Well get some damn eco-acceptable mugs," Drake said. "Doesn't Canada make mugs? Nobody ever complains about anything Canada does. Get some Canadian mugs and print 'Catastrophe' on them. That's all."

The artists were looking at one another. One said, "There's that supply house in Vancouver . . ."

"But their mugs are cream-colored . . ."

"I don't care if they're chartreuse," Drake said, his voice rising. "Just do it! Now what about the press releases?"

Another designer held up a sheet. "They're four-color banners printed in biodegradable inks on recycled bond paper."

Drake picked up a sheet. "This is recycled? It looks damn good."

"Actually, it's fresh paper." The designer looked nervous. "But no one will know."

"You didn't tell me that," Drake said. "It's essential that recycled materials look good."

"And they do, sir. Don't worry."

"Then let's move on." He turned to the PR people. "What's the timeline of the campaign?"

"It's a standard starburst launch to bring public awareness to abrupt climate change," the first rep said, standing up. "We have our initial press break on Sunday-morning talk shows and in the Sunday newspaper supplements. They'll be talking about the start of the conference Wednesday and interviewing major photogenic principals. Stanford, Levine, the other people who show well on TV. We've given enough lead time to get into all the major weekly newsbooks around the world, *Time, Newsweek, Der Spiegel, Paris Match, Oggi, The Economist.* All together, fifty news magazines to inform lead opinion makers. We've asked for cover stories, accepting banner folds with a graphic. Anything less and they didn't get us. We expect covers on at least twenty."

"Okay," Drake said, nodding.

"We start the conference on Wednesday. Well-known, charismatic environmentalists and major politicians from industrialized nations are scheduled to appear. We have delegates from around the world, so B-roll reaction shots of the audience will be satisfactorily color-mixed. Industrialized countries now include India and Korea and Japan, of course. The Chinese delegation will participate but there will be no speakers.

"Our two hundred invited television journalists will stay at the Hilton, and we will have interview facilities there as well as in the conference halls, so our speakers can spread the message to video audiences around the world. We will also have a number of print media people to carry the word to elite opinion makers, the ones that read but do not watch TV."

"Good," Drake said. He appeared pleased.

"Each day's theme will be identified by a distinctive graphic icon, emphasizing flood, fire, rising sea levels, drought, icebergs, typhoons, and hurricanes, and so on. Each day we have a fresh contingent of politicians from around the world coming to attend and give interviews explaining the high level of their dedication and concern about this newly emerging problem."

"Good, good." Drake nodded.

"The politicians will stay for only a day—some only a few hours—and they will not have time to attend the conferences beyond a brief photo-op showing them in the audience, but they are briefed and will be effective. Then we have local schoolchildren, grades four to seven, coming each day to learn about the dangers—sorry, the catastrophe—in their futures, and we have educational kits for grade-school teachers, so they can teach their kids about the crisis of abrupt climate change."

"When do those kits go out?"

"They were going out today, but now we'll hold them for re-bannering."

"Okay," Drake said. "And for high schools?"

"We have some trouble there," the PR guy said. "We showed the kits to a sample of high school science teachers and, uh . . ."

"And what?" Drake said.

"The feedback we got was they might not go over so well."

Drake's expression turned dark. "And why not?"

"Well, the high school curriculum is very college oriented, and there isn't a lot of room for electives . . ."

"This is hardly an *elective* . . ."

"And, uh, they felt it was all speculative and unsubstantiated. They kept saying things like, 'Where's the hard science here?' Just reporting, sir."

"God damn it," Drake said, "it is *not* speculative. It is *happening!*"

"Uh, perhaps we didn't get the right materials that show what you are saying . . ."

"Ah fuck. Never mind now," Drake said. "Just trust me, it's happening. Count on it." He turned, and said in a surprised voice, "Evans, how long have you been here?"

Peter Evans had been standing in the doorway for at least two minutes and had overheard a good deal of the conversation. "Just got here, Mr. Drake."

"All right." Drake turned to the others. "I think we've gone through this. Evans, you come with me."

Drake shut the door to his office. "I need your counsel, Peter," he said quietly. He walked around to his desk, picked up some papers, and slid them toward Evans. "What the fuck is this?"

Evans looked. "That is George's withdrawal of support."

"Did you draw it up?"

"I did."

"Whose idea was paragraph 3a?"

"Paragraph 3a?"

"Yes. Did you add that little bit of wisdom?"

"I don't really remember—"

"Then let me refresh your memory," Drake said. He picked up the document and started to read. " 'In the event of any claim that I am not of sound mind, there may be an attempt to obtain injunctive relief from the terms of this document. Therefore this document authorizes the payment of fifty thousand dollars per week to NERF while awaiting the judgment of a full trial. Said monies shall be deemed sufficient to pay ongoing costs incurred by NERF and shall by said payment deny injunctive relief.' Did you write this, Evans?"

"I did."

"Whose idea was it?"

"George's."

"George is not a lawyer. He had help."

"Not from me," Evans said. "He more or less dictated that clause. I wouldn't have thought of it."

Drake snorted in disgust. "Fifty thousand a week," he said. "At that rate, it will take us four years to receive the ten-million-dollar grant."

"That's what George wanted the document to say," Evans said.

"But whose idea was it?" Drake said. "If it wasn't you, who was it?"

"I don't know."

"Find out."

"I don't know if I can," Evans said. "I mean, George is dead now, and I don't know who he might have consulted—"

Drake glared at Evans. "Are you with us here, Peter, or not?" He started pacing back and forth. "Because this Vanutu litigation is undoubtedly the most significant lawsuit we have ever filed." He lapsed into his speech-making mode. "The stakes are enormous, Peter. Global warming is the greatest crisis facing mankind. You know that. I know that. Most of the civilized world knows that. We *must* act to save the planet, before it is too late."

"Yes," Evans said. "I know that."

"Do you?" Drake said. "We have a lawsuit, a very important lawsuit, that needs our help. And fifty thousand dollars a week will strangle it."

Evans was sure that was not true. "Fifty thousand is a lot of money," he said, "I don't see why it should strangle—"

"Because it will!" Drake snapped. *"Because I am telling you it will!"* He seemed surprised by his own outburst. He gripped the desk, got control of himself. "Look," he said. "We can never forget about our opponents here. The forces of industry are strong, phenomenally strong. And industry wants to be left alone to pollute. It wants to pollute here, and in Mexico, and in China, and wherever else it does its business. The stakes are huge."

"I understand," Evans said.

"Many powerful forces are taking an interest in this case, Peter."

"Yes, I'm sure."

"Forces that will stop at nothing to be sure that we lose it."

Evans frowned. What was Drake telling him?

"Their influence is everywhere, Peter. They may have influence with members of your law firm. Or other people you know. People whom you believe you can trust—but you can't. Because they are on the other side, and they don't even know it."

Evans said nothing. He was just looking at Drake.

"Be prudent, Peter. Watch your back. Don't discuss what you are doing with anyone—with *anyone*—except me. Try not to use your cell phone. Avoid e-mail. And keep an eye out in case you are followed."

"Okay. . . . But actually I've already been followed," Evans said. "There's a blue Prius—"

"Those were our guys. I don't know what they are doing. I called them off days ago."

"Your guys?"

"Yes. It's a new security firm we've been trying out. They're obviously not very competent."

"I'm confused," Evans said. "NERF has a security firm?"

"Absolutely. For years, now. Because of the danger we face. Please understand me: *We are all in danger*, Peter. Don't you understand what this lawsuit means if we win? Trillions of dollars that industry must pay in the coming years, to halt their emissions that are causing global warming. *Trillions*. With those stakes, a few lives don't matter. So: Be very damn careful."

Evans said that he would. Drake shook his hand.

"I want to know who told George about the paragraph," Drake said. "And I want that money freed up for us to use it as we see fit. This is all riding on you now," he said. "Good luck, Peter."

On his way out of the building, Evans ran into a young man who was sprinting up the stairs. They collided so hard that Evans was almost knocked down. The young man apologized hastily, and continued on his way. He looked like one of the kids working on the conference. Evans wondered what the crisis could be, now.

When he got back outside, he looked down the street. The blue Prius was gone.

He got into the car and drove back to Morton's, to see Sarah.

Traffic was heavy. He crept slowly along Sunset; he had plenty of time to think. The conversation with Drake left him feeling odd. There had been a funny quality to the actual meeting. As if it didn't really need to happen, as if Drake just wanted to make sure he was able to call Evans in, and Evans would come. As if he were asserting his authority. Or something like that.

Anyway, Evans felt, something was off.

And Evans also felt a little strange about the security firm. That just didn't seem right. After all, NERF was one of the good guys. They shouldn't be sneaking around and following people. And Drake's paranoid warnings were somehow not persuasive. Drake was overreacting, as he so often did.

Drake was dramatic by nature. He couldn't help it. Everything was a crisis, everything was desperate, everything was vitally important. He lived in a world of extreme urgency, but it wasn't necessarily the real world.

Evans called his office, but Heather had gone for the day. He called Lowenstein's office and spoke to Lisa. "Listen," he said, "I need your help."

Her voice was lower, conspiratorial. "Of course, Peter."

"My apartment was robbed."

"No—you, too?"

"Yes, me, too. And I really need to talk to the police—"

"Well, yes, you certainly do—my goodness—did they take anything?"

"I don't think so," he said, "but just to file a report, all that—I'm kind of busy right now, dealing with Sarah . . . it may go later into the night . . ."

"Well, of course, do you need me to deal with the police about your robbery?"

"Could you?" he said. "It would help so much."

"Why of course, Peter," she said. "Leave it to me." She paused. When she spoke again, it was almost a whisper. "Is there, ah, anything you don't want the police to find?"

"No," he said.

"I mean, it's all right with me, everybody in LA has a few bad habits, otherwise we wouldn't be here—"

"No, Lisa," he said. "Actually, I don't have any drugs, if that's what you mean."

"Oh, no," she said quickly. "I wasn't assuming anything. No pictures or anything like that?"

"No, Lisa."

"Nothing, you know, underage?"

"Afraid not."

"Okay, I just wanted to be sure."

"Well, thanks for doing this. Now to get in through the door—"

"I know," she said, "the key is under the back mat."

"Yes." He paused. "How'd you know that?"

"Peter," she said, sounding a little offended. "You can count on me to know things."

"All right. Well, thanks."

"Don't mention it. Now, what about Margo? How's she doing?" Lisa said.

"She's fine."

"You went to see her?"

"This morning, yes, and—"

"No, I mean at the hospital. Didn't you hear? Margo was coming back from the bank today and walked in while her apartment was being robbed. Three robberies in one day! You, Margo, Sarah! What is going on? Do you know?"

"No," Evans said. "It's very mysterious."

"It *is*."

"But about Margo . . . ?"

"Oh yes. So I guess she decided to fight these guys, which was the wrong thing to do, and they beat her up, maybe knocked her unconscious. She had a black eye, I heard, and while the cops were there interviewing her, she passed out. Got completely paralyzed and couldn't move. And she even stopped breathing."

"You're kidding."

"No. I had a long conversation with the detective who was there. He told me it just came over her, and she was unable to move and was dark blue before the paramedics showed up and took her to UCLA. She's been in intensive care all afternoon. The doctors are waiting to ask her about the blue ring."

"What blue ring?"

"Just before she became paralyzed, she was slurring her words but she said something about the blue ring, or the blue ring of death."

"The blue ring of death," Evans said. "What does that mean?"

"They don't know. She isn't able to talk yet. Does she take drugs?"

"No, she's a health nut," Evans said.

"Well, I hear the doctors say she'll be okay. It was some temporary paralysis."

"I'll go see her later," he said.

"When you do, will you call me afterward? And I'll handle your apartment, don't worry."

It was dark when he got to Morton's house. The security people were gone; the only car parked in front was Sarah's Porsche. She opened the front door when he rang. She had changed into a tracksuit. "Everything all right?" he said.

"Yes," she said. They came into the hallway, and they crossed to the living room. The lights were on, and the room was warm and inviting.

"Where are the security people?"

"They left for dinner. They'll be back."

"They *all* left?"

"They'll be back. I want to show you something," she said. She pulled out a wand with an electronic meter attached to it. She ran it over his body, like an airport security check. She tapped his left pocket. "Empty it."

The only thing in his pocket were his car keys. He dropped them on the coffee table. Sarah was running the wand over his chest, his jacket. She touched his right jacket pocket, gestured for him to empty it out.

"What's this about?" he said.

She shook her head, and didn't speak.

He pulled out a penny. Set it on the counter.

She waved her hand: more?

He felt again. Nothing.

She ran the wand over his car keys. There was a plastic rectangle on the chain, which unlocked his car door. She pried it open with a pocket-knife.

"Hey, listen . . ."

The rectangle popped open. Evans saw electronic circuits inside, a watch battery. Sarah pulled out a tiny bit of electronics hardly bigger than the tip of a lead pencil. "Bingo."

"Is that what I think it is?"

She took the electronic unit and dropped it into a glass of water. Then she turned to the penny. She examined it minutely, then twisted it in her fingers. To Evans's surprise, it broke in half, revealing a small electronic center.

She dropped that in the glass of water, too. "Where's your car?" she said.

"Out in front."

"We can check it later."

He said, "What's this about?"

"The security guys found bugs on me," she said. "And all over the house. The best guess is that was the reason for the robbery—to plant bugs. And guess what? You have bugs, too."

He looked around. "Is the house okay?"

"The house has been electronically swept and cleared. The guys found about a dozen bugs. Supposedly it's clean now."

They sat together on the couch. "Whoever is doing all this, they think we know something," she said. "And I'm beginning to believe they're right."

Evans told her about Morton's comments about the list.

"He bought a list?" she said.

Evans nodded. "That's what he said."

"Did he say what kind of a list?"

"No. He was going to tell me more, but he never got around to it."

"He didn't say anything more to you, when you were alone with him?"

"Not that I remember."

"Going up on the plane?"

"No . . ."

"At the table, at dinner?"

"I don't think so, no."

"When you walked him to his car?"

"No, he was singing all that time. It was sort of embarrassing, to tell you the truth. And then he got in his car . . . Wait a minute." Evans sat up. "He did say one funny thing."

"What was that?"

"It was some Buddhist philosophical saying. He told me to remember it."

"What was it?"

"I don't remember," Evans said. "At least not exactly. It was something like 'Everything that matters is near where the Buddha sits.'"

"George wasn't interested in Buddhism," Sarah said. "Why would he say that to you?"

"Everything that matters is near where the Buddha sits," Evans said, repeating it again.

He was staring forward, into the media room adjacent to the living room.

"Sarah . . ."

Directly facing them, under dramatic overhead lighting, was a large wooden sculpture of a seated Buddha. Burmese, fourteenth century.

Evans got up and walked into the media room. Sarah followed him. The sculpture was four feet high, and mounted on a high pedestal. Evans walked around behind the statue.

"You think?" Sarah said.

"Maybe."

He ran his fingers around the base of the statue. There was a narrow space there, beneath the crossed legs, but he could feel nothing. He crouched, looked: nothing. There were some wide cracks in the wood of the statue, but nothing was there.

"Maybe move the base?" Evans said.

"It's on rollers," Sarah said.

They slid it to one side, exposing nothing but white carpet.

Evans sighed.

"Any other Buddhas around here?" he said, looking around the room.

Sarah was down on her hands and knees. "Peter," she said.

"What?"

"Look."

He crouched down. There was a roughly one-inch gap between the base of the pedestal and the floor. Barely visible in that gap was the corner of an envelope, attached to the inside of the pedestal.

"I'll be damned."

"It's an envelope."

She slid her fingers in.

"Can you reach it?"

"I . . . think so . . . got it!"

She pulled it out. It was a business-size envelope, sealed and unmarked.

"This could be it," she said, excited. "Peter, I think we may have found it!"

The lights went out, and the house was plunged into darkness.

They scrambled to their feet.

"What happened?" Evans said.

"It's okay," she said. "The emergency generator will cut in at any second."

"Actually, it won't," a voice in the darkness said.

Two powerful flashlights shone directly in their faces. Evans squinted in the harsh light; Sarah raised her hand to cover her eyes.

"May I have the envelope, please," the voice said.

Sarah said, "No."

There was a mechanical click, like the cocking of a gun.

"We'll take the envelope," the voice said. "One way or another."

"No you won't," Sarah said.

Standing beside her, Evans whispered, "Sar-ah . . ."

"Shut up, Peter. They can't have it."

"We'll shoot if we have to," the voice said.

"Sarah, give them the fucking envelope," Evans said.

"Let them take it," Sarah said defiantly.

"Sar-ah . . ."

"Bitch!" the voice screamed, and a gunshot sounded. Evans was embroiled in chaos and blackness. There was another scream. One of the flashlights bounced on the floor and rolled, pointing in a corner. In the shadows Evans saw a large dark figure attack Sarah, who screamed and kicked. Without thinking, Evans threw himself against the attacker, grabbing an arm in a leather jacket. He could smell the man's beery breath, hear him grunting. Then someone else pulled him off, slamming him to the ground, and he was kicked in the ribs.

He rolled away, banging against the furniture, and then a new, deep voice held up a flashlight and said "Move away *now*." Immediately the attacker stopped fighting with them, and turned to this new voice. Evans looked back to see Sarah, who was on the floor. Another man got up and turned toward the flashlight.

There was a crackling sound and the man screamed and fell backward. The flashlight swung to the man who had been kicking Peter.

"You. Down."

The man immediately lay on the carpet.

"Face down."

The man rolled over.

"That's better," the new voice said. "Are you two all right?"

"I'm fine," Sarah said, panting, staring into the light. "Who the hell are you?"

"Sarah," the voice said. "I'm disappointed you don't recognize me."

Just then, the lights came back up in the room.

Sarah said, "John!"

And to Evans's astonishment, she stepped across the body of the fallen attacker to give a grateful hug to John Kenner, professor of Geoenvironmental Engineering at MIT.

"I think I deserve an explanation," Evans said. Kenner had crouched down and was handcuffing the two men lying on the floor. The first man was still unconscious.

"It's a modulated taser," Kenner said. "Shoots a five-hundred-megahertz dart that delivers a four-millisecond jolt that inactivates cerebellar functioning. Down you go. Unconsciousness is immediate. But it only lasts a few minutes."

"No," Evans said. "I meant—"

"Why am I here?" Kenner said, looking up with a faint smile.

"Yes," Evans said.

"He's a good friend of George's," Sarah said.

"He is?" Evans said. "Since when?"

"Since we all met, a while back," Kenner said. "And I believe you remember my associate, Sanjong Thapa, as well."

A compact, muscular young man with dark skin and a crew cut came into the room. As before, Evans was struck by his vaguely military bearing, and British accent. "Lights are all back on, Professor," Sanjong Thapa said. "Should I call the police?"

"Not just yet," Kenner said. "Give me a hand here, Sanjong." Together, Kenner and his friend went through the pockets of the handcuffed men. "As I thought," Kenner said, straightening at last. "No identification on them."

"Who are they?"

"That'll be a question for the police," he said. The men were beginning to cough, and wake up. "Sanjong, let's get them to the front door." They hauled the intruders to their feet, and half-led, half-dragged them out of the room.

Evans was alone with Sarah. "How did Kenner get in the house?"

"He was in the basement. He's been searching the house most of the afternoon."

"And why didn't you tell me?"

"I asked her not to," Kenner said, walking back into the room. "I wasn't sure about you. This is a complicated business." He rubbed his hands together. "Now then, shall we have a look at that envelope?"

"Yes." Sarah sat down on the couch, and tore it open. A single sheet of paper, neatly folded, was inside. She stared at it in disbelief. Her face fell.

"What is it?" Evans said.

Without a word, she handed it to him.

It was a bill from the Edwards Fine Art Display Company of Torrance, California, for construction of a wooden pedestal to support a statue of a Buddha. Dated three years ago.

Feeling dejected, Evans sat down on the couch next to Sarah.

"What?" Kenner said. "Giving up already?"

"I don't know what else to do."

"You can begin by telling me exactly what George Morton said to you."

"I don't remember exactly."

"Tell me what you do remember."

"He said it was a philosophical saying. And it was something like, 'Everything that matters is near where the Buddha sits.'"

"No. That's impossible," Kenner said, in a definite tone.

"Why?"

"He wouldn't have said that."

"Why?"

Kenner sighed. "I should think it's self-evident. If he was giving instructions—which we presume he was—he wouldn't be so inexact. So he must have said something else."

"That's all I remember," Evans said, defensively. Evans found Kenner's quick manner to be brusque, almost insulting. He was beginning not to like this man.

"That's all you remember?" Kenner said. "Let's try again. *Where* did George make this statement to you? It must have been after you left the lobby."

At first Evans was puzzled. Then he remembered: "Were you there?"

"Yes, I was. I was in the parking lot, off to one side."

"Why?" Evans said.

"We'll discuss that later," Kenner said. "You were telling me, you and George went outside . . ."

"Yes," Evans said. "We went outside. It was cold, and George stopped singing when he felt the cold. We were standing on the steps of the hotel, waiting for the car."

"Uh-huh . . ."

"And when it came, he got into the Ferrari, and I was worried he shouldn't be driving, and I asked him about that, and George said, 'This reminds me of a philosophical saying.' And I said, 'What is it?' And he said. 'Everything that matters is not far from where the Buddha sits.'"

"Not far?" Kenner said.

"That's what he said."

"All right," Kenner said. "And at this moment, you were . . ."

"Leaning over the car."

"The Ferrari."

"Yes."

"Leaning over. And when George told you this philosophical saying, what did you answer back?"

"I just asked him not to drive."

"Did you repeat the phrase?"

"No," Evans said.

"Why not?"

"Because I was worried about him. He shouldn't be driving. Anyway, I remember thinking it was sort of awkwardly phrased. 'Not remote from where the Buddha sits.'"

"Not remote?" Kenner said.

"Yes," Evans said.

"He said to you, 'not remote?'"

"Yes."

"*Much* better," Kenner said. He was moving restlessly around the room, his eyes flicking from object to object. Touching things, dropping them, moving on.

"Why is it much better?" Evans said irritably.

Kenner gestured around the room. "Look around you, Peter. What do you see?"

"I see a media room."

"Exactly."

"Well, I don't understand—"

"Sit down on the couch, Peter."

Evans sat down, still furious. He crossed his arms over his chest and glowered at Kenner.

The doorbell rang. They were interrupted by the arrival of the police. Kenner said, "Let me handle this. It's easier if they don't see you," and he again walked out of the room. From the hallway, they heard several low voices discussing the two captured intruders. It sounded all very chummy.

Evans said, "Does Kenner have something to do with law enforcement?"

"Not exactly."

"What does that mean?"

"He just seems to know people."

Evans stared at her. "He knows people," he repeated.

"Different sorts of people. Yes. He sent George off to see a lot of them. Kenner has a tremendously wide range of contacts. Particularly in the environmental area."

"Is that what the Center for Risk Analysis does? Environmental risks?"

"I'm not sure."

"Why is he on sabbatical?"

"You should ask him these things."

"Okay."

"You don't like him, do you?" she said.

"I like him fine. I just think he's a conceited asshole."

"He's very sure of himself," she said.

"Assholes usually are."

Evans got up, and walked to where he could see into the hallway. Kenner was talking to the policemen, signing some documents, and turning over the intruders. The police were joking with him. Standing to one side was the dark man, Sanjong.

"And what about the little guy with him?"

"Sanjong Thapa," she said. "Kenner met him in Nepal when he was climbing a mountain there. Sanjong was a Nepali military officer assigned to help a team of scientists studying soil erosion in the Himalaya. Kenner invited him back to the States to work with him."

"I remember now. Kenner's a mountain climber, too. And he was almost on the Olympic ski team." Evans couldn't conceal his annoyance.

Sarah said, "He's a remarkable man, Peter. Even if you don't like him."

Evans returned to the couch, sat down again, folded his arms. "Well, you're right about that," he said. "I don't."

"I have the feeling you're not alone there," she said. "The list of people who dislike John Kenner is a long one."

Evans snorted, and said nothing.

They were still sitting on the couch when Kenner came bounding back into the room. He was again rubbing his hands. "All right," he said. "All the two boys have to say is that they want to talk to a lawyer, and they seem to know one. Imagine that. But we'll know more in a few hours." He turned to Peter. "So: mystery solved? Concerning the Buddha?"

Evans glared at him. "No."

"Really? It's quite straightforward."

"Why don't you just tell us," Evans said.

"Reach your right hand out to the end table," Kenner said.

Evans put his hand out. There were five remote controls on the table. "Yes?" he said. "And?"

"What are they for?"

"It's a media room," Evans said. "I think we've established that."

"Yes," Kenner said. "But *what are they for?*"

"Obviously," Evans said, "to control the television, the satellite, the DVD, the VHS, all that."

"Which one does which?" Kenner said.

Evans stared at the table. And suddenly he got it. "Oh my God," he said. "You're absolutely right."

He was flipping them over, one after another.

"This one's the flat panel . . . DVD . . . satellite . . . high def . . ." He stopped. There was one more. "Looks like there are two DVD controllers." The second one was stubby and black and had all the usual buttons, but it was slightly lighter than the other.

Evans pulled open the battery compartment. Only one battery was there. In place of the other was a tightly rolled piece of paper.

"Bingo," he said.

He took the paper out.

All that matters is not remote from where the Buddha sits. That's what George had said. Which meant that this paper was all that matters.

Carefully, Evans unrolled the tiny sheet and pressed it flat on the coffee table with the heel of his hand, smoothing out the wrinkles.

And then he stared.

The paper contained nothing but columns of numbers and words:

662262	3982293	24FXE 62262 82293	**TERROR**
882320	4898432	12FXE 82232 54393	**SNAKE**
774548	9080799	02FXE 67533 43433	**LAUGHER**
482320	5898432	22FXE 72232 04393	**SCORPION**
ALT			
662262	3982293	24FXE 62262 82293	**TERROR**
382320	4898432	12FXE 82232 54393	**SEVER**
244548	9080799	02FXE 67533 43433	**CONCH**
482320	5898432	22FXE 72232 04393	**SCORPION**
ALT			
662262	3982293	24FXE 62262 82293	**TERROR**
382320	4898432	12FXE 82232 54393	**BUZZARD**
444548	7080799	02FXE 67533 43433	**OLD MAN**
482320	5898432	22FXE 72232 04393	**SCORPION**
ALT			
662262	3982293	24FXE 62262 82293	**TERROR**
382320	4898432	12FXE 82232 54393	**BLACK MESA**
344548	9080799	02FXE 67533 43433	**SNARL**
482320	5898432	22FXE 72232 04393	**SCORPION**

Evans said, "Is *this* what everybody's after?"

Sarah was looking at the paper over his shoulder. "I don't get it. What does it mean?"

Evans passed the paper to Kenner. He hardly glanced at it before he said, "No wonder they were so desperate to get this back."

"You know what it is?"

"There's no doubt about what it is," Kenner said, handing the paper to Sanjong. "It's a list of geographic locations."

"Locations? Where?"

"We'll have to calculate that," Sanjong said. "They're recorded in UTM, which may mean the listing was intended for pilots." Kenner saw the blank looks on the others' faces. "The world is a globe," he said, "and maps are flat. Therefore all maps are projections of a sphere onto a flat surface. One projection is the Universal Transverse Mercator grid, which divides the globe into six-degree grids. It was originally a military projection, but some pilot charts use it."

Evans said, "So these numbers are latitude and longitude in a different form?"

"Correct. A military form." Kenner ran his finger down the page. "It appears to be several alternate sets of four locations. But in every instance the first and last locations are the same. For whatever reason . . ." He frowned, and stared off into space.

"Is that bad?" Sarah said.

"I'm not sure," Kenner said. "But it might be, yes." He looked at Sanjong.

Sanjong nodded gravely. "What is today?" he said.

"Tuesday."

"Then . . . time is very short."

Kenner said, "Sarah, we're going to need George's plane. How many pilots does he have?"

"Two, usually."

"We'll need at least four. How soon can you get them?"

"I don't know. Where do you want to go?" she said.

"Chile."

"Chile! And leave when?"

"As soon as possible. Not later than midnight."

"It'll take me some time to arrange—"

"Then get started now," Kenner said. "Time is short, Sarah. Very short."

Evans watched Sarah go out of the room. He turned back to Kenner. "Okay," he said. "I give up. What's in Chile?"

"A suitable airfield, I presume. With adequate jet fuel." Kenner snapped his fingers. "Good point, Peter. Sarah," he called into the next room, "what kind of a plane is it?"

"G-five!" she called back.

Kenner turned to Sanjong Thapa, who had taken out a small handheld computer and was tapping away at it. "Are you connected to Akamai?"

"Yes."

"Was I right?"

"I've only checked the first location so far," Sanjong said. "But yes. We need to go to Chile."

"Then Terror is Terror?" Kenner said.

"I think so, yes."

Evans looked from one man to the other. "Terror is Terror?" he said, puzzled.

"That's right," Kenner said.

Sanjong said, "You know, Peter's got a point."

Evans said, "Are you guys ever going to tell me what's going on?"

"Yes," Kenner said. "But first, you have your passport?"

"I always carry it."

"Good man." Kenner turned back to Sanjong. "What point?"

"It's UTM, Professor. It's a six-degree grid."

"Of course!" Kenner said, snapping his fingers again. "What's the matter with me?"

"I give up," Evans said. "What's the matter with you?"

But Kenner didn't answer; he now seemed almost hyperactive, his fingers twitching nervously as he picked up the remote control from the table beside Peter and peered at it closely, turning it in the light. Finally, he spoke.

"A six-degree grid," Kenner said, "means that these locations are only accurate to a thousand meters. Roughly half a mile. That's simply not good enough."

"Why? How accurate should it be?"

"Three meters," Sanjong said. "About ten feet."

"Assuming they are using PPS," Kenner said, still squinting at the remote control. "In which case . . . Ah. I thought so. It's the oldest trick in the book."

He pulled the entire back of the remote off, exposing the circuit board. He lifted that away to reveal a second folded sheet of paper. It was thin, hardly more than tissue paper. It contained rows of numbers and symbols.

-2147483640,8,0*x°%ÁgKÀ__^O#_QÀ__cÁ«ªªªªªÚ?_ ___ÿÿÿ__å
-2147483640,8,0%h° â#KÀ_O,__@BÀ__cÁ«ªªªªªÚ?ÿÿÿÿ___ÿÿÿ__
-2147483640,8,0ã'»^$PNÀ_N__éxFÀ__cÁ¬ªªªªªÚ¿___ÿÿÿ__Å
-2147483640,8,0óW»1/4_OÀ   ò°q_IMÀ__cÁ«ªªªªªÚ?ÿÿÿ___ÿÿÿ__¥
-2147483640,8,0‰œ°/Ñ_LÀøø_8_ÔPÀ__cÁ«ªªªªªÚ?____ÿÿÿ__

-2147483640,8,0*x°%ÁgKÀ__^O#_QÀ__cÁ«ªªªªªÚ?_ ___ÿÿÿ__å
-2147483640,8,0%h° â#KÀ_O,__@BÀ__cÁ«ªªªªªÚ?ÿÿÿÿ___ÿÿÿ__
-2147483640,8,0óW»1/4_OÀ   ò°q_IMÀ__cÁ«ªªªªªÚ?ÿÿÿÿ___ÿÿÿ__¥
-2147483640,8,0ë{»I_´OÀã°°"d,LÀ__cÁ¬ªªªªªÚ¿___ÿÿÿ
-2147483640,8,0‰œ°/Ñ_LÀøø_8_ÔPÀ__cÁ«ªªªªªÚ?____ÿÿÿ__

-2147483640,8,0*x°%ÁgKÀ__^O#_QÀ__cÁ«ªªªªªÚ?_ ___ÿÿÿ__å
-2147483640,8,0%h° â#KÀ_O,__@BÀ__cÁ«ªªªªªÚ?ÿÿÿÿ___ÿÿÿ__
-2147483640,8,0óW»1/4_OÀ   ò°q_IMÀ__cÁ«ªªªªªÚ?ÿÿÿÿ___ÿÿÿ__¥
-2147483640,8,0ë{»I_´OÀã°°"d,LÀ__cÁ¬ªªªªªÚ¿___ÿÿÿ
-2147483640,8,0‰œ°/Ñ_LÀøø_8_ÔPÀ__cÁ«ªªªªªÚ?____ÿÿÿ__

"All right," Kenner said. "This is more like it."

"And these are?" Evans said.

"True coordinates. Presumably for the same locations."

"Terror is Terror?" Evans said. He was starting to feel foolish.

Kenner said, "Yes. We're talking about Mount Terror, Peter. An inactive volcano. You have heard of it?"

"No."

"Well, we're going there."

"Where is it?"

"I thought you'd have guessed that by now," Kenner said. "It's in Antarctica, Peter."

II

TERROR

TO PUNTA ARENAS
TUESDAY, OCTOBER 5
9:44 P.M.

Van Nuys Airport sank beneath them. The jet turned south, crossing the flat, glowing expanse of the Los Angeles Basin. The flight attendant brought Evans coffee. On the little screen, it said 6,204 miles to destination. Flying time was nearly twelve hours.

The flight attendant asked them if they wanted dinner, and went off to prepare it.

"All right," Evans said. "Three hours ago, I'm coming to help Sarah deal with a robbery. Now I'm flying to Antarctica. Isn't it time somebody told me what this is about?"

Kenner nodded. "Have you heard of the Environmental Liberation Front? ELF?"

"No," Evans said, shaking his head.

"Not me," Sarah said.

"It's an underground extremist group. Supposedly made up of ex-Greenpeace and Earth First! types who thought those organizations had gone soft. ELF engages in violence on behalf of environmental causes. They've burned hotels in Colorado, houses on Long Island, spiked trees in Michigan, torched cars in California."

Evans nodded. "I read about them. . . . The FBI and other law enforcement agencies can't infiltrate them because the organization consists of separate cells that never communicate with one another."

"Yes," Kenner said. "Supposedly. But cell phone conversations have been recorded. We've known for some time that the group was going global, planning a series of major events around the world, starting a few days from now."

"What kind of events?"

Kenner shook his head. "That, we don't know. But we have reason to think they'll be big—and destructive."

Sarah said, "What does this have to do with George Morton?"

"Funding," Kenner said. "If ELF is preparing actions around the world, they need a lot of money. The question is, where are they getting it?"

"Are you saying George has funded an extremist group?"

"Not intentionally. ELF is a criminal organization, but even so, radical groups like PETA fund them. Frankly, it's a disgrace. But the question became whether better-known environmental groups were funding them, too."

"Better-known groups? Like who?"

"Any of them," Kenner said.

"Wait a minute," Sarah said. "Are you suggesting that the Audubon Society and the Sierra Club fund terrorist groups?"

"No," Kenner said. "But I'm telling you that nobody knows exactly what any of these groups do with their money. Because government oversight of foundations and charities is extraordinarily lax. They don't get audited. The books don't get inspected. Environmental groups in the US generate half a billion dollars a year. What they do with it is unsupervised."

Evans frowned. "And George knew this?"

"When I met him," Kenner said, "he was already worrying about NERF. What it was doing with its money. It dispenses forty-four million dollars a year."

Evans said, "You're not going to tell me that NERF—"

"Not directly," Kenner said. "But NERF spends nearly sixty percent of its money on fund-raising. It can't admit that, of course. It'd look bad. It gets around the numbers by contracting nearly all of its work to out-side direct-mail advertisers and telephone solicitation groups. These groups have misleading names, like the International Wildlife Preservation Fund—that's an Omaha-based direct-mail organization, that in turn outsources the work to Costa Rica."

"You're kidding," Evans said.

"No. I am not. And last year the IWPF spent six hundred fifty thousand dollars to gather information on environmental issues, including three hundred thousand dollars to something called the Rainforest Action and Support Coalition, RASC. Which turns out to be a drop box in Elmira, New York. And an equal sum to Seismic Services in Calgary, another drop box."

"You mean . . ."

"A drop box. A dead end. That was the true basis of the disagreement between Morton and Drake. Morton felt that Drake wasn't minding the store. That's why he wanted an external audit of the organization, and when Drake refused, Morton got really worried. Morton is on the NERF board; he has liability. So he hired a team of private investigators to investigate NERF."

"He did?" Evans said.

Kenner nodded. "Two weeks ago."

Evans turned to Sarah. "Did you know this?"

She looked away, then back. "He told me I couldn't tell anyone."

"George did?"

"I did," Kenner said.

"So you were behind this?"

"No, I merely consulted with George. It was his ball game. But the point is, once you outsource the money, you no longer control how it is spent. Or, you have deniability about how it is spent."

"Jesus," Evans said. "All this time, I just thought George was worried about the Vanutu lawsuit."

"No," Kenner said. "The lawsuit is probably hopeless. It is very unlikely it will ever go to trial."

"But Balder said when he gets good sea-level data—"

"Balder already has the good data. He has had it for months."

"What?"

"The data show no rise in South Pacific sea levels for the last thirty years."

"*What?*"

Kenner turned to Sarah. "Is he always like this?"

The flight attendant set out placemats, napkins, and silverware. "I've got fusilli pasta with chicken, asparagus, and sun-dried tomatoes," she said, "and a mixed green salad to follow. Would anyone like wine?"

"White wine," Evans said.

"I have Puligny-Montrachet. I'm not sure of the year, I think it's '98. Mr. Morton usually kept '98 on board."

"Just give me the whole bottle," Evans said, trying to make a joke. Kenner had unnerved him. Earlier in the evening, Kenner had been excited, almost twitchy-nervous. But now, sitting on the airplane, he was very still. Implacable. He had the manner of a man who was telling obvious truths, even though none of it was obvious to Peter. "I had it all wrong," Evans said finally. "If what you're saying is true . . ."

Kenner just nodded slowly.

Evans thought: He's letting me put it together. He turned to Sarah. "Did you know this, too?"

"No," she said. "But I knew something was wrong. George was very upset for the last two weeks."

"You think that's why he gave that speech, and then killed himself?"

"He wanted to embarrass NERF," Kenner said. "He wanted intense media scrutiny of that organization. Because he wanted to stop what is about to happen."

The wine came in cut glass crystal. Evans gulped it, held out his glass for more. "And what is about to happen?" he said.

"According to that list, there will be four events," Kenner said. "In four locations in the world. Roughly one day apart."

"What kind of events?"

Kenner shook his head. "We now have three good clues."

Sanjong fingered his napkin. "This is real linen," he said, in an awestruck tone. "And real crystal."

"Nice, huh?" Evans said, draining his glass again.

Sarah said, "What are the clues?"

"The first is the fact that the timing is not exact. You might think a terrorist event would be precisely planned, down to the minute. These events are not."

"Maybe the group isn't that well organized."

"I doubt that's the explanation. The second clue we got tonight, and it's very important," Kenner said. "As you saw from the list, there are several alternate locations for these events. Again, you'd think a terrorist organization would pick one location and stick to it. But this group hasn't done that."

"Why not?"

"I assume it reflects the kind of events that are planned. There must be some uncertainty inherent in the event itself, or in the conditions needed for it to take place."

"Pretty vague."

"It's more than we knew twelve hours ago."

"And the third clue?" Evans said, gesturing to the flight attendant to refill his glass.

"The third clue we have had for some time. Certain government agencies track the sale of restricted high technologies that might be useful to terrorists. For example, they track everything that can be used in nuclear weapons production—centrifuges, certain metals, and so on. They track the sale of all conventional high explosives. They track certain critical biotechnologies. And they track equipment that might be used to disrupt communications networks—that generate electromagnetic impulses, for example, or high-intensity radio frequencies."

"Yes . . ."

"They do this work with neural network pattern-recognition computers that search for regularities in great masses of data—in this case, basically thousands of sales invoices. About eight months ago, the computers detected a very faint pattern that seemed to indicate a common origin for the widely scattered sale of certain field and electronic equipment."

"How did the computer decide that?"

"The computer doesn't tell you that. It just reports the pattern, which is then investigated by agents on the ground."

"And?"

"The pattern was confirmed. ELF was buying very sophisticated high technology from companies in Vancouver, London, Osaka, Helsinki, and Seoul."

"What kind of equipment?" Evans said.

Kenner ticked them off on his fingers. "Fermentation tanks for AOB primers—that's ammonia-oxidizing bacteria. Mid-level particle-dispersal units, military grade. Tectonic impulse generators. Transportable MHD units. Hypersonic cavitation generators. Resonant impact processor assemblies."

"I don't know what any of that is," Evans said.

"Few people do," Kenner said. "Some of it's fairly standard environmental technology, like the AOB primer tanks. They're used in industrial wastewater treatment. Some of it's military but sold on the open market. And some of it's highly experimental. But it's all expensive."

Sarah said, "But how is it going to be used?"

Kenner shook his head. "Nobody knows. That's what we're going to find out."

"How do you *think* it's going to be used?"

"I hate to speculate," Kenner said. He picked up a basket of rolls. "Bread, anyone?"

TO PUNTA ARENAS
WEDNESDAY, OCTOBER 6
3:01 A.M.

The jet flew through the night.

The front of the cabin was darkened; Sarah and Sanjong were sleeping on makeshift beds, but Evans couldn't sleep. He sat in the back, staring out the window at the carpet of clouds glowing silver in the moonlight.

Kenner sat opposite him. "It's a beautiful world, isn't it?" he said. "Water vapor is one of the distinctive features of our planet. Makes such beauty. It's surprising there is so little scientific understanding of how water vapor behaves."

"Really?"

"The atmosphere is a bigger mystery than anyone will admit. Simple example: No one can say for sure if global warming will result in more clouds, or fewer clouds."

"Wait a minute," Evans said. "Global warming is going to raise the temperature, so more moisture will evaporate from the ocean, and more moisture means more clouds."

"That's one idea. But higher temperature also means more water vapor in the air and therefore fewer clouds."

"So which is it?"

"Nobody knows."

"Then how do they make computer models of climate?" Evans said.

Kenner smiled. "As far as cloud cover is concerned, they guess."

"They *guess?*"

"Well, they don't call it a guess. They call it an estimate, or parameterization, or an approximation. But if you don't understand something, you can't approximate it. You're really just guessing."

Evans felt the beginnings of a headache. He said, "I think it's time for me to get some sleep."

"Good idea," Kenner said, glancing at his watch. "We still have another eight hours before we land."

The flight attendant gave Evans some pajamas. He went into the bathroom to change. When he came out, Kenner was still sitting there, staring out the window at the moonlit clouds. Against his better judgment, Evans said, "By the way. You said earlier that the Vanutu lawsuit won't go to trial."

"That's right."

"Why not? Because of the sea-level data?"

"In part, yes. It's hard to claim global warming is flooding your country if sea levels aren't rising."

"It's hard to believe sea levels aren't rising," Evans said. "Everything you read says that they are. All the television reports . . ."

Kenner said, "Remember African killer bees? There was talk of them for years. They're here now, and apparently there's no problem. Remember Y2K? Everything you read back then said disaster was imminent. Went on for months. But in the end, it just wasn't true."

Evans thought that Y2K didn't prove anything about sea levels. He felt an urge to argue that point, but found himself suppressing a yawn.

"It's late," Kenner said. "We can talk about all this in the morning."

"You're not going to sleep?"

"Not yet. I have work to do."

Evans went forward to where the others were sleeping. He lay down across the aisle from Sarah, and pulled the covers up to his chin. Now his feet were exposed. He sat up, wrapped the blanket around his toes, and then lay down again. The blanket only came to mid-shoulder. He thought about getting up and asking the flight attendant for another.

And then he slept.

He awoke to harsh, glaring sunlight. He heard the clink of silverware, and smelled coffee. Evans rubbed his eyes, and sat up. In the back of the plane, the others were eating breakfast.

He looked at his watch. He'd slept for more than six hours.

He walked to the back of the plane.

"Better eat," Sarah said, "we land in an hour."

They stepped out onto the runway of Marso del Mar, shivering in the chill wind that whipped in off the ocean. The land around them was low, green, marshy, and cold. In the distance Evans saw the jagged, snow-covered spires of the El Fogara range of southern Chile.

"I thought this was summer," he said.

"It is," Kenner said. "Late spring, anyway."

The airfield consisted of a small wooden terminal, and a row of corrugated steel hangars, like oversize Quonset huts. There were seven or eight other aircraft on the field, all four-engine prop planes. Some had skis that were retracted above the landing wheels.

"Right on time," Kenner said, pointing to the hills beyond the airport. A Land Rover was bouncing toward them. "Let's go."

Inside the little terminal, which was little more than a single large room, its walls covered with faded, stained air charts, the group tried on parkas, boots, and other gear brought by the Land Rover. The parkas were all bright red or orange. "I tried to get everybody's size right," Kenner said. "Make sure you take long johns and microfleece, too."

Evans glanced at Sarah. She was sitting on the floor, pulling on heavy socks and boots. Then she unselfconsciously stripped down to her bra, and pulled a fleece top over her head. Her movements were quick, businesslike. She didn't look at any of the men.

Sanjong was staring at the charts on the wall, and seemed particularly interested in one. Evans went over. "What is it?"

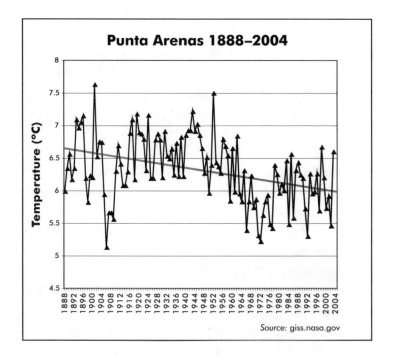

"It's the record from the weather station at Punta Arenas, near here. It's the closest city to Antarctica in the world." He tapped the chart and laughed. "There's your global warming."

Evans frowned at the chart.

"Finish up, everybody," Kenner said, glancing at his watch. "Our plane leaves in ten minutes."

Evans said, "Where exactly are we going?"

"To the base nearest Mount Terror. It's called Weddell Station. Run by New Zealanders."

"What's there?"

"Not much, mate," the Land Rover driver said, and he laughed. "But the way the weather's been lately, you'll be lucky if you can get there at all."

Evans stared out the narrow window of the Hercules. The vibration of the props made him sleepy, but he was fascinated by what he saw beneath him—mile after mile of gray ice, a vista broken by intermittent fog, and the occasional outcrop of black rock. It was a monochromatic, sunless world. And it was huge.

"Enormous," Kenner said. "People have no perspective on Antarctica, because it appears as a fringe at the bottom of most maps. But in fact, Antarctica is a major feature on the Earth's surface, and a major factor in our climate. It's a big continent, one and a half times the size of either Europe or the United States, and it holds ninety percent of all the ice on the planet."

"Ninety percent?" Sarah said. "You mean there's only ten percent in the rest of the world?"

"Actually, since Greenland has four percent, all the other glaciers in the world—Kilimanjaro, the Alps, the Himalaya, Sweden, Norway, Canada, Siberia—they all account for six percent of the planet's ice. The overwhelming majority of the frozen water of our planet is in the continent of Antarctica. In many places the ice is five or six miles thick."

"No wonder they're concerned that the ice here is melting," Evans said.

Kenner said nothing.

Sanjong was shaking his head.

Evans said, "Come on, guys. Antarctica *is* melting."

"Actually, it's not," Sanjong said. "I can give you the references, if you like."

Kenner said, "While you were asleep, Sanjong and I were talking about how to clarify things for you, since you seem to be so ill-informed."

"Ill-informed?" Evans said, stiffening.

"I don't know what else one would call it," Kenner said. "Your heart may be in the right place, Peter, but you simply don't know what you're talking about."

"Hey," he said, controlling his anger. "Antarctica *is* melting."

"You think repetition makes something true? The data show that one relatively small area called the Antarctic Peninsula is melting and calving huge icebergs. That's what gets reported year after year. But the continent as a whole is getting colder, and the ice is getting thicker."

"Antarctica is getting *colder?*"

Sanjong had taken out a laptop and was hooking it up to a small portable bubble jet printer. He flipped open his laptop screen.

"What we decided," Kenner said, "is that we're going to give you references from now on. Because it's too boring to try and explain everything to you."

A sheet of paper began to buzz out of the printer. Sanjong passed it to Evans.

Doran, P. T., Priscu, J. C., Lyons, W. B., Walsh, J. E., Fountain, A. G., McKnight, D. M., Moorhead, D. L., Virginia, R. A., Wall, D. H., Clow, G. D., Fritsen, C. H., McKay, C. P., and Parsons, A. N., 2002, "Antarctic climate cooling and terrestrial ecosystem response," *Nature* **415**: 517–20.
From 1986 to 2000 central Antarctic valleys cooled .7° C per decade with serious ecosystem damage from cold.

Comiso, J. C., 2000, "Variability and trends in Antarctic surface temperatures from *in situ* and satellite infrared measurements," *Journal of Climate* **13**: 1674–96.
Both satellite data and ground stations show slight cooling over the last 20 years.

Joughin, I., and Tulaczyk, S., 2002, "Positive mass balance of the Ross Ice Streams, West Antarctica," *Science* **295**: 476–80.
Side-looking radar measurements show West Antarctic ice is increasing at 26.8 gigatons/yr. Reversing the melting trend of the last 6,000 years.

Thompson, D. W. J., and Solomon, S., 2002, "Interpretation of recent Southern Hemisphere climate change," *Science* **296**: 895–99.
Antarctic peninsula has warmed several degrees while interior has cooled somewhat. Ice shelves have retreated but sea ice has increased.

Petit, J. R., Jouzel, J., Raynaud, D., Barkov, N. I., Barnola, J.-M., Basile, I., Bender, M., Chappellaz, J., Davis, M., Delaygue, G., Delmotte, M., Kotlyakov, V. M., Legrand, M., Lipenkov, V. Y., Lorius, C., Pepin, L., Ritz, C., Saltzman, E., and Stievenard, M., 1999, "Climate and atmospheric history of the past 420,000 years from the Vostok ice core, Antarctica," *Nature* **399**: 429–36.
During the last four interglacials, going back 420,000 years, the Earth was warmer than it is today.

Anderson, J. B., and Andrews, J. T., 1999, "Radiocarbon constraints on ice sheet advance and retreat in the Weddell Sea, Antarctica," *Geology* **27**: 179–82.
Less Antarctic ice has melted today than occurred during the last interglacial.

Liu, J., Curry, J. A., and Martinson, D. G., 2004, "Interpretation of recent Antarctic sea ice variability," *Geophysical Research Letters* **31**: 10.1029/2003 GL018732.
Antarctic sea ice has increased since 1979.

Vyas, N. K., Dash, M. K., Bhandari, S. M., Khare, N., Mitra, A., and Pandey, P. C., 2003, "On the secular trends in sea ice extent over the antarctic region based on OCEANSAT-1 MSMR observations," *International Journal of Remote Sensing* **24**: 2277–87.
Trend toward more sea ice may be accelerating.

Parkinson, C. L., 2002, "Trends in the length of the southern Ocean sea-ice season, 1979–99," *Annals of Glaciology* **34**: 435–40.
The greater part of Antarctica experiences a longer sea-ice season, lasting 21 days longer than it did in 1979.

"Okay, well, I see *slight* cooling referred to here," Evans said. "I also see warming of the peninsula of *several degrees*. That certainly seems more significant. And that peninsula's a pretty big part of the continent, isn't it?" He tossed the paper aside. "Frankly, I'm not impressed."

Sanjong said, "The peninsula is two percent of the continent. And frankly, I am surprised that you did not comment on the most significant fact in the data you were given."

"Which is?"

"When you said earlier that the Antarctic is melting," Sanjong said, "were you aware that it has been melting for the last *six thousand years?*"

"Not specifically, no."

"But generally, you knew that?"

"No," Evans said. "I wasn't aware of that."

"You thought that the Antarctic melting was something new?"

"I thought it was melting faster than previously," Evans said.

"Maybe we won't bother anymore," Kenner said.

Sanjong nodded, and started to put the computer away.

"No, no," Evans said. "I'm interested in what you have to say. I'm not closed-minded about this. I'm ready to hear new information."

"You just did," Kenner said.

Evans picked up the sheet of paper again, and folded it carefully. He slipped it into his pocket. "These studies are probably financed by the coal industry," he said.

"Probably," Kenner said. "I'm sure that explains it. But then, everybody's paid by somebody. Who pays your salary?"

"My law firm."

"And who pays them?"

"The clients. We have several hundred clients."

"You do work for all of them?"

"Me, personally? No."

"In fact, you do most of your work for environmental clients," Kenner said. "Isn't that true?"

"Mostly. Yes."

"Would it be fair to say that the environmental clients pay your salary?" Kenner said.

"You could make that argument."

"I'm just asking, Peter. Would it be fair to say environmentalists pay your salary?"

"Yes."

"Okay. Then would it be fair to say the opinions you hold are because you work for environmentalists?"

"Of course not—"

"You mean you're not a paid flunky for the environmental movement?"

"No. The fact is—"

"You're not an environmental stooge? A mouthpiece for a great fund-raising and media machine—a multi-billion-dollar industry in its own right—with its own private agenda that's not necessarily in the public interest?"

"God damn it—"

"Is this pissing you off?" Kenner said.

"You're damn right it is!"

"Good," Kenner said. "Now you know how legitimate scientists feel when their integrity is impugned by slimy characterizations such as the one you just made. Sanjong and I gave you a careful, peer-reviewed interpretation of data. Made by several groups of scientists from several different countries. And your response was first to ignore it, and then to make an ad hominem attack. You didn't answer the data. You didn't provide counter evidence. You just smeared with innuendo."

"Oh, fuck you," Evans said. "You think you have an answer for everything. But there's only one problem: Nobody agrees with you. Nobody in the world thinks that Antarctica is getting colder."

"These scientists do," Kenner said. "They published the data."

Evans threw up his hands. "The hell with it," he said. "I don't want to talk about this anymore."

He walked to the front of the plane and sat down, crossed his arms, and stared out the window.

Kenner looked at Sanjong and Sarah. "Anyone feel like coffee?"

. . .

Sarah had watched Kenner and Evans with a certain amount of uneasiness. Even though she had worked for the past two years for Morton, she had never shared her employer's passion for environmental issues. All during that time, Sarah had been in a tempestuous, exciting relationship with a handsome young actor. Their time together consisted of an unending series of passionate evenings, angry confrontations, slammed doors, tearful reconciliations, jealousies, and infidelities—and it had consumed her more than she cared to admit. The truth was that she had paid no more attention to NERF or Morton's other environmental interests than the job required. At least, until the son-of-a-bitch actor appeared in the pages of *People* magazine with a young actress from his TV show, and Sarah finally decided she had had enough, erased the guy from her cell phone, and threw herself into her work.

But she certainly held the same general view about the state of the world as Evans did. Perhaps Evans was more aggressive in stating his views, and more trusting of his assumptions, but she basically agreed with him. And here was Kenner, casting doubt after doubt.

It left her wondering whether Kenner was really correct about everything he was saying. And it also made her wonder just how he and Morton had become friends.

She asked Kenner, "Did you have these same discussions with George?"

"In the last weeks of his life, yes."

"And did he argue with you the way Evans is?"

"No." Kenner shook his head. "Because by then, he knew."

"Knew what?"

They were interrupted by the pilot's voice on the intercom. "Good news," he said. "The weather's broken over Weddell, and we will land in ten minutes. For those of you who have never made a landing on ice, seat belts should be low and tight, and all your gear safely stowed. And we really mean it."

The plane began a slow, curving descent. Sarah looked out the window at a crusty expanse of white, snow-covered ice. In the distance she saw a series of brightly colored buildings—red, blue, green—built on a cliff, overlooking the gray and choppy ocean.

"That's Weddell Station," Kenner said.

Trudging toward structures that looked like oversize children's building blocks, Evans kicked a clump of ice out of his path. He was in a grumpy mood. He felt relentlessly bullied by Kenner, whom he now recognized as one of those perpetual contrarians who argued against all conventional wisdom, simply because it was conventional.

But since Evans was stuck with this lunatic—at least for the next few days—he decided to avoid Kenner as much as possible. And certainly not engage him in any more conversations. There was no point in arguing with extremists.

He looked at Sarah, walking across the ice airfield beside him. Her cheeks were flushed in the cold air. She looked very beautiful. "I think the guy is a nut," Evans said.

"Kenner?"

"Yeah. What do you think?"

She shrugged. "Maybe."

"I bet those references he gave me are fake," he said.

"They'll be easy enough to check," she said. They stamped their feet and entered the first building.

• • •

Weddell Research Station turned out to be home to thirty-odd scientists, graduate students, technicians, and support staff. Evans was pleasantly surprised to find it was quite comfortable inside, with a cheerful cafeteria, a game room, and a large gym with a row of treadmills. There were big picture windows with views of the choppy, restless ocean. Other windows looked out over the vast, white expanse of the Ross Ice Shelf, stretching away to the west.

The head of the station greeted them warmly. He was a heavyset, bearded scientist named MacGregor who looked like Santa Claus in a Patagonia vest. Evans was annoyed that MacGregor seemed to know Kenner, at least by reputation. The two men immediately struck up a friendly conversation.

Evans excused himself, saying he wanted to check his e-mail. He was shown to a room with several computer terminals. He signed on to one, and went directly to the site for *Science* magazine.

It took him only a few moments to determine that the references Sanjong had given him were genuine. Evans read the online abstracts, and then the full text. He began to feel a little better. Kenner had summarized the raw data correctly, but he had drawn a different interpretation from that of the authors. The authors of those papers were firmly committed to the idea of global warming—and said so in the text.

Or at least, most of them did.

It was a bit complicated. In one paper, it was clear that even though the authors gave lip service to the threat of global warming, their data seemed to suggest the opposite of what they were saying in the text. But that apparent confusion, Evans suspected, was probably just the result of drawing up a paper with half a dozen authors. What they *said* was they supported the idea of global warming. And that was what counted.

More disturbing was the paper on the increase in ice thickness in the Ross Ice Shelf. Here Evans found some troubling points. First, the author did say that the shelf had been melting for the last six thousand years, ever since the Holocene era. (Though Evans could not remember reading, in any article about melting Antarctic ice, that it had been going on for the last six thousand years.) If that were true, it wasn't exactly news. On the contrary, the author suggested that the real news was the end of this long-term melting trend, and the first evidence of ice thickening. The author was hinting that this might be the first sign of the start of the next Ice Age.

Jesus!

The next *Ice Age?*

There was a knock on the door behind him. Sarah stuck her head in. "Kenner wants us," she said. "He's discovered something. Looks like we're going out on the ice."

The map covered the entire wall, showing the enormous, star-shaped continent. In the lower right-hand corner was Weddell Station, and the curving arc of the Ross Ice Shelf.

"We've learned," Kenner said, "that a supply ship docked five days ago bringing boxes of field material for an American scientist named James Brewster, from the University of Michigan. Brewster is a very recent arrival who was permitted to come at the last minute because the terms of his research grant were unusually generous in their allowance for overhead—meaning the station would get some much-needed money for operations."

"So he bought his way in?" Evans said.

"In effect."

"When did he get here?"

"Last week."

"Where is he now?"

"Out in the field." Kenner pointed to the map. "Somewhere south of the slopes of Mount Terror. And that's where we're going."

"You say this guy's a scientist from Michigan?" Sarah said.

"No," Kenner said. "We just checked with the university. They have a Professor James Brewster, all right. He's a geophysicist at the University of Michigan, and right now he's in Ann Arbor waiting for his wife to deliver a baby."

"So who is this guy?"

"Nobody knows."

"And what was his offloaded equipment?" Evans said.

"Nobody knows that, either. It was helicoptered out to the field, still in the original crates. The guy's been out there a week with two so-called graduate students. Whatever he's doing, he's apparently working across a large area, so he moves his base camp frequently. Nobody here knows precisely where he is." Kenner lowered his voice. "One of the graduate students came back yesterday to do some computer work. But we won't use him to lead us out there, for obvious reasons. We'll use one of the staff people at Weddell, Jimmy Bolden. He's very knowledgeable.

"The weather's too dicey for helicopters, so we have to take snow-tracks. It's seventeen miles to the camp. The snowtracks should get us there in two hours. The outside temperature's perfect for springtime in Antarctica—minus twenty-five degrees Fahrenheit. So, bundle up. Any questions?"

Evans glanced at his watch. "Won't it get dark soon?"

"We have much less nighttime now that spring is here. We'll have daylight all the time we're out there. The only problem we face is right here," Kenner said, pointing to the map. "We have to cross the shear zone."

THE SHEAR ZONE
WEDNESDAY, OCTOBER 6
12:09 P.M.

"The shear zone?" Jimmy Bolden said, as they trudged toward the vehicle shed. "There's nothing to it. You just have to be careful, that's all."

"But what is it?" Sarah said.

"It's a zone where the ice is subjected to lateral forces, shear forces, a bit like the land in California. But instead of having earthquakes, you get crevasses. Lots of 'em. Deep ones."

"We have to cross that?"

"It's not a problem," Bolden said. "Two years ago they built a road that crosses the zone safely. They filled in all the crevasses along the road."

They went into the corrugated steel shed. Evans saw a row of boxy vehicles with red cabs and tractor treads. "These are the snowtracks," Bolden said. "You and Sarah'll go in one, Dr. Kenner in one, and I'll be in the third, leading you."

"Why can't we all go in one?"

"Standard precaution. Keep the weight down. You don't want your vehicle to fall through into a crevasse."

"I thought you said there was a road where the crevasses were filled in?"

"There is. But the road is on an ice field, and the ice moves a couple of inches a day. Which means the road moves. Don't worry, it's clearly marked with flags." Bolden climbed up onto the tread. "Here, let me show you the features of the snowtrack. You drive it like a regular car:

clutch there, handbrake, accelerator, steering wheel. You run your heater
on this switch here—" he pointed to a switch "—and keep it on at all
times. It will maintain the cab at around ten above zero. This bulgey
orange beacon on the dashboard is your transponder. It turns on when
you push this button here. It also turns on automatically if the vehicle
shifts more than thirty degrees from horizontal."

"You mean if we fall into a crevasse," Sarah said.

"Trust me; that isn't going to happen," Bolden said. "I'm just showing you the features. Transponder broadcasts a unique vehicle code, so
we can come and find you. If for any reason you need to be rescued, you
should know the average time to rescue is two hours. Your food is here;
water here; you have enough for ten days. Medical kit here, including
morphine and antibiotics. Fire extinguisher here. Expedition equipment
in this box—crampons, ropes, carabiners, all that. Space blankets here,
equipped with mini heaters; they'll keep you above freezing for a week,
if you crawl inside 'em. That's about it. We communicate by radio.
Speaker in the cab. Microphone above the windshield. Voice-activated—
just talk. Got it?"

"Got it," Sarah said, climbing up.

"Then let's get started. Professor, you clear on everything?"

"I am," Kenner said, climbing up into the adjacent cab.

"Okay," Bolden said. "Just remember that whenever you are outside
your vehicle, it is going to be thirty below zero. Keep your hands and
face covered. Any exposed skin will get frostbite in less than a minute.
Five minutes, and you're in danger of losing anatomy. We don't want you
folks going home without all your fingers and toes. Or noses."

Bolden went to the third cab. "We proceed single file," he said.
"Three cab-lengths apart. No closer under any circumstances, and no
farther. If a storm comes up and visibility drops, we maintain the same
distance but reduce our speed. Got it?"

They all nodded.

"Then let's go."

At the far end of the shed, a corrugated door rolled up, the icy metal
screeching. Bright sunlight outside.

"Looks like a beautiful day in the neighborhood," Bolden said. And with a sputter of diesel exhaust, he drove the first snowtrack out through the door.

It was a bouncing, bone-jolting ride. The ice field that had looked so flat and featureless from a distance was surprisingly rugged when experienced up close, with long troughs and steep hillocks. Evans felt like he was in a boat, crashing through choppy seas, except of course this sea was frozen, and they were moving slowly through it.

Sarah drove, her hands confident on the wheel. Evans sat in the passenger seat beside her, clutching the dashboard to keep his balance.

"How fast are we going?"

"Looks like fourteen miles an hour."

Evans grunted as they nosed down a short trench, then up again. "We've got two hours of this?"

"That's what he said. By the way, did you check Kenner's references?"

"Yes," Evans said, in a sulky voice.

"Were they made up?"

"No."

Their vehicle was third in the row. Ahead was Kenner's snowtrack, following behind Bolden's in the lead.

The radio hissed. "Okay," they heard Bolden say, over the speaker. "Now we're coming into the shear zone. Maintain your distance and stay within the flags."

Evans could see nothing different—it just looked like more ice field, glistening in the sun—but here there were red flags on both sides of the route. The flags were mounted on six-foot-high posts.

As they moved deeper into the field, he looked beyond the road to the openings of crevasses in the ice. They had a deep blue color, and seemed to glow.

"How deep are they?" Evans said.

"The deepest we've found is a kilometer," Bolden said, over the radio. "Some of them are a thousand feet. Most are a few hundred feet or less."

"They all have that color?"

"They do, yes. But you don't want a closer look."

Despite the dire warnings, they crossed the field in safety, leaving the flags behind. Now they saw to the left a sloping mountain, with white clouds.

"That's Erebus," Bolden said. "It's an active volcano. That's steam coming from the summit. Sometimes it lobs chunks of lava, but never this far out. Mount Terror is inactive. You see it ahead. That little slope."

Evans was disappointed. The name, Mount Terror, had suggested something fearsome to him—not this gentle hill with a rocky outcrop at the top. If the mountain hadn't been pointed out to him, he might not have noticed it at all.

"Why is it called Mount Terror?" he said. "It's not terrifying."

"Has nothing to do with that. The first Antarctic landmarks were named after the ships that discovered them," Bolden said. "Terror was apparently the name of a ship in the nineteenth century."

"Where's the Brewster camp?" Sarah said.

"Should be visible any minute now," Bolden said. "So, you people are some kind of inspectors?"

"We're from the IADG," Kenner said. "The international inspection agency. We're required to make sure that no US research project violates the international agreements on Antarctica."

"Uh-huh . . ."

"Dr. Brewster showed up so quickly," Kenner went on, "he never submitted his research grant proposal for IADG approval. So we'll check in the field. It's just routine."

They bounced and crunched onward for several minutes in silence. They still did not see a camp.

"Huh," Bolden said. "Maybe he moved it."

"What type of research is he doing?" Kenner said.

"I'm not sure," Bolden said, "but I heard he's studying the mechanics of ice calving. You know, how the ice flows to the edge, and then breaks off the shelf. Brewster's been planting GPS units in the ice to record how it moves toward the sea."

"Are we close to the sea?" Evans said.

"About ten or eleven miles away," Bolden said. "To the north."

Sarah said, "If he's studying iceberg formation, why is he working so far from the coast?"

"Actually, this isn't so far," Kenner said. "Two years ago an iceberg broke off the Ross Shelf that was four miles wide and forty miles long. It was as big as Rhode Island. One of the biggest ever seen."

"Not because of global warming, though," Evans said to Sarah, with a disgusted snort. "Global warming couldn't be responsible for that. Oh no."

"Actually, it wasn't responsible," Kenner said. "It was caused by local conditions."

Evans sighed. "Why am I not surprised?"

Kenner said, "There's nothing wrong with the idea of local conditions, Peter. This is a *continent*. It would be surprising if it didn't have its own distinctive weather patterns, irrespective of global trends that may or may not exist."

"And that's very true," Bolden said. "There are definitely local patterns here. Like the katabatic winds."

"The what?"

"Katabatic winds. They're gravitational winds. You've probably noticed that it's a lot windier here than in the interior. The interior of the continent is relatively calm."

"What's a gravitational wind?" Evans said.

"Antarctica's basically one big ice dome," Bolden said. "The interior is higher than the coast. And colder. Cold air flows downhill, and gathers speed as it goes. It can be blowing fifty, eighty miles an hour when it reaches the coast. Today is not a bad day, though."

"That's a relief," Evans said.

And then Bolden said, "See there, dead ahead. That's Professor Brewster's research camp."

It wasn't much to look at: a pair of orange domed tents, one small, one large, flapping in the wind. It looked like the large one was for equipment; they could see the edges of boxes pressing against the tent fabric. From the camp, Evans could see orange-flagged units stuck into the ice every few hundred yards, in a line stretching away into the distance.

"We'll stop now," Bolden said. "I'm afraid Dr. Brewster's not here at the moment; his snowtrack is gone."

"I'll just have a look," Kenner said.

They shut the engines and climbed out. Evans had thought it was chilly in the cab, but it was a shock to feel the cold air hit him as he stepped out onto the ice. He gasped and coughed. Kenner appeared to have no reaction; he went straight for the supply tent and disappeared inside.

Bolden pointed down the line of flags. "You see his vehicle tracks there, parallel to the sensor units? Dr. Brewster must have gone out to check his line. It runs almost a hundred miles to the west."

Sarah said, "A hundred miles?"

"That's right. He has installed GPS radio units all along that distance. They transmit back to him, and he records how they move with the ice."

"But there wouldn't be much movement . . ."

"Not in the course of a few days, no. But these sensors will remain in place for a year or more. Sending back the data by radio to Weddell."

"Dr. Brewster is staying that long?"

"Oh no, he'll go back, I'm sure. It's too expensive to keep him here. His grant allows an initial twenty-one-day stay only, and then monitoring visits of a week every few months. But we'll be forwarding his data to him. Actually, we just put it up on the Internet; he takes it wherever he happens to be."

"So you assign him a secure web page?"

"Exactly."

Evans stamped his feet in the cold. "So, is Brewster coming back, or what?"

"Should be coming back. But I couldn't tell you when."

From within the tent, Kenner shouted, "Evans!"

"I guess he wants me."

Evans went to the tent. Bolden said to Sarah, "Go ahead with him, if you want to." He pointed off to the south, where clouds were darkening. "We don't want to be staying here too long. Looks like weather coming up. We have two hours ahead of us, and it won't be any fun if it socks in. Visibility drops to ten feet or less. We'd have to stay put until it cleared. And that might be two or three days."

"I'll tell them," she said.

Evans pushed the tent flap aside. The interior glowed orange from the fabric. There were the remains of wooden crates, broken down and stacked on the ground. On top of them were dozens of cardboard boxes, all stenciled identically. They each had the University of Michigan logo, and then green lettering:

> University of Michigan
> Dept. of Environmental Science
> Contents: Research Materials
> *Extremely Sensitive*
> HANDLE WITH CARE
> This Side Up

"Looks official," Evans was saying. "You sure this guy isn't an actual research scientist?"

"See for yourself," Kenner said, opening one cardboard carton. Within it, Evans saw a stack of plastic cones, roughly the size of highway cones. Except they were black, not orange. "You know what these are?"

"No." Evans shook his head.

Sarah came into the tent. "Bolden says bad weather coming, and we shouldn't stay here."

"Don't worry, we won't," Kenner said. "Sarah, I need you to go into the other tent. See if you can find a computer there. Any kind of computer—laptop, lab controller, PDA—anything with a microprocessor in it. And see if you can find any radio equipment."

"You mean transmitters, or radios for listening?"

"Anything with an antenna."

"Okay." She turned and went outside again.

Evans was still going through the cartons. He opened three, then a fourth. They all contained the same black cones. "I don't get it."

Kenner took one cone, turned it to the light. In raised lettering it said: "Unit PTBC-XX-904/8776-AW203 US DOD."

Evans said, "These are military?"

"Correct," Kenner said.

"But what are they?"

"They're the protective containers for coned PTBs."

"PTBs?"

"Precision-timed blasts. They're explosives detonated with millisecond timing by computer in order to induce resonant effects. The individual blasts are not particularly destructive, but the timing sets up standing waves in the surrounding material. That's where the destructive power comes from—the standing wave."

"What's a standing wave?" Evans said.

"You ever watch girls play jump rope? Yes? Well, if instead of spinning the rope, they shake it up and down, they generate loopy waves that travel along the length of the rope, back and forth."

"Okay . . ."

"But if the girls shake it just right, the waves appear to stop moving back and forth. The rope takes on a single curved shape and holds it.

You've seen that? Well, that's a standing wave. It reflects back and forth in perfect synchronization so it doesn't seem to move."

"And these explosives do that?"

"Yes. In nature, standing waves are incredibly powerful. They can shake a suspension bridge to pieces. They can shatter a skyscraper. The most destructive effects of earthquakes are caused by standing waves generated in the crust."

"So Brewster's got these explosives . . . set in a row . . . for a hundred miles? Isn't that what Bolden said? A hundred miles?"

"Right. And I think there's no question what he intends. Our friend Brewster is hoping to fracture the ice for a hundred miles, and break off the biggest iceberg in the history of the planet."

Sarah stuck her head in.

Kenner said, "Did you find a computer?"

"No," she said. "There's nothing there. Nothing at all. No sleeping bag, no food, no personal effects. Nothing but a bare tent. The guy's gone."

Kenner swore. "All right," he said. "Now, listen carefully. Here's what we are going to do."

"Oh no," Jimmy Bolden said, shaking his head. "I'm sorry, but I can't allow that, Dr. Kenner. It's too dangerous."

"Why is it dangerous?" Kenner said. "You take these two back to the station, and I'll follow Brewster's snowtracks until I meet up with him."

"No, sir, we all stay together, sir."

"Jimmy," Kenner said firmly, "we're not going to do that."

"With all due respect, sir, you don't know your way around this part of the world . . ."

"You forget, I am an IADG inspector," Kenner said. "I was resident in Vostok Station for six months in the winter of '99. And I was resident in Morval for three months in '91. I know exactly what I'm doing."

"Gee, I don't know . . ."

"Call back to Weddell. The station chief will confirm it."

"Well, sir, if you put it that way . . ."

"I do," Kenner said firmly. "Now get these two people back to base. Time is wasting."

"Okay, if you'll be all right . . ." Bolden turned to Evans and Sarah. "Then I guess we go. Mount up, folks, and we'll head out."

Within minutes, Evans and Sarah were jouncing along on the ice, following behind Bolden's snowtrack. Behind them, Kenner was driving parallel to the line of flags, heading east. Evans looked back just in time to see Kenner stop, get out, check one of the flags briefly, then get back in again and drive on.

Bolden saw it, too. "What is he doing?" he said in an anxious tone.

"Just looking at the unit, I guess."

"He shouldn't be getting out of his vehicle," Bolden said. "And he shouldn't be alone on the shelf. It's against regulations."

Sarah had the feeling Bolden was about to turn back. She said, "I can tell you something about Dr. Kenner, Jimmy."

"What's that?"

"You don't want to make him mad."

"Really?"

"No, Jimmy. You don't."

"Well . . . okay then."

They drove on, climbing a long rise, descending on the other side. Brewster's camp was gone, and so was Kenner's snowtrack. Ahead lay the vast white field of the Ross Ice Shelf, stretching away to the gray horizon.

"Two hours, folks," Bolden said. "And then a hot shower."

The first hour passed uneventfully. Evans started to fall asleep, only to be jolted awake by the sharp movements of the vehicle. Then he would drift off again, his head nodding until the next shock.

Sarah was driving. He said to her, "Aren't you tired?"

"No, not at all," she said.

The sun was now low on the horizon, and obscured by fog. The landscape was shades of pale gray, with almost no separation between land and sky. Evans yawned. "Want me to take over?"

"I've got it, thanks."

"I'm a good driver."

"I know you are."

He was thinking she had a definite bossy side, despite her charm and her beauty. She was the kind of woman who would want to control the remote.

"I bet you want the remote," he said.

"You think so?" She smiled.

It was irritating in a certain way, he thought, that she did not take him seriously as a man. At least, not as a man she could be interested in. In truth, she was a little too cool for his taste. A little too ice blond. A little too controlled, beneath that beautiful exterior.

The radio clicked. Bolden said, "I don't like this weather coming in. We better take a shortcut."

"What shortcut?"

"It's only half a mile, but it'll save twenty minutes on our time. Follow me." He turned his snowtrack left, leaving the packed snow road, and heading off onto the ice fields.

"Okay," Sarah said. "Right behind you."

"Good work," Bolden said. "We're still an hour from Weddell. I know this route, it's a piece of cake. Just stay directly behind me. Not to the left or right, but directly behind, you understand?"

"Got it," Sarah said.

"Good."

In a matter of minutes, they had moved several hundred yards from the road. The ice there was bare and hard, the treads of the snowtracks scratching and squeaking as they crossed it.

"You're on ice now," Bolden said.

"I noticed."

"Won't be long now."

Evans was looking out the window. He could no longer see the road. In fact, he wasn't sure anymore in which direction it lay. Everything now looked the same. He felt anxious suddenly. "We're really in the middle of nowhere."

The snowtrack slid laterally a little, across the ice. He grabbed for the dashboard. Sarah immediately brought the vehicle back under control.

"Jeez," Evans said, clinging to the dashboard.

"Are you a nervous passenger?" she said.

"Maybe a little."

"Too bad we can't get some music. Is there any way to get music?" she asked Bolden.

"You should," Bolden said. "Weddell broadcasts twenty-four hours. Just a minute." He stopped his snowtrack, and walked back to their stopped vehicle. He climbed up on the tread and opened the door, in a blast of freezing air. "Sometimes you get interference from this," he said, and unclipped the transponder from the dash. "Okay. Try your radio now."

Sarah fiddled with the receiver, twisting the knob. Bolden walked back to his red cab, carrying the transponder. His diesel engine spit a cloud of black exhaust as he put the snowtrack in gear.

"You think they'd be a little more ecologically minded," Evans said, looking at the exhaust as Bolden's snowtrack chugged forward.

"I'm not getting any music," Sarah said.

"Never mind," Evans said. "I don't care that much."

They drove another hundred yards. Then Bolden stopped again.

"Now what?" Evans said.

Bolden climbed out of his vehicle, walked to the back of it, and looked at his own treads.

Sarah was still fiddling with the radio. Punching the buttons for the different transmission frequencies, she got bursts of static for each.

"I'm not sure this is an improvement," Evans said. "Just let it go. Why have we stopped, anyway?"

"I don't know," Sarah said. "He seems to be checking something."

Now Bolden turned and looked back at them. He didn't move. He just stood there and stared.

"Should we get out?" Evans said.

The radio crackled and they heard "—is Weddell CM to—401. Are you there, Dr. Kenner? Weddell CM to—Kenner. Can you hear—?"

"Hey," Sarah said, smiling. "I think we finally got something."

The radio hissed and sputtered.

"—just found Jimmy Bolden unconscious in—maintenance room. We don't know who is—out there with—but it's not—"

"Oh shit," Evans said, staring at the man in front of them. "That guy's not Bolden? Who is he?"

"I don't know, but he's blocking the way," Sarah said. "And he's waiting."

"Waiting for what?"

There was a loud *crack!* from beneath them. Inside the cab, the sound echoed like a gunshot. Their vehicle shifted slightly.

"Screw this," Sarah said. "We're getting out of here, even if I have to ram the bastard." She put the snowtrack in gear, and started to back away from the vehicle in front of them. She shifted, starting the snowtrack forward again.

Another *crack!*

"Let's go!" Evans said. "Let's *go!*"

Crack! Crack! Their vehicle lurched beneath them, tilted sideways at an angle. Evans looked out at the guy pretending to be Bolden.

"It's the ice," Sarah said. "He's waiting for our weight to break through."

"Ram him!" Evans said, pointing ahead. The bastard was making some hand gesture to them. It took him a moment for Evans to understand what it meant. Then he got it.

The man was waving goodbye.

Sarah stomped on the accelerator and the engine rumbled forward, but in the next moment the ground gave way completely beneath them, and their vehicle nosed down. Evans saw the blue-ice wall of a crevasse. Then the vehicle began to tumble forward, and they were encased for an instant in a world of eerie blue before they plunged onward into the blackness below.

SHEAR ZONE
WEDNESDAY, OCTOBER 6
3:51 P.M.

Sarah opened her eyes and saw a huge blue starburst, streaks radiating outward in all directions. Her forehead was icy cold, and she had terrible pain in her neck. Tentatively, she shifted her body, checking each of her limbs. They hurt, but she could move all of them except her right leg, which was pinned under something. She coughed and paused, taking stock. She was lying on her side, her face shoved up against the windshield, which she had shattered with her forehead. Her eyes were just inches from the fractured glass. She eased away, and slowly looked around.

It was dark, a kind of twilight. Faint light coming from somewhere to her left. But she could see that the whole cab of the snowtrack was lying on its side, the treads up against the ice wall. They must have landed on a ledge of some kind. She looked upward—the mouth of the crevasse was surprisingly close, maybe thirty or forty yards above her. It was near enough to give her a burst of encouragement.

Next she looked down, trying to see Evans. But it was dark everywhere beneath her. She couldn't see him at all. Her eyes slowly adjusted. She gasped. She saw her true situation.

There was no ledge.

The snowtrack had tumbled into the narrowing crevasse, and wedged itself sideways within the crevasse walls. The treads were against one wall, the roof of the cab against the other, and the cab itself was suspended over the inky downward gash. The door on Evans's side hung open.

Evans was not in the cab.

He had fallen out.

Into the blackness.

"Peter?"

No answer.

"Peter, can you hear me?"

She listened. There was nothing. No sound or movement.

Nothing at all.

And then the realization hit her: *She was alone down there.* A hundred feet down in a freezing crevasse, in the middle of a trackless ice field, far off the road, miles from anywhere.

And she realized, with a chill, that this was going to be her tomb.

Bolden—or whoever he was—had planned it very well, Sarah thought. He had taken their transponder. He could drive a few miles, drop it down the deepest crevasse he could find, and then go back to the base. When the rescue parties set out, they would head for the transponder. It would be nowhere near where she was. The party might search for days in a deep crevasse before giving up.

And if they widened the search? They still wouldn't find the snow-track. Even though it was only about forty yards below the surface, it might as well be four hundred yards below. It was too deep to be seen by a passing helicopter, or even a vehicle as it drove by. Not that any vehicle would. They would think the snowtrack had gone off the marked road, and they would search along the edge of the road. Not way out here, in the middle of the ice field. The road was seventeen miles long. They would spend days searching.

No, Sarah thought. They would never find her.

And even if she could get herself to the surface, what then? She had no compass, no map, no GPS. No radio—it lay smashed beneath her knee.

She didn't even know in what direction Weddell Station might be from her present location.

Of course, she thought, she had a bright red parka that would be visible from a distance, and she had supplies, food, equipment—all the equipment that guy had talked about, before they set out. What was it, exactly? She vaguely remembered something about climbing supplies. Crampons and ropes.

Sarah bent down, managed to free herself from a toolbox that had pinned her foot to the floor, and then crawled to the rear of the cab, balancing carefully to avoid the gaping, wide-open door beneath her. In the perpetual twilight of the crevasse, she saw the supply locker. It was crumpled slightly from the impact, and she couldn't get it open.

She went back to the toolbox, opened it, took out a hammer and a screwdriver, and spent the better part of the next half hour trying to pry the locker open. At last, with a metallic screech, the door swung wide. She peered inside.

The locker was empty.

No food, no water, no climbing supplies. No space blankets, no heaters.

Nothing at all.

Sarah took a deep breath, let it out slowly. She remained calm, refusing to panic. She considered her options. Without ropes and crampons, she could not get to the surface. What could she use instead? She had a toolbox. Could she use the screwdriver as an ice axe? Probably too small. Perhaps she could disassemble the gearshift and make an ice axe out of the parts. Or perhaps she could take apart some of the tread and find parts to use.

She had no crampons, but if she could find sharp pointed things, screws or something like that, she could push them through the soles of her boots and then climb. And for a rope? Some sort of cloth perhaps . . . She looked around the interior. Maybe she could tear the fabric off the seats? Or cut it off in strips? That might work.

In this way, she kept her spirits up. She kept herself moving forward. Even if her chance of success was small, there was still a chance. A *chance*.

She focused on that.

Where was Kenner? What would he do when he heard the radio message? He probably had, already. Would he come back to Weddell? Almost certainly. And he would look for that guy, the one they thought of as Bolden. But Sarah was pretty sure that guy had disappeared.

And with his disappearance, her hopes for rescue.

The crystal of her watch was smashed. She didn't know how long she had been down there, but she noticed that it was darker than before. The gap above her was not as bright. Either the weather on the surface was changing, or the sun was low on the horizon. That would mean she had been down there for two or three hours already.

She was aware of a stiffening in her body—not just from the fall, but also, she realized, because she was cold. The cab had lost its heat.

It occurred to her that perhaps she could start the motor, and get heat going. It was worth a try. She flicked on the headlights, and one of them worked, glaring off the ice wall. So there was still electricity from the battery.

She turned the key. The generator made a grinding sound. The engine did not kick on.

And she heard a voice yell, "Hey!"

Sarah looked up, toward the surface. She saw nothing but the gap and the strip of gray sky beyond.

"Hey!"

She squinted. Was somebody really up there? She yelled back: "Hey! I'm down here!"

"I know where you are," the voice said.

And then she realized the voice was coming from *below* her.

She looked down, into the depths of the crevasse.

"Peter?" she said.

"I'm fucking freezing," he said. His voice floated up from the darkness.

"Are you hurt?"

"No, I don't think so. I don't know. I can't move. I'm wedged in some kind of cleft or something."

"How far down are you?"

"I don't know. I can't turn my head to look up. I'm stuck, Sarah." His voice trembled. He sounded frightened.

"Can you move at all?" she said.

"Just one arm."

"Can you see anything?"

"Ice. I see a blue wall. It's about two feet away."

Sarah was straddling the open door, peering down into the crevasse, straining to see. It was very dark down there. But it seemed as if the crevasse narrowed quickly, farther down. If so, he might not be that far beneath her.

"Peter. Move your arm. Can you move your arm?"

"Yes."

"Wave it."

"I am."

She didn't see anything. Just darkness.

"Okay," she said. "Stop."

"Did you see me?"

"No."

"Shit." He coughed. "It's really cold, Sarah."

"I know. Hang on."

She had to find a way to see down into the cleft. She looked under the dashboard, near where the fire extinguisher was clipped to the car wall. If there was a fire extinguisher, there was probably a flashlight there, too. They would be sure to have a flashlight . . . someplace.

Not under the dashboard.

Maybe the glove compartment. She opened it, shoved her hand in, feeling in the darkness. Crunching paper. Her fingers closed around a thick cylinder. She brought it out.

It was a flashlight.

She flicked it on. It worked. She shone it down into the depths of the crevasse.

"I see that," Peter said. "I see the light."

"Good," she said. "Now swing your arm again."

"I am."

"Now?"

"I'm doing it now."

She stared. "Peter, I don't see—wait a minute." She *did* see him—just the tips of his fingers in their red gloves, protruding briefly beyond the tractor treads, and the ice below.

"Peter."

"What."

"You're very near me," she said. "Just five or six feet below me."

"Great. Can you get me out?"

"I could, if I had a rope."

"There's no rope?" he said.

"No. I opened the supply chest. There's nothing at all."

"But it's not in the supply chest," he said. "It's under the seat."

"What?"

"Yeah, I saw it. The ropes and stuff are under the passenger seat."

She looked. The seat was on a steel base anchored firmly to the floor of the snowtrack. There were no doors or compartments in the base. It was difficult to maneuver around the seat to see, but she was sure: no doors. On a sudden impulse, she lifted up the seat cushion, and saw a compartment beneath it. The light of her flashlight revealed ropes, hooks, snow axes, crampons . . .

"Got it," she said. "You were right. It's all here."

"Whew," he said.

She brought the equipment out carefully, making sure none of it fell through the open door. Already her fingers were growing numb, and she felt clumsy as she held a fifty-foot length of nylon rope with a three-pronged ice hook at one end.

"Peter," she said. "If I lower a rope, can you grab it?"

"Maybe. I think so."

"Can you hold the rope tight, so I can pull you out?"

"I don't know. I just have the one arm free. The other one's pinned under me."

"Are you strong enough to hold the rope with one arm?"

"I don't know. I don't think so. I mean, if I got my body partway out, and lost my grip . . ." His voice broke off. He sounded on the verge of tears.

"Okay," she said. "Don't worry."

"I'm *trapped*, Sarah!"

"No, you're not."

"I am, I'm trapped, I'm fucking trapped!" Now there was panic. "I'm going to die here!"

"Peter. Stop." She was coiling the rope around her waist as she spoke. "It's going to be all right. I have a plan."

"What plan?"

"I'm going to lower an ice hook on the rope," she said. "Can you hook it onto something? Like your belt?"

"Not my belt . . . No. I'm wedged in here, Sarah. I can't move. I can't reach my belt."

She was trying to visualize his situation. He must be wedged in some sort of cleft in the ice. It was frightening just to imagine it. No wonder he was scared. "Peter," she said, "can you hook it onto anything?"

"I'll try."

"Okay, here it comes," she said, lowering the rope. The hook disappeared into the darkness. "Do you see it?"

"I see it."

"Can you reach it?"

"No."

"Okay, I'll swing it toward you." She turned her wrist gently, starting the rope in a lateral swing. The hook vanished out of sight, then swung back, then out of sight again.

"I can't . . . keep doing it, Sarah."

"I am."

"I can't get it, Sarah."

"Keep trying."

"It has to be lower."

"Okay. How much lower?"

"About a foot."

"Okay." She lowered it a foot. "How's that?"

"Good, now swing it."

She did. She heard him grunting, but each time the hook swung back into view.

"I can't do it, Sarah."

"Yes you can. Keep trying."

"I can't. My fingers are too cold."

"Keep trying," she said. "Here it is again."

"I can't, Sarah, I can't . . . Hey!"

"What?"

"I almost got it."

Looking down, she saw the hook spinning when it came back into view. He'd touched it.

"Once more," she said. "You'll do it, Peter."

"I'm trying, it's just I have so little—I got it, Sarah. *I got it!*"

She gave a long sigh of relief.

He was coughing in the darkness. She waited.

"Okay," he said. "I got it hooked on my jacket."

"Where?"

"Right on the front. Just on my chest."

She was visualizing that if the hook ripped free, it would tear right into his chin. "No, Peter. Hook it on the armpit."

"I can't, unless you pull me out a couple of feet."

"Okay. Say when."

He coughed. "Listen, Sarah. Are you strong enough to pull me out?"

She had avoided thinking about that. She just assumed that somehow she could. Of course she didn't know how hard he was wedged in, but . . . "Yes," she said. "I can do it."

"Are you sure? I weigh a hundred and sixty." He coughed again. "Maybe a little more. Maybe ten more."

"I've got you tied off on the steering wheel."

"Okay, but . . . don't drop me."

"I won't drop you, Peter."

There was a pause. "How much do you weigh?"

"Peter, you never ask a lady that question. Especially in LA."

"We're not in LA."

"I don't know how much I weigh," she said. Of course she knew exactly. She weighed a hundred and thirty-seven pounds. He weighed over thirty pounds more than that. "But I know I can pull you up," she said. "Are you ready?"

"Shit."

"Peter, are you ready or not?"

"Yeah. Go."

She drew the rope tight, then crouched down, planting her feet firmly on either side of the open door. She felt like a sumo wrestler at the start of a match. But she knew her legs were much stronger than her arms. This was the only way she could do it. She took a deep breath.

"Ready?" she said.

"I guess."

Sarah began to stand upright, her legs burning with effort. The rope stretched taut, then moved upward—slowly at first, just a few inches. But it was moving.

It was moving.

· · ·

"Okay, stop. Stop!"

"What?"

"*Stop!*"

"Okay." She was in mid-crouch. "But I can't hold this for long."

"Don't hold it at all. Let it out. Slowly. About three feet."

She realized that she must have already pulled him part of the way out of the cleft. His voice sounded better, much less frightened, though he was coughing almost continuously.

"Peter?"

"Minute. I'm hooking it on my belt."

"Okay . . ."

"I can see up now," he said. "I can see the tread. The tread is about six feet above my head."

"Okay."

"But when you pull me up, the rope's going to rub on the edge of the tread."

"It'll be okay," she said.

"And I'll be hanging right over the, uh . . ."

"I won't let you go, Peter."

He coughed for a while. She waited. He said, "Tell me when you're ready."

"I'm ready."

"Then let's get this over with," he said, "before I get scared."

There was only one bad moment. She had pulled him up about four feet, and he came free of the cleft, and she suddenly took the full weight of his body. It shocked her; the rope slid three feet down. He howled.

"*Sar-ah!*"

She gripped the rope, stopped it. "Sorry."

"Fuck!"

"Sorry." She adjusted to the added weight, started pulling again. She was groaning with the effort but it was not long before she saw his hand appear above the tread, and he gripped it, and began to haul himself over. Then two hands, and his head appeared.

That shocked her, too. His face was covered in thick blood, his hair matted red. But he was smiling.

"Keep pulling, sister."

"I am, Peter. I am."

Only after he finally had scrambled into the cab did Sarah sink to the floor. Her legs began to shake violently. Her body trembled all over. Evans, lying on his side, coughing and wheezing beside her, hardly noticed. Eventually the trembling passed. She found the first-aid kit and began to clean his face up.

"It's only a superficial cut," she said, "but you'll need stitches."

"If we ever get out of here . . ."

"We'll get out, all right."

"I'm glad you're confident." He looked out the window at the ice above. "You done much ice climbing?"

She shook her head. "But I've done plenty of rock climbing. How different can it be?"

"More slippery? And what happens when we get up there?" he said.

"I don't know."

"We have no idea where to go."

"We'll follow the guy's snowtracks."

"If they're still there. If they haven't blown away. And you know it's at least seven or eight miles to Weddell."

"Peter," she said.

"If a storm comes up, maybe we're better off down here."

"I'm not staying here," she said. "If I'm going to die, I'll die in daylight."

. . .

The actual climb up the crevasse wall was not so bad, once Sarah got used to the way she had to kick her boots with the crampons, and how hard she had to swing the axe to make it bite into the ice. It took her only seven or eight minutes to cover the distance, and clamber onto the surface.

The surface looked exactly the same as before. The same dim sunlight, the same gray horizon that blended with the ground. The same gray, featureless world.

She helped Evans up. His cut was bleeding again, and his mask was red, frozen stiff against his face.

"Shit it's cold," he said. "Which way, do you think?"

Sarah was looking at the sun. It was low on the horizon, but was it sinking, or rising? And which direction did the sun indicate, anyway, when you were at the South Pole? She frowned: She couldn't work it out, and she didn't dare make a mistake.

"We'll follow the tracks," she said at last. She took off her crampons and started walking.

She had to admit, Peter was right about one thing: It was much colder here on the surface. After half an hour, the wind came up, blowing strongly; they had to lean into it as they trudged forward. Worse, the snow began to blow across the ground beneath their feet. Which meant—

"We're losing the tracks," Evans said.

"I know."

"They're getting blown away."

"I *know*." Sometimes he was such a baby. What did he expect her to do about the wind?

"What do we do?" he said.

"I don't *know*, Peter. I've never been lost in Antarctica before."

"Well, me neither."

They trudged onward.

"But it was your idea to come up here."

"Peter. Pull yourself together."

"Pull myself together? It's fucking freezing, Sarah. I can't feel my nose or my ears or my fingers or my toes or—"

"Peter." She grabbed him by the shoulders and shook him. "*Shut up!*"

He was silent. Through slots in his facemask, he stared out at her. His eyelashes were white with ice.

"I can't feel my nose either," Sarah said. "We have to keep a grip."

She looked around, turning a full circle, trying to conceal her own growing desperation. The wind was blowing more snow now. It was becoming harder to see. The world was flatter and grayer, with almost no sense of depth. If this weather continued, they would soon not be able to see the ground well enough to avoid the crevasses.

Then they would have to stop where they were.

In the middle of nowhere.

He said, "You're beautiful when you're angry, you know that?"

"Peter, for Christ's sake."

"Well, you are."

She started walking, looking down at the ground, trying to see the tread marks. "Come on, Peter." Perhaps the tracks would return soon to the road. If they did, the road would be easier to follow in a storm. And safer for walking.

"I think I'm falling in love, Sarah."

"Peter . . ."

"I had to tell you. This may be my last chance." He started coughing again.

"Save your breath, Peter."

"Fucking freezing."

They stumbled on, no longer speaking. The wind howled. Sarah's parka was pressed flat against her body. It became harder and harder to move forward. But she pressed on. She did not know how much longer she continued in that way before she raised a hand, and stopped. Evans must not have been able to see her, because he walked into her back, grunted, and stopped.

They had to put their heads together and shout to hear each other above the wind.

"We have to stop!" she yelled.

"I know!"

And then, because she didn't know what else to do, she sat down on the ground and pulled her legs up and lowered her head to her knees, and tried not to cry. The wind grew louder and louder. Now it was shrieking. The air was thick with flying snow.

Evans sat down beside her. "We're going to fucking die," he said.

SHEAR ZONE
WEDNESDAY, OCTOBER 6
5:02 P.M.

She started shivering, little tremulous bursts at first, and then almost continuously. She felt as if she were having a seizure. From skiing, she knew what that meant. Her core temperature had dropped dangerously, and the shivering was an automatic physiological attempt to warm her body up.

Her teeth chattered. It was hard to speak. But her mind was still working, still looking for a way out. "Isn't there a way to build a snow house?"

Evans said something. The wind whipped his words away.

"Do you know how?" she said.

He didn't answer her.

But it was too late, anyway, she thought. She was losing control of her body. She could hardly even keep her arms wrapped around her knees, the shaking was so bad.

And she was starting to feel sleepy.

She looked over at Evans. He was lying on his side on the ice.

She nudged him to get up. She kicked him. He didn't move. She wanted to yell at him but she couldn't, because her teeth were chattering so badly.

Sarah fought to retain consciousness, but the desire to sleep was becoming overpowering. She struggled to keep her eyes open and, to her astonishment, began to see swift scenes from her life—her childhood, her mother, her kindergarten class, ballet lessons, the high school prom . . .

Her whole life was passing before her. Just like the books said happened, right before you died. And when she looked up, she saw a light in the distance, just like they said happened. A light at the end of a long, dark tunnel . . .

She couldn't fight it any longer. She lay down. She couldn't feel the ground anyway. She was lost in her own, private world of pain and exhaustion. And the light before her was growing brighter and brighter, and now there were two other lights, blinking yellow and green . . .

Yellow and green?

She fought the sleepiness. She tried to push herself upright again, but she couldn't. Her muscles were too weak, her arms blocks of frozen ice. She couldn't move.

Yellow and green lights, growing larger. And a white light in the center. Very white, like halogen. She was starting to see details through the swirling snow. There was a silver dome, and wheels, and large glowing letters. The letters said—

NASA.

She coughed. The thing emerged from the snow. It was some kind of small vehicle—about three feet high, no larger than those Sunday lawnmowers that people drove around on. It had big wheels and a flattened dome, and it was beeping as it came directly toward her.

In fact, it was going to drive right over her. She realized it without concern. She could do nothing to prevent it. She lay on the ground, dazed, indifferent. The wheels grew larger and larger. The last thing she remembered was a mechanical voice saying, "Hello. Hello. Please move out of the way. Thank you very much for your cooperation. Hello. Hello. Please move out of the way . . ."

And then nothing.

Darkness. Pain. Harsh voices.

Pain.

Rubbing. All over her body, arms and legs. Like fire rubbed on her body.

She groaned.

A voice spoke, rasping and distant. It sounded like "Coffee grounds."

The rubbing continued, brisk and harsh and excruciating. And a sound like sandpaper—scratching, rough, terrible.

Something struck her in the face, on the mouth. She licked her lips. It was snow. Freezing snow.

"Cousins set?" a voice said.

"Nod eely."

It was a foreign language, Chinese or something. Sarah heard several voices now. She tried to open her eyes but could not. Her eyes were held shut by something heavy over her face, like a mask, or—

She tried to reach up, but couldn't. All her limbs were held down. And the rubbing continued, rubbing, rubbing . . .

She groaned. She tried to speak.

"Thin song now whore nod?"

"Don thin song."

"Kee pub yar wok."

Pain.

They rubbed her, whoever they were, while she lay immobilized in darkness, and gradually more sensation returned to her limbs and to her face. She was not glad for it. The pain grew worse and worse. She felt as if she were burned everywhere on her body.

The voices seemed to float around her, disembodied. There were more of them now. Four, five—she was not sure anymore. All women, it sounded like.

And now they were doing something else, she realized. Violating her. Sticking something in her body. Dull and cold. Not painful. Cold.

The voices floated, slithered all around her. At her head, at her feet. Touching her roughly.

It was a dream. Or death. Maybe she was dead, she thought. She felt oddly detached about it. The pain made her detached. And then she heard a woman's voice in her ear, very close to her ear, and very distinct. The voice said:

"Sarah."

She moved her mouth.

"Sarah, are you awake?"

She nodded slightly.

"I am going to take the icepack off your face, all right?"

She nodded. The weight, the mask was lifted.

"Open your eyes. Slowly."

She did. She was in a dimly lit room with white walls. A monitor to one side, a tangle of green lines. It was like a hospital room. A woman looked down at her with concern. The woman wore a white nurse's uniform and a down vest. The room was cold. Sarah could see her breath.

She said, "Don't try to speak."

Sarah didn't.

"You're dehydrated. It'll be a few hours yet. We're bringing your temperature up slowly. You're very lucky, Sarah. You're not going to lose anything."

Not lose anything.

She felt alarmed. Her mouth moved. Her tongue was dry, thick feeling. A sort of hissing sound came from her throat.

"Don't speak," the woman said. "It's too soon. Is your pain bad? Yes? I'll give you something for it." She raised a syringe. "Your friend saved your life, you know. He managed to get to his feet, and open the radiophone on the NASA robot. That's how we knew where to find you."

Her lips moved.

"He's in the next room. We think he'll be all right, too. Now just rest."

She felt something cold in her veins.

Her eyes closed.

The nurses left Peter Evans alone to get dressed. He put on his clothes slowly, taking stock of himself. He was all right, he decided, though his ribs hurt when he breathed. He had a big bruise on the left side of his chest, another big bruise on his thigh, and an ugly purple welt on his shoulder. A line of stitches on his scalp. His whole body was stiff and aching. It was excruciating to put on his socks and shoes.

But he was all right. In fact, better than that—he felt new somehow, almost reborn. Out there on the ice, he had been certain he was going to die. How he found the strength to get to his feet, he did not know. He had felt Sarah kicking him, but he did not respond to her. Then he'd heard the beeping sound. And when he looked up, he saw the letters "NASA."

He'd realized vaguely that it was some kind of vehicle. So there must be a driver. The front tires had stopped just inches from his body. He managed to get to his knees, and haul himself up over the tires, grabbing onto the struts. He hadn't understood why the driver hadn't climbed out and helped him. Finally, he managed to get to his knees in the howling wind. He realized that the vehicle was low and bulbous, barely four feet off the ground. It was too small for any human operator—it was some kind of robot. He scraped snow away from the dome-like shell. The lettering read, "NASA Remote Vehicle Meteorite Survey."

The vehicle was talking, repeating a taped voice over and over. Evans couldn't understand what it was saying because of the wind. He brushed away the snow, thinking there must be some method of communication, some antenna, some—

Then his fingers had touched a panel with a finger hole. He pulled it open. Inside he saw a telephone—a regular telephone handset, bright red. He held it to his frozen mask. He could not hear anything from it, but he said, "Hello? Hello?"

Nothing more.

He collapsed again.

But the nurses told him what he had done was enough to send a signal to the NASA station at Patriot Hills. NASA had notified Weddell, who sent out a search party, and found them in ten minutes. They were both still alive, barely.

That had been more than twenty-four hours ago.

It had taken the medical team twelve hours to bring their body temperatures back to normal, because, the nurse said, it had to be done slowly. They told Evans he was going to be fine, but he might lose a couple of his toes. They would have to wait and see. It would be a few days.

His feet were bandaged with some kind of protective splints around the toes. He couldn't fit into his regular shoes, but they had found him an oversized pair of sneakers. They looked like they belonged to a basketball player. On Evans, they made huge clown feet. But he could wear them, and there wasn't much pain.

Tentatively, he stood. He was tremulous, but he was all right.

The nurse came back. "Hungry?"

He shook his head. "Not yet."

"Pain?"

He shook his head. "Just, you know, everywhere."

"That'll get worse," she said. She gave him a small bottle of pills. "Take one of these every four hours if you need it. And you'll probably need it to sleep, for the next few days."

"And Sarah?"

"Sarah will be another half hour or so."

"Where's Kenner?"

"I think he's in the computer room."

"Which way is that?"

She said, "Maybe you better lean on my shoulder . . ."

"I'm fine," he said. "Just tell me the way."

She pointed, and he started walking. But he was more unsteady than he realized. His muscles weren't working right; he felt shaky all over. He started to fall. The nurse quickly ducked, sliding her shoulder under his arm.

"Tell you what," she said. "I'll just show you the way."

This time he did not object.

Kenner sat in the computer room with the bearded station chief, Mac-Gregor, and Sanjong Thapa. Everybody was looking grim.

"We found him," Kenner said, pointing to a computer monitor. "Recognize your friend?"

Evans looked at the screen. "Yeah," he said. "That's the bastard."

On the screen was a photo of the man Evans knew as Bolden. But the ID form onscreen gave his name as David R. Kane. Twenty-six years old. Born Minneapolis. BA, Notre Dame; MA, University of Michigan. Current Status: PhD candidate in oceanography, University of Michigan, Ann Arbor. Research Project: Dynamics of Ross Shelf Flow as measured by GPS sensors. Thesis Advisor/Project Supervisor: James Brewster, University of Michigan.

"His name's Kane," the Weddell chief said. "He's been here for a week, along with Brewster."

"Where is he now?" Evans said darkly.

"No idea. He didn't come back to the Station today. Neither did Brewster. We think they may have gone to McMurdo and hopped the morning transport out. We have a call in to McMurdo to do a vehicle count, but they haven't gotten back to us yet."

"You're sure he's not still here?" Evans said.

"Quite sure. You need an ID tag to open the exterior doors here, so we always know who's where. Neither Kane nor Brewster opened any doors in the last twelve hours. They aren't here."

"So you think they may be on the plane?"

"McMurdo Tower wasn't sure. They're pretty casual about the daily transport—if somebody wants to go, they just hop on and leave. It's a C-130, so there's always plenty of room. You see, a lot of the research grants don't permit you to leave during the period of your research, but people have birthdays and family events back on the mainland. So they just go, and come back. It's unrecorded."

"If I recall," Kenner said, "Brewster came here with two graduate students. Where's the other one?"

"Interesting. He left from McMurdo yesterday, the day you arrived."

"So they all got out," Kenner said. "Got to give them credit: They're smart." He looked at his watch. "Now let's see what, if anything, they left behind."

The name on the door said "Dave Kane, U. Mich." Evans pushed it open, and saw a small room, an unmade bed, a small desk with a messy stack of papers, and four cans of Diet Coke. There was a suitcase lying open in the corner.

"Let's get started," Kenner said. "I'll take the bed and the suitcase. You check the desk."

Evans began to go through the papers on the desk. They all seemed to be reprints of research articles. Some were stampe U MICH GEO LIB followed by a number.

"Window dressing," Kenner said, when he was shown the papers. "He brought those papers with him. Anything else? Anything personal?"

Evans didn't see anything of interest. Some of the papers were highlighted in yellow marker. There was a stack of 3-by-5 notecards, with some notes written on them, but they seemed to be genuine, and related to the stack of papers.

"You don't suppose this guy is really a graduate student?"

"Could be, though I doubt it. Eco-terrorists aren't usually well educated."

There were pictures of glacier flows, and satellite images of various sorts. Evans shuffled through them quickly. Then he paused at one:

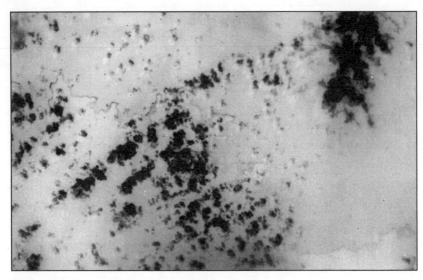

ISS006.ESC1.03003375 SCORPION B

What caught his eye was the caption. "Listen," he said, "on that list of four locations, wasn't one of them called 'Scorpion'?"

"Yes . . ."

"It's right here, in Antarctica," Evans said. "Look at this."

Kenner started to say, "But it can't be—" and abruptly broke off. "This is extremely interesting, Peter. Well done. It was in that stack? Good. Anything else?"

Despite himself, Evans felt pleased by Kenner's approval. He searched quickly. A moment later he said, "Yes. There's another one."

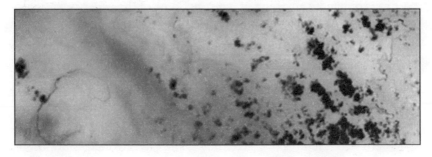

ISS006.ESC1.03003375 SCORPION B

"It's the same basic pattern of rock outcrops in the snow," Evans said, excitedly. "And, I don't know about these faint lines . . . roads? Rocks covered in snow?"

"Yes," Kenner said. "I think that's almost certainly correct."

"And if they're aerial photographs, there must be a way to trace them. Do you think these numbers are references of some kind?"

"There's no question." Kenner pulled out a small pocket magnifying glass, and scanned the image, peering closely. "Yes, Peter. Very well done."

Evans beamed.

From the doorway, MacGregor said, "You found something? Can I help?"

"I don't think so," Kenner said. "We'll deal with this ourselves."

Evans said, "But maybe he will recognize—"

"No," Kenner said. "We'll get the ID off the NASA image files. Let's continue."

They searched in silence for several minutes more. Kenner took out a pocketknife and began cutting the lining of the suitcase lying open in the corner of Brewster's office. "Ah." He straightened. In his fingers, he held two curved arcs of pale rubber.

"What are those?" Evans said. "Silicon?"

"Or something very similar. A kind of soft plastic, at any rate." Kenner seemed very pleased.

"What're they for?" Evans said.

"I have no idea," Kenner said. He resumed his search of the suitcase. Privately, Evans wondered why Kenner was so pleased. Probably he was not saying what he knew in front of MacGregor. But what could two bits of rubber mean, anyway? What could they be used for?

Evans went through the documents on the desk a second time, but found nothing more. He lifted the desk lamp and looked under the base. He crouched down and looked under the desk, in case something was taped there. He found nothing.

Kenner closed the suitcase. "As I thought, nothing more. We were very lucky to find what we did." He turned to MacGregor. "Where's Sanjong?"

"In the server room, doing what you requested—cutting Brewster and his team out of the system."

The "server room" was hardly larger than a closet. There were twin racks of processors running floor to ceiling, and the usual mesh ceiling for cabling. There was a master terminal in the room, on a small steel table. Sanjong was crowded in there with a Weddell technician at his side, looking frustrated.

Kenner and Evans stood outside, in the hallway. Evans was pleased that he felt steady enough to stand. His strength was coming back quickly.

"It hasn't been easy," Sanjong said to Kenner. "The procedure here is to give each Weddell researcher private storage space and also direct radio and Internet connections. And these three guys knew how to take advantage of it. Apparently the third man with Brewster was the computer guy. Within a day of his arrival, he got into the system as root, and installed back doors and trojans all over the place. We're not sure how many. We're trying to get them out."

"He also added a few dummy user accounts," the technician said.

"Like about twenty," Sanjong said. "But I'm not worried about those. They're probably just that—dummies. If this guy was smart—and he was—he'd have given himself access to the system through an existing user, so he'd go undetected. We're looking now for any users who have added a new secondary password in the last week. But this system doesn't have a lot of maintenance utilities. It's slow going.

"What about the trojans?" Kenner said. "How are they timed?" In computer slang, a trojan was an innocent-looking program installed in the system. It was designed to wake up at a later time and carry out some action. It derived its name from the way the Greeks won the Trojan war—by making a huge horse and presenting it to the Trojans as a gift. Once the horse was within the walls of Troy, the Greek soliders who had been hiding inside it came out and attacked the city.

The classic trojan was one installed by a disgruntled employee. It erased all the hard drives in a business three months after the employee was fired. But there were many variations.

"Timing on all of the ones I found here is short," Sanjong said. "One day, two days from now. We found one that is three days from now. Nothing after that."

"So. Just as we suspected," Kenner said.

"Exactly," Sanjong said, nodding. "They intended it to happen soon."

"Intended what?" Evans said.

"The calving of the big iceberg," Kenner said.

"Why soon? They would still have been here."

"I'm not sure they would have. But in any case the timing was determined by something else."

"Yes? What?" Evans said.

Kenner gave him a look. "We can go into it later." He turned back to Sanjong. "And what about the radio connects?"

"We disabled all the direct connects right away," he said. "And I assume you did work on the ground at the location itself."

"I did," Kenner said.

"What did you do on the ground?" Evans said.

"Random disconnects."

"Of what?"

"Tell you later."

"So we're redundant," Sanjong said.

"No. Because we can't be sure there's not someone else embedded in this place who will undo our work."

"I wish," Evans said, "I knew what the hell you guys were talking about . . ."

"*Later*," Kenner said. This time the look was sharp.

Evans was silent. He felt a little wounded.

MacGregor said, "Ms. Jones is awake, and getting dressed."

"All right," Kenner said. "I believe our work here is done. Wheels up in an hour."

"To go where?" Evans said.

"I thought that was obvious," Kenner said. "Helsinki, Finland."

EN ROUTE
FRIDAY, OCTOBER 8
6:04 A.M.

The plane flew back through the dazzling morning light. Sarah was sleeping. Sanjong was working on his laptop. Kenner stared out the window.

Evans said, "All right, what did you disconnect randomly?"

"The cone charges," Kenner said. "They were laid out in a precise pattern, four hundred meters apart. I disconnected fifty at random, mostly along the eastern end of the line. That will suffice to prevent the standing wave from being generated."

"So, no iceberg?"

"That's the idea."

"And why are we going to Helsinki?"

"We're not. I only said that for the benefit of the technician. We're going to Los Angeles."

"Okay. And why are we going to Los Angeles?"

"Because that's where the NERF Conference on Abrupt Climate Change is being held."

"This is all related to the conference?"

Kenner nodded.

"These guys are trying to break off an iceberg to coincide with the conference?"

"Exactly. All part of any good starburst media plan. You arrange an event with good visuals that reinforces the point of the conference."

"You seem awfully calm about it," Evans said.

"It's the way things are done, Peter." Kenner shrugged. "Environmental concerns don't come to the public's attention by accident, you know."

"What do you mean?"

"Well, take your favorite fear, global warming. The arrival of global warming was announced dramatically by a prominent climatologist, James Hansen, in 1988. He gave testimony before a joint House and Senate committee headed by Senator Wirth of Colorado. Hearings were scheduled for June, so Hansen could deliver his testimony during a blistering heat wave. It was a setup from the beginning."

"That doesn't bother me," Evans said. "It's legitimate to use a government hearing as a way to make the public aware—"

"Really? So you're saying that in your mind, there's no difference between a government hearing and a press conference?"

"I'm saying hearings have been used that way many times before."

"True. But it is unquestionably manipulative. And Hansen's testimony wasn't the only instance of media manipulation that's occurred in the course of the global warming sales campaign. Don't forget the last-minute changes in the 1995 IPCC report."

"IPCC? What last-minute changes?"

"The UN formed the Intergovernmental Panel on Climate Change in the late 1980s. That's the IPCC, as you know—a huge group of bureaucrats, and scientists under the thumb of bureaucrats. The idea was that since this was a global problem, the UN would track climate research and issue reports every few years. The first assessment report in 1990 said it would be very difficult to detect a human influence on climate, although everybody was concerned that one might exist. But the 1995 report announced with conviction that there was now 'a discernable human influence' on climate. You remember that?"

"Vaguely."

"Well, the claim of 'a discernable human influence' was written into the 1995 summary report after the scientists themselves had gone home.

Originally, the document said scientists couldn't detect a human influence on climate for sure, and they didn't know when they would. They said explicitly, 'we don't know.' That statement was deleted, and replaced with a new statement that a discernable human influence did indeed exist. It was a major change."

"Is that true?" Evans said.

"Yes. Changing the document caused a stir among scientists at the time, with opponents and defendants of the change coming forward. If you read their claims and counter-claims, you can't be sure who's telling the truth. But this is the Internet age. You can find the original documents and the list of changes online and decide for yourself. A review of the actual text changes makes it crystal clear that the IPCC is a political organization, not a scientific one."

Evans frowned. He wasn't sure how to answer. He'd heard of the IPCC, of course, although he didn't know much about it. . . .

"But my question is simpler, Peter. If something is real, if it is a genuine problem that requires action, why does anybody have to exaggerate their claims? Why do there have to be carefully executed media campaigns?"

"I can give you a simple answer," Evans said. "The media is a crowded marketplace. People are bombarded by thousands of messages every minute. You have to speak loudly—and yes, maybe exaggerate a little—if you want to get their attention. And try to mobilize the entire world to sign the Kyoto treaty."

"Well, let's consider that. When Hansen announced in the summer of 1988 that global warming was here, he predicted temperatures would increase .35 degrees Celsius over the next ten years. Do you know what the actual increase was?"

"I'm sure you'll tell me it was less than that."

"*Much* less, Peter. Dr. Hansen overestimated by three hundred percent. The actual increase was .11 degrees."

"Okay. But it *did* increase."

And ten years after his testimony, he said that the forces that govern climate change are so poorly understood that long-term prediction is impossible."

"He did not say that."

Kenner sighed. "Sanjong?"

Sanjong pecked at his laptop. "Proceedings of the National Academy of Sciences, October 1998."*

"Hansen didn't say that prediction was *impossible.*"

"He said quote 'The forcings that drive long-term climate change are not known with an accuracy sufficient to define future climate change' endquote. And he argued that, in the future, scientists should use multiple scenarios to define a range of possible climate outcomes."

"Well that isn't exactly—"

"Stop quibbling," Kenner said. "He said it. Why do you think Balder is worried about his witnesses in the Vanutu case? It's because of statements like these. However you attempt to reframe it, it's a clear statement of limited knowledge. And it's hardly the only one. The IPCC itself made many limiting statements."†

"But Hansen still believes in global warming."

"Yes, he does. And his 1988 prediction," Kenner said, "was wrong by three hundred percent."

"So what?"

"You are ignoring the implication of an error that large," Kenner said. "Compare it to other fields. For example, when NASA launched the rocket carrying the Mars Rover, they announced that in two hundred and fifty three days, the Rover would land on the surface of Mars at 8:11 P.M., California time. In fact, it landed at 8:35 P.M. That is an error of a few *thousandths* of a percent. The NASA people knew what they were talking about."

* James E. Hansen, Makiko Sato, Andrew Lacis, Reto Ruedy, Ina Tegen, and Elaine Matthews, "Climate Forcings in the Industrial Era," *Proceedings of the National Academy of Sciences* 95 (October 1998): 12753–58.
† IPCC. *Climate Change 2001: The Scientific Basis.* Cambridge, UK: Cambridge University Press, 2001, p. 774: "In climate research and modelling [*sic*], we should recognize that we are dealing with a coupled nonlinear chaotic system, and therefore that the long-term prediction of future climate states is not possible." See also: IPCC. *Climate Change 1995: The Science of Climate Change*, p. 330. "Natural climate variability on long time-scales will continue to be problematic for CO2 climate change analysis and detection."

"Okay, fine. But there are some things you have to estimate."

"You're absolutely right," Kenner said. "People estimate all the time. They estimate sales, they estimate profits, they estimate delivery dates, they estimate—by the way, do you estimate your taxes for the government?"

"Yes. Quarterly."

"How accurate does that estimate have to be?"

"Well, there's no fixed rule—"

"Peter. How accurate, without penalty?"

"Maybe fifteen percent."

"So if you were off by three hundred percent, you'd pay a penalty?"

"Yes."

"Hansen was off by three hundred percent."

"Climate is not a tax return."

"In the real world of human knowledge," Kenner said, "to be wrong by three hundred percent is taken as an indication you don't have a good grasp on what you are estimating. If you got on an airplane and the pilot said it was a three-hour flight, but you arrived in one hour, would you think that pilot was knowledgeable or not?"

Evans sighed. "Climate is more complicated than that."

"Yes, Peter. Climate *is* more complicated. It is so complicated that no one has been able to predict future climate with accuracy. Even though billons of dollars are being spent, and hundreds of people are trying all around the world. Why do you resist that uncomfortable truth?"

"Weather prediction is much better," Evans said. "And that's because of computers."

"Yes, weather prediction has improved. But nobody tries to predict weather more than ten days in advance. Whereas computer modelers are predicting what the temperature will be one hundred years in advance. Sometimes a thousand years, three thousand years."

"And they are doing better."

"Arguably they aren't. Look," Kenner said. "The biggest events in global climate are the El Niños. They happen roughly every four years. But climate models can't predict them—not their timing, their duration, or their intensity. And if you can't predict El Niños, the predictive value of your model in other areas is suspect."

"I heard they can predict El Niños."

"That was claimed in 1998. But it is not true."* Kenner shook his head. "Climate science simply isn't there yet, Peter. One day it will be. But not now."

---

* C. Landsea, et al., 2000, "How Much Skill Was There in Forecasting the Very Strong 1997–98 El Niño?" *Bulletin of the American Meteorological Society* 81: 2107-19. ". . . one could have even less confidence in anthropogenic global warming studies because of the lack of skill in predicting El Niño . . . the successes in ENSO forecasting have been overstated (sometimes drastically) and misapplied in other arenas."

Another hour passed. Sanjong was working continuously on the laptop. Kenner sat motionless, staring out the window. Sanjong was accustomed to this. He knew that Kenner could stay silent and immobile for several hours. He only turned away from the window when Sanjong swore.

"What's the matter?" Kenner said.

"I lost our satellite connection to the Internet. It's been in and out for a while."

"Were you able to trace the images?"

"Yes, that was no problem. I have the location fixed. Did Evans really think these were images from Antarctica?"

"Yes. He thought they showed black outcrops against snow. I didn't disagree with him."

"The actual location," Sanjong said, "is a place called Resolution Bay. It's in northeast Gareda."

"How far from Los Angeles?"

"Roughly six thousand nautical miles."

"So the propagation time is twelve or thirteen hours."

"Yes."

"We'll worry about it later," Kenner said. "We have other problems first."

• • •

Peter Evans slept fitfully. His bed consisted of a padded airplane seat laid flat, with a seam in the middle, right where his hip rested. He tossed and turned, waking briefly, hearing snatches of conversation between Kenner and Sanjong at the back of the plane. He couldn't hear the whole conversation over the drone of the engines. But he heard enough.

Because of what I need him to do.

He'll refuse, John.

. . . he likes it or not . . . Evans is at the center of everything.

Peter Evans was suddenly awake. He strained to hear now. He raised his head off the pillow so he could hear better.

Didn't disagree with him.

Actual location . . . Resolution Bay . . . Gareda.

How far . . . ?

. . . thousand miles . . .

. . . the propagation time . . . thirteen hours . . .

He thought: *Propagation time? What the hell were they talking about?* On impulse he jumped up, strode back there, and confronted them.

Kenner didn't blink. "Sleep well?"

"No," Evans said, "I did not sleep well. I think you owe me some explanations."

"About what?"

"The satellite pictures, for one."

"I couldn't very well tell you right there in the room, in front of the others," Kenner said. "And I hated to interrupt your enthusiasm."

Evans went and poured himself a cup of coffee. "Okay. What do the pictures really show?"

Sanjong flipped his laptop around to show Evans the screen. "Don't feel bad. You would never have had any reason to suspect. The images were negatives. They're often used that way, to increase contrast."

"Negatives . . ."

"The black rocks are actually white. They're clouds."

Evans sighed.

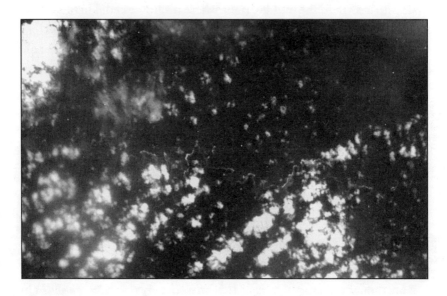

"And what is the land mass?"

"It's an island called Gareda, in the southern part of the Solomon chain."

"Which is . . ."

"Off the coast of New Guinea. North of Australia."

"So this is an island in the South Pacific," Evans said. "This guy in Antarctica had a picture of a Pacific island."

"Correct."

"And the SCORPION reference is . . ."

"We don't know," Sanjong said. "The actual location is called Resolution Bay on the charts. But it may be known locally as Scorpion Bay."

"And what are they planning down there?"

Kenner said, "We don't know that, either."

"I heard you talking about propagation times. Propagation times for what?"

"Actually, you misheard me," Kenner said smoothly. "I was talking about interrogation times."

"Interrogation times?" Evans said.

"Yes. We were hoping we'd be able to identify at least one of the three men in Antarctica, since we have good photographs of all three. And we know the photographs are accurate because people on the base saw them. But, I'm afraid we're out of luck."

Sanjong explained that they had transmitted photos of Brewster and the two graduate students to several databases in Washington, where pattern-recognition computers checked them against individuals with known criminal records. Sometimes you got lucky, and the computer found a match. But this time, no match had come back.

"It's been several hours, so I think we're out of luck."

"As we expected," Kenner said.

"Yes," Sanjong said. "As we expected."

"Because these guys don't have criminal records?" Evans said.

"No. They very well may."

"Then why didn't you get a match?"

"Because this is a netwar," Kenner said. "And at the moment, we are losing it."

TO LOS ANGELES
FRIDAY, OCTOBER 8
3:27 P.M.

In media accounts, Kenner explained, the Environmental Liberation Front was usually characterized as a loose association of eco-terrorists, operating in small groups on their own initiative, and employing relatively unsophisticated means to create havoc—starting fires, trashing SUVs in car lots, and so on.

The truth was quite different. Only one member of ELF had ever been apprehended—a twenty-nine-year-old graduate student at the University of California at Santa Cruz. He was caught sabotaging an oil rig in El Segundo, California. He denied any association with the group, and insisted he was acting alone.

But what troubled authorities was the fact that he was wearing an appliance on his forehead that changed the shape of his skull and made his eyebrows jut out prominently. He was also wearing false ears. It wasn't much of a disguise. But it was troubling, because it suggested that he knew quite a lot about the pattern-matching programs used by the government.

Those programs were tuned to look past changes in facial hair—wigs, beards, and mustaches—since that was the most common method of disguise. They were also designed to compensate for changes in age, such as increased heaviness in the face, drooping features, receding hairlines.

But ears didn't change. The shape of the forehead didn't change. So the programs were therefore weighted to rely on the configuration of ears, and the shape of the forehead. Changing these parts of the face would result in a "no-match" outcome on a computer.

The guy from Santa Cruz knew that. He knew security cameras would photograph him when he got near the rig. So he changed his appearance in a way that would prevent identification by computer.

Similarly, the three extremists at Weddell clearly had formidable backing to carry out their high-tech terrorist act. It took months of planning. Costs were high. And they obviously had in-depth support to obtain academic credentials, university stencils on their shipping boxes, shell companies for their Antarctic shipments, false websites, and dozens of other details necessary for the undertaking. There was nothing unsophisticated about their plan or the way they had executed it.

"And they would have succeeded," Kenner said, "except for that list George Morton obtained shortly before his death."

All of which suggested that if ELF was once a loose association of amateurs, it was no longer. Now it was a highly organized network—one that employed so many channels of communication among its members (e-mail, cell phones, radio, text messaging) that the network as a whole eluded detection. The governments of the world had long worried about how to deal with such networks, and the "netwars" that would result from trying to fight them.

"For a long time, the concept of a netwar was theoretical," Kenner said. "There were studies coming out of RAND, but nobody in the military was really focusing on it. The notion of a networked enemy, or terrorists, or even criminals was too amorphous to bother with."

But it was the amorphous quality of the network—fluid, rapidly evolving—that made it so difficult to combat. You couldn't infiltrate it. You couldn't listen in on it, except by accident. You couldn't locate it geographically because it wasn't in any one place. In truth, the network represented a radically new kind of opponent, and one that required radically new techniques to combat it.

"The military just didn't get it," Kenner said. "But like it or not, we're in a netwar right now."

"And how do you fight a netwar?" Evans said.

"The only way to oppose a network is with another network. You expand your listening posts. You decrypt around the clock. You employ techniques of networked deception and entrapment."

"Such as what?"

"It's technical," Kenner said vaguely. "We rely on the Japanese to spearhead that effort. They are the best at it in the world. And of course we extend our feelers in multiple directions at the same time. Based on what we've just learned at Weddell, we have lots of irons in the fire." Kenner had databases being searched. He had state organizations mobilized. He had inquiries into where the terrorists had obtained their academic credentials, their encrypted radio transmitters, their explosive charges, their computerized detonation timers. None of this was commonplace stuff and it could be traced, given enough time.

"Is there enough time?" Evans said.

"I'm not sure."

Evans could see that Kenner was worried. "So: What is it you want me to do?"

"Just one very simple thing," Kenner said.

"What's that?"

Kenner smiled.

III

ANGEL

LOS ANGELES
SATURDAY, OCTOBER 9
7:04 A.M.

"Is this really necessary?" Peter Evans said, with a worried look.

"It is," Kenner said.

"But it's illegal," Evans said.

"It's not," Kenner said firmly.

"Because you are a law-enforcement officer?" Evans said.

"Of course. Don't worry about it."

They were flying in over Los Angeles, approaching the runway at Van Nuys. The California sun shone through the windows. Sanjong was hunched over the dining table in the middle of the plane. In front of him lay Evans's cell phone, the back removed. Sanjong was attaching a thin gray plate the size of his thumbnail right on top of the battery.

"But what exactly is it?" Evans said.

"Flash memory," Sanjong said. "It'll record four hours of conversation in a compressed format."

"I see," Evans said. "And what am I supposed to do?"

"Just carry the phone in your hand, and go about your business."

"And if I get caught?" he said.

"You won't get caught," Kenner said. "You can take it anywhere. You'll go right through any security, no problem."

"But if they have bug sweepers . . ."

"They won't detect you, because you're not transmitting anything. It's got a burst transmitter. For two seconds every hour, it transmits. The rest of the time, nothing." Kenner sighed. "Look, Peter. It's just a cell phone. Everyone has them."

"I don't know," Evans said. "I feel bad about this. I mean, I'm not a stool pigeon."

Sarah came to the back, yawning, clearing her ears. "Who's a stool pigeon?"

"It's how I feel," Evans said.

"That's not the issue," Kenner said. "Sanjong?"

Sanjong took out a printed list, passed it to Evans. It was Morton's original sheet, now with additions to it:

662262	3982293	24FXE 62262 82293	**TERROR**	**Mt. Terror, Antarctica**
882320	4898432	12FXE 82232 54393	**SNAKE**	**Snake Butte, Arizona**
774548	9080799	02FXE 67533 43433	**LAUGHER**	**Laugher Cay, Bahamas**
482320	5898432	22FXE 72232 04393	**SCORPION**	**Resolution, Solomon Is.**
ALT				
662262	3982293	24FXE 62262 82293	**TERROR**	**Mt. Terror, Antarctica**
382320	4898432	12FXE 82232 54393	**SEVER**	**Sever City, Arizona**
244548	9080799	02FXE 67533 43433	**CONCH**	**Conch Cay, Bahamas**
482320	5898432	22FXE 72232 04393	**SCORPION**	**Resolution, Solomon Is.**
ALT				
662262	3982293	24FXE 62262 82293	**TERROR**	**Mt. Terror, Antarctica**
382320	4898432	12FXE 82232 54393	**BUZZARD**	**Buzzard Gulch, Utah**
444548	7080799	02FXE 67533 43433	**OLD MAN**	**Old Man Is., Turks & Caicos**
482320	5898432	22FXE 72232 04393	**SCORPION**	**Resolution, Solomon Is.**
ALT				
662262	3982293	24FXE 62262 82293	**TERROR**	**Mt. Terror, Antarctica**
382320	4898432	12FXE 82232 54393	**BLACK MESA**	**Black Mesa, New Mexico**
344548	9080799	02FXE 67533 43433	**SNARL**	**Snarl Cay, BWI**
482320	5898432	22FXE 72232 04393	**SCORPION**	**Resolution, Solomon Is.**

"As you see, Sanjong has identified the precise GPS locations," Kenner said. "You've undoubtedly noticed a pattern in the list. The first incident we know about. The second incident will take place somewhere in the American desert—either Utah, Arizona, or New Mexico. The third incident will be somewhere in the Caribbean, east of Cuba. And the fourth incident will be in the Solomon Islands."

"Yes? So?"

"Our concern right now is for the second incident," Kenner said. "And the problem is that from Utah to Arizona to New Mexico there are fifty thousand square miles of desert. Unless we can get additional information, we'll never find these guys."

"But you have exact GPS locations . . ."

"Which they will undoubtedly change, now that they know of the trouble in Antarctica."

"You think they have already changed plans?"

"Of course. Their network knew something was wrong as soon as we arrived at Weddell yesterday. I think that's why the first guy left. I think he's actually the leader of the three. The other two were just foot soldiers."

"So you want me to go see Drake," Evans said.

"Right. And find out whatever you can."

"I hate this," Evans said.

"I understand," Kenner said. "But we need you to do it."

Evans looked at Sarah, who was rubbing her eyes, still sleepy. He was annoyed to see that she had arisen from her bed perfectly composed, her face uncreased, beautiful as ever. "How are you?" he said to her.

"I need to brush my teeth," she said. "How long until we land?"

"Ten minutes."

She got up, and walked to the back of the plane.

Evans looked out the window. The sunlight was glaring, harsh. He hadn't had enough sleep. The line of stitches in his scalp pinched. His body ached from being wedged in the damned crevasse for so long. Just to rest his elbow on the armrest of the seat was painful.

He sighed.

"Peter," Kenner said, "those guys tried to kill you. I wouldn't be too careful about the niceties when you fight back."

"Maybe so, but I'm a lawyer."

"And you could be a dead lawyer," Kenner said. "I don't advise it."

• • •

It was with a sense of unreality that Peter Evans merged his hybrid car onto the San Diego freeway, twelve lanes of roaring traffic on an expanse of concrete as wide as half a football field. Sixty-five percent of the surface area of Los Angeles was devoted to cars. People had to wedge themselves in what little was left. It was an inhuman design and it was environmentally absurd. Everything was so far apart, you couldn't walk anywhere, the pollution was incredible.

And people like Kenner did nothing but criticize the good work of environmental organizations, without whose efforts the environment of a place like Los Angeles would be much, much worse.

Face it, he thought. The world needed help. It desperately needed an environmental perspective. And nothing in Kenner's smooth manipulation of facts would change that truth.

His thoughts rambled on in this way for another ten minutes, until he crossed Mulholland Pass and came down toward Beverly Hills.

He looked at the passenger seat beside him. The doctored cell phone glinted in the sunlight. He decided to take it to Drake's office right away. Get this whole thing over with.

He telephoned Drake's office and asked to talk to him; he was told Drake was at the dentist and would return later in the day. The secretary wasn't sure exactly when.

Evans decided to go to his apartment and take a shower.

He parked in the garage and walked through the little garden to his apartment. The sun was shining down between the buildings; the roses were in bloom, beautiful. The only thing that marred it, he thought, was the lingering odor of cigar smoke in the air. It was offensive to think that somebody had smoked a cigar and that what remained was—

"Sssst! Evans!"

He paused. He looked around. He could see nothing.

Evans heard an intense whisper, like a hiss: "Turn right. Pick a damn rose."

"What?"

"Don't talk, you idiot. And stop looking around. Come over here and pick a rose."

Evans moved toward the voice. The cigar smell was stronger. Behind the tangle of the bushes, he saw an old stone bench that he had never noticed before. It was crusted with algae. Hunched down on the bench was a man in a sportcoat. Smoking a cigar.

"Who are—"

"Don't talk," the man whispered. "How many times do I have to tell you. Take the rose, and smell it. That'll give you a reason to stay a minute. Now listen to me. I'm a private investigator. I was hired by George Morton."

Evans smelled the rose. Inhaling cigar smoke.

"I have something important for you," the guy said. "I'll bring it to your apartment in two hours. But I want you to leave again, so they'll follow you. Leave your door unlocked."

Evans turned the rose in his fingers, pretending to examine it. In fact, he was looking past the rose at the man on the bench. The man's face was familiar, somehow. Evans was sure he had seen him before . . .

"Yeah, yeah," the man said, as if reading his thoughts. He turned his lapel, to show a badge. "AV Network Systems. I was working in the NERF building. Now you remember, right? Don't *nod*. For Christ's sake. Just go upstairs, change your clothes, and leave for a while. Go to the gym or whatever. Just go. These assholes—" he jerked his head toward the street "have been waitin' for you. So don't disappoint them. Now *go*."

His apartment had been put back together very well. Lisa had done a good job—the slashed cushions had been flipped over; the books were back in the bookcase. They were out of order, but he would deal with that later.

From the large windows in his living room, Evans looked out toward the street. He could see nothing except the green expanse of Roxbury Park. The kids playing at midday. The clusters of gossiping nannies. There was no sign of surveillance.

It looked perfectly normal.

Self-consciously, he started unbuttoning his shirt, and turned away. He went to the shower, letting the hot spray sting his body. He looked at his toes, which were dark purple, a worrisome, unnatural color. He wiggled them. He didn't have much sensation, but other than that, they seemed to be all right.

He toweled off, and checked his messages. There was a call from Janis, asking if he was free tonight. Then another, nervous one from her, saying her boyfriend had just come back into town and she was busy (which meant, don't call her back). There was a call from Lisa, Herb Lowenstein's assistant, asking where he was. Lowenstein wanted to go over some documents with him; it was important. A call from Heather, saying that Lowenstein was looking for him. A call from Margo Lane, saying she was still in the hospital and why hadn't he called her back? A call from his client the BMW dealer, asking when he was coming to the showroom.

And about ten hang-ups. Far more than he usually had.

The hang-ups gave him a creepy feeling.

Evans dressed quickly, putting on a suit and tie. He came back into the living room and, feeling uneasy, clicked on the television set, just in time for the local noon news. He was heading for the door when he heard: "Two new developments emphasize once again the dangers of global warming. The first study, out of England, says global warming is literally changing the rotation of the Earth, shortening the length of our day."

Evans turned back to look. He saw two co-anchors, a man and a woman. The man was explaining that even more dramatic was a study that showed that the Greenland ice cap was going to melt entirely away. That would cause sea levels to rise twenty feet.

"So, I guess it's good-bye Malibu!" the anchor said cheerfully. Of course, that wouldn't happen for a few years yet. "But it's coming . . . unless we all change our ways."

Evans turned away from the television and headed for the door. He wondered what Kenner would have to say about this latest news. Changing the rotation speed of the Earth? He shook his head at the sheer enormity of it. And melting all the ice in Greenland? Evans could imagine Kenner's discomfiture.

But then, he'd probably just deny it all, the way he usually did.

Evans opened the door, carefully ensured that it would remain unlocked, closed it behind him, and headed for his office.

He ran into Herb Lowenstein in the hall, walking toward a conference room. "Jesus," Lowenstein said, "where the hell have you been, Peter? Nobody could find you."

"I've been doing a confidential job for a client."

"Well next time tell your damn secretary how to reach you. You look like shit. What happened, you get in a fight or something? And what's that above your ear? Jesus, are those stitches?"

"I fell."

"Uh-huh. What client were you doing this confidential job for?"

"Nick Drake, actually."

"Funny. He didn't mention it."

"No?"

"No, and he just left. I spent the whole morning with him. He's very unhappy about the document rescinding the ten-million-dollar grant from the Morton Foundation. Especially that clause."

"I know," Evans said.

"He wants to know where the clause came from."

"I know."

"Where did it come from?"

"George asked me not to divulge that."

"George is dead."

"Not officially."

"This is bullshit, Peter. Where did the clause come from?"

Evans shook his head. "I'm sorry, Herb. I have specific instructions from the client."

"We're in the same firm. And he's my client, too."

"He instructed me in writing, Herb."

"In *writing?* Horseshit. George didn't write anything."

"Handwritten note," Evans said.

"Nick wants the terms of the document broken."

"I'm sure he does."

"And I told him we'd do that for him," Lowenstein said.

"I don't see how."

"Morton was not in his right mind."

"But he was, Herb," Evans said. "You'll be taking ten million out of his estate and if anybody whispers in the ear of his daughter—"

"She's a total cokehead—"

"—who goes through cash like a monkey through bananas. And if anybody whispers in her ear, this firm will be liable for the ten million, and for punitive damages for conspiracy to defraud. Have you talked to the other senior partners about this course of action?"

"You're being obstructive."

"I'm being cautious. Maybe I should express my concerns in an e-mail to you."

"This is not how you advance in this firm, Peter."

Evans said, "I think I am acting in the firm's best interest. I certainly don't see how you can abrogate this document without, at the very least, first obtaining written opinions from attorneys outside the firm."

"But no outside attorney would countenance—" He broke off. He glared at Evans. "Drake is going to want to talk to you about this."

"I'll be happy to do that."

"I'll tell him you'll call."

"Fine."

Lowenstein stalked off. Then he turned back. "And what was all that business about the police and your apartment?"

"My apartment was robbed."

"For what? Drugs?"

"No, Herb."

"My assistant had to leave the office to help you with a police matter."

"That's true. As a personal favor. And it was after hours, if I recall."

Lowenstein snorted, and stomped off down the hall.

Evans made a mental note to call Drake. And get this entire business behind him.

In the hot midday sun, Kenner parked his car in the downtown lot and walked with Sarah out onto the street. Heat shimmered off the pavement. The signs there were all in Spanish, except for a few English phrases—"Checks Cashed" and "Money Loaned." From scratchy loudspeakers, mariachi music blared out.

Kenner said, "All set?"

Sarah checked the small sports bag on her shoulder. It had nylon mesh at either end. The mesh concealed the video lens. "Yes," she said. "I'm ready."

Together, they walked toward the large store on the corner, "Brader's Army/Navy Surplus."

Sarah said, "What're we doing here?"

"ELF purchased a large quantity of rockets," Kenner said.

She frowned. "Rockets?"

"Small ones. Lightweight. About two feet long. They're outdated versions of an '80s Warsaw Pact device called Hotfire. Handheld, wire-guided, solid propellant, range of about a thousand yards."

Sarah wasn't sure what all that meant. "So, these are weapons?"

"I doubt that's why they bought them."

"How many did they buy?"

"Five hundred. With launchers."

"Wow."

"Let's just say they're probably not hobbyists."

Above the doors, a banner in flaking yellow and green paint read, Camping Gear Paintball Paratrooper Jackets Compass Sleeping Bags Much, Much More!

The front door chimed as they went in.

The store was large and disorderly, filled with military stuff on racks and piled in untidy heaps on the floor. The air smelled musty, like old canvas. There were few people inside at this hour. Kenner walked directly to the kid at the cash register, flashed his wallet, and asked for Mr. Brader.

"In the back."

The kid smiled at Sarah. Kenner went to the back of the store. Sarah stayed at the front.

"So," she said. "I need a little help."

"Do my best." He grinned. He was a crew-cut kid, maybe nineteen or twenty. He had a black T-shirt that said "The Crow." His arms looked like he worked out.

"I'm trying to find a guy," Sarah said, and slid a sheet of paper toward him.

"You think any guy would be trying to find you," the kid said. He picked up the paper. It showed a photograph of the man they knew as Brewster, who had set up camp in Antarctica.

"Oh yeah," the kid said immediately. "Sure, I know him. He comes in sometimes."

"What's his name?"

"I don't know, but he's in the store now."

"Now?" She glanced around for Kenner, but he was in the back, huddled with the owner. She didn't want to call to him or do anything to cause attention.

The kid was standing on tiptoes, looking around. "Yeah, he's here. I mean, he was in here a few minutes ago. Came in to buy some timers."

"Where are your timers?"

"I'll show you." He came around the counter, and led her through the stacks of green clothing and the boxes piled seven feet high. She couldn't see over them. She could no longer see Kenner.

The kid glanced over his shoulder at her. "What are you, like a detective?"

"Sort of."

"You want to go out?"

They were moving deeper into the store when they heard the chime of the front door. She turned to look. Over stacks of flak jackets, she had a glimpse of a brown head, a white shirt with a red collar, and the door closing.

"He's leaving . . ."

She didn't think. She just turned and sprinted for the door. The bag banged against her hip. She jumped over stacked canteens, running hard.

"Hey," the kid yelled behind her. "You coming back?"

She banged through the door.

She was out on the street. Glaring hot sun and shoving crowds. She looked left and right. She didn't see the white shirt and red collar anywhere. There hadn't been time for him to cross the street. She looked around the corner, and saw him strolling casually away from her, toward Fifth Street. She followed him.

He was a man of about thirty-five, dressed in cheap golf-type clothes. His pants were rumpled. He wore dirty hiking boots. He had tinted glasses and a small, trim moustache. He looked like a guy who spent a lot of time outdoors, but not a construction guy—more of a supervisor. Maybe a building contractor. Building inspector. Something like that.

She tried to notice the details, to remember them. She gained on him, then decided that was a bad idea, and dropped back. "Brewster" stopped in front of one window and looked at it intently for a few moments, then went on.

She came to the window. It was a crockery store, displaying cheap plates. She wondered, then, if he already knew he was being followed.

· · ·

To trail a terrorist on a downtown street felt like something out of a movie, but it was more frightening than she anticipated. The surplus store seemed very far behind her. She didn't know where Kenner was. She wished he were here. Also, she was hardly inconspicuous; the crowd on the sidewalk was largely Hispanic, and Sarah's blond head stuck up above most people's.

She stepped off the curb, and walked along the street gutter, hanging at the edge of the crowd. That way she lost six inches of height. But still, she was uncomfortably aware that her hair was distinctively blonde. But there was nothing she could do about that.

She let Brewster get twenty yards ahead of her. She didn't want to allow more distance than that because she was afraid she'd lose him.

Brewster crossed Fifth Street, and continued on. He went another half a block, and then turned left, down an alley. Sarah got to the alley entrance, and paused. There were garbage bags stacked at intervals. She could smell the rotten odor from where she was. A big delivery truck blocked the far end of the alley.

And no Brewster.

He had vanished.

It wasn't possible, unless he had walked through one of the back doors that opened onto the alley. There were doors every twenty feet or so, many of them recessed into the brick wall.

She bit her lip. She didn't like the idea that she couldn't see him. But there were delivery men down at the truck. . . .

She started down the alley.

She looked at each door as she passed it. Some were boarded shut, some were locked. A few had grimy signs giving the name of the firm, and saying USE FRONT ENTRANCE or PRESS BELL FOR SERVICE.

No Brewster.

She had gotten halfway down the alley when something made her look back. She was just in time to see Brewster step out of a doorway and head back to the street, moving quickly away from her.

She ran.

As she passed the doorway, she saw an elderly woman standing in the door. The sign on the door said, Munro Silk and Fabrics.

"Who is he?" she shouted.

The old woman shrugged, shaking her head. "Wrong door. They all do—" She said something more, but by then Sarah couldn't hear.

She was back on the sidewalk, still running. Heading toward Fourth. She could see Brewster half a block ahead. He was walking quickly, almost a jog.

He crossed Fourth. A pickup truck pulled over to the side, a few yards ahead. It was battered blue, with Arizona license plates. Brewster jumped in the passenger side, and the truck roared off.

Sarah was scribbling down the license plate when Kenner's car screeched to a stop alongside her. "Get in."

She did, and he accelerated forward.

"Where were you?" she said.

"Getting the car. I saw you leave. Did you film him?"

She had forgotten all about the bag on her shoulder. "Yes, I think so."

"Good. I got a name for this guy, from the store owner."

"Yes?"

"But it's probably an alias. David Poulson. And a shipping address."

"For the rockets?"

"No, for the launch stands."

"Where?"

Kenner said, "Flagstaff, Arizona."

Ahead, they saw the blue pickup.

They followed the pickup down Second, past the *Los Angeles Times* building, past the criminal courts, and then onto the freeway. Kenner was skilled; he managed to stay well back, but always kept the truck in sight.

"You've done this before," Sarah said.

"Not really."

"What is that little card you show everybody?"

Kenner pulled out his wallet, and handed it to her. There was a silver badge, looking roughly like a police badge, except it said "NSIA" on it. And there was an official license for "National Security Intelligence Agency," with his photograph.

"I've never heard of the National Security Intelligence Agency."

Kenner nodded, took the wallet back.

"What does it do?"

"Stays below the radar," Kenner said. "Have you heard from Evans?"

"You don't want to tell me?"

"Nothing to tell," Kenner said. "Domestic terrorism makes domestic agencies uncomfortable. They're either too harsh or too lenient. Everyone in NSIA is specially trained. Now, call Sanjong and read him the license plate on that pickup, see if he can trace it."

"So you do domestic terrorism?"

"Sometimes."

Ahead, the pickup truck moved onto the Interstate 5 freeway, heading east, past the clustered yellowing buildings of County General Hospital.

"Where are they going?" she said.

"I don't know," he said. "But this is the road to Arizona."

She picked up the phone and called Sanjong.

Sanjong wrote down the license, and called back in less than five minutes. "It's registered to the Lazy-Bar Ranch, outside Sedona," he told Kenner. "It's apparently a guest ranch and spa. The truck hasn't been reported stolen."

"Okay. Who owns the ranch?"

"It's a holding company: Great Western Environmental Associates. They own a string of guest ranches in Arizona and New Mexico."

"Who owns the holding company?"

"I'm checking on that, but it'll take some time."

Sanjong hung up.

Ahead, the pickup truck moved into the right lane, and turned on its blinker.

"It's pulling off the road," Kenner said.

They followed the truck through an area of seedy industrial parks. Sometimes the signs said SHEET WORKS or MACHINE TOOLING, but most of the buildings were blocky and unrevealing. The air was hazy, almost a light fog.

After two miles, the truck turned right again, just past a sign that said LTSI CORP. And beneath that, a small picture of an airport, with an arrow.

"It must be a private airfield," Kenner said.

"What's LTSI?" she said.

He shook his head. "I don't know."

Farther down the road, they could see the little airfield, with several small prop planes, Cessnas and Pipers, parked to one side. The truck drove up and parked alongside a twin-engine plane.

"Twin Otter," Kenner said.

"Is that significant?"

"Short takeoff, large payload. It's a workhorse aircraft. Used for fire-fighting, all sorts of things."

Brewster got out of the truck, and walked to the cockpit of the plane. He spoke briefly to the pilot. Then he got back in the truck, and drove a hundred yards down the road, pulling up in front of a huge rectangular shed of corrugated steel. There were two other trucks parked alongside it. The sign on the shed said LTSI, in big blue letters.

Brewster got out of the truck, and came around the back as the driver of the truck got out.

"Son of a bitch," Sarah said.

The driver was the man they knew as Bolden. He was now wearing jeans, a baseball cap, and sunglasses, but there was no doubt about his identity.

"Easy," Kenner said.

They watched as Brewster and Bolden walked into the shed through a narrow door. The door closed behind them with a metallic clang.

Kenner turned to Sarah. "You stay here."

He got out of the car, walked quickly to the shed, and went inside.

She sat in the passenger seat, shading her eyes against the sun, and waited. The minutes dragged. She squinted at the sign on the side of the shed, because she could detect small white lettering beneath the large LTSI initials. But she was too far away to make out what it said.

She thought of calling Sanjong, but didn't. She worried about what would happen if Brewster and Bolden came out, but Kenner remained inside. She would have to follow them alone. She couldn't let them get away. . . .

That thought led her to slide over into the driver's seat. She rested her hands on the wheel. She looked at her watch. Surely nine or ten minutes had already passed. She scanned the shed for any sign of activity, but the building was clearly made to be as unobtrusive and as unrevealing as possible.

She looked at her watch again.

She began to feel like a coward, just sitting there. All her life, she had confronted the things that frightened her. That was why she had learned to ski black diamond ice, to rock climb (even though she was too tall), to scuba dive wrecks.

Now, she was just sitting in a hot car, waiting as the minutes ticked by.

The hell with it, she thought. And she got out of the car.

At the door to the shed, there were two small signs. One said LTSI LIGHTNING TEST SYSTEMS INTERNATIONAL. The second said WARNING: DO NOT ENTER TEST BED DURING DISCHARGE INTERVALS.

Whatever that meant.

Sarah opened the door cautiously. There was a reception area, but it was deserted. On a plain wooden desk was a handwritten sign and a buzzer. PRESS BUZZER FOR ASSISTANCE.

She ignored the buzzer, and opened the inner door, which was ominously marked:

**NO TRESPASSING
HIGH VOLTAGE DISCHARGE
AUTHORIZED PERSONNEL ONLY**

She went through the door and came into an open, dimly lit industrial space—pipes on the ceiling, a catwalk, rubber-tile floor underfoot. It was all quite dark except for a two-story glass-walled chamber in the center, which was brightly lit. It was a fairly large space, roughly the size of her living room. Inside the chamber she saw what looked like an airplane jet engine, mounted on a small section of wing. At the side of the room was a large metal plate, set against the wall. And outside the room was a control panel. A man was sitting in front of the panel. Brewster and Bolden were nowhere to be seen.

Inside the room, a recessed monitor screen flashed CLEAR AREA NOW. A computer voice said, "Please clear the test area. Testing begins in . . . thirty seconds." Sarah heard a slowly building whine, and the chugging of a pump. But nothing was happening that she could see.

Curious, she moved forward.

"Ssst!"

She looked around, but could not see where the sound was coming from.

"Ssst!"

She looked up. Kenner was above her, on the catwalk. He gestured for her to join him, pointing to a set of stairs at the corner of the room.

The computer voice said, "Testing begins in . . . twenty seconds."

She climbed the stairs and crouched beside Kenner. The whine had now built to a shriek, and the chugging was rapid, almost a continuous sound. Kenner pointed to the jet engine, and whispered, "They're testing airplane parts." He explained quickly that airplanes were frequently struck by lightning, and all their components had to be lightning proof.

He said something else, too, but she couldn't really hear him over the increasing noise.

Inside the center room, the lights went off, leaving just a faint blue glow over the jet engine and its smoothly curved cowling. The computer voice was counting backward from ten.

"Testing begins . . . now."

There was a *snap!* so loud it sounded like a gunshot, and a bolt of lightning snaked out from the wall and struck the engine. It was immediately followed by more bolts from the other walls, striking the engine from all sides. The lightning crackled over the cowling in jagged white-hot fingers, then abruptly shot down to the floor, where Sarah saw a dome-shaped piece of metal about a foot in diameter.

She noticed a few of the lightning bolts seemed to shoot directly to this dome, missing the engine entirely.

As the test continued, the lightning bolts grew thicker, brighter. They made a long *crack!* as they shot through the air, and etched black streaks over the metal cowl. The fan blades were struck by one bolt, causing the fan to spin silently.

As Sarah watched, it seemed as if more and more of the bolts did not strike the engine, but instead struck the small dome on the floor until finally there was a white spiderweb of lightning strikes, coming from all sides, going directly to the dome.

And then, abruptly, the test ended. The whining sound stopped, and the room lights came on. Faint, hazy smoke rose from the engine cowling. Sarah looked over at the console, and saw Brewster and Bolden standing behind the seated technician. All three men walked into the central room, where they crouched beneath the engine and inspected the metal dome.

"What is it?" Sarah whispered.

Kenner put a finger to his lips, and shook his head. He looked unhappy.

Inside the room, the men upended the dome, and Sarah had a glimpse of its complexity—green circuit boards and shiny metal attachments. But the men were clustered around it, talking excitedly, and it was hard for her to see. Then they put the dome back down on the floor again, and walked out of the room.

They were laughing and slapping each other on the back, apparently very pleased with the test. She heard one of them say something about buying a round of beer, and there was more laughter, and they walked out through the front door. The test area was silent.

They heard the outer door slam shut.

She and Kenner waited.

She looked at Kenner. He waited, motionless for a full minute, just listening. Then, when they still heard nothing, he said, "Let's have a look at that thing."

They climbed down from the catwalk.

On the ground level, they saw and heard nothing. The facility was apparently deserted. Kenner pointed to the inner chamber. They opened the door, and went inside.

The interior of the chamber was bright. There was a sharp smell in the air.

"Ozone," Kenner said. "From the strikes."

He walked directly to the dome on the floor.

"What do you think it is?" Sarah said.

"I don't know, but it must be a portable charge generator." He crouched, turned the dome over. "You see, if you can generate a strong enough negative charge—"

He broke off. The dome was empty. Its electronic innards had been removed.

With a *clang*, the door behind them slammed shut.

Sarah whirled. Bolden was on the other side of the door, calmly locking it with a padlock.

"Oh shit," she said. Over at the console she saw Brewster, turning knobs, flipping switches. He flicked an intercom.

"There's no trespassing in this facility, folks. It's clearly marked. Guess you didn't read the signs . . ."

Brewster stepped away from the console. The room lights went dark blue. Sarah heard the start of the whine, beginning to build. The screen flashed CLEAR AREA NOW. And she heard a computer voice say, "Please clear the test area. Testing begins in . . . thirty seconds."

Brewster and Bolden walked out, without looking back.

Sarah heard Bolden say, "I hate the smell of burning flesh."

And they were gone, slamming the door.

The computer voice said, "Testing begins in . . . fifteen seconds."

Sarah turned to Kenner. "What do we do?"

Outside the facility, Bolden and Brewster got into their car. Bolden started the engine. Brewster put a hand on the other man's shoulder.

"Let's just wait a minute."

They watched the door. A red light began to flash, slowly at first, then faster and faster.

"Test has started," Brewster said.

"Damn shame," Bolden said. "How long you figure they can survive?"

"One bolt, maybe two. But by the third one, they're definitely dead. And probably on fire."

"Damn shame," Bolden said again. He put the car in gear, and drove toward the waiting airplane.

IV

FLASH

Inside the test chamber, the air took on a sizzly, electric quality, like the atmosphere before a storm. Sarah saw the hairs on her arm standing up. Her clothing was sticking to her body, flattened by the electric charge.

"Got a belt?" Kenner said.

"No . . ."

"Hairclip?"

"No."

"Anything metal?"

"No! Damn it, no!"

Kenner flung himself against the glass wall, but just bounced off. He kicked it with his heel; nothing happened. He slammed his weight against the door, but the lock was strong.

"Ten seconds to test," the computer voice said.

"What are we going to do?" Sarah said, panicked.

"Take your clothes off."

"What?"

"Now. Do it." He was stripping off his shirt, ripping it off, buttons flying. "Come on, Sarah. Especially the sweater."

She had a fluffy angora sweater, and bizarrely, she recalled it had been a present from her boyfriend, one of the first things he ever bought her. She tore it off, and the T-shirt beneath.

"Skirt," Kenner said. He was down to his shorts, pulling off his shoes.

"What is this—"

"It's got a zipper!"

She fumbled, getting the skirt off. She was down to her sports bra and panties. She shivered. The computer voice was counting backward. "Ten . . . nine . . . eight . . ."

Kenner was draping the clothes over the engine. He took her skirt, draped it over, too. He arranged the angora sweater to lie on the top.

"What are you doing?"

"Lie down," he said. "Lie flat on the floor—make yourself as flat as you can—and *don't move.*"

She pressed her body against the cold concrete. Her heart was pounding. The air was bristling. She felt a shiver down the back of her neck.

"Three . . . two . . . one . . ."

Kenner threw himself on the ground next to her and the first lightning bolt crashed through the room. She was shocked by the violence of it, the blast of air rushing over her body. Her hair was rising into the air, she could feel the weight of it lift off her neck. There were more bolts—the crashing sound was terrifying—blasting blue light, so bright she saw it even though she squeezed her eyes shut. She pressed herself against the ground, willing herself to be even flatter, exhaling, thinking *Now is a time for prayer.*

But suddenly there was another kind of light in the room, yellower, flickering, and a sharp acrid smell.

Fire.

A piece of her flaming sweater fell on her bare shoulder. She felt searing pain.

"It's a fire—"

"Don't move!" Kenner snarled.

The bolts were still blasting, coming faster and faster, crackling over the room, but she could see out of the corner of her eye that the clothes heaped on the engine were aflame, the room was filling with smoke.

She thought, *My hair is burning.* And she could feel it suddenly hot at the base of her neck, along her scalp . . .

And suddenly the room was filled with blasting water, and the lightning had stopped, and the sprinkler nozzles hissed overhead. She felt cold; the fires went out; the concrete was wet.

"Can I get up now?"

"Yes," Kenner said. "You can get up now."

He spent several more minutes trying to break the glass without success. Finally he stopped and stared, his hair matted by the sizzling water. "I don't get it," he said. "You can't have a room like this without a safety mechanism to enable someone to get out."

"They locked the door, you saw it yourself."

"Right. Locking it from the outside with a padlock. That padlock must be there to make sure nobody can enter the room from the outside while the facility is closed. But there still has to be some way to get out *from the inside.*"

"If there is, I don't see it." She was shivering. Her shoulder hurt where she was burned. Her underwear was soaked through. She wasn't modest, but she was cold, and he was nattering on . . .

"There just has to be a way," he said, turning slowly, looking.

"You can't break the glass . . ."

"No," he said. "You can't." But that seemed to suggest something to him. He bent and carefully examined the glass frame, looking at the seam where the glass met the wall. Running his finger along it.

She shivered while she watched him. The sprinklers were still on, still spraying. She was standing in three inches of water. She could not understand how he could be so focused, so intent on—

"I'll be damned," he said. His fingers had closed on a small latch, flush with the mounting. He found another on the opposite side of the window, flicked it open. And then he pushed the window, which was hinged in the center, and rotated it open.

He stepped through into the outer room.

"Nothing to it," he said. He extended his hand. "Can I offer you some dry clothes?"

"Thank you," she said, and took his hand.

The LTSI washrooms weren't anything to write home about, but Sarah and Kenner dried off with paper towels and found some warm coveralls, and Sarah began to feel better. Staring in the mirror, she saw that she'd lost two inches of hair around her left side. The ends were ragged, black, twisted.

"Could have been worse," she said, thinking *Ponytails for a while.*

Kenner tended to her shoulder, which he said was just a first-degree burn with a few blisters. He put ice on it, telling her that burns were not a thermal injury but were actually a nerve response within the body, and that ice in the first ten minutes reduced the severity of the burn by numbing the nerve, and preventing the response. So, if you were going to blister, ice prevented it from happening.

She tuned out his voice. She couldn't actually see the burned area, so she had to take his word for it. It was starting to hurt. He found a first-aid kit, brought back aspirin.

"Aspirin?" Sarah said.

"Better than nothing." He dropped two tablets in her hand. "Actually, most people don't know it, but aspirin's a true wonder drug, it has more pain-killing power than morphine, and it is anti-inflammatory, anti-fever—"

"Not right now," she said. "Please." She just couldn't take another of his lectures.

He said nothing. He just put on the bandage. He seemed to be good at that, too.

"Is there anything you're not good at?" she said.

"Oh sure."

"Like what? Dancing?"

"No, I can dance. But I'm terrible at languages."

"That's a relief." She herself was good at languages. She'd spent her junior year in Italy, and was reasonably fluent in Italian and French. And she'd studied Chinese.

"And what about you?" he said. "What are you bad at?"

"Relationships," she said. Staring in the mirror and pulling at the blackened strands of her hair.

As Evans climbed the steps to his apartment, he could hear the television blaring. It seemed louder than before. He heard cheers and laughter. Some sort of show with a live studio audience.

He opened the door, and went into the living room. The private investigator from the courtyard was sitting on the couch, his back to Evans while he watched television. His jacket was off and flung over a nearby chair. He had his arm draped across the back of the sofa. His fingers drummed impatiently.

"I see you've made yourself at home," Evans said. "Pretty loud, don't you think? Would you mind turning it down?"

The man didn't answer, he just continued to stare at the TV.

"Did you hear me?" Evans said. "Turn it down, would you?"

The man did not move. Just his fingers, moving restlessly on the back of the couch.

Evans walked around to face the man. "I'm sorry, I don't know your name but—"

He broke off. The investigator hadn't turned to look at him but continued to stare fixedly at the TV. In fact, no part of his body moved. He was immobile, rigid. His eyes didn't move. They didn't even blink. The only part of his body that moved was his fingers, on the top of the couch. They almost seemed to be twitching. In spasm.

Evans stepped directly in front of the man. "Are you all right?"

The man's face was expressionless. His eyes stared forward, seeming to look straight through Evans.

"Sir?"

The investigator was breathing shallowly, his chest hardly moving. His skin was tinged with gray.

"Can you move at all? What happened to you?"

Nothing. The man was rigid.

Just like the way they described Margo, Evans thought. The same rigidity, the same blankness. Evans picked up the phone and dialed 911, called for an ambulance to his address.

"Okay, help is coming," he said to the man. The private detective gave no visible response, but even so, Evans had the impression that the man could hear, that he was fully aware inside his frozen body. But there was no way to be sure.

Evans looked around the room, hoping to find clues as to what had happened to this man. But the apartment seemed undisturbed. One chair in the corner seemed to have been moved. The guy's smelly cigar was on the floor in the corner, as if it had rolled there. It had burned the edge of the rug slightly.

Evans picked up the cigar.

He brought it back to the kitchen, ran it under the faucet, and tossed it in the wastebasket. Then he had an idea. He went back to the man. "You were going to bring me something . . ."

There was no movement. Just the fingers on the couch.

"Is it here?"

The fingers stopped. Or almost stopped. They still moved slightly. But there was clearly an effort being made.

"Can you control your fingers?" Evans said.

They started, then stopped again.

"So you can. Okay. Now: is the thing you wanted me to see here?"

Fingers moved.

Then stopped.

"I take that as a yes. Okay." Evans stepped back. In the distance, he heard an approaching siren. The ambulance would be here in a few minutes. He said, "I am going to move in one direction, and if it is the right direction, move your fingers."

The fingers started, then stopped, as if to signal "yes."

"Okay," Evans said. He turned and took several steps to his right, heading toward the kitchen. He looked back.

The fingers did not move.

"So it's not that way." He now moved toward the television, directly in front of the man.

The fingers did not move.

"All right, then." Evans turned left, walking toward the picture windows. Still the fingers did not move. There was only one direction remaining: he moved behind the investigator, heading toward the door. Since the man could not see him, Evans said, "Now I am walking away from you, toward the front door . . ."

The fingers did not move.

"Maybe you didn't understand," Evans said. "I wanted you to move your fingers if I was heading in the right direction . . ."

Fingers moved. Scratching the couch.

"Yeah, okay, but which direction? I went in all four directions and—"

The doorbell rang. Evans opened it, and two paramedics rushed in, bringing a stretcher. And now there was pandemonium, they were asking him rapid-fire questions, and loading the guy onto the stretcher. The police arrived a few moments later, with still more questions. They were the Beverly Hills police, so they were polite, but they were insistent. This man was paralyzed in Evans's apartment, and Evans did not seem to know anything about it.

Finally, a detective came through the door. He wore a brown suit and introduced himself as Ron Perry. He gave Evans his card. Evans gave him his own card. Perry looked at it, then looked at Evans and said, "Haven't I seen this card before? It looks familiar. Oh yeah, I remember. It was at that apartment on Wilshire where the lady was paralyzed."

"She was my client."

"And now it's happened again, the same paralysis," Perry said. "Is that a coincidence or what?"

"I don't know," Evans said, "because I wasn't here. I don't know what happened."

"Somehow people just become paralyzed wherever you go?"

"No," Evans said. "I told you, I don't know what happened."

"Is this guy a client, too?"

"No."

"Then who is he?"

"I have no idea who he is."

"No? How'd he get in here?"

Evans was about to say he had left the door open for him, but he realized that was going to be a long explanation, and a difficult one.

"I don't know. I, uh . . . Sometimes I don't lock my door."

"You should always lock your door, Mr. Evans. That's just common sense."

"Of course, you're right."

"Doesn't your door lock automatically, when you leave?"

"I told you, I don't know how he got in my apartment," Evans said, looking directly into the detective's eyes.

The detective returned the stare. "How'd you get those stitches in your head?"

"I fell."

"Looks like quite a fall."

"It was."

The detective nodded slowly. "You could save us a lot of trouble if you'd just tell me who this guy is, Mr. Evans. You've got a man in your apartment, you don't know who he is, you don't know how he got here. Forgive me if I feel you're maybe leaving something out."

"I am."

"Okay." Perry took out his notebook. "Go ahead."

"The guy's a private detective."

"I know that."

"You do?" Evans said.

"The paramedics checked his pockets, found a license in his wallet. Go on."

"He told me he had been hired by a client of mine."

"Uh-huh. Which client is that?" Perry was writing.

"I can't tell you that," Evans said.

He looked up from his pad. "Mr. Evans—"

"I'm sorry. That's privileged."

The detective gave a long sigh. "Okay, so this guy is a private investigator hired by a client of yours."

"Right," Evans said. "The investigator contacted me and said he wanted to see me, to give me something."

"To give you something?"

"Right."

"He didn't want to give it to the client?"

"He couldn't."

"Because?"

"The client is, uh, unavailable."

"I see. So he came to you instead?"

"Yes. And he was a bit paranoid, and wanted to meet me in my apartment."

"So you left the door to your apartment open for him."

"Yes."

"Some guy you'd never seen before?"

"Yes, well, I knew he was working for my client."

"How did you know that?"

Evans shook his head. "Privileged."

"Okay. So this guy comes into your apartment. Where are you?"

"I was at my office."

Evans quickly recounted his movements during the intervening two hours.

"People saw you at the office?"

"Yes."

"Conversations?"

"Yes."

"More than one person?"

"Yes."

"You see anybody else besides people in the law firm?"

"I stopped to get gas."

"Attendant will recognize you?"

"Yes. I had to go in to use my credit card."

"Which station?"

"Shell on Pico."

"Okay. So you were gone two hours, you come back here, and the guy is . . ."

"As you saw him. Paralyzed."

"And what was he going to give you?"

"I have no idea."

"You didn't find anything in the apartment?"

"No."

"Anything else you want to tell me?"

"No."

Another long sigh. "Look, Mr. Evans. If two people I knew were mysteriously paralyzed, I'd be a little worried. But you don't seem worried."

"Believe me, I'm worried," Evans said.

The detective frowned at him. "Okay," he said finally. "You have a client privilege you're invoking. I have to tell you that I've gotten calls from UCLA and from the CDC on this paralysis thing. Now that there's a second case, there are going to be more calls." He flipped his notebook shut. "I'm going to need you to come by the station and give us a signed statement. Can you do that later today?"

"I think so."

"Four o'clock?"

"Yes. Fine."

"The address is on the card. Just ask for me at the desk. Parking is under the building."

"Okay," Evans said.

"See you then," the detective said, and turned to leave.

. . .

Evans shut the door behind him and leaned against it. He was glad to finally be alone. He walked around the apartment slowly, trying to focus his thoughts. The television was still on, but the sound was turned off. He looked at the couch where the private investigator had been sitting. The indentation of his body was still visible.

He still had half an hour before he was supposed to meet with Drake. But he wanted to know what the PI had brought to him. Where was it? Evans had moved in every direction of the compass, and each time the man had indicated with his fingertips that it was the wrong direction.

Which meant what? He hadn't brought the thing? It was somewhere else? Or that whoever paralyzed him had taken it, so it was no longer there?

Evans sighed. The critical question—is it here?—was one he hadn't asked the detective. Evans just assumed it was there.

And suppose it was? Where would it be?

North, south, east, west. All wrong.

Which meant . . .

What?

He shook his head. He was having trouble concentrating. The truth was, the private investigator's paralysis had unnerved him more than he wanted to admit. He looked at the couch, and the indentation. The guy couldn't move. It must have been terrifying. And the paramedics had lifted him up bodily, like a sack of potatoes, and put him on the stretcher. The cushions on the couch were in disarray, a reminder of their efforts.

Idly, Evans straightened up the couch, putting the cushions in place, fluffing them . . .

He felt something. Inside a slit in one cushion. He stuck his hand deeper into the padding.

"Damn," he said.

• • •

Of course it was obvious in retrospect. Moving away in every direction was wrong, because the investigator wanted Evans to move *toward* him. The guy was sitting on the thing, which he had slipped inside the couch cushion.

It turned out to be a shiny DVD.

Evans dropped it in the DVD player, and watched as a menu came up, a list of dates. They were all in the last few weeks.

Evans clicked on the first date.

He saw a view of the NERF conference room. It was a side angle, from the corner of the room, waist high. It must have been from a camera hidden in the speaker's podium or something, Evans thought. Undoubtedly the investigator had installed the camera the day Evans had seen him in the NERF conference room.

At the bottom of the screen was a running time code, numbers flickering. But Evans stared at the image itself, which showed Nicholas Drake talking to John Henley, the PR guy. Drake was upset, throwing up his hands.

"I *hate* global warming," Drake said, almost shouting. "I fucking *hate* it. It's a goddamn disaster."

"It's been established," Henley said calmly. "Over many years. It's what we have to work with."

"To work with? But *it doesn't work*," Drake said. "That's my point. You can't raise a dime with it, especially in winter. Every time it snows people forget all about global warming. Or else they decide some warming might be a good thing after all. They're trudging through the snow, *hoping* for a little global warming. It's not like pollution, John. Pollution *worked*. It still works. Pollution scares the shit out of people. You tell 'em they'll get cancer, and the money rolls in. But nobody is scared of a little warming. Especially if it won't happen for a hundred years."

"You have ways to play it," Henley said.

"Not anymore," Drake said. "We've tried them all. Species extinction from global warming—nobody gives a shit. They've heard that most of the species that will become extinct are insects. You can't raise money on insect extinctions, John. Exotic diseases from global warming—nobody cares. Hasn't happened. We ran that huge campaign last year connecting global warming to the Ebola and Hanta viruses. Nobody went for it. Sea-level rise from global warming—we all know where that'll end up. The Vanutu lawsuit is a fucking disaster. Everybody'll assume the sea level isn't rising anywhere. And that Scandinavian guy, that sea level expert. He's becoming a pest. He's even attacking the IPCC for incompetence."

"Yes," Henley said patiently. "That's all true . . ."

"So you tell me," Drake said, "how the hell I'm supposed to *play* global warming. Because you know what I have to raise to keep this organization going, John. I need forty-two million dollars a year. The foundations will only give me a quarter of that this year. The celebrities show up at the fund-raisers, but they don't give us shit. They're so egotistical they think showing up should be payment enough. Of course we sue the EPA every year, and they may cough up three, four million. With EPA grants, maybe five total. That still leaves a big gap, John. Global warming isn't going to cut it. I need a fucking *cause*. A cause that *works!*"

"I understand," Henley said, still very calm. "But you are forgetting the conference."

"Oh, Christ, the conference," Drake said. "These assholes can't even get the posters right. Bendix is our best speaker; he's got a family problem. Wife is having chemo. Gordon was scheduled, but he's got some lawsuit about his research . . . Seems his notebooks were faked . . ."

"Those are details, Nicholas," Henley said. "I'm asking you to stay with the big picture—"

At that moment, the phone rang. Drake answered it, listened briefly. Then he put his hand over the phone and turned to Henley.

"We have to continue this later, John. I've got an emergency here."

Henley got up, and left the room.

The clip ended.

The screen went black.

Evans stared at the blank screen. He felt as if he were going to be ill. A wave of dizziness passed over him. His stomach churned. He held the remote in his hand, but he did not press the buttons.

The moment passed. He took a breath. On reflection, he realized that what he had seen wasn't really surprising. Perhaps Drake was more explicit in private—everyone was—and obviously he felt under pressure to raise money. But the frustration he expressed was perfectly under-standable. From the beginning, the movement had had to fight apathy in the broader society. Human beings didn't think in the long term. They didn't see the slow degradation of the environment. It had always been an uphill battle to rouse the public to do what was really in its own best interest.

That fight was far from over. In fact, it was just beginning.

And it was probably true that it wasn't easy to raise money for global warming. So Nicholas Drake had his work cut out for him.

And environmental organizations were really working with very small funds. Forty-four million for NERF, the same for the NRDC, maybe fifty for the Sierra Club. The big one was the Nature Conservancy, they had three quarters of a billion. But what was that compared with the zillions of dollars that could be mobilized by corporations? It was David and Goliath. And Drake was David. As he had said himself, on every occasion.

Evans glanced at his watch. In any case, it was time to go see Drake.

He took the DVD out of the player, slipped it into his pocket, and left the apartment. On his way, he reviewed what he was going to say. He went over it, again and again, trying to make it perfect. He had to do it carefully, because everything Kenner had told him to say was a lie.

"Peter, Peter," Nicholas Drake said, shaking his hand warmly. "I am very pleased to see you. You've been away."

"Yes."

"But you haven't forgotten my request."

"No, Nick."

"Have a seat."

Evans sat down and Drake sat behind the desk. "Go ahead."

"I traced the origin of that clause."

"Yes?"

"Yes. You were right. George did get the idea from a lawyer."

"I knew it! Who?"

"An outside attorney, not in our firm." Evans spoke carefully, saying just what Kenner had instructed him to say.

"Who?"

"Unfortunately, Nick, there's documentation. Red-lined drafts with George's handwritten comments."

"Ah, shit. From when?"

"Six months ago."

"Six months!"

"Apparently George has been concerned for some time about . . . things. The groups he supports."

"He never told me."

"Nor me," Evans said. "He chose an outside attorney."

"I want to see this correspondence," Drake said.

Evans shook his head. "The attorney will never permit it."

"George is dead."

"Privilege continues after death. *Swidler and Berlin v. United States.*"

"This is bullshit, Peter, and you know it."

Evans shrugged. "But this attorney plays by the book. And I have arguably overstepped proper bounds by saying as much as I have."

Drake drummed his fingers on the desk top. "Peter, the Vanutu lawsuit is desperately in need of that money."

"I keep hearing," Evans said, "that that lawsuit may be dropped."

"Nonsense."

"Because the data sets don't show any rise in Pacific sea level."

"I'd be careful about saying things like that," Drake said. "Where did you hear that? Because that has to be disinformation from industry, Peter. There is *no question* sea levels are rising around the world. It's been scientifically demonstrated time and again. Why, just the other day I was looking at the satellite measurements of sea level, which are a relatively new way to make those measurements. The satellites show a rise of several millimeters, just in the last year."

"Was that published data?" Evans said.

"I don't remember offhand," Drake said, giving him an odd look. "It was in one of the briefing summaries I get."

Evans hadn't planned to ask questions like these. They had just somehow come out of his mouth, unbidden. And he was uncomfortably aware that his tone was skeptical. No wonder Drake was giving him an odd look.

"I don't mean anything," Evans said quickly. "It's just that I heard these rumors . . ."

"And you wanted to get to the bottom of it," Drake said, nodding. "As is only natural. I'm glad you brought this to my attention, Peter. I'll get on the horn with Henley and find out what's being disseminated. Of course it's an endless battle. You know we have those Neanderthals at the Competitive Enterprise Institute, and the Hoover Foundation, and the

Marshall Institute to deal with. Groups financed by right-wing radicals and brain-dead fundamentalists. But, unfortunately, they have a tremendous amount of money at their disposal."

"Yes, I understand," Evans said. He turned to go. "Do you need me for anything else?"

"I'll be frank," Drake said, "I'm not happy. Are we back to fifty thousand a week?"

"Under the circumstances, I think we have no option."

"Then we will have to manage," Drake said. "The lawsuit's going fine, by the way. But I have to focus my energies on the conference."

"Oh, right. When does that start?"

"Wednesday," Drake said. "Four days from now. Now, if you'll excuse me . . ."

"Of course," Evans said. He walked out of the office, leaving his cell phone on the side table across from the desk.

Evans had gone all the way down the stairs to the ground floor before he realized Drake hadn't asked him about his stitches. Everyone else he had seen that day had made some comment about them, but not Drake.

Of course, Drake had a lot on his mind, with the preparations for the conference. Directly ahead, Evans saw the ground-floor conference room bustling with activity. The banner on the wall read, ABRUPT CLIMATE CHANGE — THE CATASTROPHE AHEAD. Twenty young people clustered around a large table, on which stood a scale model of the interior of an auditorium, and the surrounding parking lot. Evans paused to watch for a moment.

One of the young people was putting wooden blocks in the parking lot, to simulate cars.

"He won't like that," another one said. "He wants the slots nearest the building reserved for news vans, not buses."

"I left three spaces over here for news," the first kid said. "Isn't that enough?"

"He wants ten."

"Ten spaces? How many news crews does he think are going to show up for this thing?"

"I don't know, but he wants ten spaces and he's told us to arrange extra power and phone lines."

"For an academic conference on abrupt climate change? I don't get it. How much can you say about hurricanes and droughts? He'll be lucky to have three crews."

"Hey, he's the boss. Mark off the ten slots and be done with it."

"That means the buses have to go way in the back."

"Ten slots, Jake."

"Okay, okay."

"Next to the building, because the line feeds are very expensive. The auditorium's charging us an arm and a leg for the extra utilities."

At the other end of the table, a girl was saying, "How dark will it be in the exhibition spaces? Will it be dark enough to project video?"

"No, they're limited to flat panels."

"Some of the exhibitors have all-in-one projectors."

"Oh, that should be all right."

A young woman came up to Evans as he was standing looking into the room. "Can I help you, sir?" She looked like a receptionist. She had that bland prettiness.

"Yes," he said, nodding toward the conference room. "I was wondering how I arrange to attend this conference."

"It's by invitation only, I'm afraid," she said. "It's an academic conference, not really open to the public."

"I've just left Nick Drake's office," Evans said, "and I forgot to ask him—"

"Oh. Well, actually, I have some comp tickets at the reception desk. Do you know which day you'll be attending?"

"All of them," Evans said.

"That's quite a commitment," she said, smiling. "If you'll come this way, sir . . ."

· · ·

It was only a short drive from NERF to the conference headquarters, in downtown Santa Monica. Workmen on a cherry picker were placing letters on the large sign: so far it said, ABRUPT CLIMATE CHA, and beneath, THE CATASTR.

His car was hot in the midday sun. Evans called Sarah on the car phone. "It's done. I left my phone in his office."

"Okay. I was hoping you'd call earlier. I don't think that matters anymore."

"No? Why?"

"I think Kenner already found out what he needed."

"He did?"

"Here, talk to him."

Evans thought, she's with him?

"Kenner speaking."

"It's Peter," he said.

"Where are you?"

"In Santa Monica."

"Go back to your apartment and pack some hiking clothes. Then wait there."

"For what?"

"Change all the clothes you are wearing now. Take nothing with you that you are wearing right now."

"Why?"

"Later."

Click. The phone was dead.

Back in his apartment, he hastily packed a bag. Then he went back to the living room. While he waited, he put the DVD back into the player and waited for the menu of dates.

He chose the second date on the list.

On the screen, he once again saw Drake and Henley. It must have been the same day, because they were dressed in the same clothes. But now it was later. Drake had his jacket off, hung over a chair.

"I've listened to you before," Drake was saying. He sounded resentful. "And your advice didn't work."

"Think structurally," Henley said, leaning back in his chair, staring up at the ceiling, fingertips tented.

"What the hell does that mean?" Drake said.

"Think structurally, Nicholas. In terms of how information functions. What it holds up, what holds it up."

"This is just PR bullshit."

"Nicholas," Henley said, sharply. "I am trying to help you."

"Sorry." Drake looked chastened. He hung his head a little.

Watching the video, Evans thought: *Is Henley in charge here?* For a moment, it certainly appeared that way.

"Now then," Henley said. "Let me explain how you are going to solve your problem. The solution is simple. You have already told me—"

There was a loud pounding on Evans's door. Evans stopped the DVD, and just to be safe, removed it from the player and slipped it into his pocket. The pounding continued, impatient, as he went to the door.

It was Sanjong Thapa. He looked grim.

"We have to leave," he said. "Right now."

V

SNAKE

DIABLO
SUNDAY, OCTOBER 10
2:43 P.M.

The helicopter thumped over the Arizona desert, twenty miles east of Flagstaff, not far from Canyon Diablo. In the back seat, Sanjong handed Evans pictures and computer printouts. Speaking of the Environmental Liberation Front, he said, "We assume their networks are up, but so are ours. All our networks are running," he said, "and we picked up an unexpected clue from one of them. Of all things, the Southwestern Parks Management Association."

"Which is?"

"It's an organization of state park managers from all the western states. And they discovered that something very odd had happened." A large percentage of the state parks in Utah, Arizona, and New Mexico were booked in advance, and paid for, to reserve them for company picnics, school celebrations, institutional birthday parties, and so on, for this weekend. In each case they were family affairs, involving parents and kids, sometimes grandparents, too.

True, this was a long three-day weekend. But nearly all the advance bookings were for Monday. Only a handful had been for Saturday or Sunday. None of the park superintendents could remember such a thing happening before.

"I don't get it," Evans said.

"They didn't either," Sanjong said. "They thought it might be some cult thing, and because the parks can't be used for religious purposes, they got on the phone and called some of the organizations. And they found in every case that the organization had received a special donation to fund the function on this particular weekend."

"Donation from whom?"

"Charitable organizations. In every case the situation was the same. They'd receive a letter saying 'Thank you for your recent request for funding. We are pleased to say we can support your get-together at such-and-such park on Monday, October eleventh. The check has already been sent in your name. Enjoy your gathering.' "

"But the groups never requested the booking?"

"No. So they'd call the charity, and someone would tell them it must have been a mixup, but since the checks were already sent out, they might as well go ahead and use the park that day. And a lot of the groups decided they would."

"And these charitable organizations were?"

"None you ever heard of. The Amy Rossiter Fund. The Fund for a New America. The Roger V. and Eleanor T. Malkin Foundation. The Joiner Memorial Foundation. All together, about a dozen charities."

"Real charities?"

Sanjong shrugged. "We assume not. But we're checking that now."

Evans said, "I still don't get it."

"Somebody wants those parks used this weekend."

"Yes, but why?"

Sanjong handed him a photograph. It was an aerial shot in false colors, and it showed a forest, the trees bright red against a dark blue ground. Sanjong tapped the center of the picture. There, in a clearing in the forest, Evans saw what looked like a spiderweb on the ground—a series of concentric lines connecting fixed points. Like a spiderweb.

"And that is?"

"It's a rocket array. The launchers are the fixed points. The lines are the power cables to control the launch." His finger moved across the picture. "And you see, there's another array here. And a third one here. The three arrays form a triangle, approximately five miles on each side."

Evans could see it. Three separate spiderwebs, set in clearings in the forest.

"Three rocket arrays . . ."

"Yes. We know they have purchased five hundred solid-state rockets. The rockets themselves are quite small. Close analysis of the picture elements indicates that the launchers are four to six inches in diameter, which means the rockets are capable of going up about a thousand feet or so. Not more than that. Each array has about fifty rockets, wired together. Probably not set to fire at the same time. And you notice the launchers are placed quite far apart . . ."

"But for what purpose?" Evans said. "These things are out in the middle of nowhere. They shoot up a thousand feet, and then fall back down? Is that it? What's the point of that?"

"We don't know," Sanjong said. "But we have another clue. The picture you're holding in your hands was taken yesterday. But here is a picture from a flyby this morning." He handed Evans a second picture, showing the same terrain.

The spiderwebs were gone.

"What happened?" Evans said.

"They packed up and left. You see in the first picture, there are vans parked at the edge of the clearings. Apparently, they just put everything in the vans and moved."

"Because they were spotted?"

"It's unlikely they know they were spotted."

"Then what?"

"We think they had to move to a more favorable setting."

"More favorable for what?" Evans said. "What's going on?"

"It may be significant," Sanjong said, "that at the time they purchased the rockets, they also purchased a hundred and fifty kilometers of microfilament wire."

He was nodding to Evans, as if that was supposed to explain everything.

"A hundred and fifty kilometers . . ."

Sanjong flicked his eyes toward the helicopter pilot, and shook his head. "We can go into it in greater detail later on, Peter."

And then he looked out the window.

Evans stared out the opposite window. He saw mile after mile of eroded desert landscape, cliffs brown with streaks of orange and red. The helicopter rumbled northward. He could see the helicopter's shadow racing over the sand. Distorted, twisted, then recognizable again.

Rockets, he thought. Sanjong had given him this information as if he were supposed to figure it out on his own. Five hundred rockets. Groups of fifty launchers, set widely apart. One hundred and fifty kilometers of microfilament wire.

Perhaps that was supposed to mean something, but Peter Evans didn't have the faintest idea what it could possibly be. Groups of small rockets, for what?

Microfilament, for what?

In his head, it was easy enough to calculate that if this microfilament was attached to the rockets, each rocket would have about a third of a kilometer of wire. And a third of a kilometer was . . . roughly a thousand feet.

Which was how high Sanjong said the rockets could go, anyway.

So these rockets were flying a thousand feet into the air, dragging a microfilament wire behind them? What was the point of that? Or was the wire intended to be used to retrieve them, later on? But no, he thought, that couldn't be. The rockets would fall back into the forest, and any microfilament would snap.

And why were the rockets spaced widely apart? If they were only a few inches in diameter, couldn't they be packed closer together?

He seemed to recall that the military had rocket launchers where the rockets were so close together the fins almost touched. So why should these rockets be far apart?

A rocket flies up . . . dragging a thin wire . . . and it gets to a thousand feet . . . and . . .

And what?

Perhaps, he thought, there was some instrumentation in the nose of each rocket. The wire was a way to transmit information back to the ground. But what instrumentation?

What was the point of all this?

He glanced back at Sanjong, who was now hunched over another photograph.

"What're you doing?"

"Trying to figure out where they've gone."

Evans frowned as he saw the picture in Sanjong's hand. It was a satellite weather map.

Sanjong was holding a weather map.

Did all this have to do with weather?

"Yes," Kenner said, leaning forward in the booth of the restaurant. They were in the back of a steakhouse in Flagstaff. The jukebox at the bar was playing old Elvis Presley: "Don't Be Cruel." Kenner and Sarah had showed up just a few minutes before. Sarah, Evans thought, looked drawn and worried. Not her usual cheerful self.

"We think this is all about the weather," Kenner was saying. "In fact, we're sure it is." He paused while a waitress brought salads, then continued. "There are two reasons to think so. First, ELF has bought a considerable amount of expensive technology that seems to have no use in common, except perhaps attempts to influence the weather. And second, the—"

"Hold on, hold on," Evans said. "You said attempts to influence the weather?"

"Exactly."

"Influence how?"

"Control it," Sanjong said.

Evans leaned back in the booth. "This is crazy," he said. "I mean, you're telling me these guys think they can control the weather?"

"They can," Sarah said.

"But how?" Evans said. "How could they do it?"

"Most of the research is classified."

"Then how do they get it?"

"Good question," Kenner said. "And we'd like to know that answer. But the point is, we assume that these rocket arrays are designed to produce major storms, or to amplify the power of existing storms."

"By doing what?"

"They cause a change in the electric potentials of the infra-cumulus strata."

"I'm glad I asked," Evans said. "That's very clear."

"We don't really know the details," Kenner said, "although I'm sure we'll find out soon enough."

"The strongest evidence," Sanjong said, "comes from the pattern of park rentals. These guys have arranged for lots of picnics over a large area—three states, in point of fact. Which means they are probably going to decide at the last minute where to act, based on existing weather conditions."

"Decide what?" Evans said. "What are they going to do?"

Nobody spoke.

Evans looked from one to another.

"Well?"

"We know one thing," Kenner said. "They want it documented. Because if there's one thing you can count on at a school picnic or a company outing with families and kids, it's lots of cameras. Lots of video, lots of stills."

"And then of course the news crews will come," Sanjong said.

"They will? Why?"

"Blood draws cameras," Kenner said.

"You mean they're going to hurt people?"

"I think it's clear," Kenner said, "that they're going to try."

An hour later they all sat on lumpy motel beds while Sanjong hooked a portable DVD player to the television set in the room. They were in a crappy motel room in Shoshone, Arizona, twenty miles north of Flagstaff.

On the screen, Evans once again saw Henley talking to Drake.

"I've listened to you before," Drake said resentfully. "And it didn't work."

"Think structurally," Henley answered. He was leaning back in his chair, staring up at the ceiling, fingertips tented.

"What the hell does that mean?" Drake said.

"Think structurally, Nicholas. In terms of how information functions. What it holds up, what holds it up."

"This is just PR bullshit."

"Nicholas," Henley said, sharply. "I am trying to help you."

"Sorry." Drake looked chastened. He hung his head a little.

Watching the screen, Evans said, "Does it look like Henley is in charge here?"

"He's always been in charge," Kenner said. "Didn't you know that?"

On the screen, Henley was saying, "Let me explain how you are going to solve your problem, Nicholas. The solution is simple. You have already told me that global warming is unsatisfactory because whenever there is a cold snap, people forget about it."

"Yes, I told you—"

"So what you need," Henley said, "is to structure the information so that whatever kind of weather occurs, it always confirms your message. That's the virtue of shifting the focus to abrupt climate change. It enables you to use everything that happens. There will always be floods, and freezing storms, and cyclones, and hurricanes. These events will always get headlines and airtime. And in every instance, you can claim it is an example of abrupt climate change caused by global warming. So the message gets reinforced. The urgency is increased."

"I don't know," Drake said doubtfully. "That's been tried, the last couple of years."

"Yes, on a scattered, individual basis. Isolated politicians, making claims about isolated storms or floods. Clinton did it, Gore did it, that blithering science minister in England did it. But we're not talking about isolated politicians, Nicholas. We are talking about an organized campaign throughout the world to make people understand that global warming is responsible for abrupt and extreme weather events."

Drake was shaking his head. "You know," he said, "how many studies show no increase in extreme weather events."

"Please." Henley snorted. "Disinformation from skeptics."

"That's hard to sell. There are too many studies . . ."

"What are you talking about, Nicholas? It's a snap to sell. The public already believes that industry is behind any contrary view." He sighed. "In any case, I promise you there will soon be more computer models showing that extreme weather *is* increasing. The scientists will get behind this and deliver what is needed. You know that."

Drake paced. He looked unhappy. "But it just doesn't make sense," he said. "It's not logical to say that freezing weather is caused by global warming."

"What's logic got to do with it?" Henley said. "All we need is for the media to report it. After all, most Americans believe that crime in their country is increasing, when it has actually been declining *for twelve years.* The US murder rate is as low as it was in the early 1970s, but Americans are more frightened than ever, because so much more airtime is devoted to crime, they naturally assume there is more in real life, too." Henley sat up in his chair. "Think about what I am saying to you, Nicholas. A twelve-year trend, and they still don't believe it. There is no greater proof that all reality is media reality."

"The Europeans are more sophisticated—"

"Trust me—it'll be even easier to sell abrupt climate change in Europe than in the US. You just do it out of Brussels. Because bureaucrats *get it,* Nicholas. They'll see the advantages of this shift in emphasis."

Drake did not reply. He walked back and forth, hands in his pockets, staring at the floor.

"Just think how far we have come!" Henley said. "Back in the 1970s, all the climate scientists believed an ice age was coming. They thought the world was getting colder. But once the notion of global *warming* was raised, they immediately recognized the advantages. Global warming creates a crisis, a call to action. A crisis needs to be studied, it needs to be funded, it needs political and bureaucratic structures around the world. And in no time at all, a huge number of meteorologists, geologists, oceanographers suddenly became 'climate scientists' engaged in the management of this crisis. This will be the same, Nicholas."

"Abrupt climate change has been discussed before, and it hasn't caught on."

"That's why you are holding a conference," Henley said patiently. "You hold a well-publicized conference and it happens to coincide with some dramatic evidence for the dangers of abrupt climate. And by the end of the conference, you will have established abrupt climate change as a genuine problem."

"I don't know . . ."

"Stop whining. Don't you remember how long it took to establish the global threat of nuclear winter, Nicholas? It took *five days*. On one Saturday in 1983, nobody in the world had ever heard of nuclear winter. Then a big media conference was held and by the following Wednesday the entire world was worried about nuclear winter. It was established as a bona fide threat to the planet. Without a single published scientific paper."

Drake gave a long sigh.

"Five days, Nicholas," Henley said. "They did it. You'll do it. Your conference is going to change the ground rules for climate."

The screen went black.

"My God," Sarah said.

Evans said nothing. He just stared at the screen.

Sanjong had stopped listening some minutes before. He was working with his laptop.

Kenner turned to Evans. "When was that segment recorded?"

"I don't know." Evans slowly came out of his fog. He looked around the room in a daze. "I have no idea when it was recorded. Why?"

"You've got the remote in your hand," Kenner said.

"Oh, sorry." Evans pressed the buttons, brought the menu up, saw the date. "It was two weeks ago."

"So Morton's been bugging Drake's offices for two weeks," Kenner said.

"Looks like it."

Evans watched as the recording ran again, this time with the sound off. He stared at the two men, Drake pacing and worried, Henley just sitting there, sure of himself. Evans was struggling to assimilate what he had heard. The first recording had seemed reasonable enough to him. There, Drake was complaining about the problems of publicizing a genuine environmental threat, global warming, when everybody naturally ceased to care about the topic in the middle of a snowstorm. All that made sense to Evans.

But this conversation . . . He shook his head. This one worried him.

Sanjong clapped his hands together and said, "I got it! I have the location!" He turned his laptop so everyone could see the screen. "This is NEXRAD radar from Flagstaff-Pulliam. You can see the precipitation center forming northeast of Payson. There should be a storm there by midday tomorrow."

"How far is that from us?" Sarah said.

"About ninety miles."

Kenner said, "I think we better get in the helicopter."

"And do what?" Evans said. "It's ten o'clock at night, for God's sake."

"Dress warmly," Kenner said.

The world was green and black, the trees slightly fuzzy through the lenses. The night-vision goggles pressed heavily against his forehead. There was something wrong with the straps: they cut into his ears and were painful. But everybody was wearing them, looking out the windows of the helicopter at the miles of forest below.

They were looking for clearings, and had already passed a dozen or more. Some were inhabited, the houses dark rectangles with glowing windows. In a couple of clearings, the buildings were completely black—ghost towns, abandoned mining communities.

But they hadn't yet found what they were looking for.

"There's one," Sanjong said, pointing.

Evans looked off to his left, and saw a large clearing. The familiar spiderweb pattern of launchers and cables was partially obscured in tall grass. To one side stood a large trailer truck of the size used to deliver groceries to supermarkets. And indeed, in black lettering, he saw "A&P" printed on the side panels.

"Food terrorists," Sarah said. But no one laughed.

And then the clearing had flashed past, the helicopter continuing onward. The pilot had explicit instructions not to slow down or to circle any clearing.

"That was definitely one," Evans said. "Where are we now?"

"Tonto Forest, west of Prescott," the pilot said. "I've marked the coordinates."

Sanjong said, "We should find two more, in a five-mile triangle."

The helicopter thumped onward into the night. It was another hour before they located the remaining spiderwebs, and the helicopter headed home.

The morning was warm and sunny, although dark clouds threatened to the north. At McKinley State Park, the Lincoln Middle School was having its annual outing. There were balloons attached to the picnic tables, the barbecue grills were smoking, and about three hundred kids and their families were playing on the grassy field beside the waterfall, throwing Frisbees and baseballs. More were playing along the banks of the nearby Cavender River, which meandered peacefully through the park. The river was low at the moment, with sandy banks on either side, and small rocky pools where the younger children played.

Kenner and the others were parked to one side, watching.

"When that river overflows," Kenner said, "it'll take out the entire park and everyone in it."

"It's a pretty big park," Evans said. "Will it really overflow that much?"

"Doesn't take much. The water will be muddy and fast moving. Six inches of fast water is enough to knock a person off his feet. Then they slide; it's slippery, they won't be able to get back up again. There're rocks and debris in the water; mud blinds them, they hit things, lose consciousness. Most drownings occur because people try to move across very low water."

"But six inches . . ."

"Muddy water has power," Kenner said. "Six inches of mud will take a car, no problem. Lose traction, sweep it right off the road. Happens all the time."

Evans found this hard to believe, but Kenner was now talking about some famous flood in Colorado, the Big Thompson, where a hundred and forty people died in a matter of minutes. "Cars crushed like beer cans," he said. "People with clothes ripped off their bodies by mud. Don't kid yourself."

"But here," Evans said, pointing to the park. "If the water starts to rise, there will be enough time to get out. . . ."

"Not if it's a flash flood. Nobody here will know until it's too late. That's why we're going to make sure they don't have a flash flood."

He checked his watch, looked up at the darkening sky, and then walked back to the cars. They had three SUVs in a row. Kenner would drive one; Sanjong would drive one; Peter and Sarah would drive the third.

Kenner opened the back door to his car. He said to Peter, "Do you have a gun?"

"No."

"You want one?"

"You think I need one?"

"You might. When was the last time you were on a range?"

"Uh, it's been a while." In truth, Evans had never fired a gun in his life. And until this moment, he was proud of it. He shook his head. "I'm not much of a gun guy."

Kenner had a revolver in his hands. He had opened the round barrel-thing and was checking it. Sanjong was over by his own car, checking an evil-looking rifle, matte black stock with a telescopic sight. His manner was quick, practiced. A soldier. Uneasily, Evans thought: *What is this, the O.K. Corral?*

"We'll be all right," Sarah said to Kenner. "I have a gun."

"You know how to use it?"

"I do."

"What is it?"

"A 9-millimeter Beretta."

Kenner shook his head. "Can you handle a .38?"

"Sure."

He gave her a gun and a holster. She clipped the holster to the waistband of her jeans. She seemed to know what she was doing.

Evans said, "Do you really expect us to shoot somebody?"

"Not unless you have to," Kenner said. "But you may need to defend yourself."

"You think they'll have guns?"

"They might. Yes."

"Jesus."

"It's okay," Sarah said. "Personally, I'll be happy to shoot the bastards." Her voice was hard, angry.

"All right, then," Kenner said. "That about does it. Let's mount up."

Evans thought, *Mount up*. Jesus. This *was* the O.K. Corral.

Kenner drove to the other side of the park and spoke briefly to a state trooper, whose black-and-white patrol car stood at the edge of a clearing. Kenner had arranged radio contact with the trooper. In fact, they were all going to be in radio contact, because the plan required a high degree of coordination. They would have to hit the three spiderweb sites at the same time.

As Kenner explained it, the rockets were intended to do something called "charge amplification" of the storm. It was an idea from the last ten years, when people first began to study lightning in the field, in actual storms. The old idea was that each lightning strike decreased the storm's intensity, because it reduced the difference in electrical charge between the clouds and the ground. But some researchers had concluded that lightning strikes had the opposite effect—they increased the power of storms dramatically. The mechanism for this was not known, but was presumed to be related to the sudden heat of the lightning bolt, or the shockwave it created, adding turbulence to the already turbulent storm center. In any case, there was now a theory that if you could make more lightning, the storm would get worse.

"And the spiderwebs?" Evans said.

"They're little rockets with microfilaments attached. They go up a thousand feet into the cloud layer, where the wire provides a low-resistance conduction pathway and creates a lightning strike."

"So the rockets cause more lightning? That's what they're for?"

"Yes. That's the idea."

Evans remained doubtful. "Who pays for all this research?" he said. "The insurance companies?"

Kenner shook his head. "It's all classified," he said.

"You mean it's military?"

"Correct."

"The military pays for weather research?"

"Think about it," Kenner said.

Evans was not inclined to do so. He was deeply skeptical of all things military. The notion that they were paying for weather research struck him as the same sort of ludicrous excess as the six-hundred-dollar toilet seats and thousand-dollar wrenches that had become so notorious. "If you ask me, it's all a waste of money."

"ELF doesn't think so," Kenner said.

It was then that Sanjong spoke, with considerable intensity. Evans had forgotten that he was a soldier. Sanjong said that whoever could control the weather would control the battlefield. It was an age-old military dream. Of course the military would spend money on it.

"You're saying it actually works."

"Yes," Sanjong said. "Why do you think we are here?"

The SUV wound up into the wooded hills north of McKinley Park. This was an area of intermittent dense forest and open grassy fields. In the passenger seat, Sarah looked at Peter. He was good-looking, and he had the strong physique of an athlete. But sometimes he behaved like such a wimp.

"You ever do any sports?" she said.

"Sure."

"What?"

"Squash. A little soccer."

"Oh."

"Hey," he said. "Just because I don't shoot guns . . . I'm a lawyer, for Christ's sake."

She was disappointed with him and not even sure why. Probably, she thought, because she was nervous and wanted somebody competent to be with her. She liked being around Kenner. He was so knowledgeable, so skilled. He knew what was going on. He was quick to respond to any situation.

Whereas Peter was a nice guy, but . . .

She watched his hands on the wheel. He drove well. And that was important today.

It was no longer sunny. They were close to the storm clouds. The day was dark, gloomy, threatening. The road ahead was deserted as it wound through the forests. They hadn't seen a car since they left the park.

"How much farther?" Evans said.

Sarah consulted the GPS. "Looks like another five miles."

He nodded. Sarah shifted in her seat, moving so the holstered gun would not press against her hip. She glanced at the passenger-side mirror.

"Oh shit."

"What?"

Behind them was a battered blue pickup truck. With Arizona plates.

AURORAVILLE
MONDAY, OCTOBER II
10:22 A.M.

"We've got trouble," Sarah said.

"Why?" Evans said. He glanced in the rearview mirror, saw the truck. "What is it?"

Sarah had the radio in her hand. "Kenner. They spotted us."

"Who did?" Evans said. "Who are they?"

The radio clicked. "Where are you?" Kenner said.

"On Highway 95. We're about four miles away."

"Okay," Kenner said. "Stick with the plan. Do your best."

"Who is it?" Evans said, looking in the mirror.

The blue pickup was advancing fast. Very fast. In the next instant, it banged into the back of their car. Evans was startled, swerved, got control again. "What the *fuck?*" he said.

"Just drive, Peter."

Sarah took the revolver from its holster. She held the gun on her lap, looked out the side mirror.

The blue truck had dropped back for a moment, but now raced forward again.

"Here he comes—"

Perhaps because Peter stepped on the gas, the impact was surprisingly gentle. It was hardly more than a nudge. Peter careened around the curves, glancing at the rearview mirror.

Again, the blue truck dropped back. It followed them for the next half mile, but it was never closer than five or six car lengths.

"I don't get it," Evans said. "Are they going to ram us or not?"

"Guess not," she said. "See what happens if you slow down."

He slowed the SUV, dropping their speed to forty.

The blue truck slowed too, falling back farther.

"They're just following us," she said.

Why?

The first scattered drops of rain spattered the windshield. The road ahead was spotted. But they weren't yet in full rain.

The blue truck dropped even farther back now.

They came around a curve, and immediately ahead of them saw a big silver eighteen-wheeler, with a big trailer. It was rumbling slowly along the road, not going more than thirty miles an hour. On its back doors it said, "A&P."

"Oh shit," Evans said. In the back mirror, they saw the blue truck, still following. "They've got us front and back."

He swerved out, trying to pass the big trailer, but as soon as he did, the driver moved toward the center of the road. Evans immediately fell back.

"We're trapped," he said.

"I don't know," she said. "I don't get it."

The trailer blocked them at the front, but behind them the blue truck was farther back than ever, several hundred yards down the road.

She was still puzzling over this situation when a bolt of lightning crashed down at the side of the road as they drove past. It couldn't have been more than ten yards away, a white-hot, dazzling blast of light and sound. They both jumped.

"Jesus, that was close," Evans said.

"Yes . . ."

"I've never seen one that close."

Before she could answer, a second bolt crashed down, directly in front of them. The sound was explosive; Evans swerved involuntarily, even though the bolt was gone.

"Holy shit."

By then Sarah had a suspicion, just as the third bolt hit the car itself, a deafening crash and a sudden pressure that made knife pains in her ears and a blast of white that enveloped the car. Evans screamed in fear and let go of the wheel; Sarah grabbed it and straightened the car in the road.

A fourth bolt smashed down by the driver's side, just inches from the car. The driver's-side window cracked and splintered.

"Holy shit," Evans was saying. "Holy shit! What is this?"

To Sarah, it was only too obvious.

They were attracting lightning.

The next bolt cracked down, and was immediately followed by another, which smashed into the hood and spread burning white, jagged fingers over the car, and then was gone. There was a huge black indentation in the hood.

"I can't do this," Evans was saying. "I can't, I can't do this."

"Drive, Peter," Sarah said, grabbing his arm and squeezing hard. *"Drive."*

Two more bolts hit them, in rapid succession. Sarah smelled the odor of something burning—she wasn't sure what. But now she understood why they had been so gently rammed.

The blue pickup had stuck something onto their car. Some kind of electronic thing. And it was drawing the lightning to them.

"What do we do? What do we do?" Evans was whimpering. He howled as each new bolt struck.

But they were trapped, driving on a narrow road, hemmed in by dense pine forest on both sides of the road . . .

Something she should know.

Forest . . . What about the forest?

A lightning bolt cracked the rear window with explosive force. Another bolt struck them so hard it bounced the car on the macadam, as if it had been hit by a hammer.

"The hell with this," Evans said, and spun the wheel, turning off the highway and onto a dirt track in the forest. Sarah saw a sign flash by, the

name of a town on a battered post. They were plunged into near darkness under the huge, green pines. But the lightning immediately stopped.

Of course, she thought. *The trees.*

Even if their car was attracting lightning, it would strike the taller
trees first.

A moment later, it did. They heard a sharp crack just behind them,
and lightning flashed down the side of a tall pine, splitting the trunk open
with what looked like steam and bursting the tree into flames.

"We're going to start a forest fire."

"I don't care," Evans said. He was driving fast. The vehicle was
bouncing over the dirt road, but it was an SUV and it rode high so Sarah
knew they would be all right.

Looking back, she saw the tree burning, and the fire spreading laterally in fingers along the ground.

Kenner on the radio: "Sarah, what's happening?"

"We had to leave the road. We're being struck by lightning."

"A lot!" Evans yelled. "All the time!"

"Find the attractor," Kenner said.

"I think it's attached to the car," Sarah said. As she spoke, a bolt
smashed down on the road just ahead of them. The glare was so bright
she saw green streaks before her eyes.

"Then dump the car," Kenner said. "Go out as low as you can."

He clicked off. Evans continued to race forward, the SUV bouncing
on the ruts. "I don't want to leave," he said. "I think we're safer inside.
They always say don't leave your car because you're safer inside. The
rubber tires insulate you."

"But something's on fire," she said, sniffing.

The car jolted and bounced. Sarah tried to keep her balance, just
holding onto her seat, not touching the metal of the doors.

"I don't care, I think we should stay," Evans said.

"The gas tank might explode . . ."

"I don't want to leave," he said. "I'm not leaving." His knuckles were
white, gripping the wheel. Ahead, Sarah saw a clearing in the forest. It
was a large clearing, with high, yellow grass.

A lightning bolt smashed down with a fearsome crack, shattering the side mirror, which blew apart like a bomb. A moment later, they heard a soft *whump*. The car tilted to one side. "Oh shit," Evans said. "It blew a tire."

"So much for the insulation," she said.

The car was now grinding, the underside scraping over a dirt rut, metal squealing.

"Peter," she said.

"All right, all right, just let me get to the clearing."

"I don't think we can wait."

But the rut ended, the road flattened, and Evans drove forward, creaking on the rim, into the clearing. Raindrops spattered the windshield. Above the grass, Sarah saw the roofs of wooden buildings bleached by the sun. It took her a moment to realize that this was a ghost town. Or a mining town.

Directly ahead was a sign, AURORAVILLE, POP. 82. Another lightning bolt crashed down, and Evans hit the sign, knocking it over.

"Peter, I think we're here."

"Okay, yeah, let me get a little closer—"

"*Now, Peter!*"

He stopped the car, and they flung open their doors in unison. Sarah threw herself bodily onto the ground, and another bolt crashed so close to her that the blast of hot air knocked her sideways and sent her rolling on the ground. The roar of the lightning was deafening.

She got up on hands and knees, and scrambled around to the back of the vehicle. Evans was on the other side of the SUV, yelling something, but she couldn't hear him. She examined the rear bumper. There was no attachment, no device.

There was nothing there.

But she had no time to think, because another bolt struck the back of the SUV, rocking it, and the rear window shattered, sprinkling her with shards of glass. She fought panic and scrambled forward, staying low as she moved around the SUV and through the grass toward the nearest building.

Evans was somewhere ahead, yelling to her. But she couldn't hear him over the rumbling thunder. She just didn't want another bolt, not now, if she could just go a few more seconds . . .

Her hands touched wood. A board.

A step.

She crawled forward quickly, pushing aside the grass, and now she saw a porch, a dilapidated building, and swinging from the roof a sign bleached so gray she couldn't see what it said. Evans was inside, and she scrambled forward, ignoring the splinters in her hands, and he was yelling, yelling.

And she finally heard what he was saying:

"Look out for the scorpions!"

They were all over the wooden porch—tiny, pale yellow, with their stingers in the air. There must have been two dozen. They moved surprisingly fast, scampering sideways, like crabs.

"Stand up!"

She got to her feet, and ran, feeling the arachnids crunch under her feet. Another lightning bolt smashed into the building's roof, knocking down the sign, which fell in a cloud of dust onto the porch.

But then she was inside the building. And Evans was standing there, fists raised, yelling, "Yes! Yes! We did it!"

She was gasping for breath. "At least they weren't snakes," she said, chest heaving.

Evans said, "What?"

"There're always rattlers in these old buildings."

"Oh Jesus."

Outside, thunder rumbled.

And the lightning started again.

Through the shattered, grimy window Sarah was looking at the SUV, and thinking that now that they had left the car, there were no more lightning strikes on the SUV . . . thinking . . . nothing on the bumper . . . then why had the pickup nudged the SUV? What was the point? She turned to ask Evans if he had noticed—

And a lightning bolt blasted straight down through the roof, smashing it open to the dark sky, sending boards flying in all directions, and blasting into the ground right where she had been standing. The lightning left a blackened pattern of jagged streaks, like the shadow of a thorn bush on the floor. The ozone smell was strong. Wisps of smoke drifted up from the dry floorboards.

"This whole building could go," Evans said. He was already flinging a side door open, heading outside.

"Stay low," Sarah said, and followed him out.

The rain was coming down harder, big splattering drops that struck her back and shoulders as she ran to the next building. It had a brick chimney, and looked generally better built. But the windows were the same, broken and thickly coated with dust and grime.

They tried the nearest door, but it was jammed shut, so they ran around to the front, and found that door wide open. Sarah ran inside. A lightning bolt smashed down behind her, sagging the roof over the porch, splintering one of the side posts as it streaked down into the ground. The shockwave blasted the front windows in a shower of dirty glass. Sarah turned away, covering her face, and when she looked out again, she realized she was in a blacksmith's shop. There was a large firepit in the center of the room, and above it all sorts of iron implements hanging from the ceiling.

And on the walls, she saw horseshoes, tongs, metal of all sorts.

This room was full of metal.

The thunder rumbled ominously. "We have to get out of here," Evans shouted. "This is the wrong place to—"

He never finished. The next bolt knocked him off his feet as it came crashing down through the ceiling, spinning the iron implements, then smashing into the firepit, blasting the bricks outward in all directions. Sarah ducked, covering her head and ears, felt bricks striking her shoulders, back, legs—knocking her over—and then there was a burst of pain in her forehead, and she saw brief stars before blackness settled over her and the rumble of thunder faded to endless silence.

FOREST
MONDAY, OCTOBER 11
11:11 A.M.

Kenner was fifteen miles away, driving east on Route 47, listening to Sarah's radio. Her transmitter was still on, clipped to her belt. It was hard to be sure what was happening because each lightning strike produced a burst of static that lasted for the next fifteen seconds. Nevertheless he understood the most important point—Evans and Sarah had gotten away from the SUV, but the lightning hadn't stopped. In fact it seemed that the lightning was following them.

Kenner had been yelling into his handset, trying to get Sarah's attention, but apparently she had turned her volume down, or was too busy dealing with what was happening in the ghost town. He kept saying, "It's following you!" over and over.

But she never answered.

Now there was a long burst of static, followed by silence. Kenner switched channels.

"Sanjong?"

"Yes, Professor."

"Have you been listening?"

"Yes."

"Where are you?" Kenner said.

"I am on Route 190, going north. I estimate I am three miles from the web."

"Any lightning yet?"

"No. But the rain has just started here. First drops on the windshield."

"Okay. Hang on."

He went back to Sarah's channel. There was still static, but it was fading.

"Sarah! Are you there? Sarah! Sarah!"

Kenner heard a cough, a distant cough.

"Sarah!"

A click. A bang. Someone fumbling with the radio. A cough. "This is Peter. Evans."

"What's happening there?"

"—dead."

"What?"

"She's dead. Sarah's dead. She got hit with a brick, and she fell and then there was a lightning strike that hit her full on the body and she's dead. I'm right here beside her. She's dead, oh shit, she's dead . . ."

"Try mouth-to-mouth."

"I'm telling you, she's dead."

"Peter. *Mouth-to-mouth.*"

"Oh God . . . She's *blue* . . ."

"That means she's alive, Peter."

"—like a corpse, a—corpse—"

"Peter, listen to me."

But Evans wasn't hearing anything. The idiot had his finger on the radio button. Kenner swore in frustration. And then suddenly a new blast of static. Kenner knew what it meant.

There had been another lightning strike. A bad one.

"Sanjong?"

Now, Kenner heard nothing but static on Sanjong's channel, too. It lasted ten seconds, fifteen seconds. So Sanjong had a strike, too. Only then did Kenner realize what must be causing it.

Sanjong came back, coughing.

"Are you all right?"

"I had a lightning strike. Very near the car. I cannot imagine, so close."

"Sanjong," Kenner said. "I think it's the radios."

"You think?"

"Where'd we get them?"

"I had them FedExed from DC."

"Package delivered to you personally?"

"No. To the motel. The owner gave it to me when I checked in . . . But the box was sealed . . ."

"Throw your radio away," Kenner said.

"There's no cellular net, we won't be in communic—"

Nothing more. Just a blast of static.

"Peter."

There was no answer. Only silence on the radio. Not even static now.

"Peter. Answer me. Peter. Are you there?"

Nothing. Dead.

Kenner waited a few moments. There was no answer from Evans.

The first drops of rain splashed on Kenner's windshield. He rolled down his window, and threw his radio away. It bounced on the pavement, and went into the grass on the other side of the road.

Kenner had gone another hundred yards down the road when a bolt of lightning crashed down behind him on the opposite side of the road.

It was the radios, all right.

Somebody had gotten to the radios. In DC? Or in Arizona? It was hard to know for sure, and at this point it didn't matter. Their carefully coordinated plan was now impossible to carry out. The situation was suddenly very dangerous. They had planned to hit all three rocket arrays at the same time. That would not happen now. Of course Kenner could still hit his array. If Sanjong was still alive, he might get to the second array, but their attack would not be coordinated. If one of them were later than the other, the second rocket team would have been informed by radio, and would be waiting with guns ready. Kenner had no doubt about that.

And Sarah and Evans were either dead or unable to function. Their car was broken down. Certainly they would never make it to the third array.

So. Just one rocket array taken out. Maybe two.

Would that be enough?

Maybe, he thought.

Kenner looked at the road ahead, a pale strip under dark skies. He did not think about whether his friends were alive or not. Perhaps all three were dead. But if Kenner did not stop the storm, there would be hundreds dead. Children, families. Paper plates in the mud, while the searchers dug out the bodies.

Somehow he had to stop it.

He drove forward, into the storm.

MCKINLEY
MONDAY, OCTOBER 11
11:29 A.M.

"Mommy! Mommy! Brad hit me! Mommy! Make him stop!"

"All right, kids . . ."

"Bradley? How many times do I have to tell you? Leave your sister alone!"

Standing to one side of McKinley Park, Trooper Miguel Rodriguez of the Arizona Highway Patrol stood by his car and watched the picnic in progress. It was now eleven-thirty in the morning, and the kids were getting hungry. They were starting to fight. All around the park, barbecues were going, the smoke rising into an ever-darkening sky. Some of the parents looked upward with concern, but nobody was leaving the park. And the rain hadn't started here, even though they had heard the crack of lightning and the rumble of thunder a few miles to the north.

Rodriguez glanced at the bullhorn resting on the seat of his car. For the last half hour, he had waited impatiently for the radio call from Agent Kenner, telling him to clear the park.

But the call hadn't yet come.

And Agent Kenner had given him explicit instructions. Do not clear McKinley Park before he was given the word.

Trooper Rodriguez didn't understand why it was necessary to wait, but Kenner had been insistent. He said it was a matter of national security. Rodriguez didn't understand that either. How was a damn picnic in a park a matter of national security?

But he knew an order when he heard one. So Rodriguez waited, impatient and uneasy, and watched the sky. Even when he heard the weather service announce a flash flood advisory for the eastern counties from Kayenta to Two Guns and Camp Payson—an area that included McKinley—Rodriguez still waited.

He could not know that the radio call he was waiting for would never come.

AURORAVILLE
MONDAY, OCTOBER 11
11:40 A.M.

In retrospect, what saved Peter Evans was the slight tingling he had felt, holding the radio in his sweating palm. In the minutes before, Evans had realized that something was causing the lightning to follow them wherever they went. He didn't know any science, but assumed it must be something metallic or electronic. Talking to Kenner, he had felt the faint electric tingle from the handset—and on an impulse he had flung it across the room. It landed against a large iron viselike contraption that looked like a bear trap.

The lightning crashed down a moment later, glaring white and roaring, and Evans threw himself flat, across Sarah's dead body. Lying there, dizzy with fear, his ears ringing from the blast, he thought for a moment that he felt some movement from her body beneath him.

He got up quickly and began to cough. The room was full of smoke. The opposite wall was on fire, the flames still small, but already licking up the wall. He looked back at Sarah, blue and cold. There was no question in his mind that she was dead. He must have imagined her movement, but—

He pinched her nose and began to give her mouth-to-mouth. Her lips were cold. It frightened him. He was sure she was dead. He saw hot embers and ash floating in the smoky air. He would have to leave before the entire building came down around him. He was losing his count, blowing into her lungs.

There was no point anyway. He heard the flames crackling around him. He looked up and saw that the ceiling timbers were starting to burn.

He felt panic. He jumped to his feet, ran to the door, and threw it open and went outside.

He was stunned to feel hard rain coming down—pelting him, soaking him instantly. It shocked him to his senses. He looked back and saw Sarah lying on the floor. He couldn't leave her.

He ran back, grabbed both her arms, and dragged her out of the house. Her inert body was surprisingly heavy. Her head sagged back, eyes closed, her mouth hanging open. She was dead, all right.

Out in the rain once more, he dropped her in the yellow grass, got down on his knees, and gave her more mouth-to-mouth. He was not sure how long he kept up his steady rhythm. One minute, two minutes. Maybe five. It was clearly pointless, but he continued long past any reason, because in a strange way the rhythm relieved his own sense of panic, it gave him something to concentrate on. He was out there in the middle of a pelting downpour with a ghost town in flames around him anyway, and—

Sarah retched. Her body rose up suddenly, and he released her in astonishment. She had a spasm of dry heaves, and then fell into a fit of coughing.

"Sarah . . ."

She groaned. She rolled over. He grabbed her in his arms, and held her. She was breathing. But her eyes fluttered wildly. She didn't seem to be conscious.

"Sarah, come on . . ."

She was coughing, her body shaking. He wondered if she was choking to death.

"Sarah . . ."

She shook her head, as if to clear it. She opened her eyes and stared at him. "Oh man," she said. "Do I have a *headache*."

He thought he was going to cry.

• • •

Sanjong glanced at his watch. The rain was coming down harder now, the wipers flicking back and forth. It was very dark, and he had turned on his headlights.

He had thrown his radio away many minutes before, and the lightning had stopped around his car. But it was continuing elsewhere—he heard the rumble of distant thunder. Checking the GPS, he realized he was only a few hundred yards from the spiderweb he was meant to disrupt.

He scanned the road ahead, looking for the turnoff. That was when he saw the first cluster of rockets firing skyward, like black birds streaking straight up into the dark and roiling clouds.

And in a moment, a cluster of lightning bolts came blasting downward, carried on the wires.

Ten miles to the north, Kenner saw the rocket array fire upward from the third spiderweb. He guessed there were only about fifty rockets in that array, which meant there were another hundred still on the ground.

He came to the side road, turned right, and came instantly into a clearing. There was a large eighteen-wheeler parked to one side. There were two men in yellow rain slickers standing beside the cab. One of them held a box in his hands—the firing device.

Kenner didn't hesitate. He spun the wheel of the SUV and drove right for the cab. The men were stunned for a moment, and at the last moment jumped aside just as Kenner scraped along the side of the cab, screeching metal, and then turned into the rocket field itself.

In his rearview mirror he saw the men scrambling up, but by now he was within the spiderweb array, driving along the line of wires, trying to crush the launch tubes under his wheels. As he hit them he could hear: *Thunk! Thunk! Thunk!* He hoped that would disrupt the firing pattern, but he was wrong.

Directly ahead, he saw another fifty rockets spout flames, and rush upward into the sky.

• • •

Sanjong was inside the second clearing. He saw a wooden cabin off to the right, and a large truck parked beside it. There were lights in the cabin, and he saw shapes moving in the windows. There were men in there. Wires came out from the front door of the cabin and disappeared in the grass.

He drove straight for the cabin, and he pushed the cruise control on the steering wheel.

From the front door he saw one man come out, cradling a machine gun. Flame spurted from the barrel and Sanjong's windshield shattered. He threw open his door and jumped out of the SUV, holding his rifle away from his body, then landing and rolling in the grass.

He looked up just in time to see the SUV smash into the cabin. There was a lot of smoke and shouting. Sanjong was only about twenty yards away. He waited. After a moment, the man with the machine gun came running around to the side of the SUV, to look for the driver. He was shouting excitedly.

Sanjong fired once. The man fell backward.

He waited. A second man came out, yelling in the rain. He saw the fallen man, and jumped back, huddling behind the front bumper of the SUV. He leaned forward and called to the fallen man.

Sanjong shot at him. The man disappeared, but Sanjong was not certain he had hit him.

He had to change position now. The rain had matted down the grass, so there was not as much cover as he would have liked. He rolled quickly, moving laterally about ten yards, and then crawled forward cautiously, trying to get a view into the cabin. But the car had smashed in the front door, and the lights inside were now out. He was sure there were more men in the cabin but he did not see anyone now. The shouting had stopped. There was just the rumble of thunder and the patter of rain.

He strained, listening. He heard the crackle of radios. And voices.

There were still men in the cabin.

He waited in the grass.

. . .

Rain dripped in Evans's eyes as he spun the wrench, tightening the lug nuts on the front wheel of the SUV. The spare tire was now securely in place. He wiped his eyes, and then briefly tightened each lug nut in turn. Just to be sure. It was a rough road going back to the main highway, and now with this rain it would be muddy. He didn't want the wheel coming loose.

Sarah was waiting for him in the passenger seat. He had half-dragged, half-carried her back to the vehicle. She was still dazed, out of it, so he was surprised to hear her shouting something over the sound of the rain.

Evans looked up.

He saw headlights, in the distance. On the far side of the clearing.

He squinted.

It was the blue pickup truck.

"Peter!"

He dropped the lug wrench and ran for the driver's side. Sarah had already started the engine. He got behind the wheel and put the SUV in gear. The blue truck was gaining on them, coming across the clearing.

"Let's go," Sarah said.

Evans stepped on the gas, turned, and drove into the forest—heading back the way they had come. Behind them, the burning building had been put out by the rain. It was now a smoldering wreck, hissing clouds of steam.

The blue pickup drove past the building without a pause. And came down the road after them.

Kenner turned, and came back toward the eighteen-wheeler. The men were standing there, holding the firing box. One had a pistol out, and began firing at Kenner. Kenner accelerated hard, driving straight at them. He hit the man with the pistol. His body was thrown into the air, over the top of the SUV. The second man had somehow gotten away. Kenner spun the wheel.

As he came back he saw the man he had hit staggering to his feet in the grass. The other man was nowhere to be seen. The staggering man raised his gun just as Kenner hit him again. He went down, and the SUV bounced over his body. Kenner was looking for the other man—the man with the firing box.

He didn't see him anywhere.

He spun the wheel. There was only one place the man could have gone.

Kenner drove straight for the truck.

Sanjong was waiting in the grass when he heard the sound of a truck engine. His view was blocked by his own crashed SUV. The truck was behind the SUV. He heard someone put it into gear, backing up.

Sanjong got to his feet and began to run. A bullet whined past him. He dropped to the ground again.

They had left someone in the house.

He stayed low in the grass, and crawled forward, heading for the truck. Bullets snapped in the grass all around him. Somehow they had his position, even in the grass. That meant . . .

He twisted, turning to face the house. He wiped the rain out of his eyes and looked through the sights of his rifle.

The guy was on the roof of the cabin. Barely visible, except when he rose up to fire.

Sanjong fired just below the roofline. He knew the bullet would pass right through the wood. He didn't see the man again. But the man's rifle slid down the roof as Sanjong watched.

He got to his feet and ran toward the truck, but it was already driving away, heading out from the clearing, a pair of red taillights in the rain, disappearing onto the main road.

Kenner was out of his SUV, and on the ground. He could see the last guy, a silhouette under the big eighteen-wheeler.

"Don't shoot me, don't shoot me!" the guy was yelling.

"Come out slowly, with your hands empty," Kenner shouted. "I want to see your hands."

"Just don't shoot . . ."

"Come out. Real slow and—"

A sudden burst of machine gun fire. The wet grass around him snapped.

Kenner pressed his face into the wet earth, and waited.

"Go faster!" Sarah said, looking over her shoulder.

Their SUV bounced in the mud, headlights jumping wildly.

"I don't think I can . . ." Evans said.

"They're gaining!" she said. "You have to go faster!"

They were almost out of the forest. Evans could see the highway just a few dozen yards ahead. He remembered that the last section of the dirt track was less eroded, and he accelerated, heading there.

And came out onto the highway, going south.

"What are you doing?" Sarah said. "We have to go to the rocket field."

"It's too late now," he said. "We're going back to the park."

"But we promised Kenner—"

"It's too late," he said. "Look at the storm. It's already full blown. We have to get back to help those families in the park."

He turned the windshield wipers on full force, and raced down the road in the storm.

Behind them, the pickup truck turned and followed them.

Trooper Miguel Rodriguez had been watching the waterfall. An hour ago, it had been a clear mist, coming over the cliff's edge. Now it was tinged with brown, and it had more volume. The river, too, was starting to rise. It was flowing faster, and beginning to turn a muddy brown.

But it was still not raining at the park. The air had turned distinctly humid, and there had been scattered raindrops for a few minutes, but then the rain had stopped. A few families had abandoned their barbecues. A half-dozen more were packing up their cars in anticipation of the coming storm. But most had chosen to ignore it. The school principal was walking among the picnickers, telling people the weather would pass, urging everyone to stay.

Rodriguez was edgy. He tugged at his uniform collar, uncomfortable in the dampness. He paced back and forth beside his open car door. He heard the police radio announce flash flood warnings for Clayton County, which was where McKinley Park was located. He didn't want to wait any longer, but still he hesitated.

He couldn't understand why Kenner hadn't called him. The park was located in a canyon, and there was every sign of a potential flash flood. Rodriguez had lived in northern Arizona his whole life. He knew he should clear the park now.

Why hadn't Kenner called?

He drummed his fingers on the door of the car.

He decided to give it five more minutes.

Five minutes. No more.

What worried him most at the moment was the waterfall. The brown tinge had put people off, and most of the crowd had moved away. But a few teenagers were still playing in the pool at the base of the fall. Rodriguez knew that rocks could come over the cliff any minute now. Even small rocks would have enough force to kill a person at the bottom.

Rodriguez was thinking about clearing the waterfall area when he noticed something strange. Up at the top of the cliff, where the water came over the lip, he saw a van with an antenna. It looked like a TV station van. There was no lettering on the side, but there was a logo of some kind. Still he couldn't make it out from this distance. He saw a cameraman get out of the van and take a position by the waterfall, crouching down with a camera mounted on his shoulder and looking down into the park. A woman in a skirt and blouse stood by his side, pointing in this direction and that. Apparently telling him where to film, because he was turning the camera where she pointed.

It was definitely a news crew.

He thought: *A news crew for a school picnic?*

Rodriguez squinted, trying to identify the van's logo. It was yellow and blue, sort of swirly interlocking circles. He didn't recognize it as one of the local stations. But there was something distinctly creepy about this crew, coming here right as the storm was descending on the park. He decided he'd better walk over and have a talk with them.

Kenner didn't want to kill the guy now huddled beneath the semi. No member of ELF had ever been captured, and this one seemed a likely candidate. Kenner could tell from the sound of the guy's voice that he was scared. And he sounded young, maybe in his twenties. Probably he was shaken by the death of his friend. Certainly he couldn't handle a machine gun very well.

Now this guy was afraid he was going to die, too. Maybe he was having second thoughts about his cause.

"Come out now," Kenner yelled to him. "Come out, and everything will be all right."

"Fuck you," the guy said. "Who the fuck are you, anyway? What is your fucking problem? Don't you get it, man? We're trying to save the planet."

"You're breaking the law," Kenner said.

"The *law*," the guy said contemptuously. "The law's owned by the corporations that pollute the environment and destroy human life."

"The only one killing people is you," Kenner said. Thunder was rumbling and lightning flickered dimly behind the inky clouds. It was absurd to be having this conversation in the middle of a storm.

But it was worth it to get the guy alive.

"Hey, I'm not killing anyone," the guy said. "Not even you."

"You're killing little kids," Kenner said, "in the park. You're killing families on a picnic."

"Casualties are inevitable in accomplishing social change. History tells us that."

Kenner wasn't sure whether the guy believed what he was saying, had been fed it at college, or was just distracted by fear. Then again, maybe it was meant to be a distraction . . .

He looked to his right, beneath his own vehicle. And he saw a pair of feet moving around the SUV and heading toward him.

Ah hell, he thought. It was disappointing. He aimed carefully and shot once, hitting the man behind the SUV in the ankle. The guy screamed in pain and went down on his back. Kenner could see him under the car. He wasn't young, maybe forty or forty-five. Bearded. He carried a machine gun, and he was rolling over to shoot—

Kenner fired twice. The man's head jerked back. He dropped the machine gun and did not move, his body sprawled awkwardly in the grass.

The man under the semi began to fire his own machine gun. The bullets were flying wildly. Kenner heard several *thunk* into his SUV. Kenner lay in the grass, head down.

When the shooting stopped, he yelled, "Last chance!"

"Fuck you!"

Kenner waited. There was a long pause. He listened to the sound of the rain. It was coming down very hard, now.

He waited.

The guy yelled, "Did you hear me, you fucking asshole?"

"I heard you," Kenner said, and shot once.

It was a real desert downpour, Evans thought, gripping the steering wheel. The rain was coming down in dense sheets. Even with the windshield wipers going as fast as they could, he found it almost impossible to see the road ahead. He had dropped his speed to fifty, then forty. Now he was down to thirty. The pickup truck behind them had slowed, too. There was no real choice.

He passed one or two other cars, but they were all pulled over to the side of the road. It was the sensible thing to do.

The pavement was awash in water, and whenever the pavement dipped a little, it formed a lake, or a rushing rivulet. Sometimes he could not tell how deep the water was, and he didn't want to soak his ignition. He gunned the engine to keep it dry.

He didn't see any road signs. It was almost as dark as night out there, and he had his headlights on, but they seemed to make no difference. He could see only a few yards ahead through the rain.

He looked over at Sarah, but she was just staring forward. Not moving, not speaking. He wondered if she was all right.

Looking in the rearview mirror, he could sometimes see the lights of the pickup truck following him, and sometimes not. There was that much rain.

"I think we're almost to the park," he said. "But I can't be sure."

The interior of the windshield was starting to fog up. He rubbed it with the back of his arm and his elbow, making a squeaking sound on the glass. Now he could see a little better. They were at the top of a gentle hill, heading down toward—

"Oh shit."

"What?" Sarah said.

"Look."

At the bottom of the hill was a fifteen-foot culvert, the road passing over a series of large pipes carrying water from a small stream. Earlier, the stream had been little more than a silvery trickle in a rocky bed. But it had broadened and risen so that it now flowed over the surface of the road, the water moving swiftly.

Evans couldn't tell how deep it was. Probably not very deep.

"Peter," Sarah said. "You've stopped the car."

"I know."

"You can't stop."

"I don't know if I can go through this," he said. "I don't know how deep—"

Six inches of water is enough to carry away a car.

"You've got no choice."

In his rearview mirror, he saw the lights of the pickup truck. He headed down the hill, toward the culvert. He kept his eyes on the mirror, waiting to see what the truck did. It had slowed as well, but it was still following as he drove the SUV down the hill.

"Keep your fingers crossed," Evans said.

"I've got everything crossed."

He entered the water. It was whooshing up on the sides of the car, spraying up as high as the windows, and gurgling under the floorboards. He was terrified that he would lose the ignition, but so far, so good.

He gave a sigh. He was approaching the middle now, and it wasn't that deep. No more than two, two and a half feet. He would make it okay.

"Peter . . ." Sarah pointed ahead.

There was a large eighteen-wheeler coming down the road toward them. Its lights were flaring. It wasn't slowing down at all.

"He's an idiot," Evans said.

Moving slowly in the water, he turned right, moving farther toward his side of the road, to make room.

In response, the truck moved directly into his lane.

It did not slow down.

Then he saw the logo above the cab.

It said in red letters, "A&P."

"Peter, *do something!*"

"Like *what?*"

"*Do something!*"

Several tons of roaring steel were coming right at him. He glanced in the rearview mirror. The blue pickup truck was still behind him, closing in.

They had him front and back.

They were going to drive him off the road.

The semi was in deeper water now, roaring forward. The water plumed high on both sides.

"*Peterrrrr!*"

There wasn't any choice.

He spun the wheel and drove off the road, plunging into the water of the rushing stream.

The SUV nosed down, and water came over the hood, up to the windshield, and for a moment he thought they were going to sink right there. Then the bumper crunched against the rocks of the streambed, and the wheels gained purchase, and the car straightened.

For a thrilling moment he thought he was going to be able to drive the car along the streambed—the river wasn't that deep, not really—but almost at once, the engine died, and he felt the rear end pull loose and spin around.

And they were carried helplessly along in the river.

Evans turned the ignition, trying to start the engine again, but it wasn't working. The SUV moved gently, rocking and bumping against rocks. Occasionally it would stop, and he considered getting out, but then it would begin to float downstream again.

He looked over his shoulder. The road was surprisingly far back. Now that the engine was out, the car was fogging up quickly. He had to rub all the windows, to see out.

Sarah was silent. Gripping the arms of her seat.

The car came to a stop again, against a rock. "Should we get out?" she said.

"I don't think so," he said. He could feel the car shuddering in the moving water.

"I think we should," she said.

The car started to move again. He tried the ignition, but it would not start up. The alternator whirred and sputtered. Then he remembered.

"Sarah," he said. "Open your window."

"What?"

"Open your window."

"Oh." She flicked the switch. "It doesn't work."

Evans tried his own window on the driver's side. It didn't work, either. The electrical systems were shot.

On a chance, he tried the rear windows. The left window opened smoothly.

"Hey! Success."

Sarah said nothing. She was looking forward. The stream was moving faster, the car picking up speed.

He kept rubbing the fogged windows, trying to see, but it was difficult and suddenly the car gave a sharp jolt, and afterward the movement was different. It went swiftly ahead, turning slowly in circles. The wheels no longer touched rock.

"Where are we? What happened?" Together, they rubbed the windshield frantically to get it clean.

"Oh Jesus," Sarah said, when she saw.

They were in the middle of a rushing river. Muddy brown, and moving fast, standing waves of churning water. There were big tree branches and debris moving swiftly along. The car was going faster and faster every second.

And water was coming in through the floor now. Their feet were wet. Evans knew what that meant.

They were sinking.

"I think we should get out, Peter."

"No." He was looking at the standing waves of churning water. There were rapids, big boulders, sinkholes. Maybe if they had helmets and body protection, they might try to go into the current. But without helmets they would die.

The car tilted to the right, then came back up. But he had the feeling that sooner or later it would roll onto its side and sink. And he had the feeling it would sink fast.

He looked out the window and said, "Does this look familiar? What river is this?"

"Who cares?" Sarah yelled.

And then Evans said, "Look!"

• • •

Trooper Rodriguez saw the SUV bouncing and spinning down the river and immediately hit his car siren. He grabbed the bullhorn and turned to the picnickers.

"Folks, please clear the area! We have a flash flood *now*. Everybody move to higher ground, and do it now!"

He hit the siren again.

"Now, folks! Leave your things for later. *Go now!*"

He looked back at the SUV, but it was already almost out of sight, headed down the river toward the McKinley overpass. And right beyond McKinley overpass was the cliff's edge, a ninety-foot drop.

The car and its occupants wouldn't survive it.

And there was nothing they could do about it.

Evans couldn't think, couldn't plan—it was all he could do to hang on. The SUV rolled and turned in the churning water. The vehicle was sinking lower, and the water now sloshing at knee height was freezing cold, and seemed to make the car more unstable, its movements more unpredictable.

At one point he banged heads with Sarah, who grunted, but she was not saying anything either. Then he banged his head on the door post, saw stars briefly.

Ahead, he saw an overpass, a roadway held up with big concrete stanchions. Each stanchion had caught debris floating downriver; the pylons were now wrapped with a tangled mat of tree branches, burned trunks, old boards, and floating junk, so that there was little room to pass by.

"Sarah," he yelled, "unbuckle your seat belt." His own belt was now under the chilly water. He fumbled with it, as the car rolled.

"I can't," she said. "I can't get it."

He bent to help her.

"What are we going to do?'

"We're going to get out," he said.

The car raced forward, then slammed into a mass of branches. It shuddered in the current, but held position. It clanged against an old refrigerator (*a refrigerator?* Evans thought) that bobbed in the water nearby. The pylon loomed above them. The river was so high, the road overpass was only about ten feet above them.

"We have to get out, Sarah," he said.

"My belt is stuck; I can't."

He bent to help her, plunging his hands into the water, fumbling for the belt. He couldn't see it in the mud. He had to do it by feel.

And he felt the car begin to move.

It was going to break free.

Sanjong was driving furiously along the upper road. He saw Peter and Sarah in their SUV, riding the current toward the bridge. He saw them crash against the pylon, and hold precariously there.

The traffic on the bridge was swarming away from the park, passengers panicking, honking horns, confusion. Sanjong drove across the bridge, and jumped out of his car. He began to run across the bridge, toward the car in the water below.

Evans hung on desperately as the SUV rolled and spun in the churning water. The refrigerator clanged against them, again and again. Branches stuck through the shattered windows, the tips quivering like fingers. Sarah's seat belt was jammed, the latch was crumpled or something. Evans's fingers were numb in the cold. He knew that the car wouldn't stay in position very long. He could feel the current pulling at it, dragging it laterally.

"I can't get it open, Sarah," he said.

The water had risen; it was now almost chest high.

"What do we do?" she said. Her eyes were panicky.

For an instant he didn't know, and then he thought *I'm an idiot* and he threw himself bodily across her, plunged his head underwater, and felt for the door post on her side of the car. He dragged a three-foot length of the seat belt away from the post, and brought his head back up, gasping for air.

"Slide out!" he yelled. "Slide out!"

She understood immediately, putting her hands on his shoulder and shoving as she slithered out from the belt. His head went back under the water, but he could feel her getting free. She moved into the backseat, kicking him in the head as she went.

He was back up above the water, gasping.

"Now climb out!" he yelled.

The car was starting to move. The branches creaking. The refrigerator clanging.

Sarah's athleticism stood her in good stead. She slipped through the rear window, and hung onto the car.

"Go for the branches! Climb!" He was afraid the current would take her if she held onto the car. He was scrambling back into the rear seat, then squeezing himself through the window. The car was pulling loose, trembling at first, then distinctly moving, rolling around the debris pile, and he was still half out the window.

"Peter!" Sarah shouted.

He lunged, throwing himself forward into the branches, scratching his face but feeling his hands close around large branches and he pulled his body clear of the car just as the current ripped it away, dragging it under the bridge.

The car was gone.

He saw Sarah climbing up the debris stack, reaching up for the concrete railing of the roadway. He followed her, shivering from cold and fear. In a few moments, he felt a strong hand reach down and pull him up the rest of the way. He looked up and saw Sanjong grinning at him.

"My friend. You are a lucky one."

Evans came over the railing and toppled onto the ground, gasping, exhausted.

Distantly, he heard the sound of a police siren, and a bullhorn barking orders. He became aware of the traffic on the bridge, the honking horns, the panic.

"Come on," Sarah said, helping him up. "Somebody's going to run over you if you stay here."

Trooper Rodriguez was still getting everybody into their cars, but there was pandemonium in the parking lot and a traffic jam on the bridge. The rain was starting to come down hard. That was making people move faster.

Rodriguez cast a worried eye at the waterfall, noting that it was a darker brown, and flowing more heavily than before. He saw then that the TV crew had gone. The van was no longer atop the cliff. That was odd, he thought. You'd think they'd have stayed to film the emergency exit.

Cars were honking on the bridge, where traffic was stalled. He saw a number of people standing there, looking over the other side. Which could only mean that the SUV had gone over the cliff.

Rodriguez slipped behind the wheel to radio for an ambulance. That was when he heard that an ambulance had already been called to Dos Cabezas, fifteen miles to the north. Apparently a group of hunters had gotten into a drunken argument, and there had been some shooting. Two men were dead and a third was injured. Rodriguez shook his head. Damn guys went out with a rifle and a bottle of bourbon each, and then had to sit around drinking because of the rain, and before you knew it, couple of them were dead. Happened every year. Especially around the holidays.

"I don't see why this is necessary," Sarah said, sitting up in bed. She had electrodes stuck to her chest and legs.

"Please don't move," the nurse said. "We're trying to get a record."

They were in a small, screened-off cubicle in the Flagstaff hospital emergency room. Kenner, Evans, and Sanjong had insisted she come there. They were waiting outside. She could hear them talking softly.

"But I'm twenty-eight years old," Sarah said. "I'm not going to have a heart attack."

"The doctor wants to check your conduction pathways."

"My conduction pathways?" Sarah said. "There's nothing wrong with my conduction pathways."

"Ma'am? Please lie down and don't move."

"But this is—"

"And don't talk."

She lay down. She sighed. She glanced at the monitor, which showed squiggly white lines. "This is ridiculous. There's nothing wrong with my heart."

"No, there doesn't seem to be," the nurse said, nodding to the monitor. "You're very lucky."

Sarah sighed. "So, can I get up now?"

"Yes. And don't you worry yourself about those burn marks," the nurse said. "They'll fade over time."

Sarah said, "What burn marks?"

The nurse pointed to her chest. "They're very superficial."

Sarah sat up and looked down her blouse. She saw the white adhesive tags of the electrodes. But she also saw pale brown streaks, jagged marks that ran across her chest and abdomen. Like zigzags or something—

"What is this?" she said.

"It's from the lightning."

She said, "What?"

"You were struck by lightning," the nurse said.

"What are you talking about?"

The doctor came in, an absurdly young man, prematurely balding. He seemed very busy and preoccupied. He said, "Don't worry about those burn marks, they'll fade in no time at all."

"It's from lightning?"

"Pretty common, actually. Do you know where you are?"

"In Flagstaff hospital."

"Do you know what day it is?"

"Monday."

"That's right. Very good. Look at my finger, please." He held his finger up in front of her face, moved it left and right, up and down. "Follow it. That's good. Thank you. You have a headache?"

"I did," she said. "Not anymore. Are you telling me I was struck by lightning?"

"You sure as heck were," he said, bending to hit her knees with a rubber hammer. "But you're not showing any signs of hypoxia."

"Hypoxia . . ."

"Lack of oxygen. We see that when there's a cardiac arrest."

She said, "What are you talking about?"

"It's normal not to remember," the doctor said. "But according to your friends out there, you arrested and one of them resuscitated you. Said it took four or five minutes."

"You mean I was dead?"

"Would have been, if you hadn't gotten CPR."

"*Peter* resuscitated me?" It had to be Peter, she thought.

"I don't know which one." Now he was tapping her elbows with the hammer. "But you're a very lucky young woman. Around here, we get three, four deaths a year from strikes. And sometimes very serious burns. You're just fine."

"Was it the young guy?" she said. "Peter Evans? Him?"

The doctor shrugged. He said, "When was your last tetanus?"

"I don't understand," Evans said. "On the news report it said they were hunters. A hunting accident or an argument of some kind."

"That's right," Kenner said.

"But you're telling me you guys shot them?" Evans looked from Kenner to Sanjong.

"They shot first," Kenner said.

"Jesus," Evans said. "Three deaths?" He bit his lip.

But in truth, he was feeling a contradictory reaction. He would have expected his native caution to take over—a series of killings, possibly murders, he was an accomplice or at the very least a material witness, he could be tied up in court, disgraced, disbarred. . . . That was the path his mind usually followed. That was what his legal training had emphasized.

But at this moment he felt no anxiety at all. Extremists had been discovered and they had been killed. He was neither surprised nor disturbed by the news. On the contrary, he felt quite satisfied to hear it.

He realized then that his experience in the crevasse had changed him—and changed him permanently. Someone had tried to kill him. He could never have imagined such a thing growing up in suburban Cleveland, or in college, or in law school. He could never have imagined such a thing while living his daily life, going to work at his firm in Los Angeles.

And so he could not have predicted the way that he felt changed by it now. He felt as if he had been physically moved—as if someone had picked him up and shifted him ten feet to one side. He was no longer standing in the same place. But he had also been changed internally. He felt a kind of solid impassivity he had not known before. There were unpleasant realities in the world, and previously he had averted his eyes from them, or changed the subject, or made excuses for what had occurred. He had imagined that this was an acceptable strategy in life—in fact, that it was a more humane strategy. He no longer believed that.

If someone tried to kill you, you did not have the option of averting your eyes or changing the subject. You were forced to deal with that person's behavior. The experience was, in the end, a loss of certain illusions.

The world was not how you wanted it to be.

The world was how it was.

There were bad people in the world. They had to be stopped.

"That's right," Kenner was saying, nodding slowly. "Three deaths. Isn't that right, Sanjong?"

"That's right," Sanjong said.

"Screw 'em," Evans said.

Sanjong nodded.

Kenner said nothing.

The jet flew back to Los Angeles at six o'clock. Sarah sat in the front, staring out the window. She listened to the men in the back. Kenner was talking about what would happen next. The dead men were being ID'd. Their guns and trucks and clothes were being traced. And the television film crew had already been found: it was a truck from KBBD, a cable station in Sedona. They'd gotten an anonymous call saying that the highway patrol had been derelict and had allowed a picnic to proceed despite flash flood warnings, and disaster was probable. That was why they had gone to the park.

Apparently it never occurred to anyone to question why they'd got an anonymous call half an hour before a flash flood warning had been issued from the NEXRAD center. The call had been traced, however. It had been placed from a pay phone in Calgary, Canada.

"That's organization," Kenner said. "They knew the phone number of the station in Arizona before they ever started this thing."

"Why Calgary?" Evans said. "Why from there?"

"That seems to be one primary location for this group," Kenner said.

Sarah looked at the clouds. The jet was above the weather. The sun was setting, a golden band in the west. The view was serene. The events of the day seemed to have occurred months before, years before.

She looked down at her chest and saw the faint brownish markings from the lightning. She'd taken an aspirin, but it was still beginning to hurt slightly, to burn. She felt marked. A marked woman.

She no longer listened to what the men were saying, only to the sound of their voices. She noticed that Evans's voice had lost its boyish hesitancy. He was no longer protesting everything Kenner said. He sounded older somehow, more mature, more solid.

After a while, he came up to sit with her. "You mind company?"

"No." She gestured to a seat.

He dropped into it, wincing slightly. He said, "You feel okay?"

"I'm okay. You?"

"A little sore. Well. Very sore. I think I got banged around in the car."

She nodded, and looked out the window for a while. Then she turned back. "When were you going to tell me?" she said.

"Tell you what?"

"That you saved my life. For the second time."

He shrugged. "I thought you knew."

"I didn't."

She felt angry when she said it. She didn't know why it should make her angry, but it did. Maybe because now she felt a sense of obligation, or . . . or . . . she didn't know what. She just felt angry.

"Sorry," he said.

"Thanks," she said.

"Glad to be of service." He smiled, got up, and went to the back of the plane again.

It was odd, she thought. There was something about him. Some surprising quality she hadn't noticed before.

When she looked out the window again, the sun had set. The golden band was turning richer, and darker.

TO LOS ANGELES
MONDAY, OCTOBER 11
6:25 P.M.

In the back of the plane, Evans drank a martini and stared at the monitor mounted on the wall. They had the satellite linkup of the news station in Phoenix. There were three anchors, two men and a woman, at a curved table. The graphic behind their heads read "Killings in Canyon Country" and apparently referred to the deaths of the men in Flagstaff, but Evans had come in too late to hear the news.

"There's other news from McKinley State Park, where a flash flood warning saved the lives of three hundred schoolchildren on a school picnic. Officer Mike Rodriguez told our own Shelly Stone what happened."

There followed a brief interview with the highway patrol officer, who was suitably laconic. Neither Kenner nor his team was mentioned.

Then there was footage of Evans's overturned SUV, smashed at the bottom of the cliff. Rodriguez explained that fortunately no one was in the car when it was carried away by the floodwater.

Evans gulped his martini.

Then the anchors came back onscreen, and one of the men said, "Flood advisories remain in effect, even though it is unseasonable for this time of year."

"Looks like the weather's changing," the anchorwoman said, tossing her hair.

"Yes, Marla, there is no question the weather is changing. And here, with that story, is our own Johnny Rivera."

They cut to a younger man, apparently the weatherman. "Thanks, Terry. Hi, everybody. If you're a longtime resident of the Grand Canyon State, you've probably noticed that our weather is changing, and scientists have confirmed that what's behind it is our old culprit, global warming. Today's flash flood is just one example of the trouble ahead—more extreme weather conditions, like floods and tornadoes and droughts—all as a result of global warming."

Sanjong nudged Evans, and handed him a sheet of paper. It was a printout of a press release from the NERF website. Sanjong pointed to the text: ". . . scientists agree there will be trouble ahead: more extreme weather events, like floods and tornadoes and drought, all as a result of global warming."

Evans said, "This guy's just reading a press release?"

"That's how they do it, these days," Kenner said. "They don't even bother to change a phrase here and there. They just read the copy outright. And of course, what he's saying is not true."

"Then what's causing the increase in extreme weather around the world?" Evans said.

"There is no increase in extreme weather."

"That's been studied?"

"Repeatedly. The studies show no increase in extreme weather events over the past century. Or in the last fifteen years. And the GCMs don't predict more extreme weather. If anything, global warming theory predicts *less* extreme weather."

"So he's just full of shit?" Evans said.

"Right. And so is the press release."

Onscreen, the weatherman was saying, "—is becoming so bad, that the latest news is—get this—glaciers on Greenland are melting away and will soon vanish entirely. Those glaciers are three miles thick, folks. That's a lotta ice. A new study estimates sea levels will rise twenty feet or more. So, sell that beach property now."

Evans said, "What about that one? It was on the news in LA yesterday."

"I wouldn't call it news," Kenner said. "Scientists at Reading ran computer simulations that suggested that Greenland *might* lose its ice pack in the next thousand years."

"Thousand years?" Evans said.

"Might."

Evans pointed to the television. "He didn't say it could happen a thousand years from now."

"Imagine that," Kenner said. "He left that out."

"But you said it isn't news . . ."

"You tell me," Kenner said. "Do you spend much time worrying about what might happen a thousand years from now?"

"No."

"Think anybody should?"

"No."

"There you are."

When he had finished his drink he suddenly felt sleepy. His body ached; however he shifted in his seat, something hurt—his back, his legs, his hips. He was bruised and exhausted. And a little tipsy.

He closed his eyes, thinking of news reports of events a thousand years in the future.

All reported as if it were up-to-the-minute, important life-and-death news.

A thousand years from now.

His eyes were heavy. His head fell to his chest, then jerked up abruptly as the intercom came on.

"Fasten your seat belts," the captain said. "We are landing in Van Nuys."

All he wanted to do was sleep. But when he landed, he checked his cell phone messages and discovered that he had been missed, to put it mildly:

"Mr. Evans, this is Eleanor in Nicholas Drake's office. You left your cell phone. I have it for you. And Mr. Drake would like to speak to you."

"Peter, it's Jennifer Haynes at John Balder's office. We'd like you to come to the office no later than ten o'clock tomorrow please. It's quite important. Call me if for some reason you can't make it. See you then."

"Peter, call me. It's Margo. I'm out of the hospital."

"Mr. Evans, this is Ron Perry at the Beverly Hills police department. You've missed your four o'clock appointment to dictate a statement. I don't want to issue a warrant for your arrest. Call me. You have the number."

"This is Herb Lowenstein. Where the hell are you? We don't hire junior associates to have them disappear day after day. There is work to be done here. Balder's office has been calling. They want you at the Culver City office tomorrow morning by ten A.M. sharp. My advice is, be there, or start looking for another job."

"Mr. Evans, this is Ron Perry from Beverly Hills police. Please return my call ASAP."

"Peter, call me. Margo."

"Peter, want to get together tonight? It's Janis. Call me."

"Mr. Evans, I have Mr. Drake for you, at the NERF office."

"Peter, it's Lisa in Mr. Lowenstein's office. The police have been calling for you. I thought you would want to know."

"Peter, it's Margo. When I call my lawyer I expect to get a call back. Don't be an asshole. Call me."

"This is Ron Perry from the Beverly Hills police department. If I do not hear from you I will have to ask the judge to issue a warrant for your arrest."

"Evans, it's Herb Lowenstein. You really are a dumb shit. The police are going to issue a warrant for your arrest. Deal with it at once. Members of this firm do not get arrested."

Evans sighed, and hung up.

Sarah said, "Trouble?"

"No. But it doesn't look like I will be getting any sleep for a while."

He called the detective, Ron Perry, and was told that Perry was gone for the day, and would be in court in the morning. His cell phone would be off. Evans left a number for him to call back.

He called Drake, but he was gone for the day.

He called Lowenstein, but he was not in the office.

He called Margo, but she did not answer.

He called Jennifer Haynes and said that he would be there tomorrow, at ten o'clock.

"Dress professionally," she said.

"Why?"

"You're going to be on television."

There were two white camera trucks parked outside the offices of the Vanutu litigation team. Evans went inside and found workmen setting up lights and changing fluorescent light bulbs in the ceiling. Four different video crews were walking around, inspecting different angles. But nobody was shooting yet.

The offices themselves, he noticed, had been considerably transformed. The graphs and charts on the walls were now much more complicated and technical looking. There were huge, blowup photographs of the Pacific nation of Vanutu, as seen from the air and from the ground. Several featured the erosion of the beaches, and houses leaning at an angle, ready to slide into the water. There was a school picture from the Vanutu school, beautiful brown-skinned kids with smiling faces. In the center of the room, there was a three-dimensional model of the main island, specially lit for cameras.

Jennifer was wearing a skirt and blouse and heels. She looked startlingly beautiful in a dark, mysterious way. Evans noticed that everyone was better dressed than at his first visit; all the researchers were now in jackets and ties. The jeans and T-shirts were gone. And there seemed to be a lot more researchers.

"So," Evans said, "what is this about?"

"B-roll," Jennifer said. "We're shooting B-roll for the stations to use as background and cutaways. And of course we're making a video press kit as well."

"But you haven't announced the lawsuit yet."

"That happens this afternoon, here outside the warehouse. Press conference at one P.M. You'll be there, of course?"

"Well, I didn't—"

"I know John Balder wants you there. Representing George Morton."

Evans felt uneasy. This could create a political problem for him at the firm. "There are several attorneys more senior than I who handled George's—"

"Drake specifically asked for you."

"He did?"

"Something about your involvement in getting the papers signed to finance this suit."

So that was it, Evans thought. They were putting him on television so he would not be able later to say anything about the gift of ten million dollars to NERF. No doubt they would stick him in the background for the announcement ceremony, maybe make a brief acknowledgment of his presence. Then Drake would say that the ten million was coming, and unless Evans stood up and contradicted him, his silence would be taken as acquiescence. Later, if he developed any qualms, they could say, But you were there, Evans. Why didn't you speak up then?

"I see," Evans said.

"You look worried."

"I am . . ."

"Let me tell you something," she said. "Don't worry about it."

"But you don't even know—"

"Just listen to me. Don't worry about it." She was looking directly into his eyes.

"Okay . . ."

Of course she meant well, but despite her words, Evans was experiencing an unpleasant, sinking feeling. The police were threatening to issue a warrant for his arrest. The firm was complaining about his absences. Now this effort to force him into silence—by putting him on television.

He said, "Why did you want me here so early?"

"We need you to sit in the hot seat again, as part of our test for jury selection."

"I'm sorry, I can't—"

"Yes. You have to. Same thing as before. Want some coffee?"

"Sure."

"You look tired. Let's get you to hair and makeup."

Half an hour later he was back in the deposition room, at the end of the long table. There was again a crew of eager young scientific types looking down at him.

"Today," Jennifer said, "we would like to consider issues of global warming and land use. Are you familiar with this?"

"Only slightly," Evans said.

Jennifer nodded to one of the researchers at the far end. "Raimundo? Will you give him the background?"

The researcher had a heavy accent, but Evans could follow him. "It is well known," he said, "that changes in land use will cause changes in average ground temperature. Cities are hotter than the surrounding countryside—what is called the 'urban heat island' effect. Croplands are warmer than forested lands, and so on."

"Uh-huh," Evans said. Nodding. He hadn't heard about these land use concepts, but it certainly stood to reason.

Raimundo continued, "A high percentage of weather stations that were out in the countryside forty years ago are now surrounded by concrete and skyscrapers and asphalt and so on. Which makes them register warmer."

"I understand," Evans said. He glanced away, through the glass wall. He saw film crews moving around the warehouse, shooting various things. He hoped the crews wouldn't come in. He didn't want to sound stupid in front of them.

"These facts," Raimundo said, "are well known within the field. So researchers take the raw temperature data from stations near cities and reduce them by some amount to compensate for the urban heat island effect."

Evans said, "And how is this reduction calculated?"

"Different ways, depending on who does it. But most algorithms are based on population size. The larger the population, the greater the reduction."

Evans shrugged. "That sounds like the right way to do it."

"Unfortunately," he said, "it probably isn't. Do you know about Vienna? It was studied by Bohm a few years back. Vienna has had no increase in population since 1950, but it has more than doubled its energy use and increased living space substantially. The urban heat island effect has increased, but the calculated reduction is unchanged, because it only looks at population change."[*]

"So the heating from cities is being underestimated?" Evans said.

"It's worse than that," Jennifer said. "It used to be assumed that urban heating was unimportant because the urban heat island effect was only a fraction of total warming. The planet warmed about .3 degrees Celsius in the last thirty years. Cities are typically assumed to have heated by around .1 degree Celsius."

"Yes? So?"

"So those assumptions are wrong. The Chinese report that Shanghai warmed 1 degree Celsius in the last twenty years alone.[†] That's more than the total global warming of the planet in the last hundred years. And Shanghai is not unique. Houston increased .8 degrees Celsius in the last twelve years.[‡] Cities in South Korea are heating

---

[*] R. Bohm, "Urban bias in temperature time series—a case study for the city of Vienna, Austria," *Climatic Change* 38, (1998): 113–1128. Ian G. McKendry, "Applied Climatology," *Progress in Physical Geography* 27, 4 (2003): 597–606. "Population-based adjustments for the UHI in the USA may be underestimating the urban effect."

[†] L. Chen, et al., 2003, "Characteristics of the heat island effect in Shanghai and its possible mechanism," *Advances in Atmospheric Sciences* 20: 991–1001.

[‡] D. R. Streutker, "Satellite-measured growth of the urban heat island of Houston, Texas," *Remote Sensing of Environment* 85 (2003): 282–289. "Between 1987 and 1999, the mean nighttime surface temperature heat island of Houston increased 0.82 ± 0.10 °C."

rapidly.* Manchester, England, is now 8 degrees warmer than the surrounding countryside.† Even small towns are much hotter than the surrounding areas."

Jennifer reached for her charts. "Anyway," she said, "the point is that the graphs you see are not raw data. They have already been adjusted with fudge factors to compensate for urban heating. But probably not enough."

At that moment, the door opened and one of the four video crews came in, their camera light shining. Without hesitation, Jennifer reached for some charts, and brought them up. She whispered, "B-roll is silent, so we need to be active and provide visuals."

She turned toward the camera and said, "Let me show you some examples of weather station data. Here, for instance, is a record of the average temperature for Pasadena since 1930."‡

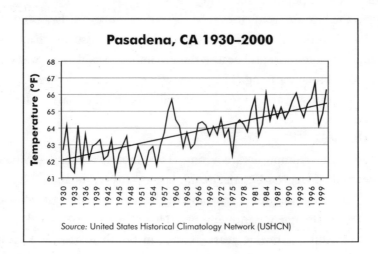

Pasadena, CA 1930–2000

Source: United States Historical Climatology Network (USHCN)

"As you see," Jennifer said, "a dramatic rise in temperature. And here is Berkeley since 1930."

* Y. Choi, H.-S. Jung, K.-Y. Nam, and W.-T. Kwon, "Adjusting urban bias in the regional mean surface temperature series of South Korea, 1968–99," *International Journal of Climatology* 23 (2003): 577–91.
† http://news.bbc.co.uk/1/hi/in_depth/sci_tech/2002/leicester_2002/2253636.stm. The BBC gives no scientific reference for the eight-degree claim.
‡ LA population is 14,531,000; Berkeley is 6,250,000; New York is 19,345,000.

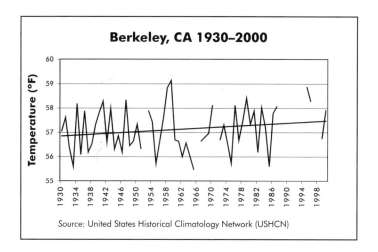

"A surprisingly incomplete record. But we are using raw data, so you can see missing years. And you see a clear warming trend. Indisputable, wouldn't you agree?"

"I would," Evans said, thinking that it wasn't much of a trend—less than a degree.

"Now, here is Death Valley, one of the hottest, driest places on Earth. No urbanization has occurred here. Again, missing years."

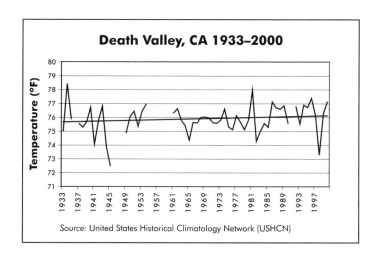

Evans said nothing. It must be an anomaly, he thought. Jennifer put up more graphs:

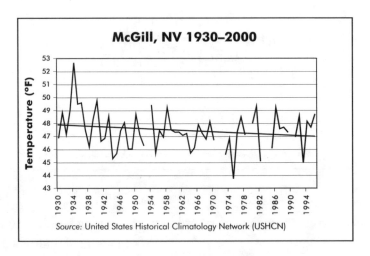

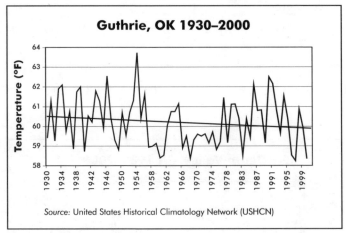

"These are stations from the Nevada desert and the Oklahoma plains," she said. "They show temperatures that are flat, or declining. And not only rural areas. Here is Boulder, Colorado. It's only of interest because NCAR is located there—the National Center for

Atmospheric Research, where so much global warming research is done."

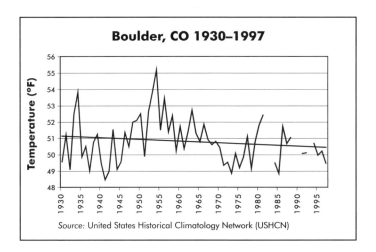

Boulder, CO 1930–1997

Source: United States Historical Climatology Network (USHCN)

"Here are some more small cities. Truman, Missouri, where the buck stops . . ."

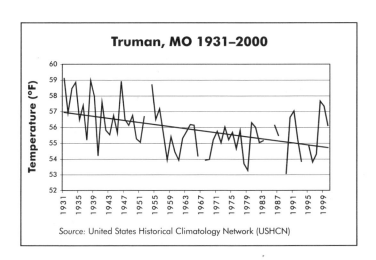

Truman, MO 1931–2000

Source: United States Historical Climatology Network (USHCN)

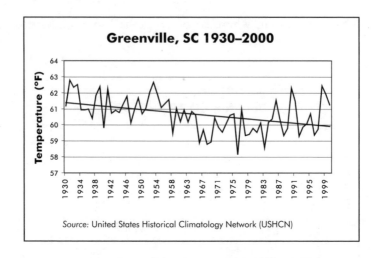

Source: United States Historical Climatology Network (USHCN)

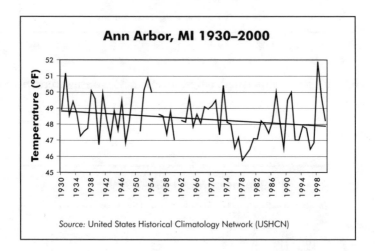

Source: United States Historical Climatology Network (USHCN)

Evans said, "Well, you have to admit, it's not very dramatic."

"I'm not sure what you consider dramatic. Truman has gotten colder by 2.5 degrees, Greenville by 1.5 degrees, Ann Arbor by one degree since 1930. If the globe is warming, these places have been left out."

"Let's look at some bigger places," Evans said, "like Charleston."

"I happen to have Charleston." She thumbed through her graphs.

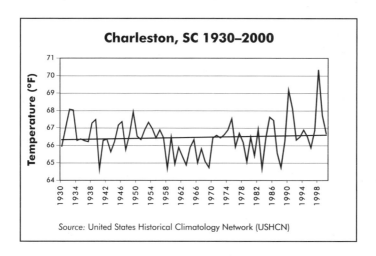

Evans said, "So, a bigger city gets warmer. What about New York?"
"I have several records from New York, city and state."

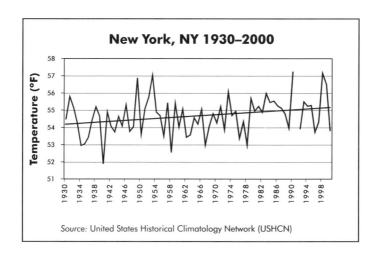

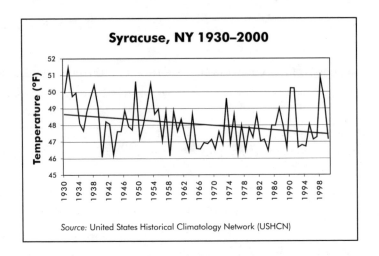

Syracuse, NY 1930–2000

Source: United States Historical Climatology Network (USHCN)

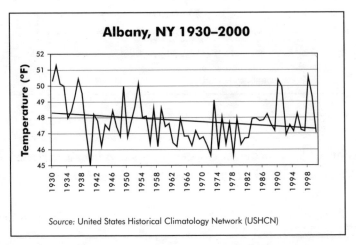

Albany, NY 1930–2000

Source: United States Historical Climatology Network (USHCN)

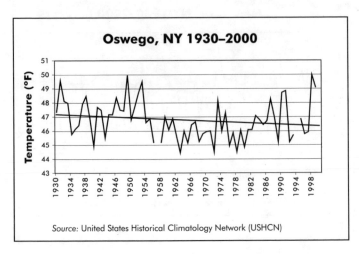

Oswego, NY 1930–2000

Source: United States Historical Climatology Network (USHCN)

"As you see," Jennifer said, "New York City is warmer, but many other parts of the state, from Oswego to Albany, have become colder since 1930."

Evans was acutely aware of the cameras on him. He nodded in what he hoped was a judicious, thoughtful manner and said, "And where does this data come from?"

"From the Historical Climatology Network data set," she said. "It's a government dataset, maintained at Oak Ridge National Laboratories."

"Well," Evans said. "It's quite interesting. However, I'd like to see the data from Europe and Asia. This is, after all, a global phenomenon."

"Certainly," Jennifer said. She, too, was playing to the cameras. "But before we do that, I'd like your reaction to the data so far. As you can see, many places in the United States do not seem to have become warmer since 1930."

"I'm sure you cherry-picked your data," Evans said.

"To some degree. As we can be sure the defense will do."

"But the results do not surprise me," Evans said. "Weather varies locally. It always has and always will." A thought occurred to him. "By the way, why are all these graphs since 1930? Temperature records go much further back than that."

"Your point is well taken," Jennifer said, nodding. "It definitely makes a difference how far back you go. For example . . ."

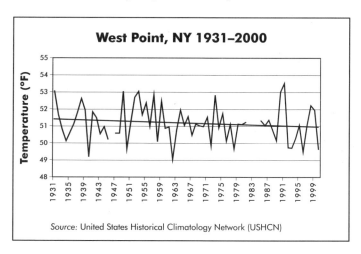

Source: United States Historical Climatology Network (USHCN)

"Here is West Point, New York, from 1931 to 2000. Trending down. And . . ."

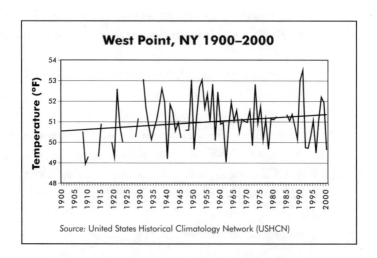

West Point, NY 1900–2000

Source: United States Historical Climatology Network (USHCN)

"Here is West Point from 1900 to 2000. This time the trend is up, not down."

"Ah-ha," Evans said. "So you *were* massaging the data. You picked the interval of years that made you look good!"

"Absolutely," Jennifer said, nodding. "But the trick only works because temperatures in many parts of the US were warmer in the 1930s than they are today."

"It's still a trick."

"Yes, it is. The defense will not miss the opportunity to show the jury numerous examples of this trick from environmental fund-raising literature. Selecting specific years that appear to show things are getting worse."

Evans registered her insult to environmental groups. "In that case," he said, "let's not permit any tricks at all. Use the full and complete temperature record. How far back does it go?"

"At West Point, back to 1826."

"Okay. Then suppose you use that?" Evans felt confident proposing this, because it was well known that a worldwide warming trend had begun at about 1850. Every place in the world had gotten warmer since then, and the graph from West Point would reflect that.

Jennifer seemed to know it too, because she suddenly appeared very hesitant, turning away, thumbing through her stack of graphs, frowning as if she couldn't find it.

"You don't have that particular graph, do you?" Evans said.

"No, no. Believe me, I have it. Yes. Here." And then she pulled it out.

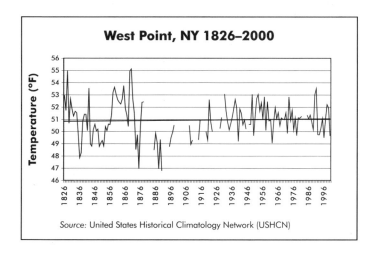

West Point, NY 1826–2000

Source: United States Historical Climatology Network (USHCN)

Evans took one look and saw that she had sandbagged him.

"As you predicted, this graph is quite telling," she said. "For the last one hundred seventy-four years, there has been no change in the average temperature at West Point. It was 51 degrees Fahrenheit in 1826, and it is 51 degrees in 2000."

"But that's just one record," Evans said, recovering quickly. "One of many. One of hundreds. Thousands."

"You're saying that other records will show other trends?"

"I'm sure they will. Especially using the *full* record from 1826."

"And you are correct," she said. "Different records do show different trends."

Evans sat back, satisfied with himself. Hands crossed over his chest.

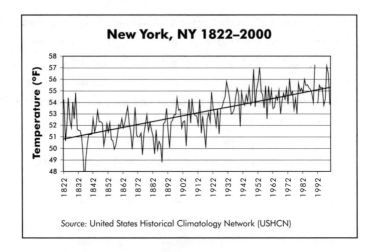

Source: United States Historical Climatology Network (USHCN)

"New York City, a rise of 5 degrees Fahrenheit in a hundred seventy-eight years."

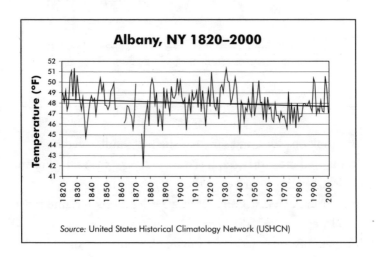

Source: United States Historical Climatology Network (USHCN)

"Albany, a decline of half a degree in a hundred eighty years."

Evans shrugged. "Local variations, as I said before."

"But I wonder," Jennifer said, "how these local variations fit into a theory of *global* warming. As I understand it, global warming is caused by an increase in so-called greenhouse gases, such as carbon dioxide, that trap heat in the Earth's atmosphere and prevent it from escaping into space. Is that your understanding?"

"Yes," Evans said, grateful he did not have to summon a definition on his own.

"So, according to the theory," Jennifer said, "the atmosphere itself gets warmer, just as it would inside a greenhouse?"

"Yes."

"And these greenhouse gases affect the entire planet."

"Yes."

"And we know that carbon dioxide—the gas we all worry about—has increased the same amount everywhere in the world . . ." She pulled out another graph:*

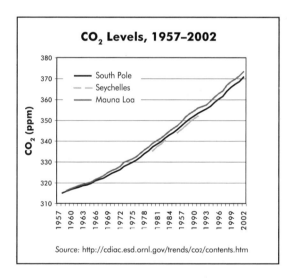

"Yes . . ."

"And its effect is presumably the same everywhere in the world. That's why it's called *global* warming."

---

* South Pole, Mauna Loa: C. D. Keeling, T. P. Whorf, and the Carbon Dioxide Research Group, Scripps Institute of Oceanography (SIO), University of California, La Jolla, CA 92093, U.S.A.; Seychelles: Thomas J. Conway, Pieter Tans, Lee S. Waterman, National Oceanic and Atmospheric Administration, Climate Monitoring and Diagnostics Laboratory, 325 Broadway, Boulder CO 80303. See http://cdiac.esd.ornl.gov/trends/co2/contents.htm.

"Yes . . ."

"But New York and Albany are only a hundred forty miles apart. You can drive between them in three hours. Their carbon dioxide levels are identical. Yet one got a lot warmer and the other got slightly colder. Is that evidence for *global* warming?"

"Weather is local," Evans said. "Some places are warmer or colder than others. And always will be."

"But we are talking about climate, not weather. Climate is weather over a long time period."

"Yes . . ."

"So I would agree with you if both locations got warmer, albeit by different amounts. But here, one got warmer and one got colder. And as we saw, West Point—which is midway between them—remained unchanged."

Evans said, "I think the theory of global warming predicts that some places will get colder."

"Really? Why is that?"

"I'm not sure, but I read it somewhere."

"The Earth's entire atmosphere warms, and as a result some places get colder?"

"I believe so."

"As you think about it now, does that claim make sense to you?"

"No," Evans said, "but you know, climate is a complex system."

"Which means what, to you?"

"It means it's, uh, complicated. It doesn't always behave the way you think it will."

"That's certainly true," Jennifer said. "But going back to New York and Albany. The fact that these two locations are so close, yet their temperature records are so different, could lead a jury to wonder whether we're really measuring something other than a *global* effect. You would agree that in the last hundred eighty-five years, New York has grown to a city of eight million, whereas Albany has grown much less?"

"Yes," Evans said.

"And we know that the urban heat island effect makes cities hotter than the surrounding countryside."

"Yes . . ."

"And this urban heat effect is a local effect, unrelated to global warming?"

"Yes . . ."

"So, tell me: how do you know that the dramatic increase in temperature in New York is caused by global warming, and not just from an excess of concrete and skyscrapers?"

"Well." Evans hesitated. "I don't know the answer to that. But I assume it is known."

"Because if cities like New York become larger and hotter than they were before, they will raise the average global temperature, will they not?"

"I assume they will."

"In which case, as cities expand all around the world, we might see an increase in average ground temperature simply because of urbanization. Without any global atmospheric effect at all."

"I am sure the scientists have thought of that already," Evans said. "I'm sure they can answer that."

"Yes, they can. Their answer is that they have subtracted a factor from the raw data to compensate for the urban heat effect."

"Well, there you are."

"Excuse me? Mr. Evans, you're a lawyer. Surely you are aware of the extraordinary efforts that are made in a lawsuit to be certain the evidence is untainted."

"Yes, but—"

"You don't want anybody to be able to change it."

"Yes . . ."

"But in this case, the evidence is the raw temperature data. And it is tainted by the very scientists who claim global warming is a worldwide crisis."

"Tainted? It's adjusted *downward*."

"But the question the defense will ask is, have they adjusted downward *enough?*"

"I don't know," Evans said, "this is getting very specialized and nitpicky."

"Hardly. It's a core issue. Urbanization versus greenhouse gases as the cause of the increased average surface temperature. And the defense will have a good argument on their side," Jennifer said. "As I said before, several recent studies suggest the reduction for urban bias has, in fact, been too small.* At least one study suggests that half of the observed temperature change comes from land use alone. If that's true, then global warming in the past century is less than three tenths of a degree. Not exactly a crisis."

Evans said nothing. He tried to look intelligent for the cameras.

"Of course," Jennifer continued, "that study can be debated, too. But the point remains: as soon as anybody adjusts the data, they open themselves to the claim that their adjustment was incorrect. That's better ground for the defense. And the larger point the defense will make is that we have allowed the data to be adjusted by the very people who have the most to gain from that adjustment."

"You're saying that climate scientists are unethical?"

"I'm saying it is never a good policy for the fox to guard the hen house. Such procedures are never allowed in medicine, for example, where double-blind experimental designs are required."

"So you're saying climate scientists *are* unethical."

"No, I'm saying that there are good reasons why double-blind procedures are instituted. Look: Every scientist has some idea of how his experiment is going to turn out. Otherwise he wouldn't do the experiment in the first place. He has an expectation. But expectation works in mysterious ways—and totally unconsciously. Do you know any of the studies of scientific bias?"

"No." Evans shook his head.

"Okay. Simple example. A group of genetically identical rats are sent to two different labs for testing. One lab is told that the rats were bred for intelligence and will run a maze faster than normal. The other lab is told that the rats are dumb and will run a maze slowly. Results come

* For a summary, see Ian G. McKendry, 2003, "Applied climatology," *Progress in Physical Geography* 27, 4:597–606. "Recent studies suggest that attempts to remove the 'urban bias' from long-term climate records (and hence identify the magnitude of the enhanced greenhouse effect) may be overly simplistic."

back—faster in one lab, slower in the other. Yet the rats are genetically identical."

"Okay, so they fudged."

"They said they didn't. Anyway, there's much more," she said. "Next example. A group of survey takers are told, Look, we know that pollsters can influence results in subtle ways. We want to avoid that. So you knock on the door, and the minute someone answers you start reading only what is on this card: 'Hello, I am doing a survey, and I am reading from this card in order not to influence you . . . et cetera.' The poll takers say nothing except what is on the card. One group of pollsters is told, this questionnaire will get seventy percent positive answers. They tell another group, you can expect thirty percent positive answers. Identical questionnaires. The results come back—seventy and thirty."

"How?" Evans said.

"It doesn't matter," she said. "All that matters is that hundreds of studies prove again and again that expectations determine outcome. People find what they think they'll find. That's the reason for 'double-blind' experiments. To eliminate bias, the experiment is divided up among different people *who do not know each other.* The people who prepare the experiment do not know the people who conduct the experiment or the people who analyze the results. These groups never communicate in any way. Their spouses and children never meet. The groups are in different universities and preferably in different countries. That's how new drugs are tested. Because that's the only way to prevent bias from creeping in."

"Okay . . ."

"So now we're talking about temperature data. It has to be adjusted in all kinds of ways. Not just for urban heat bias. Lots of other things. Stations move. They upgrade, and the new equipment may read hotter or colder than before. The equipment malfunctions and you have to decide whether to throw out certain data. You deal with lots of judgment calls in putting together the temperature record. And that's where the bias creeps in. Possibly."

"Possibly?"

"You don't know," Jennifer said, "but whenever you have one team doing all the jobs, then you're at risk for bias. If one team makes a model and also tests it and also analyzes the results, those results are at risk. They just are."

"So the temperature data are no good?"

"The temperature data are *suspect*. A decent attorney will tear them apart. To defend them, what we intend to do is—"

Abruptly, the camera crew got up and left the room. Jennifer rested her hand on his arm. "Don't worry about any of that, the footage they shot was without sound. I just wanted it to look like a lively discussion."

"I feel foolish."

"You looked good. That's all that matters for TV."

"No," he said, leaning closer to her. "I mean, when I gave those answers, I wasn't saying what I really think. I'm, uh . . . I'm asking some— I'm changing my mind about a lot of this stuff."

"Really?"

"Yes," he said, speaking quietly. "Those graphs of temperature, for instance. They raise obvious questions about the validity of global warming."

She nodded slowly. Looking at him closely.

He said, "You, too?"

She continued to nod.

They lunched at the same Mexican restaurant as before. It was almost empty, as before; the same Sony film editors laughing at the corner table. They must come here every day, Evans thought.

But somehow everything was different, and not just because his body ached and he was on the verge of falling asleep any moment. Evans felt as if he had become a different person. And their relationship was different, too.

Jennifer ate quietly, not saying much. Evans had the sense she was waiting for him.

After a while, he said, "You know, it would be crazy to imagine that global warming wasn't a real phenomenon."

"Crazy," she said, nodding.

"I mean, the whole world believes it."

"Yes," she said. "The whole world does. But in that war room, we think only about the jury. And the defense will have a field day with the jury."

"You mean, the example you told me?"

"Oh, it's much worse than that. We expect the defense to argue like this: Ladies and gentlemen of the jury, you've all heard the claim that something called 'global warming' is occurring because of an increase in carbon dioxide and other greenhouse gases in the atmosphere. But what you haven't been told is that carbon dioxide has increased by only a tiny amount. They'll show you a graph of increasing carbon dioxide that looks like the slope of Mount Everest. But here's the reality. Carbon dioxide has increased from 316 parts per million to 376 parts per million. *Sixty parts per million* is the total increase. Now, that's such a small change in our entire atmosphere that it is hard to imagine. How can we visualize that?"

Jennifer sat back, swung her hand wide. "Next, they'll bring out a chart showing a football field. And they'll say, Imagine the composition of the Earth's atmosphere as a football field. Most of the atmosphere is nitrogen. So, starting from the goal line, nitrogen takes you all the way to the seventy-eight-yard line. And most of what's left is oxygen. Oxygen takes you to the ninety-nine-yard line. Only one yard to go. But most of what remains is the inert gas argon. Argon brings you within three and a half inches of the goal line. That's pretty much the thickness of the chalk stripe, folks. And how much of that remaining three inches is carbon dioxide? One inch. That's how much CO_2 we have in our atmosphere. One inch in a hundred-yard football field."

She paused dramatically, then continued. "Now, ladies and gentlemen of the jury," she said, "you are told that carbon dioxide has increased in the last fifty years. Do you know how much it has increased, on our football field? It has increased by three-eighths of an inch—less than the thickness of a pencil. It's a lot more carbon dioxide, but it's a minuscule change in our total atmosphere. Yet you are asked to believe that this tiny change has driven the entire planet into a dangerous warming pattern."

Evans said, "But that's easily answered—"

"Wait," she said. "They're not done. First, raise doubts. Then, offer alternative explanations. So, now they take out that temperature chart for New York City that you saw before. A five-degree increase since 1815. And they say, back in 1815 the population of New York was a hundred twenty thousand. Today it's eight million. The city has grown by *six thousand percent.* To say nothing of all those skyscrapers and air-conditioning and concrete. Now, I ask you. Is it reasonable to believe that a city that has grown by six thousand percent is hotter because of a *tiny* increase in little old carbon dioxide around the world? Or is it hotter because it is now much, much bigger?"

She sat back in her chair.

"But it's easy to counter that argument," Evans said. "There are many examples of small things that produce big effects. A trigger represents a small part of a gun, but it's enough to fire it. And anyway, the preponderance of the evidence—"

"Peter," she said, shaking her head. "If you were on the jury and you were asked that question about New York City, what would you conclude? Global warming or too much concrete? What *do* you think, anyway?"

"I think it's probably hotter because it's a big city."

"Right."

"But you still have the sea-level argument."

"Unfortunately," she said, "the sea levels at Vanutu are not significantly elevated. Depending on the database, either they're flat or they've increased by forty millimeters. Half an inch in thirty years. Almost nothing."

"Then you can't possibly win this case," Evans said.

"Exactly," she said. "Although I have to say your trigger argument is a nice one."

"If you can't win," Evans said, "then what is this press conference about?"

. . .

"Thank you all for coming," John Balder said, stepping up to a cluster of microphones outside the offices. Photographers' strobes flashed. "I am John Balder, and standing with me is Nicholas Drake, the president of the National Environmental Resource Fund. Here also is Jennifer Haynes, my lead counsel, and Peter Evans, of the law firm of Hassle and Black. Together we are announcing that we will be filing a lawsuit against the Environmental Protection Agency of the United States on behalf of the island nation of Vanutu, in the Pacific."

Standing in the back, Peter Evans started to bite his lip, then thought better of it. No reason to make a facial expression that might be construed as nervous.

"The impoverished people of Vanutu," Balder said, "stand to become even more impoverished by the greatest environmental threat of our times, global warming, and the danger of abrupt climate changes that will surely follow."

Evans recalled that just a few days before, Drake had called abrupt climate change a possibility on the horizon. Now it had been transformed into a certainty in less than a week.

Balder spoke in vivid terms about how the people of Vanutu were being flooded out of their ancestral homeland, emphasizing the tragedy of young children whose heritage was washing away in raging surf caused by a callous industrial giant to the north.

"It is a matter of justice for the people of Vanutu, and of the future of the entire world now threatened by abrupt weather, that we're announcing this lawsuit today."

Then he opened the floor to questions.

The first one was, "When exactly are you filing this lawsuit?"

"The issue is technically complex," Balder said. "Right now, we have in our offices forty research scientists working on our behalf day and night. When they have finished their labors, we will make our filing for injunctive relief."

"Where will you file?"

"In Los Angeles federal district court."

"What damages are you asking?" another said.

"What is the administration's response?"

"Will the court hear it?"

The questions were coming quickly now, and Balder was in his element. Evans glanced over at Jennifer, standing on the other side of the podium. She tapped her watch. Evans nodded, then looked at his own watch, made a face, and exited the podium. Jennifer was right behind him.

They went inside the warehouse and past the guards.

And Evans stared in amazement.

The lights were turned down. Most of the people Evans had seen earlier were gone. The rooms were being stripped, the furniture stacked up, the documents packed into legal storage boxes. Movers were carrying out stacks of boxes on rolling dollies. Evans said, "What's going on?"

"Our lease is up," Jennifer said.

"So you're moving?"

She shook her head. "No. We're leaving."

"What do you mean?"

"I mean, we're leaving, Peter. Looking for new jobs. This litigation is no longer being actively pursued."

Over a loudspeaker, they heard Balder say, "We fully expect to seek an injunction within the next three months. I have complete confidence in the forty brilliant men and women who are assisting us in this ground-breaking case."

Evans stepped back as movers carried a table past him. It was the same table he had been interviewed at just three hours before. Another mover followed, lugging boxes of video equipment.

"How is this going to work?" Evans said, hearing Balder over the loudspeaker. "I mean, people are going to know what's happening . . ."

"What's happening is perfectly logical," Jennifer said. "We will file a request for a preliminary injunction. Our pleading has to work its way through the system. We expect it will be rejected by the district court for jurisdiction, so we will take it to the Ninth Circuit, and then we expect to go to the Supreme Court. The litigation cannot proceed until the issue of injunction is resolved, which could take several years. Therefore we sensibly put our large research staff on hold and close our expensive offices while we wait with a skeleton legal team in place."

"Is there a skeleton team in place?"

"No. But you asked how it would be handled."

Evans watched as the boxes rolled out the back door. "Nobody ever intended to file this lawsuit, did they?"

"Let's put it this way," she said. "Balder has a remarkable winning record in the courtroom. There's only one way to build a record like that—you dump the losers long before you ever get to trial."

"So he's dumping this one?"

"Yeah. Because I guarantee you, no court is going to grant injunctive relief for excess carbon dioxide production by the American economy." She pointed to the loudspeaker. "Drake got him to emphasize abrupt climate change. That nicely dovetails with Drake's conference, which starts tomorrow."

"Yes, but—"

"Look," she said. "You know as well as I do that the whole purpose of this case was to generate publicity. They've got their press conference. There's no need to pursue it further."

She was asked by movers where to put things. Evans wandered back into the interrogation room and saw the stack of foam core graphs in the corner. He had wanted to see the ones she *hadn't* shown him, so he pulled a few out. They showed foreign weather stations around the world.

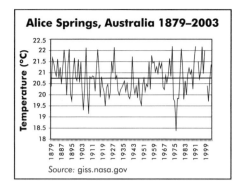

Alice Springs, Australia 1879–2003

Source: giss.nasa.gov

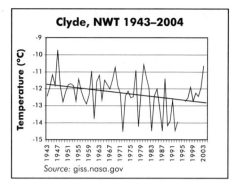

Clyde, NWT 1943–2004

Source: giss.nasa.gov

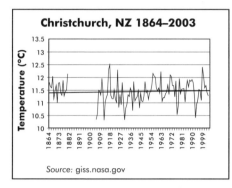

Christchurch, NZ 1864–2003

Source: giss.nasa.gov

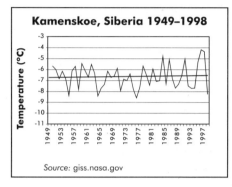

Kamenskoe, Siberia 1949–1998

Source: giss.nasa.gov

Of course, he knew that these particular charts had been chosen to prove the opposition's point. So they showed little or no warming. But still, it troubled him that there should be so many like these, from all around the world.

He saw a stack marked "Europe" and shuffled through them quickly:

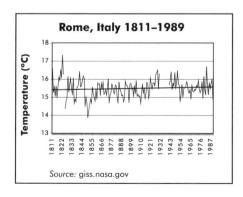

Rome, Italy 1811–1989

Source: giss.nasa.gov

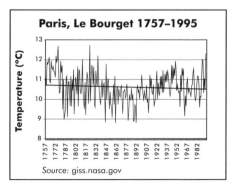

Paris, Le Bourget 1757–1995

Source: giss.nasa.gov

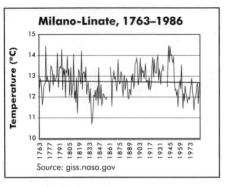

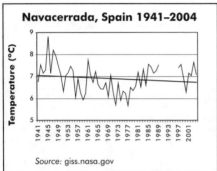

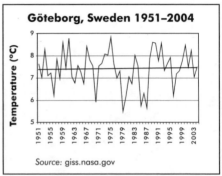

There was another stack marked "Asia." He flipped through it.

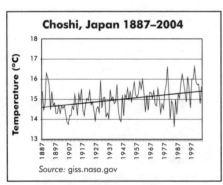

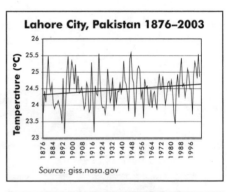

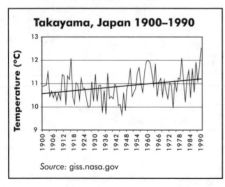

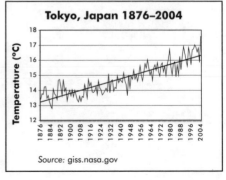

"Peter?"

She was calling him.

Her own office was already packed up. She had only a few boxes of things. He helped her carry them out to her car.

"So," he said, "what're you doing now? Going back to DC and your boyfriend?"

"I don't think so," she said.

"Then what?"

"Actually, I thought I'd go with you."

"With me?"

"You're working with John Kenner, aren't you?"

Evans said, "How did you know that?"

She just smiled.

Heading out the back door, they heard the loudspeaker from the conference. Drake was talking now, thanking the press for coming, urging them to attend his forthcoming conference, and saying that the real danger from global warming was its potential for abrupt climate change.

And then he said, "Excuse me, but I regret to say, I have an extremely sad announcement to make. I have just been handed a note that says the body of my dear friend George Morton has just been found."

The full story was on the news that afternoon. The body of millionaire financier George Morton had washed up on the shore near Pismo Beach. The identification was made from clothing and from a watch on the victim's wrist. The body itself was mutilated, the result of shark attacks, the newscaster said.

The family of the philanthropist had been notified, but no date for the memorial service had been set. There was a statement from Morton's close friend Nicholas Drake, director of NERF. Drake said that Morton had devoted his life to the environmental movement and to the work of organizations like NERF, which had just recently named him their Concerned Citizen of the Year.

"If anyone was concerned about the terrible changes that are taking place around our globe, it was George Morton," Drake said. "Ever since we learned he was missing, we have been hoping against hope that he would be found in good spirits and good health. I am saddened to learn that this is not the case. I mourn the loss of my dear and dedicated friend. The world is poorer without him."

Evans was driving when Lowenstein called him on the car phone. "What're you doing?"

"Coming back from the press conference I was ordered to attend."

"Well, you're going to San Francisco."

"Why?"

"Morton's been found. Somebody has to identify the body."

"What about his daughter?"

"She's in rehab."

"What about his ex-wife? What about—"

"Evans, you're officially assigned. Make your arrangements. The forensic guys don't want to delay the autopsy so they need him ID'd before dinner."

"But—"

"Get your ass up there. I don't know what you're bitching about. Take the guy's plane, for Christ's sake. You've certainly been helping yourself to it lately, from what I hear. Now that he's dead you'd better be more careful. Oh, one more thing. Since you're not family, they'll need two people to ID him."

"Well, I can take Sarah, his secretary—"

"No. Drake wants you to take Ted Bradley."

"Why?"

"How the hell do I know? Bradley wants to go. Drake wants to indulge him, keep him happy. Bradley probably thinks there'll be news cameras there. He is an actor, after all. And he was George's close friend."

"Sort of."

"He was at the banquet table with you."

"But Sarah would be—"

"Evans, what part of this do you not understand? You're going to San Francisco and you are taking Bradley with you. Period."

Evans sighed. "Where is he?"

"He's in Sequoia. You have to stop and get him."

"Sequoia?"

"National Park. It's on the way."

"But—"

"Bradley's already been notified. My secretary will give you the number for the San Francisco morgue. Good-bye, Evans. Don't screw up."

Click.

Jennifer said, "Problem?"

"No. But I have to go to San Francisco."

"I'll come with you," she said. "Who is Sarah?"

"Morton's personal secretary. His old assistant."

"I've seen pictures of her," Jennifer said. "She doesn't look very old."

"Where did you see pictures?"

"In a magazine. They were at a tennis tournament. She's a championship tennis player, something like that?"

"I guess."

"I would have thought that since you spent so much time with Morton, you'd know her well."

"Not really," he said, shrugging. "I mean, we've spent a little time in the last few days."

"Uh-huh." She looked at him, amused. "Peter," she said. "I don't care. She's very pretty. It's only natural."

"No, no," he said, reaching for the phone. "It's nothing like that." Desperate to put an end to this conversation, he dialed the Beverly Hills police and asked for Detective Perry. The detective was not yet back from court. Evans left a message and hung up. He turned to Jennifer. "How does it work if they issue a warrant for your arrest?"

"Criminal," she said. "Not my area. Sorry."

"Me neither."

"Somebody going to arrest you?"

"I hope not."

Then Lisa, Herb Lowenstein's chatty assistant, called. "Hi, Peter. I have the numbers for Mr. Bradley and for the San Francisco morgue. They close at eight. Can you make it by then? Herb wants to know. He's very upset."

"About what?"

"I've never seen him this way. I mean, not for a few weeks."

"What's the matter?"

"I think he's upset about George. Such a shock. And then Drake is giving him fits. He must have called five times today. And I think they were discussing you."

"Me?"

"Yes." Lisa lowered her voice, taking on a conspiratorial tone. "Herb had his door closed while he was talking, but I, uh, I heard a few things."

"Like what?" Evans said.

"Don't say anything."

"I won't."

"I mean I wasn't—I just thought that you would want to know."

"I do."

"Because there's a lot of talk here," she said, dropping her voice even lower, "about whether you have to leave."

"Leave the firm?"

"Be, uh, let go. I thought you would want to know."

"I do. Thanks. Who's talking?"

"Well, Herb. And Don Blandings, and a couple of other senior partners. Bob and Louise. Because for some reason Nick Drake is furious with you. And somebody you are spending time with, a person named Kanner or Connor?"

"I see."

"Mr. Drake is very upset about Mr. Connor."

"Why is that?"

"He says he is a spy. For industry. For *polluters*."

"I see."

"Anyway, the feeling is Mr. Drake is an important client and you've pissed him off. Even so, they would never dare fire you if Morton were alive. But he's not, anymore. And you're gone all the time. And the police are calling here for you, which I have to tell you is *not good*. It makes everybody nervous. And then they—what are you doing with this Mr. Connor, anyway?"

"It's a long story."

"Peter. I told *you*." She sounded sulky. He knew he would have to trade information.

"Okay," he said, trying to sound reluctant. "I'm carrying out an assignment that Morton gave me, before he died."

"Really? What is it?"

"It's a secret, I can't tell you yet."

"George Morton gave you an assignment?"

"In writing," he said. Thinking: That will cool their jets.

"Wow. Really. They don't dare fire you if you're on the business of the firm."

"Lisa, I have to go."

"And if they did, you would have *such* a wrongful termination action."

"Lisa . . ."

"Okay, okay. I know you can't talk. But just . . . good luck!"

He hung up. Jennifer was smiling. "That was very skillfully done," she said.

"Thank you."

But he wasn't smiling back. As far as he was concerned, the world was closing in around him. It didn't feel good. And he was still very, very tired.

He called Sarah to arrange for the plane, but got her voice mail. He called the pilot and was told that he was in the air.

"What do you mean?"

"He's flying, right now."

"Where?"

"I can't tell you that, sir. Would you like his voice mail?"

"No," Evans said. "I need to charter a plane."

"When would you like it?"

"In half an hour. To go to San Francisco, with a stop at whatever the airport is nearest Sequoia. Returning tonight."

"I'll see what I can do."

And then fatigue overcame him. He pulled over to the side of the road and got out of the car.

Jennifer said, "What's the matter?"

"You know the way to Van Nuys?"

"Sure."

"Then you drive."

He dropped into the passenger seat and fastened his seat belt. He watched her pull into traffic, and then closed his eyes and slept.

SEQUOIA
TUESDAY, OCTOBER 12
4:30 P.M.

The forest floor was dark and cool. Shafts of sunlight filtered down from the magnificent trees rising all around them. The air smelled of pine. The ground was soft underfoot.

It was a pleasant spot, with sunlight dappling the forest floor, but even so the television cameras had to turn on their lights to film the third-grade schoolchildren who sat in concentric circles around the famous actor and activist Ted Bradley. Bradley was wearing a black T-shirt that set off his makeup and his dark good looks.

"These glorious trees are your birthright," he said, gesturing all around him. "They have been standing here for centuries. Long before you were born, before your parents or your grandparents or your great-grandparents were born. Some of them, before Columbus came to America! Before the Indians came! Before anything! These trees are the oldest living things on the planet; they are the guardians of the Earth; they are wise; and they have a message for us: *Leave the planet alone*. Don't mess with it, or with us. And we must listen to them."

The kids stared open-mouthed, transfixed. The cameras were trained on Bradley.

"But now these magnificent trees—having survived the threat of fire, the threat of logging, the threat of soil erosion, the threat of acid rain—

now face their greatest threat ever. Global warming. You kids know what global warming is, don't you?"

Hands went up all around the circle. "I know, I know!"

"I'm glad you do," Bradley said, gesturing for the kids to put their hands down. The only person talking today would be Ted Bradley. "But you may not know that global warming is going to cause a very sudden change in our climate. Maybe just a few months or years, and it will suddenly be much hotter or much colder. And there will be hordes of insects and diseases that will take down these wonderful trees."

"What kind of insects?" one kid asked.

"Bad ones," Bradley said. "The ones that eat trees, that worm inside them and chew them up." He wiggled his hands, suggesting the worming in progress.

"It would take an insect a long time to eat a whole tree," a girl offered.

"No, it wouldn't!" Bradley said. "That's the trouble. Because global warming means lots and lots of insects will come—a plague of insects—and they'll eat the trees fast!"

Standing to one side, Jennifer leaned close to Evans. "Do you believe this shit?"

Evans yawned. He had slept on the flight up, and had dozed off again in the ride from the airport to this grove in Sequoia National Park. He felt groggy now, looking at Bradley. Groggy and bored.

By now the kids were fidgeting, and Bradley turned squarely to the cameras. He spoke with the easy authority he had mastered while playing the president for so many years on television. "The threat of abrupt climate change," he said, "is so devastating for mankind, and for all life on this planet, that conferences are being convened all around the world to deal with it. There is a conference in Los Angeles starting tomorrow, where scientists will discuss what we can do to mitigate this terrible threat. But if we do nothing, catastrophe looms. And these mighty, magnificent trees will be a memory, a postcard from the past, a snapshot of man's inhumanity to the natural world. We're responsible for catastrophic climate change. And only we can stop it."

He finished, with a slight turn to favor his good side, and a piercing stare from his baby blues, right into the lens.

"I have to pee-pee," one girl said.

The plane lifted off the runway and rose over the forest.

"Sorry to rush you," Evans said. "But we have to get to the morgue before six."

"No problem, no problem." Bradley smiled indulgently. After his talk, he had taken a few minutes to sign autographs for the kids. The cameras filmed that as well. He turned to Jennifer, giving her his best smile. "And what do you do, Miss Hadley?"

"I'm on the global warming legal team."

"Good, so you're one of us. How's the lawsuit going?"

"Just fine," she said, glancing at Evans.

"I get the feeling you're as brilliant as you are beautiful," Bradley said.

"Actually, no," she said. Evans could see that the actor was annoying her.

"You're being modest. It's very charming."

"I'm being honest," she said, "and telling you I don't like flattery."

"Hardly flattery, in your case," he said.

"And hardly honest, in yours," she replied.

"Believe me when I say that I genuinely admire what you're doing," Bradley said. "I can't wait for you people to stick it to the EPA. We have to keep the pressure on. That's why I did this thing with the kids. It's a sure-fire television segment for abrupt climate change. And I thought it went extremely well, didn't you?"

"Reasonably well, considering."

"Considering?"

"That it was all bullshit," Jennifer said.

Bradley's smile remained fixed, but his eyes narrowed. "I'm not sure what you're referring to," he said.

"I'm referring to all of it, Ted. The whole speech. Sequoias are sentinels and guardians of the planet? They have a message for us?"

"Well, they do—"

"They're *trees*, Ted. Big *trees*. They have about as much of a message for mankind as an eggplant."

"I think you are missing—"

"And they've managed to survive forest fires? Hardly—they're *dependent* on fires, because that's how they reproduce. Redwoods have tough seeds that only burst open in the heat of a fire. Fires are essential for the health of the redwood forest."

"I think," Bradley said rather stiffly, "that you may have missed my point."

"Really? What did I miss?"

"I was trying to convey—perhaps a bit lyrically—the timeless quality of these great primeval forests, and—"

"Timeless? Primeval? Do you know anything about these forests?"

"Yes. I think I do." His voice was tight. He was visibly angry now.

"Look out the window," Jennifer said, pointing to the forest as they flew above it. "How long do you think your primeval forest has looked the way it does now?"

"Obviously, for hundreds of thousands of years—"

"Not true, Ted. Human beings were here for many thousands of years before these forests ever appeared. Did you know that?"

He was clenching his jaw. He did not answer.

"Then let me lay it out for you," she said.

Twenty thousand years ago, the Ice Age glaciers receded from California, gouging out Yosemite Valley and other beauty spots as they left. As the ice walls withdrew, they left behind a gunky, damp plain with lots of lakes fed by the melting glaciers, but no vegetation at all. It was basically wet sand.

After a few thousand years, the land dried as the glaciers continued to move farther north. This region of California became arctic tundra, with tall grasses supporting little animals, like mice and squirrels. Human beings had arrived here by then, hunting the small animals and setting fires. "Okay so far?" Jennifer said. "No primeval forests yet."

"I'm listening," Ted growled. He was clearly trying to control his temper.

She continued. "At first, arctic grasses and shrubs were the only plants that could take hold in the barren glacial soil. But when they died they decomposed, and over thousands of years a layer of topsoil built up. And that initiated a sequence of plant colonization that was basically the same everywhere in post-glacial North America.

"First, lodgepole pine comes in. That's around fourteen thousand years ago. Later it's joined by spruce, hemlock, and alder—trees that are hardy but can't be first. These trees constitute the real 'primary' forest, and they dominated this landscape for the next four thousand years. Then the climate changed. It got much warmer, and all the glaciers in California melted. There were no glaciers at all in California back then. It was warm and dry, there were lots of fires, and the primary forest burned. It was replaced by a plains-type vegetation of oak trees and prairie herbs. And a few Douglas fir trees, but not many, because the climate was too dry for fir trees.

"Then, around six thousand years ago, the climate changed again. It became wetter, and the Douglas fir, hemlock, and cedar moved in and took over the land, creating the great closed-canopy forests that you see now. But someone might refer to these fir trees as a pest plant—an oversized weed—that invaded the landscape, crowding out the native plants that had been there before them. Because these big canopy forests made the ground too dark for other trees to survive. And since there were frequent fires, the closed-canopy forests were able to spread like mad. So they're not timeless, Ted. They're merely the last in line."

Bradley snorted. "They're still six thousand years old, for God's sake."

But Jennifer was relentless. "Not true," she said. "Scientists have shown that the forests continuously changed their composition. Each thousand-year period was different from the one before it. The forests changed constantly, Ted. And then, of course, there were the Indians."

"What about them?"

"The Indians were expert observers of the natural world, so they realized that old-growth forests sucked. Those forests may look impressive, but they're dead landscapes for game. So the Indians set fires, making sure the forests burned down periodically. They made sure there were only islands of old-growth forest in the midst of plains and meadows. The forests that the first Europeans saw were hardly primeval. They were *cultivated*, Ted. And it's not surprising that one hundred fifty years ago, there was less old-growth forest than there is today. The Indians were realists. Today, it's all romantic mythology."*

She sat back in her chair.

"Well, that's a very nice speech," Bradley said. "But those are technical objections. People aren't interested. And it's a good thing, because you're saying that these forests aren't really old and therefore aren't worth preserving. Whereas I say they are reminders of the beauty and power of the natural world and should be preserved at all costs. Especially from the dire threat of global warming."

Jennifer blinked. She said, "I need a drink."

"I'll join you there," Bradley said.

For Evans—who had intermittently been attempting to call Detective Perry while this discussion was taking place—the most disturbing aspect was the implication of constant change. Evans had never really focused on the idea that Indians had lived at the same time as the glaciers. Of course, he knew that this was true. He knew that early Indians had hunted the mammoth and other large mammals to extinction. But he had never considered the possibility that they would also have burned forests and changed the environment to suit their purposes.

But of course they had.

Equally disturbing was the image of so many different forests taking over, one after another. Evans had never wondered what had existed before the redwood forests. He, too, had considered them primeval.

* Alston Chase, *In a Dark Wood*, p. 157ff. See also p. 404ff.

Nor had he ever thought about the landscape that the glaciers would have left behind. Thinking about it now, he realized that it probably looked like the land he had recently seen in Iceland—cold, wet, rocky, and barren. It stood to reason that generations of plants would have to grow there, building up a layer of topsoil.

But in his mind, he had always imagined a sort of animated movie in which the glaciers receded and redwood trees popped up immediately along the receding edge. The glaciers pulled away leaving redwood forest behind.

He realized now how silly that view had been.

And Evans had also noticed, in passing, how frequently Jennifer had spoken of a changing climate. First it was cold and wet, then it was warm and dry and the glaciers melted, then it was wetter again, and the glaciers came back. Changing, and changing again.

Constant change.

After a while, Bradley excused himself and went to the front of the plane to call his agent. Evans said to Jennifer, "How did you know all that stuff?"

"For the reason Bradley himself mentioned. The 'dire threat of global warming.' We had a whole team researching dire threats. Because we wanted to find everything we could to make our case as impressive as possible."

"And?"

She shook her head. "The threat of global warming," she said, "is essentially nonexistent. Even if it were a real phenomenon, it would probably result in a net benefit to most of the world."

The pilot clicked on the intercom, telling them to take their seats because they were on their final approach to San Francisco.

The anteroom was gray, cold, and smelled of disinfectant. The man behind the desk wore a lab coat. He typed at his keyboard. "Morton . . . Morton . . . Yes. George Morton. Okay. And you are . . ."

"Peter Evans. I'm Mr. Morton's attorney," Evans said.

"And I'm Ted Bradley," Ted said. He started to extend his hand, then thought better of it, pulled it back.

"Oh. Hey," the technician said. "I thought you looked familiar. You're the secretary of state."

"Actually, I'm the president."

"Right, right, the president. I knew I'd seen you before. Your wife is a drunk."

"No, actually, the secretary of state's wife is a drunk."

"Oh. I don't get to see the show that often."

"It's off the air now."

"That explains it."

"But it's in syndication in all the major markets."

Evans said, "If we could make the identification now . . ."

"Okay. Sign here, and I'll get you visitor tags."

Jennifer remained in the anteroom. Evans and Bradley walked into the morgue. Bradley looked back. "Who is she anyway?"

"She's an attorney working on the global warming team."

"I think she's a plant for industry. She's obviously some kind of extremist."

"She works right under Balder, Ted."

"Well, I can understand *that*," Bradley said, snickering. "I'd like her working under me, too. But did you listen to her, for God's sake? Old-growth forests 'suck?' That's industry talking." He leaned closer to Evans. "I think you should get rid of her."

"Get rid of her?"

"She's up to no good. Why is she with us now anyway?"

"I don't know. She wanted to come. Why are you with us, Ted?"

"I have a job to do."

The sheet draping the body was spotted with gray stains. The technician lifted it back.

"Oh Jesus," Ted Bradley said, turning quickly away.

Evans forced himself to gaze at the body. Morton had been a large man in life, and now he was even larger, his torso purple gray and bloated. The odor of decay was strong. Indenting the puffy flesh was an inch-wide ring around one wrist. Evans said, "The watch?"

"Yeah, we took it off," the technician said. "Barely got it over the hand. You need to see it?"

"Yes, I do." Evans leaned closer and stiffened his body against the smell. He wanted to look at the hands and the nails. Morton had had a childhood injury to the fourth nail on his right hand, leaving the nail dented, deformed. But one of the hands of this body was missing, and the other was gnawed and mangled. There was no way he could be sure of what he was seeing.

Behind him, Bradley said, "Are you done yet?"

"Not quite."

"Je-sus, man."

The technician said, "So, will the show go back on the air?"

"No, it's been canceled."

"Why? I liked that show."

"They should have consulted you," Bradley said.

Evans was looking at the chest now, trying to recall the pattern of chest hair that Morton had had. He'd seen him often enough in a bathing suit. But the bloating, the stretching of the skin made it difficult. He shook his head. He could not be sure it was Morton.

"Are you done yet?" Bradley said.

"Yes," Evans said.

The drape went back on, and they walked out. The technician said, "Lifeguards in Pismo made the discovery, called the police. The police ID'd him from the clothes."

"He still had clothes on?"

"Uh-huh. One leg of the pants and most of the jacket. Custom made. They called the tailor in New York and he confirmed that they had been made for George Morton. Will you be taking his effects with you?"

"I don't know," Evans said.

"Well, you're his lawyer . . ."

"Yes, I guess I will."

"You have to sign for them."

They went back outside, where Jennifer was waiting. She was talking on her cell phone. She said, "Yes, I understand. Yes. Okay, we can do that." She flipped the phone shut when she saw them. "Finished?"

"Yes."

"And was it . . ."

"Yes," Ted said. "It was George."

Evans said nothing. He went down the hall and signed for the personal effects. The technician brought out a bag and handed it to Evans. Evans fished in it and pulled out the shreds of the tuxedo. There was a small NERF pin on the inside pocket of the jacket. He reached in and came out with the watch, a Rolex Submariner. It was the same watch Morton wore. Evans looked at the back. It was engraved GM 12–31–89. Evans nodded, put it back in the bag.

All these things belonged to George. Just touching them now made him feel inexpressibly sad.

"I guess that does it," he said. "Time to go."

They all walked back to the waiting car. After they got in, Jennifer said, "We have to make another stop."

"Oh?" Evans said.

"Yes. We have to go to the Oakland Municipal Garage."

"Why?"

"The police are waiting for us."

OAKLAND
TUESDAY, OCTOBER 12
7:22 P.M.

It was an enormous concrete structure, adjacent to a vast parking lot on the outskirts of Oakland. It was lit by harsh halogen lights. Behind the cyclone fence, most of the cars in the lot were junkers, but a few Cadillacs and Bentleys were there, too. Their limousine pulled up to the curb.

"Why are we here?" Bradley said. "I don't understand."

A policeman came to the window. "Mr. Evans? Peter Evans?"

"That's me."

"Come this way, please."

They all started to get out of the car. The cop said, "Just Mr. Evans."

Bradley sputtered, "But we are—"

"Sorry, sir. They just want Mr. Evans. You'll have to wait here."

Jennifer smiled at Bradley. "I'll keep you company."

"Great."

Evans got out of the car and followed the policeman through the metal door into the garage itself. The interior space was divided into long bays, where cars were worked on in a row. Most of the bays seemed to be given over to the repair of police cars. Evans smelled the sharp odor of acetylene torches. He sidestepped patches of motor oil and gobs of grease on the floor. He said to the cop accompanying him, "What's this about?"

"They're waiting for you, sir."

They were heading for the rear of the garage. They passed several crushed and blood-covered wrecks. Seats drenched in blood, shattered windows dark red. Some wrecks had pieces of string that stretched out from them in various directions. One wreck was being measured by a pair of technicians in blue lab coats. Another crash was being photographed by a man with a camera on a tripod.

"Is he a policeman?" Evans said.

"Nah. Lawyer. We have to let 'em in."

"So you deal with car wrecks here?"

"When it's appropriate."

They came around the corner and Evans saw Kenner standing with three plainclothes policemen, and two workers in blue lab coats. They were all standing around the crushed body of Morton's Ferrari Spyder, now raised on a hydraulic lift, with bright lights shining up at it.

"Ah, Peter," Kenner said. "Did you make the identification of George?"

"Yes."

"Good man."

Evans came forward to stand beneath the car. Various sections of the underside had been marked with yellow cloth tags. Evans said, "Okay, what's up?"

The plainclothesmen looked at one another. Then one of them began to speak. "We've been examining this Ferrari, Mr. Evans."

"I see that."

"This is the car that Mr. Morton recently bought in Monterey?"

"I believe so."

"When was that purchase made?"

"I don't know exactly." Evans tried to think back. "Not long ago. Last month or so. His assistant, Sarah, told me George had bought it."

"Who bought it?"

"She did."

"What was your involvement?"

"I had none. She merely informed me that George had bought a car."

"You didn't make the purchase or arrange insurance, anything like that?"

"No. All that would have been done by George's accountants."

"You never saw paperwork on the car?"

"No."

"And when did you first see the actual car itself?"

"The night George drove it away from the Mark Hopkins Hotel," Evans said. "The night he died."

"Did you ever see the car prior to that evening?"

"No."

"Did you hire anyone to work on the car?"

"No."

"The car was transported from Monterey to a private garage in Sonoma, where it remained for two weeks, before being taken to San Francisco. Did you arrange the private garage?"

"No."

"The rental was in your name."

Evans shook his head. "I don't know anything about that," he said. "But Morton often put rentals and leases in the name of his accountants or attorneys, if he didn't want the owner or lessee to be publicly known."

"But if he did that, he would inform you?"

"Not necessarily."

"So you didn't know your name was being used?"

"No."

"Who worked on the car, in San Jose?"

"I have no idea."

"Because, Mr. Evans, somebody did rather extensive work on this Ferrari before Morton ever got into it. The frame was weakened at the places you see marked by the yellow tags. Anti-skid—primitive, in a vehicle this old—was disabled, and the discs were cross-loosened on the left front, right rear. Are you following me, here?"

Evans frowned.

"This car was a death trap, Mr. Evans. Someone used it to kill your client. Lethal changes were made in a garage in Sonoma. And your name is on the lease."

• • •

Downstairs in the car, Ted Bradley was grilling Jennifer Haynes. She might be pretty, but everything about her was wrong—her manner, her tough-guy attitude, and most of all her opinions. She had said she was working on the lawsuit, and that her salary was paid by NERF, but Ted didn't think it was possible. For one thing, Ted Bradley was very publicly associated with NERF, and as a hired employee she should have known that, and she should have treated his opinions with respect.

To call the information he had shared with those kids "bullshit"—a talk he didn't have to give, a moment he had offered out of the goodness of his heart and his dedication to the environmental cause—to call that "bullshit" was outrageous. It was confrontational in the extreme. And it showed absolutely no respect. Plus, Ted knew that what he had said was true. Because, as always, NERF had given him a talking points memo listing the various things to be emphasized. And NERF would not have told him to say anything that was untrue. And the talking points said nothing about the fucking Ice Age. Everything Jennifer had said was irrelevant.

Those trees *were* magnificent. They *were* sentinels of the environment, just as the talking points claimed. In fact, he pulled the talking points out of his jacket pocket to be sure.

"I'd like to see that," Jennifer said.

"I bet you would."

"What is your problem?" she said.

See? he thought. That kind of attitude. Aggressive and confrontational.

She said, "You're one of those television stars who thinks everyone wants to touch your dick. Well, guess what, oh Big Swinging One, I don't. I think you're just an actor."

"And I think you're a plant. You're a corporate spy."

"I must not be a very good one," she said, "because you found me out."

"Because you shot your mouth off, that's why."

"It's always been my problem."

All during this conversation, Bradley felt a peculiar tension building in his chest. Women did not argue with Ted Bradley. Sometimes they were hostile for a while, but that was only because they were intimidated by him, his good looks, and his star power. They wanted to screw him, and often he'd let them. But they did not *argue* with him. This one was arguing, and it excited him and angered him in equal proportions. The tension building up inside him was almost unbearable. Her calmness, just sitting there, the direct way she looked into his eyes, the complete lack of intimidation—it was an indifference to his fame that drove him wild. All right, hell, she was beautiful.

He grabbed her face in both hands and kissed her hard on the mouth.

He could tell she liked it. To complete his dominance he stuck his tongue down her throat.

Then there was a blinding flash of pain—in his neck, his head—and he must have lost consciousness for a moment. Because the next thing he knew he was sitting on the floor of the limousine, gasping and watching blood drip all over his shirt. Ted was not sure how he had gotten there. He was not sure why he was bleeding or why his head was throbbing. Then he realized that his tongue was bleeding.

He looked up at her. She crossed her legs coolly, giving him a glimpse up her skirt, but he didn't care. He was resentful. "You bit my tongue!"

"No, asshole, you bit your own tongue."

"You assaulted me!"

She raised an eyebrow.

"You did! You assaulted me!" He looked down. "Jesus, this was a new shirt, too. From Maxfield's."

She stared at him.

"You assaulted me," he repeated.

"So sue me."

"I think I will."

"Better consult your lawyer first."

"Why?"

She nodded her head toward the front of the car. "You're forgetting the driver."

"What about him?"

"He saw it all."

"So what? You encouraged me," he said, hissing. "You were being seductive. Any guy knows the signs."

"Apparently you didn't."

"Hostile ballbreaker?" He turned and took the vodka bottle from the rack. He needed it to rinse out his mouth. He poured himself a glass, and looked back.

She was reading the talking points. She held the paper in her hands. He lunged for it. "That's not yours."

She was quick, holding the paper away from him. She raised her other hand, edge on, like a chopping knife.

"Care to try your luck again, Ted?"

"Fuck you," he said, and took a big gulp of the vodka. His tongue was on fire. What a bitch, he thought. What a goddamned bitch. Well, she'd be looking for a new job tomorrow. He'd see to that. This bimbo lawyer couldn't fuck around with Ted Bradley and get away with it.

Standing beneath the crashed Ferrari, Evans endured another ten minutes of grilling by the plainclothesmen who encircled him. Fundamentally, the story didn't make sense to him.

Evans said, "George was a good driver. If all these changes were made to the car, wouldn't he have noticed something was wrong?"

"Perhaps. But not if he was drinking heavily."

"Well, he was drinking, that's for sure."

"And who got him the drinks, Mr. Evans?"

"George got his own drinks."

"The waiter at the banquet said you were pushing drinks at Morton."

"That's not true. I was trying to limit his drinking."

Abruptly, they changed course. "Who worked on the Ferrari, Mr. Evans?"

"I have no idea."

"We know you rented a private garage outside Sonoma on Route 54.

It was fairly quiet and out of the way. Any person or persons who worked on the car would have been able to come and go as they wished, without being seen. Why would you choose such a garage?"

"I didn't choose it."

"Your name is on the lease."

"How was the lease arranged?"

"By phone."

"Who paid for it?"

"It was paid in cash."

"By whom?"

"Delivered by messenger."

"You have my signature on anything? Fingerprints?"

"No. Just your name."

Evans shrugged. "Then I'm sorry, but I don't know anything about this. It's well known that I'm George Morton's attorney. Anybody could have used my name. If anything was done to this car, it was done without my knowledge."

He was thinking that they should have been asking Sarah about all this, but then, if they were good at their jobs, they'd already have talked to her.

And sure enough, she appeared from around the corner, talking on a cell phone and nodding to Kenner.

That was when Kenner stepped forward. "Okay, gentlemen. Unless you have further questions, I'll take Mr. Evans into custody on my recognizance. I don't believe he is a flight risk. He will be safe enough with me."

The cops grumbled, but in the end they agreed. Kenner handed out his card, and then he headed back toward the entrance, his arm firmly on Evans's shoulder.

Sarah followed some distance behind. The cops stayed with the Ferrari.

As they neared the door, Kenner said, "Sorry about all that. But the police didn't tell you everything. The fact is, they photographed the car from various angles and fed the shots into a computer that simulates crashes. And the computer-generated simulation didn't match the photos of the actual crash."

"I didn't know you could do that."

"Oh yes. Everybody uses computer models these days. They are *de rigueur* for the modern organization. Armed with their computer simulation, the police went back to the wreck itself, where they now decided that it had been monkeyed with. They never imagined this during their previous examinations of the wreck, but now they do. Clear example of using a computer simulation to alter your version of reality. They trusted the simulation and not the data from the ground."

"Uh-huh."

"And of course their simulation was optimized for the most common vehicle types on American roads. The computer had no ability to model the behavior of a forty-year-old, limited-production Italian racing car. They ran the simulation anyway."

Evans said, "But what's all this about a garage in Sonoma?"

Kenner shrugged. "You don't know. Sarah doesn't know. Nobody can even verify if the car was ever there. But the garage was rented—I'd guess by George himself. Though we'll never know for sure."

Back outside, Evans threw open the door to his limo and climbed in. He was astonished to see Ted Bradley covered in blood, all down his chin and shirt front.

"What happened?"

"He slipped," Jennifer said. "And hurt himself."

On the flight back, Sarah Jones was overcome with confused feelings. First of all, she was profoundly distressed by the fact that George Morton's body had been recovered; in some part of her mind, she had been hoping against hope that he would turn up alive. Then there was the question of Peter Evans. Just as she was starting to like him—starting to see a side of him that was not wimpy, but rather tough and resilient in his own bumbling way—just as she was beginning, in fact, to have the first stirrings of feelings toward the man who had saved her life, suddenly there was this new woman, Jennifer somebody, and Peter was obviously taken with her.

And in addition, there was the arrival of Ted Bradley. Sarah had no illusions about Ted; she had seen him in action at innumerable NERF gatherings, and she had even once allowed him to work his charms on her—she was a sucker for actors—but at the last moment decided he reminded her too much of her ex. What was it about actors, anyway? They were so engaging, so personal in their approach, so intense in their feelings. It was hard to realize that they were just self-absorbed people who would do anything to get you to like them.

At least, Ted was.

And how had he been injured? Bitten his own tongue? Sarah had the feeling it had to do with this Jennifer. Undoubtedly, Ted had made a pass at her. The woman was pretty enough in a street-smart kind of way;

dark hair, toughish face, compact body, muscular but skinny. A typical speeded-up New York type—in every way Sarah's opposite.

And Peter Evans was fawning over her.

Fawning.

It was sort of disgusting, but she had to admit she was disappointed personally as well. Just as she had started to like him. She sighed.

As for Bradley, he was talking to Kenner about environmental issues, showing off his extensive knowledge. And Kenner was looking at Bradley the way a python looks at a rat.

"So," Kenner said, "global warming represents a threat to the world?"

"Absolutely," Bradley said. "A threat to the whole world."

"What sort of threat are we talking about?"

"Crop failures, spreading deserts, new diseases, species extinction, all the glaciers melting, Kilimanjaro, sea-level rise, extreme weather, tornadoes, hurricanes, El Niño events—"

"That sounds extremely serious," Kenner said.

"It is," Bradley said. "It really is."

"Are you sure of your facts?"

"Of course."

"You can back your claims with references to the scientific literature?"

"Well, I can't personally, but scientists can."

"Actually, scientific studies do not support your claims. For example, crop failure—if anything, increased carbon dioxide *stimulates* plant growth. There is some evidence that this is happening. And the most recent satellite studies show the Sahara has shrunk since 1980.* As for new diseases—not true. The rate of emergence of new diseases has not changed since 1960."

"But we'll have diseases like malaria coming back to the US and Europe."

---

* Fred Pearce, "Africans go back to the land as plants reclaim the desert," *New Scientist* 175, 21 September 2002, pp. 4–5. "Africa's deserts are in retreat . . . Analysis of satellite images . . . reveals that dunes are retreating right across the Sahel region . . . Vegetation is ousting sand across a swathe of land stretching . . . 6000 kilometers. . . . Analysts say the gradual greening has been happening since the mid 1980s, though has gone largely unnoticed."

"Not according to malaria experts."*

Bradley snorted and folded his hands across his chest.

"Species extinction hasn't been demonstrated either. In the 1970s, Norman Myers predicted a million species would be extinct by the year 2000. Paul Ehrlich predicted that fifty percent of all species would be extinct by the year 2000. But those were just opinions.† Do you know what we call opinion in the absence of evidence? We call it prejudice. Do you know how many species there are on the planet?"

"No."

"Neither does anybody else. Estimates range from three million to one hundred million. Quite a range, wouldn't you say? Nobody really has any idea."‡

"Your point being?"

"It's hard to know how many species are becoming extinct if you don't know how many there are in the first place. How could you tell if you were robbed if you didn't know how much money you had in your wallet to begin with? And fifteen thousand new species are described every year. By the way, do you know what the known rate of species extinction is?"

"No."

"That's because there is no known rate. Do you know how they measure numbers of species and species extinctions? Some poor bastard marks off a hectare or an acre of land and then tries to count all the bugs and animals and plants inside it. Then he comes back in ten years and counts again. But maybe the bugs have moved to an adjacent acre in the meantime. Anyway, can you imagine trying to count all the bugs in an acre of land?"

---

* Paul Reiter, et al., "Global warming and malaria: a call for accuracy," *Lancet*, 4, no. 1 (June 2004). "Many of these much-publicized predictions are ill informed and misleading."
† Discussion in Lomborg, p. 252.
‡ Morjorie L. Reaka-Kudia, et al., *Biodiversity II, Understanding and Protecting our Biological Resources*, Washington: National Academies Press, 1997. "Biologists have come to recognize just how little we know about the organisms with which we share the planet Earth. In particular, attempts to determine how many species there are in total have been surprisingly fruitless." Myers: "We have no way of knowing the actual extinction rate in the tropical forests, let alone an approximate guess." In Lomborg, p. 254.

"It would be difficult."

"To put it mildly. And very inaccurate," Kenner said, "which is the point. Now, about all the glaciers melting—not true. Some are, some aren't."*

"Nearly all of them are."

Kenner smiled thinly. "How many glaciers are we talking about?"

"Dozens."

"How many glaciers are there in the world, Ted?"

"I don't know."

"Guess."

"Maybe, uh, two hundred."

"There are more than that in California.† There are one hundred sixty thousand glaciers in the world, Ted. About sixty-seven thousand have been inventoried, but only a few have been studied with any care. There is mass balance data extending five years or more for only seventy-nine glaciers in the entire world. So, how can you say they're all melting? Nobody knows whether they are or not."‡

"Kilimanjaro is melting."

"Why is that?"

"Global warming."

"Actually, Kilimanjaro has been rapidly melting since the 1800s—long before global warming. The loss of the glacier has been a topic of scholarly concern for over a hundred years. And it has always been something of a mystery because, as you know, Kilimanjaro is an equatorial volcano, so it exists in a warm region. Satellite measurements of that region show no warming trend at the altitude of the Kilimanjaro glacier. So why is it melting?"

---

* Roger J. Braithwaite, "Glacier mass balance, the first 50 years of international monitoring," *Progress in Physical Geography* 26, no. 1 (2002): 76–95. "There is no obvious common global trend of increasing glacier melt in recent years."
† California has 497 glaciers; Raub, et al., 1980; Guyton: 108 glaciers and 401 glacierets, *Glaciers of California*, p. 115.
‡ H. Kieffer, et al., 2000, "New eyes in the sky measure glaciers and ice sheets," *EOS, Transactions, American Geophysical Union* 81: 265, 270–71. See also R. J. Braithwaite and Y. Zhang, "Relationships between interannual variability of glacier mass balance and climate," *Journal of Glaciology* 45 (2000): 456–62.

Sulking: "You tell me."

"Because of deforestation, Ted. The rain forest at the base of the mountain has been cut down, so the air blowing upward is no longer moist. Experts think that if the forest is replanted the glacier will grow again."

"That's bullshit."

"I'll give you the journal references.* Now then—sea-level rise? Was that the next threat you mentioned?"

"Yes."

"Sea level is indeed rising."

"Ah-hah!"

"As it has been for the last six thousand years, ever since the start of the Holocene. Sea level has been rising at the rate of ten to twenty centimeters—that's four to eight inches—every hundred years."[†]

"But it's rising faster now."

"Actually, not."

"Satellites prove it."

"Actually, they don't."[‡]

"Computer models prove it's rising faster."[§]

"Computer models can't *prove* anything, Ted. A prediction can't ever be proof—it hasn't happened yet. And computer models have failed to accurately predict the last ten or fifteen years. But if you want to believe in them anyway, there is no arguing with faith. Now, what was next on

---

* Betsy Mason, "African Ice Under Wraps," *Nature*, 24, November 2003. "Although it's tempting to blame the ice loss on global warming, researchers think that deforestation of the mountain's foothills is the more likely culprit," http://www.nature.com/nsu/031117/031117–8.html.

    Kaser, et al., "Modern glacier retreat on Kilimanjaro as evidence of climate change: Observations and facts," *International Journal of Climatology* 24: (2004): 329–39. "In recent years, Kilimanjaro and its vanishing glaciers have become an 'icon' of global warming . . . [but] processes other than air temperature control the ice recession . . . A drastic drop in atmospheric moisture at the end of the 19th century and the ensuing drier climate conditions are likely forcing glacier retreat."

† See, for example, http://www.csr.utexas.edu/gmsl/main.html. "Over the last century, global sea-level change has typically been estimated from tide gauge measurements by long-term averaging. Most recent estimates of global mean sea-level rise from tide gauge measurements range from 1.7 to 2.4 mm/yr" [that is, 6″ to 9″ every hundred years—MC].

‡ Op. cit. Global mean sea-level rise as measured by satellite is 3.1 mm/yr for the last decade or slightly more than 12″ a century. However, satellites show considerable variation. Thus the northern Pacific has risen, but the southern Pacific has fallen by several millimeters in recent years.

§ Lomborg, pp. 289–90 on inadequacy of IPCC sea-level models.

your list? Extreme weather—again, not true. Numerous studies show there is no increase."*

"Look," Ted said, "you may enjoy putting me down, but the fact is, lots of people think there will be more extreme weather, including more hurricanes and tornadoes and cyclones, in the future."

"Yes, indeed, lots of people think so. But scientific studies do not bear them out.† That's why we *do* science, Ted, to see if our opinions can be verified in the real world, or whether we are just having fantasies."

"All these hurricanes are not fantasies."

Kenner sighed. He flipped open his laptop.

"What are you doing?"

"One moment," Kenner said. "Let me bring it up."

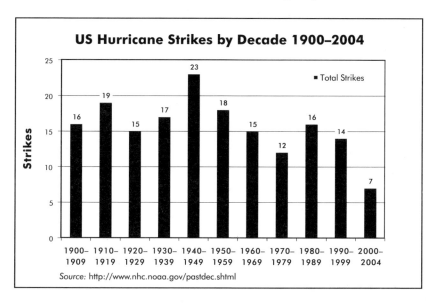

US Hurricane Strikes by Decade 1900–2004

Source: http://www.nhc.noaa.gov/pastdec.shtml

* See Henderson-Sellers, et al., 1997, "Tropical Cyclones and Global Climate Change: a post-IPCC assessment," *Bulletin of the American Meteorological Society* 79:9–38. C. Nicholls Landsea, et al. "Downward Trend in the Frequency of Intense Atlantic Hurricanes during the past five decades," *Geophysical Research Letters* 23:527–30. 1996. According to the United Nations Intergovernmental Panel on Climate Change, "Examination of meteorological data fails to support the perception [of increased frequency and severity of extreme climate events] in the context of a long-term climate change." IPCC 1995, p. 11. "Overall, there is no evidence that extreme weather events, or climate variability, has increased, in a global sense, throughout the twentieth century . . ." IPCC, *Climate Change 1995.* In the 2001 IPCC report, "No long-term trends evident" for tropical and extratropical storms, and no systematic changes in the "frequency of tornadoes, thunder days, or hail." *Executive summary*, p.2. For fuller discussion, see Lomborg, p. 292ff.
† Richard Feynman: "Science is what we have learned about how not to fool ourselves."

"Here is the actual data, Ted," Kenner said. "US hurricane strikes over the last hundred years are clearly not increasing. And similarly, extreme weather is not more frequent globally. The data simply do not agree with you. Now, you also mentioned El Niño events."

"Yes . . ."

"As you know, El Niño is a global weather pattern that begins when ocean temperatures along the west coast of South America remain above normal for several months. Once it's triggered, El Niño lasts about a year and a half, affecting weather around the world. El Niño occurs roughly every four years—twenty-three times in the last century. And it has been occurring for thousands of years. So it long precedes any claim of global warming.* But what threat does El Niño represent to the US, Ted? There was a major El Niño in 1998."

"Floods, crops ruined, like that."

"All that happened. But the net economic effect of the last El Niño was a gain of fifteen billion dollars because of a longer growing season and less use of winter heating oil. That's after deducting $1.5 billion for flooding and excess rain in California. Still a net benefit."

"I'd like to see that study," Bradley said.

"I'll make sure you get it.† Because of course it also suggests that if global warming really does occur, it will probably benefit most nations of the world."

"But not *all*."

"No, Ted. Not all."

"So what exactly is your point?" Bradley said. "You're saying that we don't need to pay any attention to the environment, that we can just leave it alone and let industry pollute and everything will be hunky-dory?"

---

* Lomborg, p. 292.
† Stanley A. Changnon, 1999: "Impacts of 1997–98 El Niño–Generated Weather in the United States," *Bulletin of the American Meteorological Society* 80, no. 9: pp. 1819–28. ("The net economic benefit was surprisingly positive . . . direct losses nationally were about $4 billion and the benefits were approximately $19 billion.")

. . .

For a moment, it looked to Sarah as if Kenner would get angry, but he did not. He said, "If you oppose the death penalty, does it also mean you are in favor of doing nothing at all about crime?"

"No," Ted said.

"You can oppose the death penalty but still favor punishing criminals."

"Yes. Of course."

"Then I can say that global warming is not a threat but still favor environmental controls, can't I?"

"But it doesn't sound like you are saying that."

Kenner sighed.

Sarah was listening to this exchange, thinking Bradley wasn't really hearing what Kenner had to say. As if to prove her thoughts, Bradley continued: "Well? Aren't you saying that the environment needs no protection from us? Isn't that what you are *really* saying?"

Kenner said, "No," in a way that suggested that the conversation was over.

Sarah thought: Ted really is a fool. He has a severely limited understanding of what he is talking about. Ted was an actor with a script, at a loss if the conversation moved away from scripted lines.

She turned away and looked toward the front of the cabin. She saw Peter talking to Jennifer, their heads together. There was a sort of intimacy in their gestures that was instantly recognizable.

She was glad when the pilot announced they were landing in Los Angeles.

Sanjong Thapa was waiting at the airport, looking worried. He and Kenner got immediately into a car and drove off. Sarah went home to her apartment. Bradley climbed into an SUV limo and left with an irritable wave. He was already on his cell phone. Peter Evans drove Jennifer to her car, which was back in Culver City. There was an awkward moment saying good-bye. He wanted to kiss her but sensed some reserve, and didn't. She promised she would call him in the morning.

He drove home, thinking of her. Sarah did not enter his mind.

It was almost midnight when Evans got back to his apartment. He was very tired and was stripping off his shirt when the phone rang. It was Janis, the exercise instructor. "Where have you *been*, you cute thing?"

"Traveling," he said.

"I have called you *every single day*," she said. "Sometimes more. Sometimes every hour."

"Uh-huh. What's up?"

"My boyfriend broke up with me."

"I'm sorry to hear that," Evans said. "Was it very—"

"Can I come over?" she said.

He sighed. "You know, Janis, I'm really tired . . ."

"I need to talk to you. I promise I won't stay, if you don't want me to. I'm only about a block away. Five minutes?"

He sighed again, louder this time. "Janis, tonight is not—"

"Okay, good, see you in five."

Click.

He sighed. He took his shirt off and tossed it in the hamper. She never listened, that was the trouble. He decided that when she got to his apartment, he would just tell her to leave. That's all. Just go.

Or then again, maybe he wouldn't.

Janis was uncomplicated. He was ready for an uncomplicated exchange. He pulled off his shoes and dropped them on the floor. On the other hand, he didn't want Janis around in the morning if Jennifer called. Would Jennifer call? She said she would. Did Jennifer know his home number? He wasn't sure. Maybe not.

He decided to take a shower. He might not hear Janis in the shower, so he unlocked the front door for her and headed for the bathroom. The hallway was dark and he had just a fleeting glimpse of a dark shadow before something hit him on the head, very hard. Evans yelled. The pain was intense, making him gasp, and he fell to his knees. He groaned. Someone hit him again, this time in the ear, and he fell over on his side.

Disoriented, he found himself staring at a pair of feet in dirty socks. He was being dragged into the living room. He was dropped unceremoniously on the floor. There were three men, moving around him. They had dark masks over their faces, like ski masks. One of them stepped on both his arms, pinning him down, flat on his back. Another one sat on his legs and said, "Don't talk. Don't move." A growly menacing voice.

Evans couldn't move anyway. He still felt disoriented. He looked around for the third man. He heard sloshing water. He glimpsed what looked like a plastic baggie.

"Hold him good." The third man spoke in a whisper. He crouched by Evans's shoulder, pulled up the shirtsleeve, exposing the flesh of his arm. He was wheezing softly behind the black mask. In the same whisper, he said, "You know what this is?"

He held up the baggie. The water was cloudy. Evans saw what looked like a fleshy ball, and in a panic he thought, *Oh God, they cut somebody's balls off.* But then he saw the ball moving, undulating. It was brown with white spots, about the size of a golf ball.

"You know?" the man said.

Evans shook his head.

"You will," the man whispered, and unzipped the baggie. He pushed it against the underside of Evans's arm. Evans felt wetness. The man was manipulating the baggie, squeezing the ball. Evans was trying to see, but it was hard to see exactly what was—

The ball moved. It spread, extended what looked like wings. No, not wings. It was a tiny octopus! Tiny! It could not have weighed more than a few ounces. Brownish with white rings. The man was squeezing the baggie, compressing it, pushing the little octopus toward the flesh of Evans's arm.

And then he understood.

Evans moaned and began to struggle, trying to move against his captors, but they had him firmly, and he felt the touch of the octopus, a kind of sticky sensation, like cellophane or Sticky Putty or something. He lifted his head in horror and saw that the man was snapping the baggie with his finger, trying to goad the octopus, which had wrapped itself against the skin of Evans's arm, and in a flash the rings on the octopus changed from white to blue.

The blue ring of death.

"That means he's mad." The third man holding the baggie said, "You won't feel it," but Evans did. It was a bite from the tiny beak, a single sting, almost like the sting of a needle. Evans jerked his arm and the man withdrew the baggie and sealed it again. He whispered, "Hold him good."

He went away a moment, then came back with a kitchen rag. He wiped the underside of Evans's arm, wiped the water off the floor. Still whispering, he said, "You won't feel anything for a few minutes." He walked over to the phone. "Don't try to call anybody," he said, and ripped the phone off the wall, smashing it on the floor.

The men released him. They moved quickly to the door, opened it, and were gone.

. . .

He coughed, and got to his hands and knees. He looked at his underarm; the bite looked like a dimple in the flesh, a small pink spot just at the edge of the hairs of his armpit. Nobody would ever see it.

He did not feel anything except a sort of dull tingling at the spot where the bite had occurred. His mouth was dry, but that was probably from fear. His head hurt. He reached up, felt blood, realized that they had torn open some of his stitches.

Jesus. He tried to get to his feet but his arm gave way, and he fell down again, rolling on the floor. He was still disoriented. He stared into the lights in the ceiling. His apartment had that cottage-cheese kind of ceiling. He hated that ceiling. He wanted to do something about it but it was too expensive. Anyway, he had always thought he would be moving soon. He was still disoriented. He got onto his elbows. His mouth was very dry now. It was the effect of the poison.

Some kind of a toad. No, he thought, that wasn't right. It wasn't a toad. It was a . . .

He couldn't remember.

Octopus.

That's right. It was a little octopus, hardly bigger than a thumbnail. Cute little thing.

The Indians in the Amazon used them for poison for their arrowheads. No, he thought, that was toads. No octopus in the Amazon. Or were there?

He was confused. Becoming more confused. He broke into a cold sweat. Was that part of it, too? He had to get to a phone. He might only have a few minutes of consciousness left.

He crawled to the nearest object, which was an easy chair . . . he'd had it in law school, it was pretty ratty, he had intended to get rid of it when he moved here but he hadn't gotten around to it yet . . . the living room needed a chair right in this spot . . . he'd had it re-covered in fabric his second year in law school . . . pretty dirty now . . . who had time to go shopping? With his mind racing, he pulled himself up until his chin was resting on the seat of the chair. He was gasping for breath, it felt as if he had climbed a mountain. He thought, Why am I here? Why is my chin on the chair? Then he remembered that he was trying to climb up, to sit in it.

Sit in the chair.

He got the elbow of his good arm up onto the seat and began to press himself up. Finally he was able to heave his chest onto the chair, then the rest of his body. His limbs were getting numb, and cold, and heavier by the minute. They were becoming too heavy to move. His whole body was getting heavy. He managed to get himself almost upright in the chair. There was a phone on the table beside him, but his arm was too heavy to reach for it. He tried, but he could not reach out at all now. His fingers moved slightly, but that was all. His body was very cold and very heavy.

He began to lose his balance, slowly at first and then sliding over sideways, until his chest rested on the arm of the chair and his head hung over the side. And there he stayed, unable to move. He could not lift his head. He could not move his arms. He could not even move his eyes. He stared at the fabric of the chair and the carpet on the floor and he thought, *This is the last thing I will see before I die.*

VI

BLUE

How long Peter Evans stared at the carpet he did not know. The arm of the chair pressing against his chest impeded his breathing, but it was becoming more difficult to breathe in any case. Images from his life flashed into consciousness—the basement where he played with his first computer, the blue bicycle that was stolen the same day he got it, the boxed corsage for his senior prom date, standing up in Professor Whitson's con law class, his legs shaking, while old Whitson took him apart—

"Peter? Hel-*lo*? Peter?"

—and terrorized him, they were all terrorized by Whitson, and the dinner that was the final interview for his LA job, where he spilled soup all over his shirt and the partners pretended not to notice, and—

"Peter? *Peter!* What are you doing there? Peter? Get up, Peter."

He felt hands on his shoulders, burning hot hands, and with a grunt he was hauled back into sitting position. "There, that's better." Janis peered at him, her face inches from his. "What's the matter with you? What did you take? Talk to me."

But he could not talk. He could not move at all. She was wearing a leotard top and jeans and sandals. If she moved to one side, she was out of his field of view.

"Peter?" A puzzled tone. "I think something is really wrong. Have you been doing ecstasy? Did you have a stroke? You're too young for a stroke. But it could happen, I guess. Especially with your diet. I told you no more than sixty-five grams of fat a day. If you were a vegetarian you would never have a stroke. Why don't you answer me?"

She touched his jaw, a questioning look on her face. Evans was feeling distinctly lightheaded because he could hardly breathe anymore. It was as if he had a twenty-ton stone on his chest. Even though he was sitting up, the great stone weighed on him.

He thought, *Call the hospital!*

"I don't know what to do, Peter," she said. "I just wanted to talk to you tonight, and now you're like this. I mean, I guess it's a bad time. But it's kind of scary, too. I have to be honest. I wish you would answer me. Can you answer me?"

Call the hospital!

"Maybe you'll hate me for this, but I don't know what you took that makes you this way, so I'm going to call 911 and get an ambulance. I'm really sorry and I don't want to get you into trouble, but this is freaking me out, Peter."

She went out of his field of view but he heard her picking up the phone on the table next to his chair. He thought, *Good. Hurry.*

She said, "Something is wrong with your phone."

Oh Jesus.

She stepped back into his field of view. "Your phone is not working, did you know that?"

Use your cell phone.

"Do you have your cell phone? I left mine in the car."

Go get it.

"Maybe one of the other phones in your apartment is working. You need to call your service provider, Peter. It's not safe to be without phones—what's this? Somebody tore the phone out of the wall? Have we been having a fit of pique?"

Knocking on the door. It sounded like the front door. "Hell-lo? Anybody here? Hello? Peter?" A woman's voice. He couldn't see who it was.

He heard Janis say, "Who are you?"

"Who are *you*?"

"I'm Janis. I'm Peter's friend."

"I'm Sarah. I work with Peter."

"You're tall."

"Where is Peter?" Sarah said.

"He's over there," Janis said. "Something's wrong with him."

Evans could see none of this, because he could not move his eyes. And now he saw the first gray spots that signaled the impending loss of consciousness. It took every ounce of energy he possessed to move his chest and fill his lungs the tiniest bit.

"Peter?" Sarah said.

She moved into his field of view. She looked at him.

"Are you paralyzed?" she said.

Yes! Call the hospital!

"He's sweating," Sarah said. "Cold sweats."

"He was that way when I found him," Janis said. She turned to Sarah. "What are you doing here anyway? How well do you know Peter?"

"Did you call an ambulance?" Sarah said.

"No, because my phone is in my car, and—"

"I'll do it."

Sarah flipped open her cell phone. It was the last thing Evans remembered.

It was late. The house was dark all around him. Nicholas Drake was sitting at his desk in his home in Brentwood, near Santa Monica. He was precisely 2.9 miles from the beach (he had recently measured it in his car), so he felt secure there. It was a good thing, too, because NERF had bought this house for him only one year before. There had been some discussion about that, because they had also bought him a townhouse in Georgetown. But Drake had pointed out that he needed a residence on the West Coast in which to entertain celebrities and important contributors.

California was, after all, the most environmentally conscious state in the nation. It had been the first to pass anti-smoking laws, almost ten years before New York or any other Eastern state did. And even when a Federal Court overturned the EPA on the issue of secondhand smoke in 1998, saying that the EPA had violated its own rules of evidence and banned a substance they had failed to prove caused any harm at all—the Federal Judge was from a tobacco state, *obviously*—even then, California did not budge. The anti-smoking laws stayed. In fact, Santa Monica was about to ban all smoking outdoors, even at the beach! Now *that* was progress!

It was easy here.

But as for getting *major* funds . . . well, that was another matter. There were some rich people in the entertainment industry who could be counted on, but for the real money in California—the investment bankers, portfolio managers, CEOs, real estate, trust funders, people with five hundred million to a couple billion, *serious* money—well, those people weren't so easy. Those people inhabited a different California. Those people belonged to golf courses that didn't allow actors to join. The big money was in the hands of pioneers and tech entrepreneurs, and they were very smart and very tough. A lot of them knew their science. Christ, a lot of them *were* scientists.

Which was why they presented such a challenge to Drake, if he wanted that bonus for making his numbers for the year. He was staring at the screen, thinking it was time for a Scotch, when a new window opened and the cursor blinked:

SCORPIO_L: Can you talk?

Speaking of dimwits, he thought. He typed:

Yes I can.

Drake shifted in his seat, adjusting the light over his desk so it would illuminate his face. He looked at the camera lens mounted just above his screen.

The window opened up. He saw Ted Bradley, sitting at his desk in his house in the San Fernando Valley.

"Well?"

"It was just as you said," Bradley said. "Evans has gone over to the dark side."

"And?"

"He was with that girl, Jennifer, who works on the lawsuit . . ."

"Jennifer Haynes?"

"Yeah. She's a wise-ass bitch."

Drake said nothing. He was listening to the sound of the voice. Bradley had been drinking again. He said, "Ted, we've talked about this before. Not everybody likes it when you come on to them."

"Yeah, they do. I mean, mostly they do."

"Ted, this is not the impression we want to make."

"Well, she insulted me."

"All right. So Jennifer Haynes was there . . ."

"She's a stooge for big oil and coal. Gotta be."

"And who else was there?"

"Sarah Jones."

"Uh-huh. She flew up to see the body?"

"I don't know why she was there. She was with a guy named Kenner, a real asshole. Another know-it-all."

"Describe him."

"Forties, dark, kind of butch. Looks military to me."

"Uh-huh. Anyone else?"

"No."

"Nobody foreign? No other people?"

"No, just the ones I described."

"Would you say that Peter Evans knew Kenner?"

"Yeah. Pretty well, I would say."

"So, it was your impression they were working together?"

"Yes. I would say very much together."

"All right, Ted," Drake said. "I like your instincts here." He watched as Bradley preened on the monitor. "I think you may be on to something. Evans could prove a problem to us."

"I'll say."

"He's been one of our trusted attorneys. Why, he was in my office just the other day, getting an assignment from me. If he's turned on us, he could do damage."

"Damn turncoat," Ted said. "He's another Bennett Arnold."

"I want you to stick close to him for the next week or so."

"My pleasure."

"Hang out with him, stay by his side. Buddy-buddy. You know."

"I got you, Nick. I'll be on him like glue."

"I'm sure he'll be at the opening of the conference later this morning," Drake said. And he thought, *Or then again, he might not make it.*

WESTWOOD
WEDNESDAY, OCTOBER 13
3:40 A.M.

Kenner said, "I must say, it was an excellent choice. *Hapalochlaena fasci-ata*, the most deadly of the three species of blue-ringed octopus. So named because when it is threatened it changes color and produces bright blue rings on its skin. It's found everywhere in the coastal waters of Australia. The animal is very tiny, the bite is small and almost unde-tectable, and envenomation is often deadly. There is no antivenom. And a bite's not likely to be quickly recognized at a hospital in Los Angeles. Really, a masterful choice."[*]

Evans, who was lying in the emergency room at UCLA with a res-pirator on his face, just stared. He was still unable to speak. But he was no longer so frightened. Janis had gone home in a huff, mentioning something about teaching an early class. Sarah was sitting by his bed, rubbing his hand gently and looking beautiful. "Where would they have gotten one?"

"I imagine they have several," Kenner said. "They're delicate, and don't live very long anyway. But they are captured in fairly large numbers because the Aussies are trying to make an antivenin. You probably know the Australians lead the world in deadly poisonous animals. The most

[*] See S. K. Sutherland, et al., "Toxins and mode of envenomation of the common ringed or blue-banded octo-pus," *Med. J.Aust.* 1 (1969): 893–98. Also H. Flecker, et al., "Fatal bite from octopus," *Med. J.Aust.* 2 (1955): 329–31.

poisonous snake, the most poisonous mollusk, the most poisonous fish—
all from Australia or found there."

Evans thought, *Great.*

"But now of course UCLA has seen three cases. They're on it."

"Yes, we are," an intern said, coming into the room. He checked
Evans's IV and his respirator. He said, "We have your preliminary blood
work. It's a tetrodotoxin, like the others. You should be up and around in
about three more hours. Lucky guy." He smiled winningly at Sarah, then
walked out again.

"Anyway, I'm glad you're all right," Kenner said. "It would have been
embarrassing to lose you."

Evans thought, *What is he talking about?* He was increasingly able to
use his eye muscles, and he glanced over at Sarah. But she just smiled.

"Oh yes," Kenner said. "I need you alive, Peter. At least for a while."

Sitting in a corner of the room on his cell phone, Sanjong said,
"Okay, we have some action."

Kenner said, "Is it where we thought?"

"Yes."

"What happened?"

"We just got the receipt notice. They rented an aircraft last month.
A C-57 transport."

"Whew," Kenner said.

"What does that mean?" Sarah said.

"Big aircraft. They probably need it to spray."

She looked puzzled. "Spray?"

Sanjong said, "It's pretty clear they're going to disseminate AOB,
ammonia-oxidizing bacteria, in large quantities. And perhaps some
hydrophilic nanoparticles as well."

"To do what?"

"Control the path of a storm," Kenner said. "There's some evidence
that disseminated AOB at altitude can shift a hurricane or cyclone track.
Hydrophilic nanoparticles potentiate the effect. At least in theory. I don't
know if it's been tried on a large system."

"They're going to control a hurricane?"

"They're going to try."

"Maybe not," Sanjong said. "Tokyo says some recent cellular and Internet traffic suggests that the project may be canceled."

"Then they don't have the initial conditions?"

"Looks like they don't, no."

Evans coughed. "Oh good," Kenner said. "You're coming around." He patted his arm. "Just rest now, Peter. Try and sleep if you can. Because, as you know, today is the big day."

"The big day?" Sarah said.

"The conference begins in about five and a half hours," Kenner said. He stood to go, then turned back to Evans. "I'm going to have Sanjong stay with you the rest of the night," he said. "I think you'll be all right here, but they've already made one attempt on your life, and I don't want them to try another."

Sanjong smiled and sat on the chair beside the bed, a stack of magazines beside him. He opened the latest issue of *Time* magazine. The cover story was "Climate Change Doomsday Ahead." He also had *Newsweek:* "Abrupt Climate Change—A New Scandal for the Administration?" And *The Economist:* "Climate Change Rears Its Ugly Head." And *Paris-Match:* "Climat: Le Nouveau Péril Américain."

Sanjong smiled cheerfully. "Just rest now," he said.

Evans closed his eyes.

At nine o'clock that morning, the invited attendees to the conference were milling around on the floor, not taking their seats. Evans was standing near the entrance, drinking coffee. He felt incredibly tired, but he was all right. He'd been a little shaky in his legs earlier, but that had passed.

The delegates were clearly academic types, many dressed casually in a manner to suggest an outdoorsy lifestyle—khakis and L.L.Bean shirts, hiking boots, Patagonia vests. "It looks like a lumberjack convention, doesn't it?" Jennifer said, standing beside Evans. "You'd never know these guys spend most of their time in front of computer monitors."

"Is that true?" Evans said.

"A lot of them, yes."

"And the hiking shoes?"

She shrugged. "The rugged look is in, at the moment."

At the podium, Nicholas Drake tapped the microphone. "Good morning, everyone," he said. "We will begin in ten minutes." Then he stepped away, and huddled with Henley.

"Waiting for the TV cameras," Jennifer said. "They had some electrical problems this morning. Crews are still setting up."

"So, of course, everything waits for television."

At the entrance to the convention hall, there was a commotion and shouting. Evans looked over and saw an elderly man in a tweed coat and tie struggling with two security guards. "But I have been invited!" he said. "I am supposed to be here."

"Sorry, sir," the guards were saying, "your name is not on the sheet."

"But, I tell you, I have been invited!"

"Oh boy," Jennifer said, shaking her head.

"Who's that?"

"That is Professor Norman Hoffman. Ever heard of him?"

"No, why?"

"The ecology of thought? He's a famous sociologist, or should I say a notorious one. Extremely critical of environmental beliefs. A bit of a mad dog. We had him over to the war room to ask him his views. That was a mistake. The guy never shuts up. He talks a mile a minute and goes off on tangents—in every direction—and you can't turn him off. It's like a TV set that changes channels every few seconds, and there's no remote."

"No wonder they don't want him here."

"Oh yes, he would cause trouble. He already is."

Over by the entrance, the old man was struggling with the security guards. "Let go of me! How dare you! I was invited! By George Morton himself. He and I are personal friends. George Morton invited me!"

The mention of George Morton sparked something. Evans went over to the old man.

Jennifer said, "You'll be sor-ry . . ."

He shrugged. "Excuse me," he said, coming up to the guards. "I'm Mr. Morton's attorney. Can I help you?"

The old man writhed in the grip of the guards. "I'm Professor Norman Hoffman and George Morton invited me!" Up close, Evans saw that the old man was messily shaven, unkempt, his hair wild. "Why do you think I would come to this horrible convocation? For one reason only: George asked me to. He wanted my *impression* of it. Although I could have told him weeks ago: There are no surprises to be had here, I can assure you. It will unfold with all the stately ceremony of any cheap funeral."

Evans was thinking Jennifer had been right to warn him about this guy. He said politely, "Do you have a ticket, sir?"

"No, I don't have a *ticket*. I don't *need* a ticket. What don't you understand, young man? I am Professor Norman Hoffman and I am a personal friend of George Morton's. Anyway," he said, "they took my ticket."

"Who did?"

"One of those guards."

Evans said to the guards, "Did you take his ticket?"

"He didn't have a ticket."

"Do you have a stub?" Evans said to Hoffman.

"No, damn it, I do not have a *stub*. I do not need a *stub*. I do not need any of this, frankly."

"I'm sorry, Professor, but—"

"However, I managed to hold on to *this*." He gave Evans the torn corner of a ticket. It was a genuine ticket.

"Where is the rest?"

"I told you, they took it."

A guard standing to one side beckoned to Evans. Evans went over to him. The guard turned his cupped hand, revealing the rest of the ticket in his palm. "I'm sorry, sir," he said, "but Mr. Drake gave specific orders this gentleman was not to be allowed in."

"But he has a ticket," Evans said.

"Perhaps you'd like to take it up with Mr. Drake."

By now, a television crew had wandered over, drawn by the commotion. Hoffman immediately played to the cameras, struggling anew.

"Don't bother with Drake!" Hoffman yelled to Evans. "Drake won't let truth into these proceedings!" He turned to the camera. "Nicholas Drake is an immoral fraud, and these proceedings are a travesty to the poor of the world. I bear witness to the dying children of Africa and Asia! Breathing their last because of conferences like this! Fearmongers! Immoral fearmongers!" He struggled maniacally. His eyes were wild. There was spittle on his lips. He certainly appeared crazy, and the cameras switched off; the crews turned away, seemingly embarrassed. At once, Hoffman stopped his struggle. "Never mind. I've said my piece.

No one is interested, as usual." He turned to his guards. "You can let me go. I have had enough of this chicanery. I cannot bear to be here another minute. Let me go!"

Evans said, "Let him go."

The guards released Hoffman. He immediately dashed into the center of the room, where a crew was now interviewing Ted Bradley. Hoffman stepped in front of Bradley and said, "This man is a pimp! He is an eco-pimp for a corrupt establishment that makes its living by spreading false fears! Don't you understand? False fears are a plague, a modern plague!"

Then the guards were on Hoffman again, dragging him bodily out of the hall. He didn't struggle this time. He just went limp, his heels scraping on the ground as he was carried out. All he said was, "Be careful, I have a bad back. You hurt me and I'll sue you for assault."

They set him outside on the curb, dusted him off, released him.

"Have a good day, sir."

"I intend to. My days are numbered."

Evans hung back with Jennifer, watching Hoffman. "I won't say I told you," Jennifer said.

"Just who is he, anyway?"

"He's a professor *emeritus* at USC. He was one of the first people to study in a rigorous statistical fashion the media and its effect on society. He's quite interesting, but as you see he has developed, uh, strong opinions."

"You think Morton really invited him here?"

"Peter, I need your help," a voice said. Evans turned and saw Drake striding toward him.

"What is it?"

"That *nut*," Drake said, nodding to Hoffman, "is probably going to go straight to the police and claim he was assaulted. We don't need that this morning. Go talk to him. See if you can calm him down."

Cautiously, Evans said, "I don't know what I can do . . ."

"Get him to explain his nutty theories," Drake said. "That'll keep him busy for *hours*."

"But then I'll miss the conf—"

"We don't need you here. We need you *there*. With the cuckoo."

There was a large crowd outside the conference center. The overflow was watching the proceedings on a big TV screen, with subtitles running underneath the speaker. Evans pushed through the gathering. "I know why you are following me," Hoffman said, when he saw Evans. "And it won't work."

"Professor—"

"You're the bright young *poseur* Nick Drake sent to put me off my purpose."

"Not at all, sir."

"Yes, you are. Don't lie to me. I don't like to be lied to."

"All right," Evans said, "it's true. I was sent by Drake."

Hoffman stopped. He seemed startled by the honesty. "I knew it. And what did he tell you to do?"

"Stop you from going to the police."

"All right then, you've succeeded. Go and tell him, I am not going to the police."

"It looks like you are."

"Oh. It *looks like* I am. You're one of those people who care what it *looks like*."

"No, sir, but you—"

"I don't care what it *looks like*. I care what *is*. Do you have any idea what is?"

"I'm not sure I follow you."

"What is your line of work?"

"I'm a lawyer."

"I should have known. Everybody is a lawyer these days. Extrapolating the statistical growth of the legal profession, by the year 2035 every single person in the United States will be a lawyer, including newborn infants. They will be *born* lawyers. What do you suppose it will be like to live in such a society?"

"Professor," Evans said, "you made some interesting comments in the hall—"

"*Interesting?* I accused them of flagrant immorality, and you call that *interesting?*"

"I'm sorry," Evans said, trying to move the discussion toward Hoffman's views. "You didn't explain why you think—"

"I do not *think* anything, young man. I *know.* That is the purpose of my research—to know things, not to surmise them. Not to theorize. Not to hypothesize. But to *know* from direct research in the field. It's a lost art in academia these days, young man—you are not *that* young—what is your name, anyway?"

"Peter Evans."

"And you work for Drake, Mr. Evans?"

"No, for George Morton."

"Well, *why didn't you say so!*" Hoffman said. "George Morton was a great, *great* man. Come along, Mr. Evans, and I will buy you some coffee and we can talk. Do you know what I do?"

"I'm afraid I don't, sir."

"I study the ecology of thought," Hoffman said. "And how it has led to a State of Fear."

They were sitting on a bench across the street from the conference hall, just beyond the milling crowds near the entrance. It was a busy scene, but Hoffman ignored everything around him. He spoke rapidly, with great animation, moving his hands so wildly that he often slapped Evans in the chest, but he never seemed to notice.

"Ten years ago, I began with fashion and slang," he said, "the latter being of course a kind of verbal fashion. I wanted to know the determinants of change in fashion and speech. What I quickly found is that there are no identifiable determinants. Fashions change for arbitrary reasons and although there are regularities—cycles, periodicities, and correlations— these are merely descriptive, not explanatory. Are you following me?"

"I think so," Evans said.

"In any case, I realized that these periodicities and correlations could be regarded as systems in themselves. Or if you will, ecosystems. I tested that hypothesis and found it heuristically valuable. Just as there is an ecology of the natural world, in the forests and mountains and oceans, so too there is an ecology of the man-made world of mental abstractions, ideas, and thought. That is what I have studied."

"I see."

"Within modern culture, ideas constantly rise and fall. For a while everybody believes something, and then, bit by bit, they stop believing it. Eventually, no one can remember the old idea, the way no one can remember the old slang. Ideas are themselves a kind of fad, you see."

"I understand, Professor, but why—"

"Why do ideas fall out of favor, you are wondering?" Hoffman said. He was talking to himself. "The answer is simply—they do. In fashion, as in natural ecology, there are disruptions. Sharp revisions of the established order. A lightning fire burns down a forest. A different species springs up in the charred acreage. Accidental, haphazard, unexpected, abrupt change. That is what the world shows us on every side."

"Professor . . ."

"But just as ideas can change abruptly, so, too, can they hang on past their time. Some ideas continue to be embraced by the public long after scientists have abandoned them. Left brain, right brain is a perfect example. In the 1970s, it gains popularity from the work of Sperry at Caltech, who studies a specific group of brain-surgery patients. His findings have no broader meaning beyond these patients. Sperry denies any broader meaning. By 1980, it is clear that the left and right brain notion is just wrong—the two sides of the brain do not work separately in a healthy person. But in the popular culture, the concept does not die for another twenty years. People talk about it, believe it, write books about it for decades after scientists have set it aside."

"Yes, all very interesting—"

"Similarly, in environmental thought, it was widely accepted in 1960 that there is something called 'the balance of nature.' If you just left nature alone it would come into a self-maintaining state of balance. Lovely idea with a long pedigree. The Greeks believed it three thousand years ago, on the basis of nothing. Just seemed nice. "However, by 1990, no scientist believes in the balance of nature anymore. The ecologists have all given it up as simply wrong. Untrue. A fantasy. They speak now of dynamic disequilibrium, of multiple equilibrium states. But they now understand that nature is *never* in balance. Never has been, never will be. On the contrary, nature is always *out of* balance, and that means—"

"Professor," Evans said, "I'd like to ask you—"

"That means that mankind, which was formerly defined as the great disrupter of the natural order, is nothing of the sort. The whole environment is being constantly disrupted all the time anyway."

"But George Morton . . ."

"Yes, yes, you wonder what I discussed with George Morton. I am coming to that. We are not off topic. Because of course, Morton wanted to know about environmental ideas. And particularly the idea of environmental crisis."

"What did you tell him?"

"If you study the media, as my graduate students and I do, seeking to find shifts in normative conceptualization, you discover something extremely interesting. We looked at transcripts of news programs of the major networks—NBC, ABC, CBS. We also looked at stories in the newspapers of New York, Washington, Miami, Los Angeles, and Seattle. We counted the frequency of certain concepts and terms used by the media. The results were very striking." He paused.

"What did you find?" Evans said, taking his cue.

"There was a major shift in the fall of 1989. Before that time, the media did not make excessive use of terms such as *crisis, catastrophe, cataclysm, plague,* or *disaster.* For example, during the 1980s, the word *crisis* appeared in news reports about as often as the word *budget.* In addition, prior to 1989, adjectives such as *dire, unprecedented, dreaded* were not common in television reports or newspaper headlines. But then it all changed."

"In what way?"

"These terms started to become more and more common. The word *catastrophe* was used five times more often in 1995 than it was in 1985. Its use doubled again by the year 2000. And the stories changed, too. There was a heightened emphasis on fear, worry, danger, uncertainty, panic."

"Why should it have changed in 1989?"

"Ah. A good question. *Critical* question. In most respects 1989 seemed like a normal year: a Soviet sub sank in Norway; Tiananmen Square in China; the *Exxon Valdez;* Salmon Rushdie sentenced to death; Jane Fonda, Mike Tyson, and Bruce Springsteen all got divorced; the Episcopal Church hired a female bishop; Poland allowed striking unions;

Voyager went to Neptune; a San Francisco earthquake flattened high-ways; and Russia, the US, France, and England all conducted nuclear tests. A year like any other. But in fact the rise in the use of the term *crisis* can be located with some precision in the autumn of 1989. And it seemed suspicious that it should coincide so closely with the fall of the Berlin Wall. Which happened on November ninth of that year."

Hoffman fell silent again, looking at Evans in a significant way. Very pleased with himself.

Evans said, "I'm sorry, Professor. I don't get it."

"Neither did we. At first we thought the association was spurious. But it wasn't. The Berlin Wall marks the collapse of the Soviet empire. And the end of the Cold War that had lasted for half a century in the West."

Another silence. Another pleased look.

"I'm sorry," Evans said finally. "I was thirteen years old then, and . . ." He shrugged. "I don't see where you are leading."

"I am leading to the notion of social control, Peter. To the require-ment of every sovereign state to exert control over the behavior of its cit-izens, to keep them orderly and reasonably docile. To keep them driving on the right side of the road—or the left, as the case may be. To keep them paying taxes. And of course we know that social control is best managed through fear."

"Fear," Evans said.

"Exactly. For fifty years, Western nations had maintained their citi-zens in a state of perpetual fear. Fear of the other side. Fear of nuclear war. The Communist menace. The Iron Curtain. The Evil Empire. And within the Communist countries, the same in reverse. Fear of us. Then, suddenly, in the fall of 1989, it was all finished. Gone, vanished. *Over.* The fall of the Berlin Wall created a vacuum of fear. Nature abhors a vacuum. Something had to fill it."

Evans frowned. "You're saying that environmental crises took the place of the Cold War?"

"That is what the evidence shows. Of course, now we have radical fundamentalism and post–9/11 terrorism to make us afraid, and those are certainly real reasons for fear, but that is not my point. My point is, there is always a cause for fear. The cause may change over time, but the fear is always with us. Before terrorism we feared the toxic environment. Before that we had the Communist menace. The point is, although the specific cause of our fear may change, we are never without the fear itself. Fear pervades society in all its aspects. Perpetually."

He shifted on the concrete bench, turning away from the crowds.

"Has it ever occurred to you how astonishing the culture of Western society really is? Industrialized nations provide their citizens with unprecedented safety, health, and comfort. Average life spans increased fifty percent in the last century. Yet modern people live in abject fear. They are afraid of strangers, of disease, of crime, of the environment. They are afraid of the homes they live in, the food they eat, the technology that surrounds them. They are in a particular panic over things they can't even see—germs, chemicals, additives, pollutants. They are timid, nervous, fretful, and depressed. And even more amazingly, they are convinced that the environment of the entire planet is being destroyed around them. Remarkable! Like the belief in witchcraft, it's an extraordinary delusion—a global fantasy worthy of the Middle Ages. Everything is going to hell, and we must all live in fear. Amazing.

"How has this world view been instilled in everybody? Because although we imagine we live in different nations—France, Germany, Japan, the US—in fact, we inhabit exactly the same state, the State of Fear. How has that been accomplished?"

Evans said nothing. He knew it wasn't necessary.

"Well, I shall tell you how," he said. "In the old days—before your time, Peter—citizens of the West believed their nation-states were dominated by something called the military-industrial complex. Eisenhower warned Americans against it in the 1960s, and after two world wars Europeans knew very well what it meant in their own countries. But the military-industrial complex is no longer the primary driver of society. In reality, for the last fifteen years we have been under the control of an entirely new complex, far more powerful and far more pervasive. I call it the politico-legal-media complex. The PLM. And it is dedicated to promoting fear in the population—under the guise of promoting safety."

"Safety is important."

"Please. Western nations are fabulously safe. Yet people do not feel they are, because of the PLM. And the PLM is powerful and stable, precisely because it unites so many institutions of society. Politicians need fears to control the population. Lawyers need dangers to litigate, and make money. The media need scare stories to capture an audience. Together, these three estates are so compelling that they can go about their business even if the scare is totally groundless. If it has no basis in fact at all. For instance, consider silicon breast implants."

Evans sighed, shaking his head. "Breast implants?"

"Yes. You will recall that breast implants were claimed to cause cancer and autoimmune diseases. Despite statistical evidence that this was not true, we saw high-profile news stories, high-profile lawsuits, high-profile political hearings. The manufacturer, Dow Corning, was hounded out of the business after paying $3.2 billion, and juries awarded huge cash payments to plaintiffs and their lawyers.

"Four years later, definitive epidemiological studies showed beyond a doubt that breast implants did not cause disease. But by then the crisis had already served its purpose, and the PLM had moved on, a ravenous machine seeking new fears, new terrors. I'm telling you, *this is the way modern society works*—by the constant creation of fear. And there is no countervailing force. There is no system of checks and balances, no restraint on the perpetual promotion of fear after fear after fear. . . ."

"Because we have freedom of speech, freedom of the press."

"That is the classic PLM answer. That's how they stay in business," Hoffman said. "But think. If it is not all right to falsely shout 'Fire!' in a crowded theater, why is it all right to shout 'Cancer!' in the pages of *The New Yorker?* When that statement is not true? We've spent more than twenty-five billion dollars to clear up the phony power-line cancer claim.* 'So what?' you say. I can see it in your face. You're thinking, we're rich, we can afford it. It's only twenty-five billion dollars. But the fact is that twenty-five billion dollars is more than the total GDP of the poorest fifty nations of the world *combined.* Half the world's population lives on two dollars a day. So that twenty-five billion would be enough to support thirty-four million people for a year. Or we could have helped all the people dying of AIDS in Africa. Instead, we piss it away on a fantasy published by a magazine whose readers take it very seriously. Trust it. It is a *stupendous* waste of money. In another world, it would be a criminal waste. One could easily imagine another Nuremberg trial—this time for the relentless squandering of Western wealth on trivialities—and complete with pictures of the dead babies in Africa and Asia that result."

He hardly paused for breath. "At the very least, we are talking about a moral outrage. Thus we can expect our religious leaders and our great humanitarian figures to cry out against this waste and the needless deaths around the world that result. But do any religious leaders speak out? No. Quite the contrary, *they join the chorus.* They promote 'What Would Jesus Drive?' As if they have forgotten that what Jesus would drive is the false prophets and fearmongers out of the temple."

He was getting quite heated now.

"We are talking about a situation that is *profoundly* immoral. It is *disgusting,* if truth be told. The PLM callously ignores the plight of the poorest and most desperate human beings on our planet in order to keep fat politicians in office, rich news anchors on the air, and conniving lawyers in Mercedes-Benz convertibles. Oh, and university professors in Volvos. Let's not forget *them.*"

"How's that?" Evans said. "What does this have to do with university professors?"

"Well, that's another discussion."

"Is there a short version?" Evans said.

"Not really. That's why headlines aren't news, Peter. But I will try to

---

* Estimate from the White House Science Office for all costs of the scare, including property devaluation and relocation of power lines. Cited in Park, *Voodoo Science*, p. 161. (Park was a participant in the controversy.)

be succinct," he said. "The point is this: the world has changed in the last fifty years. We now live in the knowledge society, the information society, whatever you want to call it. And it has had enormous impact on our universities.

"Fifty years ago, if you wanted to lead what was then called 'the life of the mind,' meaning to be an intellectual, to live by your wits, you had to work in a university. The society at large had no place for you. A few newspaper reporters, a few magazine journalists could be considered as living by their wits, but that was about it. Universities attracted those who willingly gave up worldly goods to live a cloistered intellectual life, teaching timeless values to the younger generation. Intellectual work was the exclusive province of the university.

"But today, whole sectors of society live the life of the mind. Our entire economy is based on intellectual work, now. Thirty-six percent of workers are knowledge workers. That's more than are employed in manufacturing. And when professors decided they would no longer teach young people, but leave that task to their graduate students who knew much less than they did and spoke English poorly—when that happened, the universities were thrown into crisis. What good were they anymore? They had lost their exclusive hold on the life of the mind. They no longer taught the young. Only so many theoretical texts on the semiotics of Foucault could be published in any single year. What was to become of our universities? What relevance did they have in the modern era?"

He stood up, as if energized by this question. Then abruptly, he sat down again.

"What happened," he continued, "is the universities transformed themselves in the 1980s. Formerly bastions of intellectual freedom in a world of Babbittry, formerly the locus of sexual freedom and experimentation, they now became the most restrictive environments in modern society. Because they had a new role to play. They became the creators of new fears for the PLM. Universities today are factories of fear. They invent all the new terrors and all the new social anxieties. All the new restrictive codes. Words you can't say. Thoughts you can't think. They produce a steady stream of new anxieties, dangers, and social terrors to be used by politicians, lawyers, and reporters. Foods that are bad for you. Behaviors that are unacceptable. Can't smoke, can't swear, can't screw, can't *think*. These institutions have been stood on their heads in a generation. It is really quite extraordinary.

"The modern State of Fear could never exist without universities feeding it. There is a peculiar neo-Stalinist mode of thought that is required to support all this, and it can thrive only in a restrictive setting, behind closed doors, without due process. In our society, only universities have created that—so far. The notion that these institutions are *liberal* is a cruel joke. They are fascist to the core, I'm telling you."

He broke off and pointed down the walkway. "Who is this fellow pushing toward us through the crowd? He looks oddly familiar."

Evans said, "That's Ted Bradley, the actor."

"Where have I seen him?"

"He plays the president on television."

"Oh yes. *Him.*"

Ted came to a halt in front of them, panting. "Peter," he said, "I've been looking everywhere for you. Is your cell phone on?"

"No, because—"

"Sarah has been trying to reach you. She says it's important. We have to leave town right away. And bring your passport."

Evans said, "We? What does this have to do with you?"

"I'm coming with you," Ted said.

As they started to walk away, Hoffman clutched at Evans's sleeve, holding him back. He had a new thought. "We haven't talked about *involution,*" he said.

"Professor—"

"It is the next step in the development of nation-states. Indeed it is already happening. You must see the irony. After all, twenty-five billion dollars and ten years later the same rich elitists who were terrified of power-line cancer are buying magnets to strap to their ankles or put on their mattresses—imported Japanese magnets are the best, the most expensive—in order to enjoy the *healthful effects of magnetic fields.* The same magnetic fields—only now they can't get enough of them!"

"Professor," Evans said, "I have to go."

"Why don't these people just lie back against a TV screen? Snuggle up to a kitchen appliance? All the things that terrified them before."

"We'll talk later," Evans said, pulling his arm away.

"They even sell magnets in the *health* magazines! Healthy living through magnetic fields! Insanity! No one remembers even a few years ago! George Orwell. No memory!"

"Who is that guy?" Bradley said, as they headed off. "He seems a little wound up, doesn't he?"

"The record of catastrophe is contained within the ice cores," the speaker said, droning on at the podium. He was Russian and spoke with a heavy accent. "These ice cores from Greenland show that, in the last one hundred thousand years, there have been four abrupt climate change events. Some have occurred very quickly, in a few years. While the mechanisms by which these events occurred are still being studied, they demonstrate that there can be 'trigger' effects in climate, whereby small changes—including man-made changes—can produce catastrophically large effects. We have seen a foretaste of such effects in recent days with the calving of the world's largest iceberg, and the terrible loss of life from the flash flood in the American Southwest. And it is no difficulty to predict we will see more—"

He paused, as Drake hurried up onto the stage, whispered in his ear, then stepped down again, looking at his watch.

"Uh, I must beg the forgiveness of you," the speaker said. "I seem to have brought up an outdated version of my remarks. Word processors! That was a part from an old talk from 2001. What I wanted to say was that the calving of the iceberg in 2001—larger than many American states—and the dangerously unseasonal weather around the world, including the sunny Southwest, portends further climate instability. It is just beginning."

Sarah Jones, standing in the back, was talking with Ann Garner, the wife of a prominent Hollywood lawyer and a major contributor to NERF. Ann was emphatic as always, and talking nonstop.

"I'll tell you what I heard," Ann was saying. "I heard there is an industry-sponsored campaign to discredit NGOs. Industry is afraid of the growing power of the environmental movement and they are desperate, *desperate* to stop it. We have had our modest successes in recent years, and it is driving them crazy, and—"

"I'm sorry," Sarah said. "Just a minute, Ann." She turned to look at the Russian speaker at the podium. *What did he say?* she thought.

She walked quickly to the press table, where reporters were lined up with their laptops open. They were getting real-time transcripts of the conference.

She looked over the shoulder of Ben Lopez, the reporter for the *Los Angeles Times*. Ben didn't mind; he had been after her for months.

"Hi ya, sweet thing."

"Hi, Ben. Mind if I look at something?"

She touched the mouse, scrolling up the screen.

"Sure, be my guest. Nice perfume."

She read:

CAN BE TRIGGER EFFECTS IN CLIMATE, WHEREBY SMALL CHANGES
INCLUDING MAN-MADE CHANGES CAN PRODUCE CATASTROPHICALLY
LARGE EFFECTS. WE HAVE HAD A FORETASTE OF SUCH EFFECTS ~~IN~~
~~RECENT DAYS WITH THE CALVING OF THE WORLD'S LARGEST ICEBERG~~
~~AND THE TERRIBLE LOSS OF LIFE FROM THE FLASH FLOOD IN THE~~
~~AMERICAN SOUTHWEST. AND IT IS NO DIFFICULTY TO PREDICT WE WILL~~
~~SEE MORE~~

While she watched, the text changed, the strikeout disappearing, and replaced with new text:

CAN BE TRIGGER EFFECTS IN CLIMATE, WHEREBY SMALL CHANGES
INCLUDING MAN-MADE CHANGES CAN PRODUCE CATASTROPHICALLY
LARGE EFFECTS. WE HAVE HAD A FORETASTE OF SUCH EFFECTS WITH
THE CALVING OF THE ICEBERG IN 2001 LARGER THAN MANY AMERICAN
STATES AND THE DANGEROUSLY UNSEASONAL WEATHER AROUND THE
WORLD INCLUDING THE SUNNY SOUTHWEST PORTENDS FURTHER CLIMATE
INSTABILITY

"Holy shit," she said.

"Something wrong?" Ben said.

"Did you see what he said?"

"Yeah. Poor guy. Probably has jet lag to beat hell. And obviously, he's struggling with English . . ."

The original remarks were gone. The record was corrected. But there was no doubt about it: *the Russian had known in advance about the iceberg and the flash flood.* It was written into his speech. And somebody had forgotten to tell him, when he got off the plane, that it never happened.

He knew in advance.

But now the record was corrected, the remarks stricken. She glanced at the video camera in the back, recording the proceedings. No doubt the remarks would disappear from the video record as well.

The son of a bitch knew in advance.

"Hey," Ben said, "I don't know what you're so upset about. Clue me in, will you?"

"Later," she said. "I promise." She patted his shoulder, and went back to Ann.

"So," Ann said, "what we are facing is an industry-promoted campaign, well orchestrated, well financed, pervasive and ultra right-wing, that is intent on destroying the environmental movement that stands in its way."

After what she had just seen, Sarah was in no mood to put up with this blather. "Ann," she said. "Did it ever cross your mind you might be paranoid?"

"No. Anyway, even paranoids have enemies."

"How many industry executives serve on the NERF board right now?" Sarah said.

"Uh, not that many."

Sarah knew that there were thirty board members, of whom twelve were industry figures. This was the case with all modern environmental groups. They had all had industry representatives over the last twenty years.

"Did you ask your corporate board members about this secret industry campaign?"

"No," she said. She was looking at Sarah oddly.

"Do you think," Sarah said, "that it is possible that NGOs like NERF could be the ones who are engaged in a secret campaign?"

"What are you talking about?" Ann said, stiffening. "Sarah. We're the good guys."

"Are we?"

"Yes. We are," Ann said. "What's going on with you, Sarah?"

In the parking lot outside the convention hall, Sanjong Thapa sat in the car with his laptop on his knees. He had easily hacked the WiFi network used by the journalists and was receiving the conference transcript, which was instantaneously saved. He had done it that way because he was afraid he might be discovered and locked out at any moment, but now it meant that he had the complete transcript, including the revisions. Kenner, he thought, was going to love this.

On another screen, Sanjong was monitoring the satellite images from the western Atlantic, off the coast of Florida. A large high-pressure mass was beginning to rotate, forming the ragged beginnings of a hurricane. Clearly an event was scheduled around a hurricane, but for some reason it had been abandoned.

And now he was tracking other investigative leads. In particular, Kenner was concerned about a small research submarine known as DOEV/2, and the tender ship *AV Scorpio*. That submarine and its tender ship had been leased by CanuCo, a natural gas corporation based in Calgary, to conduct research in the South Pacific, looking for undersea gas deposits. The tender had sailed to Port Moresby, New Guinea, some two months before, and had subsequently left that harbor and had been spotted near Bougainville, in the Solomon Islands.

Nothing of great interest there, until it became known that CanuCo was not a registered Canadian corporation, and that it had no assets other than a website and web address. The owner of the site was CanuCo Leasing Corp, another nonexistent company. The lease payments had been made from a Cayman Island account and paid in euros. The name of the account was Seismic Services, also in Calgary, and sharing the same postal address as CanuCo.

They were obviously the same entity. And it was Seismic Services that had originally attempted to lease a submarine. And presumably had later caused the death of Nat Damon in Vancouver.

Now there were agencies in Washington searching satellite maps, trying to find the *AV Scorpio*, somewhere in the Solomon Island chain. But the Solomons had scattered cloud cover, and the satellite passes had not yet revealed the ship's location.

That in itself was worrisome. It suggested that the ship had already hidden itself in some way, perhaps by going into a covered dock.

Somewhere in the South Pacific.

And it was a big ocean.

Equally worrisome was the fact that the tender had sailed first to Vancouver, where it had taken on thirty tons of "industrial equipment," in five-ton cartons. The Canadian government had thought the company was illegally transporting automobiles in the cartons, so they opened one. The customs officers instead found some complex equipment that they listed as "diesel generators."

Generators!

Sanjong didn't know what was in those cartons, but he was sure they weren't diesel generators. Because you didn't have to go to Vancouver to get a bunch of generators. So it was worrisome—

"Hey! You!"

He looked up and saw two security guards walking across the parking lot toward his car. Obviously his WiFi hack had been detected. It was time to go. He turned the key in the ignition and drove away, waving cheerfully to the security guards as he passed them.

"Sarah? What's going on? You're just staring into space."

"Nothing, Ann." Sarah shook her head. "Just thinking."

"About what? And what do you mean about my being paranoid?" Ann put her hand on Sarah's arm. "Really. I'm a little concerned about you."

Sarah thought, *And I'm concerned about you.*

In truth, it was Sarah who was feeling a distinct paranoid chill. She looked around the room, and her eyes met Drake's. He was staring at her, studying her from across the room. For how long? Had he seen her quick dash to the reporters' desk? Had he deduced the meaning of it? Did he know she knew?

"Sarah," Ann said, shaking her arm.

"Listen," Sarah said. "I'm really sorry, but I have to go."

"Sarah. I'm worried about you."

"I'll be fine." She started to leave the room.

"I'll just come with you," Ann said, falling into step with her.

"I'd rather you didn't."

"I'm concerned for your welfare."

"I think I need to be alone for a while," Sarah said.

"Is that any way to treat a friend?" Ann said. "I insist, darling. You need a little mothering, I can see that. And I'm here for you."

Sarah sighed.

Nicholas Drake watched as Sarah left the room. Ann was sticking with her, just as he had asked. Ann was dedicated and tenacious. Sarah would be no match for her, unless she elected to turn and literally run. But if she did that . . . well, they would have to take stronger action. These were critical times, and sometimes strong action was essential. Just as in wartime.

But Drake suspected dire action would not prove necessary. True, Kenner had managed to disrupt the first two events, but only because ELF was a bunch of amateurs. Their brand of do-it-yourself schoolboy spontaneity was unsuited to the demands of modern media. Drake had said that to Henley a dozen times. Henley shrugged it off; he was concerned about deniability. Well, NERF could certainly deny they knew these clowns. What a bunch of fuckups!

But this last event was different. It had been planned far more carefully—it had to be—and it was in professional hands. Kenner would never be able to disrupt it. He could not even get there in time, Drake thought. And between Ted Bradley and Ann, Drake had lots of eyes and ears on that team as they progressed. And just to be sure, he had other surprises in store for Kenner as well.

He flipped open his phone and dialed Henley. "We've got them covered," he said.

"Good."

"Where are you?"

"I am about to deliver the news to V.," Henley said. "I am pulling up to his house now."

Through binoculars, Kenner watched as the silver Porsche convertible pulled into the driveway of the beach house. A tall, dark man in a blue golf shirt and tan slacks got out. He wore a baseball cap and dark glasses, but Kenner recognized him at once as Henley, the head of PR for NERF.

That closed the circle, he thought. He put the binoculars down on the fence and paused to consider the implications.

"Do you know who he is, sir?" the young FBI agent said, standing by his side. He was just a kid, no more than twenty-five.

"Yes," Kenner said. "I know who he is."

They were standing on the cliffs of Santa Monica, overlooking the beach and the ocean. The beach here was several hundred yards wide, from the shore to the bike path. Then a line of houses, packed close together along the coast highway. Then six lanes of roaring traffic.

Even though they abutted the highway, the houses were phenomenally expensive—twenty or thirty million dollars each, it was said, and perhaps much more. They were inhabited by some of the wealthiest people in California.

Henley was putting up the cloth top on his Porsche. He moved in a precise, almost fussy way. Then he went to the gate and buzzed it. The house he was entering was ultra-modern, curving shapes of glass. It glistened like a jewel in the morning sun.

Henley went inside. The gate closed behind him.

"But you don't care about people *entering* the house," the FBI agent said.

"That's right," Kenner said. "I don't."

"You don't want a list, or a record of who—"

"No."

"But it might prove—"

"No," Kenner said. The kid was trying to be helpful, but it was annoying. "I don't care about any of that. I just want to know when they all leave."

"Like, if they go on vacation or something?"

"Yes," Kenner said.

"What if they leave a maid behind?"

"They won't," Kenner said.

"Actually, sir, I'm pretty sure they will. These guys always leave somebody to watch the house."

"No," Kenner said. "This house will clear out. Everybody will go."

The kid frowned. "Whose house is it, anyway?"

"It belongs to a man named V. Allen Willy," Kenner said. He might as well tell him. "He's a philanthropist."

"Uh-huh. What is he, mixed up in the mob or something?"

"You might say," Kenner said. "Sort of a protection racket."

"It figures," the kid said. "Nobody makes that much money without a story behind it, you know what I mean?"

Kenner said he did. In fact, V. Allen Willy's story was as typically American as Horatio Alger's. Al Willy had started a chain of inexpensive clothing stores, taking clothes sewn in Third-World sweatshops and selling them in Western cities for thirty times the cost. After ten years, he sold his company for $400 million. Soon after, he became (by his own definition) a radical socialist, a crusader for a sustainable world, and an advocate for environmental justice.

The exploitations he had found so profitable he now attacked with the money he had made from them. He was fiery and righteous, and with the V. added to his name, memorable too. However, his attacks often led companies to pull out of their Third World factories, which were then taken over by Chinese corporations that paid local workers even less than before. Thus, by any sensible account, V. Allen Willy was exploiting workers twice—once to make his fortune, and a second time to assuage his guilty conscience at their expense. He was a strikingly handsome man and not stupid, just an egotistical and impractical do-gooder. Currently, he was said to be writing a book on the precautionary principle.

He had also started the V. Allen Willy Foundation, which supported the cause of environmental justice through dozens of organizations, including NERF. And he was important enough to rate a personal visit from Henley himself.

"So he's a rich environmentalist?" the FBI kid said.

"That's right," Kenner said.

The kid nodded. "Okay," he said. "But I still don't get it. What makes you think a rich guy would leave his house empty?"

"I can't tell you that," Kenner said. "But he will. And I want to know the minute it happens." He handed the agent a card. "Call this number."

The kid looked at the card. "That's it?"

"That's it," Kenner said.

"And when is this going to happen?"

"Soon," Kenner said.

His phone buzzed. He flipped it open. It was a text message from Sanjong.

THEY FOUND AV SCORPIO.

"I have to go," Kenner said.

"Nonsense," Ted Bradley said, sitting back in the passenger seat as Evans drove to Van Nuys. "You can't have all the fun, Pietro. I know you've been going on these secret excursions for the last week. I'm coming, too."

"You can't come, Ted," Evans said. "They won't allow it."

"Let me worry about that, okay?" he said, grinning.

Evans thought: What's going on? Bradley was staying so close, he was practically holding his hand. He refused to leave him alone.

Evans's cell phone rang. It was Sarah.

"Where are you?" she said.

"Almost to the airport. I have Ted with me."

"Uh-huh," she said, in the vague tone that meant she couldn't talk. "Well, we just got to the airport, and there seems to be a problem."

"What kind of a problem?"

"Legal," she said.

"What does that mean?" Evans said. But even as he spoke, he was turning off the road toward the gate leading to the runway, and he could see for himself.

Herb Lowenstein was standing there with eight security guards. And it looked like they were sealing the doors to Morton's jet.

Evans went through the gate and got out of the car. "What's going on, Herb?"

"The aircraft is being sealed," Herb said, "as required by law."

"What law?"

"George Morton's estate is now in probate, in case you've forgotten, and the contents of said estate, including all bank accounts and real property, must be sealed pending federal evaluation and assessing of death taxes. This aircraft will remain sealed until the conclusion of that evaluation. Six to nine months from now."

At that moment, Kenner pulled up in a town car. He introduced himself, shook hands with Lowenstein. "So it's a matter of probate," he said.

"That's right," Lowenstein said.

Kenner said, "I'm surprised to hear you say that."

"Why? George Morton is deceased."

"Is he? I hadn't heard."

"They found his body yesterday. Evans and Bradley went up and made the identification."

"And the medical examiner concurred?"

Lowenstein hesitated fractionally. "I presume so."

"You presume? Surely you've received documentation from the medical examiner to that effect. The autopsy was performed last night."

"I presume—I believe that we have the documentation."

"May I see it?"

"I believe it is at the office."

Kenner said, "May I see it?"

"That would merely cause unnecessary delay of my work here." Lowenstein turned to Evans. "Did you or did you not make a positive identification of Morton's body?"

"I did," Evans said.

"And you, Ted?"

"Yeah," Bradley said. "I did. It was him, all right. It was George. Poor guy."

Kenner said to Lowenstein, "I'd still like to see the medical examiner's notification."

Lowenstein snorted. "You have no basis for such a request, and I formally deny it. I am the senior attorney in charge of the estate. I am his

STATE OF FEAR ▶ 473

designated executor, and I have already told you that my office has the documentation in hand."

"I heard you," Kenner said. "But I seem to remember that to falsely declare probate is fraud. That could be quite serious for an officer of the court such as you."

"Look," Lowenstein said, "I don't know what your game is—"

"I merely want to see the document," Kenner said calmly. "There's a fax machine in the flight office, right there." He pointed to the building, near the airplane. "You can have the document sent over in a few seconds and resolve this matter without difficulty. Or, barring that, you can call the medical examiner's office in San Francisco and confirm that they have, in fact, made a positive identification."

"But we are in the presence of two eyewitnesses who—"

"These are the days of DNA testing," Kenner said, looking at his watch. "I recommend that you make the calls." He turned to the security officers. "You can open the aircraft."

The security officers looked nonplussed. "Mr. Lowenstein?"

"Just a minute, just a goddamned minute," Lowenstein said, and stalked off toward the office, putting his cell phone to his ear as he went.

"Open the plane," Kenner said. He flipped open his wallet and showed the guards his badge.

"Yes, sir," they said.

Another car pulled up, and Sarah got out with Ann Garner. Ann said, "What's the fuss?"

"Just a little misunderstanding," Kenner said. He introduced himself to her.

"I know who you are," she said, with barely concealed hostility.

"I thought you might," Kenner said, smiling.

"And I have to say," she continued, "it's guys like you—smart and unscrupulous and immoral—who have made our environment the polluted mess that it now is. So let's just get that on the table right away. I don't like you, Mr. Kenner. I don't like you personally, and I don't like what you do in the world, and I don't like anything you stand for."

"Interesting," Kenner said. "Perhaps some day you and I could have a detailed and specific conversation about exactly what is wrong with our environment, and exactly who is responsible for making it a polluted mess."

"Whenever you want," she said, angrily.

"Good. You have legal training?"

"No."

"Scientific training?"

"No."

"What is your background?"

"I worked as a documentary film producer. Before I quit to raise my family."

"Ah."

"But I am very dedicated to the environment, and I have been all my life," she said. "I read everything. I read the 'Science' section of the *New York Times* every Tuesday *cover to cover*, of course *The New Yorker*, and the *New York Review*. I am extremely well informed."

"Well then," Kenner said, "I look forward to our conversation."

The pilots were driving up to the gate; they waited while it opened. "I think we can leave in a few minutes," Kenner said. He turned to Evans. "Why don't you confirm that that is all right with Mr. Lowenstein."

"Okay," Evans said, and headed toward the flight office.

"Just so you know," Ann said, "we're going with you. I am, and so is Ted."

"That will be delightful," Kenner said.

Inside the flight office, Evans found Lowenstein hunched over a phone in the back room reserved for pilots. "But I'm telling you, the guy isn't going for it, he wants documentation," Lowenstein said. And then after a pause, "Look, Nick, I'm not going to lose my license over this one. The guy's got a law degree from Harvard."

Evans knocked on the door. "Everything okay for us to leave?"

"Just a minute," Lowenstein said into the phone. He put his hand over the receiver. "You're going to leave now?"

"That's right. Unless you have the document . . ."

"It seems there is some confusion about the exact status of Morton's estate."

"Then we're going, Herb."

"Okay, okay."

He turned back to the phone. "They're leaving, Nick," he said. "You want to stop them, do it yourself."

In the cabin, everyone was sitting down. Kenner went around passing out sheets of paper. "What's this?" Bradley said, with a glance to Ann.

"It's a release," Kenner said.

Ann was reading aloud, "'. . . not liable in the event of death, serious bodily injury, disability, dismemberment'—*dismemberment?*"

"That's right," Kenner said. "You need to understand that where we are going is extremely dangerous. I strongly advise both of you not to come. But if you insist on ignoring my advice, you need to sign that."

"Where are we going?" Bradley said.

"I can't tell you that until the plane is in the air."

"Why is it dangerous?"

"Do you have a problem signing the form?" Kenner said.

"No. Hell." Bradley scrawled his signature.

"Ann?"

Ann hesitated, bit her lip, and signed.

The pilot closed the doors. The engines whined as they taxied up the runway. The flight attendant asked what they would like to drink.

"Puligny-Montrachet," Evans said.

Ann said, "Where are we going?"

"To an island off the coast of New Guinea."

"Why?"

"There is a problem," Kenner said, "that has to be dealt with."

"You want to be any more specific?"

"Not right now."

The plane rose above the cloud layer in Los Angeles, and turned west, over the Pacific.

EN ROUTE
WEDNESDAY, OCTOBER 13
4:10 P.M.

Sarah felt relieved when Jennifer Haynes went to the front of the cabin to take a nap, falling instantly asleep. But she found it awkward to have Ann and Ted onboard. Conversation in the cabin was stilted; Kenner was not saying much. Ted was drinking heavily. He said to Ann, "Just so you know, Mr. Kenner doesn't believe in anything that normal people believe in. Not even global warming. Or Kyoto."

"Of course he doesn't believe in Kyoto," Ann said. "He's an industry hit man. Representing coal and oil interests."

Kenner said nothing. He just handed her his card.

"Institute for Risk Analysis," Ann read aloud. "That's a new one. I'll add it to the list of phony right-wing fronts."

Kenner said nothing.

"Because it's *all* disinformation," Ann said. "The studies, the press releases, the flyers, websites, the organized campaigns, the big-money smears. Let me tell you, industry was *thrilled* when the US didn't sign Kyoto."

Kenner rubbed his chin, and said nothing.

Ann said, "We're the world's largest polluter, and our government doesn't give a damn."

Kenner smiled blandly.

"So now the United States is an international pariah, isolated from the rest of the world and justifiably despised because we failed to sign the Kyoto Protocol to attack a global problem."

She continued to goad him in this way, and finally, it seemed, he had had enough. "Tell me about Kyoto, Ann," he said. "Why should we have signed it?"

"Why? Because we have a moral obligation to join the rest of the civilized world in reducing carbon emissions to below 1990 levels."

"What effect would that treaty have?"

"The whole world knows that. It would reduce global temperatures in the year 2100."

"By how much?"

"I don't know what you're driving at."

"Don't you? The answer is well known. The effect of Kyoto would be to reduce warming by .04 degrees Celsius in the year 2100. Four hundredths of a degree. Do you dispute that outcome?"

"I certainly do. Four what? Hundredths of a degree? That's ridiculous."

"So you don't believe that would be the effect of the Kyoto Protocol?"

"Well, maybe because the United States didn't sign it—"

"No, that would be the effect if we *did* sign it. Four hundredths of a degree."

"No," she said, shaking her head. "I don't believe that's true."

"The figure has been published a number of times in scientific journals. I can give you the references."*

Raising his glass, Bradley said to Ann, "This guy is real big on references."

"As opposed to rhetoric," Kenner said, nodding. "Yes. I am."

Bradley belched. "Four hundredths of a degree? In a hundred years? What a bunch of bullshit."

"One could say so."

---

* Most recently, *Nature* 22 (October 2003): 395–741, stated, with Russia signed on, temperature affected by Kyoto would be −.02 degrees C by 2050. IPCC models estimate more, but none exceed .15 C. Lomborg, p. 302. Wigley, 1998: "Global warming reductions are small, .08–.28 C."

"I just did," Bradley said.

"But Kyoto's a first step," Ann said, "that's the point. Because if you believe in the precautionary principle, as I do—"

"I didn't think the purpose of Kyoto was to take a first step," Kenner said. "I thought the purpose was to reduce global warming."

"Well, it is."

"Then why make a treaty that won't accomplish that? That won't, in effect, do anything at all?"

"It's a first step, as I said."

"Tell me: do you think it's *possible* to reduce carbon dioxide?"

"Of course. There are a host of alternative energy sources just waiting to be adopted. Wind power, solar, waste, geothermal—"

"Tom Wigley and a panel of seventeen scientists and engineers from around the world made a careful study and concluded it is not possible. Their paper was published in *Science*. They said there is no known technology capable of reducing carbon emissions, or even holding them to levels many times higher than today. They conclude that wind, solar, and even nuclear power will not be sufficient to solve the problem. They say totally new and undiscovered technology is required."*

"That's crazy," Ann said. "Amory Lovins laid it all out twenty years ago. Wind and solar, conservation, energy efficiency. There's no problem."

"Apparently there is. Lovins predicted that thirty-five percent of US power would come from alternative energy by the year 2000. The actual figure turned out to be six percent."

"Not enough subsidies."

"No country in the world produces thirty-five percent renewable energy, Ann."

"But countries like Japan do much better than we do."

Kenner said, "Japan is five percent renewable. Germany is five percent. England two percent."

---

* Martin Hoffert, et al., "Advanced Technology Paths to Global Climate Stability: Energy for a Greenhouse Planet," *Science* 298 (Nov. 1, 2002): 981–87. "Energy sources that can produce 100 to 300% of present world power consumption without greenhouse emissions do not exist."

"Denmark."

"Eight percent."

"Well," she said, "it just means we have more work to do."

"No question about that. Wind farms chop birds to pieces, so they might not be so popular. But solar panels would work. Silent, efficient . . ."

"Solar is great," she said.

"Yes," Kenner said. "And all we need is about twenty-seven thousand square kilometers of panels to do the job. Just cover the state of Massachusetts with solar panels and we'd be done. Of course by 2050 our energy needs will triple, so maybe New York would be a better choice."

"Or Texas. Nobody I know cares about Texas," Ann said.

"Well, there you are," Kenner said. "Cover ten percent of Texas, and you're in business. Although," he added, "Texans would probably prefer to cover Los Angeles first."

"You're making a joke."

"Not at all. Let's settle on Nevada. It's all desert anyway. But I'm curious to hear about your personal experience with alternative energy. What about you yourself, Ann? Have you adopted alternative sources?"

"Yes. I have solar heating for my swimming pool. The maid drives a hybrid."

"What do you drive?"

"Well, I need a bigger car for the kids."

"How big?"

"Well, I drive an SUV. Sometimes."

"What about your residence? You have solar panels for your electricity?"

"Well, I had consultants come to the house. Only, Jerry—my husband—says it's too expensive to install. But I'm working on him."

"And your appliances . . ."

"Every single one is Energystar. Every one."

"That's good. And how large is your family?"

"I have two boys. Seven and nine."

"Wonderful. How big is your house?"

"I don't know exactly."

"How many square feet?"

She hesitated.

"Ah hell, tell him, Ann," Bradley said. "She has a *huge* fucking house. Must be ten, fifteen thousand square feet. Absolutely *beautiful*. And the grounds! Got to be an acre, acre and a half. Sprinklers going day and night. And such gorgeous landscaping—she has fund-raisers there all the time. Always wonderful events."

Kenner looked at her.

"Twelve thousand," Ann said. "Square feet."

"For four people?" Kenner said.

"Well, my mother-in-law lives with us, sometimes. And of course the maid in the back."

"And do you have a second home?" Kenner said.

"Shit, she's got *two*," Bradley said. "Got a *fabulous* place in Aspen, and a great house in Maine as well."

"That we inherited," Ann said. "My husband—"

"And that apartment in London," Bradley said, "is that yours or your husband's company or what?"

"The company."

Kenner said, "How about travel? You use private jets?"

"Well, I mean we don't *own* one, but we catch rides, whatever. We go when people are going anyway. We fill the plane up. Which is a *good* thing."

"Of course," Kenner said. "But I must admit I'm a little confused about the philosophy—"

"Hey," she said, suddenly angry. "I live in a milieu where I have to keep up a certain standard. It's necessary for my husband's business, and—anyway, where do you live?"

"I have an apartment in Cambridge."

"How big?"

"Nine hundred square feet. I do not own a car. I fly coach."

"I don't believe you," she said.

"I think you'd better," Bradley said. "This guy knows what he's—"

"Shut up, Ted," Ann said. "You're drunk."

"Not yet, I'm not," he said, looking wounded.

"I'm not judging you, Ann," Kenner said quietly. "I know you're a dedicated advocate. I'm just trying to figure out what your real position is on the environment."

"My position is human beings are heating the planet and poisoning the planet and we have a moral obligation to the biosphere—to all the plants and animals that are being destroyed, and to the unborn generations of human beings—to keep these catastrophic changes from taking place." She sat back, nodding her head.

"So our moral obligation is to others—other plants, animals, and other people."

"Exactly."

"We need to do what is in their interest?"

"What is in the interest of all of us."

"Conceivably their interest is not the same as ours. Conflict of interest is the usual case."

"Every creature has a right to live on the planet."

"Surely you don't believe that," Kenner said.

"I do. I'm not speciesist. Every living creature."

"Even the malaria parasite?"

"Well, it *is* part of nature."

"Then do you oppose the elimination of polio and smallpox? They were part of nature, too."

"Well, I would have to say it's part of the arrogant pattern of mankind, changing the world to suit his purposes. A testosterone-driven impulse, not shared by women—"

"You didn't answer me," Kenner said. "Do you oppose the elimination of polio and smallpox?"

"You're playing with words."

"Hardly. Is changing the world to suit one's purposes unnatural?"

"Of course. It is interfering with nature."

"Ever seen a termite mound? A beaver dam? Those creatures change the environment dramatically, affecting many other creatures. Are they interfering with nature?"

"The world is not in danger," she said, "from termite mounds."

"Arguably it is. The total weight of termites exceeds the total weight of all the humans in the world. A thousand times greater, in fact. Do you know how much methane termites produce? And methane is a more potent greenhouse gas than carbon dioxide."

"I can't continue this," Ann said. "You enjoy arguing. I don't. I just want to make the world a better place. I'm going to go read a magazine now." She went to the front of the plane and sat down, her back to Kenner.

Sarah stayed where she was. "Her intentions are good," she said.

"And her information is bad," Kenner said. "A prescription for disaster."

Ted Bradley roused himself. He had watched the debate between Kenner and Ann. He liked Ann. He was pretty sure he had gone to bed with her; when he was drinking, he sometimes couldn't remember, but he had a vaguely fond memory of Ann, and he assumed that was the reason for it.

"I think you're being harsh," Bradley said, in his presidential tone. "Why should you call someone like Ann 'a prescription for disaster?' She cares very much about these issues. She has devoted her life to them, really. She cares."

"So what?" Kenner said. "*Caring* is irrelevant. Desire to do good is irrelevant. All that counts is *knowledge* and *results*. She doesn't have the knowledge—and, worse, she doesn't know it. Human beings don't know how to do the things she believes ought to be done."

"Like what?"

"Like managing the environment. We don't know how to do that."

"What are you talking about?" Bradley said, throwing his hands in the air. "This is nonsense. Of course we can manage the environment."

"Really? Do you know anything about the history of Yellowstone Park? The first national park?"

"I've been there."

"That's not what I asked."

"Could you just get to the point?" Bradley said. "It's pretty late for Q-and-A, Professor. You know what I mean?"

"All right, then," Kenner said. "I'll tell you."

Yellowstone Park, he explained, was the first wilderness to be set aside as a natural preserve anywhere in the world. The region around the Yellowstone River in Wyoming had long been recognized for its wondrous scenic beauty. Lewis and Clark sang its praises. Artists like Bierstadt and Moran painted it. And the new Northern Pacific Railroad wanted a scenic attraction to draw tourists west. So in 1872, in part because of railroad pressure, President Ulysses Grant set aside two million acres and created Yellowstone National Park.

There was only one problem, unacknowledged then and later. No one had any experience trying to preserve wilderness. There had never been any need to do it before. And it was assumed to be much easier than it proved to be.

When Theodore Roosevelt visited the park in 1903, he saw a landscape teeming with game. There were thousands of elk, buffalo, black bear, deer, mountain lions, grizzlies, coyotes, wolves, and bighorn sheep. By that time there were rules in place to keep things as they were. Soon after that, the Park Service was formed, a new bureaucracy whose sole job was to maintain the park in its original condition.

Yet within ten years, the teeming landscape that Roosevelt saw was gone forever. And the reason for this was the park managers—charged with keeping the park in pristine condition—had taken a series of steps that they thought were in the best interest of preserving the park and its animals. But they were wrong.

"Well," Bradley said, "our knowledge has increased with time . . ."

"No, it hasn't," Kenner said. "That's my point. It's a perpetual claim that we know more today, and it's not borne out by what actually happened."

Which was this: the early park managers mistakenly believed that elk were about to become extinct. So they tried to increase the elk herds within the park by eliminating predators. To that end, they shot and poisoned all the wolves in the park. And they prohibited Indians from hunting in the park, though Yellowstone was a traditional hunting ground.

Protected, the elk herds exploded, and ate so much of certain trees and grasses that the ecology of the area began to change. The elk ate the trees that the beavers used to make dams, so the beavers vanished. That was when the managers discovered beavers were vital to the overall water management of the region.

When the beavers disappeared, the meadows dried up; the trout and otter vanished; soil erosion increased; and the park ecology changed even further.

By the 1920s it had become abundantly clear there were too many elk, so the rangers began to shoot them by the thousands. But the change in plant ecology seemed to be permanent; the old mix of trees and grasses did not return.

It also became increasingly clear that the Indian hunters of old had exerted a valuable ecological influence on the park lands by keeping down the numbers of elk, moose, and bison. This belated recognition came as part of a more general understanding that native Americans had strongly shaped the "untouched wilderness" that the first white men saw—or thought they were seeing—when they first arrived in the New World. The "untouched wilderness" was nothing of the sort. Human beings on the North American continent had exerted a huge influence on the environment for thousands of years—burning plains grasses, modifying forests, thinning specific animal populations, and hunting others to extinction.

In retrospect, the rule forbidding Indians from hunting was seen as a mistake. But it was just one of many mistakes that continued to be made in an unbroken stream by park managers. Grizzlies were protected, then killed off. Wolves were killed off, then brought back. Animal research involving field study and radio collars was halted, then resumed after certain species were declared endangered. A policy of fire prevention was instituted, with no understanding of the regenerative effects of fire. When the policy was finally reversed, thousands of acres burned so hotly that the ground was sterilized, and the forests did not grow back without reseeding. Rainbow trout were introduced in the 1970s, soon killing off the native cutthroat species.

And on and on.

And on.

"So what you have," Kenner said, "is a history of ignorant, incompetent, and disastrously intrusive intervention, followed by attempts to repair the intervention, followed by attempts to repair the damage caused by the repairs, as dramatic as any oil spill or toxic dump. Except in this case there is no evil corporation or fossil fuel economy to blame. This disaster was caused by environmentalists charged with protecting the wilderness, who made one dreadful mistake after another—and, along the way, proved how little they understood the environment they intended to protect."

"This is absurd," Bradley said. "To preserve a wilderness, you just preserve it. You leave it alone and let the balance of nature take over. That's all that is required."

"Absolutely wrong," Kenner said. "Passive protection—leaving things alone—doesn't preserve the status quo in a wilderness, any more than it does in your backyard. The world is alive, Ted. Things are constantly in flux. Species are winning, losing, rising, falling, taking over, being pushed back. Merely setting aside wilderness doesn't freeze it in its present state, any more than locking your children in a room will prevent them from growing up. Ours is a changing world, and if you want to preserve a piece of land in a particular state, you have to decide what that state is, and then actively, even aggressively, manage it."

"But you said we don't know how to do that."

"Correct. We don't. Because any action you take causes change in the environment, Ted. And any change hurts some plant or animal. It's inevitable. Preserving old-growth forest to help the spotted owl means Kirtland's warbler and other species are deprived of the new-growth forest they prefer. There is no free lunch."

"But—"

"No buts, Ted. Name an action that had only positive consequences."

"Okay, I will. Banning CFCs for the ozone layer."

"That harmed Third World people by eliminating cheap refrigerants so that their food spoiled more often and more of them died of food poisoning."

"But the ozone layer is more important—"

"Perhaps to you. They might disagree. But we're talking about whether you can take an action that does not have harmful consequences."

"Okay. Solar panels. Water recycling systems for houses."

"Enables people to put houses in remote wilderness areas where formerly they could not because of lack of water and power. Invades wilderness and thus endangers species that were previously unmolested."

"Banning DDT."

"Arguably the greatest tragedy of the twentieth century. DDT was the best agent against mosquitoes, and despite the rhetoric there was nothing anywhere near as good or as safe. Since the ban, two million people a year have died unnecessarily from malaria, mostly children. All together, the ban has caused more than fifty million needless deaths.* Banning DDT killed more people than Hitler, Ted. And the environmental movement pushed hard for it."[†]

"But DDT was a carcinogen."

"No, it wasn't. And everybody knew it at the time of the ban."[‡]

"It was unsafe."

"Actually, it was so safe you could eat it. People did just that for two

---

* Some estimates put the number at 30 million deaths.

[†] Full discussion of DDT in Wildavsky, 1994, pp. 55–80.

[‡] Sweeney Committee, 25 April 1972, "DDT is not a carcinogenic hazard to man." Ruckelshaus banned it two months later, saying, DDT "poses a carcinogenic risk" to man. He never read the Sweeney report.

years, in one experiment.* After the ban, it was replaced by parathion, which is *really* unsafe. More than a hundred farm workers died in the months after the DDT ban, because they were unaccustomed to handling really toxic pesticides."†

"We disagree about all this."

"Only because you lack the relevant facts, or are unwilling to face up to the consequences of the actions of organizations you support. Banning DDT will someday be seen as a scandalous blunder."

"DDT was never banned."

"You're right. Countries were just told that if they used it, they wouldn't get foreign aid." Kenner shook his head. "But the unarguable point, based on UN statistics, is that before the DDT ban, malaria had become almost a minor illness. Fifty thousand deaths a year worldwide. A few years later, it was once again a global scourge. Fifty million people have died since the ban, Ted. Once again, there can be no action without harm."

A long silence followed. Ted shifted in his seat, started to speak, then closed his mouth again. Finally he said, "Okay. Fine." He adopted his most lofty, presidential manner. "You have persuaded me. I grant you the point. So?"

"So the real question with any environmental action is, do the benefits outweigh the harm? Because there is always harm."

"Okay, okay. So?"

"When do you hear any environmental group speak that way? Never. They're all absolutists. They go before judges arguing that regulations should be imposed with no consideration of costs at all.‡ The requirement that regulations show a cost-benefit was imposed on them by the courts after a period of wretched excess. Environmentalists screamed bloody murder about cost-benefit requirements and they're still screaming. They don't want people to know how much their forays into regulation actually cost society and the world. The most egregious

* Hayes, 1969.
† John Noble Wilford, "Deaths from DDT Successor Stir Concern," *New York Times*, 21 August 1970, p. 1; Wildavsky, 1996, p. 73.
‡ Case references in Sunstein, pp. 200–1.

example was the benzene regulations in the late 1980s that were so expensive for so little benefit that they ended up costing twenty billion dollars for every year of life saved.* Do you agree with that regulation?"

"Well, when you put it in those terms, no."

"What other terms are there, Ted, besides the truth? Twenty billion dollars *to save one year of life*. That was the cost of the regulation. Should you support organizations that push for such wasteful regulation?"

"No."

"The lead benzene lobbying group in Congress was NERF. Are you going to resign from its board?"

"Of course not."

Kenner just nodded slowly. "And there we have it."

Sanjong was pointing to the computer screen, and Kenner came over, sliding into the seat next to him. The screen showed an aerial image of a tropical island, heavily forested, and a broad curving bay of blue water. The photo seemed to be taken from a low-flying airplane. Around the bay were four weathered wood shacks.

"Those are new," Sanjong said. "They went up in the last twenty-four hours."

"They look old."

"Yes, but they're not. Close inspection suggests that they are artificial. They may be made out of plastic instead of wood. The largest one appears to be a residence, and the other three house equipment."

"What kind of equipment?" Kenner said.

"Nothing has been visible in the photographs. The equipment was probably offloaded at night. But I went back and got a decent description from Hong Kong customs. The equipment consists of three hypersonic

* See the Harvard Center for Risk Analysis study: Tengs, et al., 1995. For full discussion, see Lomborg, p. 338ff. He concludes: "When we ignore the cost of our environmental decisions . . . on other areas . . . we are in reality committing statistical murder." He puts the number of unnecessary dead at 60,000 per year in the US alone.

cavitation generators. Mounted in carbon matrix resonant impact assembly frames."

"Hypersonic cavitation equipment is for sale?"

"They got it. I don't know how."

Kenner and Sanjong were huddled together, speaking in low tones. Evans drifted over, leaned in close. "What's a hypersonic whatever-it-is?" he said quietly.

"Cavitation generator," Kenner said. "It's a high-energy acoustic device the size of a small truck that produces a radially symmetric cavitation field."

Evans looked blank.

"Cavitation," Sanjong explained, "refers to the formation of bubbles in a substance. When you boil water, that's cavitation. You can boil water with sound, too, but in this case the generators are designed to induce cavitation fields in a solid."

Evans said, "What solid?"

"The earth," Kenner said.

"I don't get it," Evans said. "They're going to make bubbles in the ground, like boiling water?"

"Something like that, yes."

"Why?"

They were interrupted by the arrival of Ann Garner. "Is this a boys-only meeting?" she said. "Or can anyone sit in?"

"Of course," Sanjong said, tapping the keyboard. The screen showed a dense array of graphs. "We were just reviewing the carbon dioxide levels of ice cores taken from Vostok and from North GRIP in Greenland."

"You guys can't keep me in the dark forever, you know," Ann said. "Sooner or later we will land this plane. And then I'm going to find out what you're really up to."

"That's true," Kenner said.

"Why not tell me now?"

Kenner just shook his head.

The pilot clicked the radio. "Check your seat belts, please," he said. "Prepare for landing in Honolulu."

Ann said, "Honolulu!"

"Where did you think we were going?"

"I thought—"

And then she broke off.

Sarah thought: *She knows where we are going.*

While they refueled at Honolulu, a customs inspector came onboard and asked to see their passports. He seemed amused by the presence of Ted Bradley, whom he referred to as "Mr. President"; Bradley in turn was pleased by the attention from a man in uniform.

After the customs officer checked their passports, he said to the group, "Your destination is filed as Gareda in the Solomon Islands. I just want to make sure you're aware of the travel advisory for Gareda. Most embassies have warned visitors against going there in view of the current conditions."

"What current conditions?" Ann said.

"There are rebels active on the island. There have been a number of murders. The Australian army went in last year and captured most of the rebels, but not all. There have been three murders in the last week, including two foreigners. One of the corpses was, uh, mutilated. And the head was taken."

"What?"

"The head was taken. Not while he was alive."

Ann turned to Kenner. "That's where we are going? Gareda?"

Kenner nodded slowly.

"What do you mean, the head was taken?"

"Presumably, it was for the skull."

"The skull," she repeated. "So . . . you're talking about head-hunters . . ."

Kenner nodded.

"I'm getting off this plane," she said, and gathering up her hand bag, walked down the stairs.

Jennifer was just waking up. "What's her problem?"

"She doesn't like good-byes," Sanjong said.

Ted Bradley was stroking his chin in what he imagined was a thoughtful manner. He said, "A foreigner had his head cut off?"

"Apparently, it was worse than that," the customs officer said.

"Jesus. What's worse than that?" Bradley said, laughing.

The customs officer said, "The situation on the ground is not entirely clear. The reports are conflicting."

Bradley stopped laughing. "No. Seriously: I want to know. What's worse than beheading?"

There was a brief silence.

"They ate him," Sanjong said.

Bradley rocked back in his chair. "They *ate* him?"

The customs officer nodded. "Parts of him," he said. "At least, that's the report."

"Holy shit," Bradley said. "Which parts? Never mind, I don't want to know. Jesus Christ. They *ate* the guy."

Kenner looked at him. "You don't have to go, Ted," he said. "You can leave, too."

"I have to admit, I'm thinking about it," he said, in his judicious, pres-idential tone. "Getting eaten is not a distinguished end to a career. Think of any of the greats. Think of Elvis—eaten. John Lennon—eaten. I mean, it's not how we want to be remembered." He fell silent, lowering his chin to his chest, sunk deep in thought, then raising it again. It was a gesture he'd done a hundred times on television. "But, no," he said finally. "I'll accept the danger. If you're going, I'm going."

"We're going," Kenner said.

It was nine hours flight time to Kontag Airport in Gareda. The cabin was dark; most of them slept. Kenner as usual stayed awake, sitting in the back with Sanjong, talking quietly.

Peter Evans woke up about four hours into the flight. His toes still burned from the Antarctic episode and his back was very sore from his being bounced around in the flash flood. But the pain in his toes reminded him that he was supposed to check them daily, to see if they were becoming infected. He got up and went to the back of the plane, where Kenner was sitting. He pulled off his socks and inspected his toes.

"Sniff 'em," Kenner said.

"What?"

"Smell them. You have any gangrene, you'll smell it first. They hurt?"

"Burn. Mostly just at night."

Kenner nodded. "You'll be all right. I think you'll keep them all."

Evans sat back, thinking how strange it was to have a conversation about losing his toes. Somehow it made his back hurt more. He went into the bathroom at the back of the plane and rummaged through the drawers looking for painkillers. All they had was Advil, so he took that, then came back.

"That was a clever story you arranged in Honolulu," he said. "Too bad it didn't work on Ted."

Kenner just stared.

"It's not a story," Sanjong said. "There were three murders yesterday."

"Oh. And they ate somebody?"

"That was the report."

"Oh," Evans said.

Going forward into the dark cabin, Evans saw Sarah sitting up. She whispered, "Can't sleep?"

"No. A little achy. You?"

"Yeah. Toes hurt. From the frostbite."

"Me, too."

She nodded toward the galley. "Any food back there?"

"I think so."

She got up, headed back. He trailed after her. She said, "The tops of my ears hurt, too."

"Mine are okay," he said.

She rummaged around, found some cold pasta. She held a plate out to him. He shook his head. She spooned out a plate for herself and began to eat. "So, how long have you known Jennifer?"

"I don't really know her," he said. "I just met her recently, at the law office."

"Why is she coming with us?"

"I think she knows Kenner."

"She does," Kenner said, from his chair.

"How?"

"She's my niece."

"Really?" Sarah said. "How long has she been your nie—never mind. I'm sorry. It's late."

"She's my sister's kid. Her parents died in a plane crash when she was eleven."

"Oh."

"She's been on her own a lot."

"Oh."

Evans looked at Sarah and thought once again that it was a kind of trick, how she could get up from sleeping and appear beautiful, and perfect. And she had on that perfume that had driven him quietly crazy from the moment he first smelled it.

"Well," Sarah said. "She seems very nice."

"I don't, uh, there's nothing . . ."

"It's fine," she said. "You don't have to pretend with me, Peter."

"I'm not pretending," he said, leaning slightly closer, smelling her perfume.

"Yes, you are." She moved away from him, and sat down opposite Kenner. "What happens when we get to Gareda?" she said.

The thing about her, Evans thought, was that she had the most chilling ability to instantly behave as if he did not exist. Right now she was not looking at him; she was focusing all her attention on Kenner, talking with apparent concentration to Kenner and behaving as if no one else were there.

Was that supposed to be provocative? he thought. Was that supposed to be a turn-on, to get him excited and start the chase? Because it didn't make him feel that way at all. It pissed him off.

He wanted to slap his hand down on the counter, make a big noise, and say, "Hel-lo! Earth to Sarah!" Or something like that.

But somehow he thought that that would make things worse. He could imagine her annoyed glance. *You're such a baby*. Something like that. It made him long for somebody uncomplicated, the way Janis was uncomplicated. Just a great body and a voice you could tune out. That was exactly what he needed now.

He gave a long sigh.

She heard it, glanced up at him, and then patted the seat beside her. "Come sit here, Peter," she said, "and join the conversation." And she gave him a big, dazzling smile.

He thought: *I am very confused.*

• • •

"This is Resolution Bay," Sanjong said, holding out his computer screen. It showed the bay, then zoomed back to show a map of the entire island. "It's on the northeast side of the island. The airport is on the west coast. It's about twenty-five miles away."

The island of Gareda looked like a big avocado immersed in the water, with jagged edges along the shore. "There is a mountain spine running along the center of the island," Sanjong said. "In places, it's three thousand feet high. The jungle in the interior of the island is very dense, essentially impenetrable, unless you follow the roads or one of the footpaths through the jungle. But we can't make our way cross country."

"So we take a road," Sarah said.

"Maybe," Sanjong said. "But the rebels are known to be in this area here—" he circled the center of the island with his finger "—and they have split up in two or possibly three groups. Their exact locations are not known. They have taken over this small village here, Pavutu, near the north coast. That seems to be their headquarters. And they presumably have roadblocks up, and probably patrols on the jungle paths."

"Then how do we get to Resolution Bay?"

Kenner said, "By helicopter, if we can. I've arranged for one, but this is not the most reliable part of the world. If we can't do that, we'll head out by car. See how far we can get. But at this point we just don't know how we're going to do it."

Evans said, "And when we get to Resolution Bay?"

"There are four new structures on the beach. We have to take them down and dismantle the machinery inside. Make them inoperable. We also have to find their submarine tender and dismantle the submarine."

"What submarine?" Sarah said.

"They leased a small two-man research sub. It's been in the region for the last two weeks."

"Doing what?"

"We're pretty sure we know now. The whole Solomon Island chain of more than nine hundred islands is located within a very active geological part of the world in terms of plate tectonics. The Solomons are a part of the world where plates crunch together. That's why they have many volcanoes there, and so many earthquakes. It's a very unstable region. The Pacific Plate collides and slides under the Oldowan Java Plateau. The result is the Solomon Trench, a huge undersea feature that curves in an arc all along the northern side of the island chain. It's very deep, between two thousand and six thousand feet. The trench is just north of Resolution Bay, too."

"So it's an active geological region with a deep trench," Evans said. "I still don't see the game."

"Lot of undersea volcanoes, lot of slope debris, and therefore the potential for landslides," Kenner said.

"Landslides." Evans rubbed his eyes. It was late.

"Undersea landslides," Kenner said.

Sarah said, "They're trying to cause an undersea landslide?"

"We think so. Somewhere along the slope of the Solomon Trench. Probably at the five-hundred- to one-thousand-foot depth."

Evans said, "And what would that do? An undersea landslide?"

Kenner said to Sanjong, "Show them the big map." Sanjong brought up a map of the entire Pacific basin, from Siberia to Chile, Australia to Alaska.

"Okay," Kenner said. "Now draw a straight line out from Resolution Bay and see where it takes you."

"California!"

"Right. In about eleven hours."

Evans frowned. "An undersea landslide . . ."

"Displaces an enormous volume of water very quickly. That is the most common way a tsunami is formed. Once propagated, the wave front will travel right across the Pacific at five hundred miles an hour."

"Holy shit," Evans said. "How big a wave are we talking?"

"Actually, it's a series, what's called a wave train. The undersea landslide in Alaska in 1952 generated a wave forty-seven feet high. But the height of this one is impossible to anticipate because wave height is a function of the shoreline it hits. In parts of California it could be up to sixty feet high. A six-story building."

"Oh boy," Sarah said.

"And how much time do we have before they do this?" Evans said.

"The conference runs two more days. The wave will take a day to cross the Pacific. So . . ."

"We have one day."

"At most, yes. One day to land, make our way to Resolution Bay, and stop them."

"Stop who?" Ted Bradley said, yawning and coming back toward them. "Je-sus! Do I have a headache or what! How about a little hair of the dog?" He paused, stared at the group, looking from face to face. "Hey, what's going on here? You guys look like I interrupted a funeral."

TO GAREDA
THURSDAY, OCTOBER 14
5:30 A.M.

Three hours later, the sun came up and the plane began its descent. Now it was flying low, passing over green forested islands fringed in an unearthly pale blue. They saw few roads and few towns, mostly small villages.

Ted Bradley looked out the window. "Isn't it beautiful?" he said. "Truly unspoiled paradise. This is what is vanishing in our world."

Seated opposite him, Kenner said nothing. He, too, was staring out the window.

"Don't you think the problem," Bradley said, "is that we have lost contact with nature?"

"No," Kenner said. "I think the problem is I don't see many roads."

"Don't you think," Bradley said, "that's because it's the white man, not the natives, who wants to conquer nature, to beat it into submission?"

"No, I don't think that."

"I do," Bradley said. "I find that people who live closer to the earth, in their villages, surrounded by nature, that those people have a natural ecological sense and a feeling for the fitness of it all."

"Spent a lot of time in villages, Ted?" Kenner said.

"As a matter of fact, yes. I shot a picture in Zimbabwe and another one in Botswana. I know what I am talking about."

"Uh-huh. You stayed in villages all that time?"

"No, I stayed in hotels. I had to, for insurance. But I had a lot of experiences in villages. There is no question that village life is best and ecologically soundest. Frankly, I think everyone in the world should live that way. And certainly, we should not be encouraging village people to industrialize. That's the problem."

"I see. So you want to stay in a hotel, but you want everybody else to stay in a village."

"No, you're not hearing—"

"Where do you live now, Ted?" Kenner said.

"Sherman Oaks."

"Is that a village?"

"No. Well, it's a sort of a village, I suppose you could say . . . But I have to be in LA for my work," Bradley said. "I don't have a choice."

"Ted, have you ever stayed in a Third-World village? Even for one night?"

Bradley shifted in his seat. "As I said before, I spent a lot of time in the villages while we were shooting. I know what I'm talking about."

"If village life is so great, why do you think people want to leave?"

"They shouldn't leave. That's my point."

"You know better than they do?" Kenner said.

Bradley paused, then blurted: "Well, frankly, if you must know, yes. I do know better. I have the benefit of education and broader experience. And I know firsthand the dangers of industrial society and how it is making the whole world sick. So, yes, I think I do know what is best for them. Certainly I know what is ecologically best for the planet."

"I have a problem," Kenner said, "with other people deciding what is in my best interest when they don't live where I do, when they don't know the local conditions or the local problems I face, when they don't even live in the same country as I do, but they still feel—in some far-off Western city, at a desk in some glass skyscraper in Brussels or Berlin or New York—they still feel that they know the solution to all my problems and how I should live my life. I have a problem with that."

"What's your problem?" Bradley said. "I mean, look: You don't seriously believe everybody on the planet should do whatever they want, do you? That would be terrible. These people need help and guidance."

"And you're the one to give it? To 'these people?'"

"Okay, so it's not politically correct to talk this way. But do you want all these people to have the same horrific, wasteful living standard that we do in America and, to a lesser extent, Europe?"

"I don't see you giving it up."

"No," Ted said, "but I conserve where I can. I recycle. I support a carbon-neutral lifestyle. The point is, if all these other people industrialize, it will add a terrible, terrible burden of global pollution to the planet. That should not happen."

"I got mine, but you can't have yours?"

"It's a question of facing realities," Bradley said.

"Your realities. Not theirs."

At that point, Sanjong beckoned to Kenner. "Excuse me," Kenner said, and got up.

"Walk away if you want," Bradley said, "but you know I speak truth!" He gestured to the flight attendant and held up his glass. "Just one more, sweetie. One more for the road."

Sanjong said, "The helicopter's not there yet."

"What's the matter?"

"It was coming over from another island. They've closed the air space because they're worried the rebels have surface-to-air missiles."

Kenner frowned. "How long until we land?"

"Ten minutes."

"Keep your fingers crossed."

Abandoned, Ted Bradley slid to the other side of the plane, to sit with Peter Evans. "Isn't it gorgeous?" he said. "Look at that water. Crystalline and pure. Look at the depth of that blue. Look at those beautiful villages, in the heart of nature."

Evans was staring out the window but saw only poverty. The villages were clusters of corrugated tin shacks, the roads red mud ruts. The people looked poorly dressed and moved slowly. There was a depressing, disconsolate feeling about them. He imagined sickness, disease, infant death . . .

"Gorgeous," Bradley said. "Pristine! I can't wait to get down there. This is as good as a vacation! Did anyone here know the Solomons were so beautiful?"

From the front, Jennifer said, "Inhabited by headhunters, for most of history."

"Yes, well, that's all in the past," Bradley said. "If it ever existed at all. I mean, all that talk about cannibalism. Everybody knows it is not true. I read a book by some professor.* There never were any cannibals, anywhere in the world. It's all a big myth. Another example of the way the white man demonizes people of color. When Columbus came to the West Indies, he thought they told him there were cannibals there, but it wasn't true. I forget the details. There are no cannibals anywhere. Just a myth. Why are you staring at me that way?"

Evans turned. Bradley was talking to Sanjong, who was indeed staring.

"Well?" Bradley said. "You're giving me a look. Okay, buddy boy. Does that mean you disagree with me?"

"You're truly a fool," Sanjong said, in an astonished voice. "Have you ever been to Sumatra?"

"Can't say that I have."

"New Guinea?"

"No. Always wanted to go, buy some tribal art. Great stuff."

"Borneo?"

"No, but I always wanted to go there, too. That Sultan What's his name, he did a great job remodeling the Dorchester in London—"

"Well," Sanjong said, "if you go to Borneo you will see the Dyak longhouses where they still display the skulls of the people they killed."

---

* William Arens, *The Man-Eating Myth*.

"Oh, that's just tourist-attraction stuff."

"In New Guinea, they had a disease called *kuru,* transmitted by eating the brains of their enemies."

"That's not true."

"Gajdusek won a Nobel Prize for it. They were eating brains, all right."

"But that was a long time ago."

"Sixties. Seventies."

"You guys just like to tell scare stories," Bradley said, "at the expense of the indigenous people of the world. Come on, face the facts, human beings are not cannibals."*

Sanjong blinked. He looked at Kenner. Kenner shrugged.

"Absolutely beautiful down there," Bradley said, looking out the window. "And it looks like we're going to land."

---

* Cannibalism in the American southwest: http://www.nature.com/nature/fow/000907.html; Richard A. Marlar, Leonard L. Banks, Brian R. Billman, Patricia M. Lambert, and Jennifer Marlar, "Biochemical evidence of cannibalism at a prehistoric Puebloan site in southwestern Colorado, *Nature* 407, 74078 (7 Sept. 2000). Among Celts in England: http://www.bris.ac.uk/Depts/Info-Office/news/archive/cannibal.htm. Among Neanderthals: http://news.bbc.co.uk/1/hi/sci/tech/462048.stm; same issue, Jared M. Diamond, "Archeology, talk of cannibalism" ("Incontrovertible evidence of cannibalism has been found at a 900-year-old site in the southwestern United States. Why do horrified critics deny that many societies have found cannibalism acceptable?").

VII

RESOLUTION

GAREDA
THURSDAY, OCTOBER 14
6:40 A.M.

Kotak Field was sticky with humid heat. They walked to the small open shack that was marked KASTOM in roughly painted letters. To one side of the building was a wooden fence and a gate marked with a red hand-print and a sign that said, NOGOT ROT.

"Ah, nougat rot," Bradley said. "Must be a local tooth problem."

"Actually," Sanjong said, "the red hand means *kapu*. 'Forbidden.' The sign says 'No Got Right,' which is Pidgin for 'You don't have permission to pass.'"

"Huh. I see."

Evans found the heat almost unbearable. He was tired after the long plane ride, and anxious about what lay ahead of them. Alongside him, Jennifer walked casually, seemingly fresh and energetic. "You're not tired?" Evans said to her.

"I slept on the plane."

He looked back at Sarah. She, too, seemed to have plenty of energy, striding forward.

"Well, I'm pretty tired."

"You can sleep in the car," Jennifer said. She didn't seem very interested in his condition. He found it a little irritating.

And it was certainly debilitatingly hot and humid. By the time they reached the customs house, Evans's shirt was soaked. His hair was wet.

Sweat was dripping off his nose and chin onto the papers he was supposed to fill out. The pen from the ink ran in the puddles of his sweat. He glanced up at the customs officer, a dark, muscular man with curly hair and wearing pressed white trousers and a white shirt. His skin was dry; he looked almost cool. He met Evans's eyes, and smiled. *"Oh, waitman, dis no taim bilong san. You tumas hotpela."*

Evans nodded. "Yes, true," he said. He had no idea what the man had said.

Sanjong translated. "It's not even the hot time of summer. But you're too much hot. You *tumas hot.* Ya?"

"He got that right. Where'd you learn Pidgin?"

"New Guinea. I worked there a year."

"Doing what?"

But Sanjong was hurrying on with Kenner, who was waving to a young man who had driven up in a Land Rover. The man jumped out. He was dark, wearing tan shorts and a T-shirt. His shoulders were covered in tattoos. His grin was infectious. "Hey, Jon Kanner! *Hamamas klok!*" He pounded his chest with his fist and hugged Kenner.

"He has a happy heart," Sanjong said. "They know each other."

The newcomer was introduced all around as Henry, with no other name. "Hanri!" he said, grinning broadly, pumping their hands. Then he turned to Kenner.

"I understand there is trouble with the helicopter," Kenner said.

"What? No *trabel. Me got klostu long.*" He laughed. "It's just over there, my friend," he said, in perfectly accented British English.

"Good," Kenner said, "we were worried."

"Yas, but serious Jon. We better *hariyap. Mi yet harim planti yangpelas, krosim, pasim birua, got plenti masket, noken stap gut, ya?*"

Evans had the impression Henry was speaking Pidgin so the rest of them would not understand.

Kenner nodded. "I heard that, too," he said. "Lots of rebels here. They're mostly young boys? And angry? And well armed. Figures."

"I worry for the helicopter, my friend."

"Why? Do you know something about the pilot?"

"Yes, I do."

"Why? Who is the pilot?"

Henry giggled, and slapped Kenner on the back. "I am!"

"Well, then, we should go."

They all started down the road, away from the airfield. The jungle rose up on both sides of the road. The air buzzed with the sound of cicadas. Evans looked back with longing at the beautiful white Gulf-stream jet, poised on the runway against a blue sky. The pilots in their white shirts and black trousers were checking the wheels. He wondered if he would ever see the airplane again.

Kenner was saying, "And we heard, Henry, some people were killed?"

Henry made a face. "No just killed, Jon. *Olpela.* Ya?"

"So we heard."

"Ya. *Distru.*"

So it was true. "The rebels did it?"

Henry nodded. "Oh! this new *chif,* him name Sambuca, like a drink. Don't ask why this name. Him crazy man, Jon. *Longlong man tru.* Every-thing back to *olpela* for dis guy. Old ways are better. *Allatime allatime.*"

"Well, the old ways are better," Ted Bradley said, trudging along behind, "if you ask me."

Henry turned. "You got cell phones, you got computers, you got antibiotics, medicines, hospitals. And you say the old ways are better?"

"Yes, because they are," Bradley said. "They were more human, they allowed more of the human texture to life. Believe me, if you ever had a chance to experience these so-called modern miracles yourself, you would know that they're not so great—"

"I got a degree at the University of Melbourne," Henry said. "So I have some familiarity."

"Oh, well, then," Bradley said. And under his breath, he muttered, "Might have told me. Asshole."

"By the way," Henry said, "take my advice, don't do that here. Don't talk under your breath."

"Why not?"

"In this country, some *pelas* think it means you've been possessed by a demon and they'll get scared. And they might kill you."

"I see. Charming."

"So, in this country, if you have something to say, you speak up!"

"I'll remember that."

Sarah walked alongside Bradley, but she was not listening to the conversation. Henry was a character, caught between worlds, sometimes speaking in an Oxbridge accent, sometimes dropping into Pidgin. It didn't bother her.

She was looking at the jungle. The air on the road was hot and still, trapped between the huge trees that rose up on both sides of the path. The trees were forty, fifty feet high, covered in twisted vines. And at ground level, in the darkness beneath the canopy above, huge ferns grew so thickly they presented an impenetrable barrier, a solid green wall.

She thought: You could walk five feet into that and get lost forever. You'd never find your way out again.

Along the road were the rusted hulks of long-abandoned cars, windshields smashed, chassis crumpled and corroded brown and yellow. As she walked past she saw ripped upholstery, old dashboards with clocks and speedometers ripped out, leaving gaping holes.

They turned right onto a side path and she saw the helicopter ahead. She gasped. It was beautiful, painted green with a crisp white stripe, the metal blades and struts gleaming. Everybody commented on it.

"Yes, the outside is good," Henry said. "But I think the inside, the engine, maybe is not so good." He wiggled his hand. "So so."

"Great," Bradley said. "Speaking for myself, I'd prefer it the other way around."

They opened the doors to get in. In the back were stacks of wooden crates, with sawdust. They smelled of grease. "I got the supplies you wanted," he said to Kenner.

"And enough ammunition?"

"Oh ya. All things you asked for."

"Then we can go," Kenner said.

In the back, Sarah buckled her belt. She put on headphones. The engines whined, and the blades spun faster. The helicopter shuddered as it started to lift off. "We have too many people," Henry said, "so we will have to hope for the best! Cross your fingers!"

And giggling maniacally, he lifted off into the blue sky.

TO RESOLUTION
THURSDAY, OCTOBER 14
9:02 A.M.

The jungle slid beneath them, mile after mile of dense canopy forest. In places, wisps of mist clung to the trees, particularly at the higher altitudes. Sarah was surprised at how mountainous the island was, how rugged the terrain. She saw no roads at all. From time to time, they passed over a small village in a jungle clearing. Otherwise, nothing but miles of trees. Henry was flying due north, intending to drop them off along the coast a few miles west of Resolution Bay.

"Charming villages," Ted Bradley said, as they flew over another one. "What do the people grow here?"

"Nothing. Land's no good here. They work the copper mines," Henry said.

"Oh, that's too bad."

"Not if you live here. Biggest money they ever saw. People kill to work in the mines. What I mean to say is, they kill. Some murders occur every year."

Bradley was shaking his head. "Terrible. Just terrible. But look down there," he said, pointing. "There's a village has actual thatched huts. Is that the old style, the old way of doing things, still kept alive?"

"No man," Henry said. "That's a rebel village. That's *new* style. Big thatch *haus*, very impressive, big house for *chif*." He explained that Sambuca had instructed the people in every village to build these huge, three-story structures of thatch, complete with ladders going up to high walk-ways at the third level. The idea was to give rebels a view over the jungle, so they could see the arrival of Australian troops.

But in the old days, Henry said, the people never had such buildings in Gareda. The architecture was low and open, erected mostly to protect against rain and let smoke out. There was no need for high buildings, which were impractical since they would blow down in the next cyclone anyway. "But Sambuca, he wants them now, so he makes the *yangpelas*, the young fellows, build them. There may be six or eight on this island now, in rebel territory."

"So we're going over rebel territory now?" Bradley said.

"So far, so good," Henry said. And he giggled again. "Not so long now, we'll see the coast in four, five minutes and—Oh damn shit!"

"What?" They were skimming the forest canopy.

"I made a big mistake."

"What mistake?" Bradley said.

"*Tumas longwe es.*"

"You're too far east?" Kenner said.

"Damn shit. Damn damn shit. Hang on!" Henry banked the heli-copter steeply, but not before they all glimpsed a huge clearing, with four of the enormous thatch structures interspersed with the more common houses of wood and corrugated tin. There were a half-dozen trucks clus-tered in the muddy center of the clearing. Some of the trucks had machine guns mounted on their backs.

"What is this?" Bradley said, looking down. "This is much bigger than the others—"

"This Pavutu! Rebel headquarters!"

And then the clearing was gone, the helicopter moving swiftly away. Henry was breathing hard. They could hear his breath over the earphones.

Kenner said nothing. He was staring intently at Henry.

"Well, I think we're all right," Bradley said. "It looks like they didn't see us."

"Oh yeah," Henry said. "Nice wish."

"Why?" Bradley said. "Even if they did see us—what can they do?"

"They have radios," Henry said. "They're not stupid, these *yangpelas.*"

"What do you mean?"

"They want this helicopter."

"Why? Can they fly it?"

"*Orait orait!* Yes! Because they want me, too." Henry explained that for months now, no helicopters had been allowed on the island. This one had been brought over only because Kenner had pulled some very important strings. But it was specifically not to fall into rebel hands.

"Well, they probably think we're going south," Bradley said. "I mean, we are, aren't we?"

"These boys know better," Henry said. "They know."

"They know what?" Bradley said.

Kenner said, "The ELF would have had to buy off the rebels in order to land on the island. So the rebels know there's something going on at Resolution Bay. When they saw this helicopter, they knew where it was going."

"These boys aren't stupid," Henry said again.

"I never said they were," Bradley protested.

"Ya. But you think it. I know you, *waitman.* This in the back of your tongue. You think it."

"I promise you, I did not," Bradley said. "Really. I have no such feelings at all. You simply didn't understand me."

"Ya," Henry said.

Sarah was sitting in the middle of the second seat, wedged between Ted and Jennifer. Peter and Sanjong were behind in the little backseat, with all the boxes. She couldn't really see out the windows, so she had trouble following the discussion. She wasn't sure what it was all about.

So she asked Jennifer. "Do you understand what's going on?"

Jennifer nodded. "As soon as the rebels saw the helicopter they knew it was going to Resolution. Now, whatever we do, they'll be expecting it to show up in that area. They have radios, and they're in different groups scattered around. They can keep an eye on us. And they'll be there when we land."

"I am very sorry," Henry said. "So very sorry."

"Never mind," Kenner said. His voice was neutral.

"What do we do now?" Henry said.

Kenner said, "Continue exactly as planned. Go north and put us down on the coast."

There was no mistaking the urgency in his voice.

In the backseat, pushed up against Sanjong, smelling the grease that coated the machine guns, Peter Evans wondered where this urgency came from. He looked at his watch. It was nine in the morning, which meant that of their original twenty-four hours, only twenty remained. But this was a small island, and it should allow plenty of time—

And then he had a thought. "Wait a minute," he said. "What time is it in Los Angeles?"

Sanjong said, "They're on the other side of the dateline. Twenty-seven hours behind."

"No, I mean elapsed time. Actual time difference."

"Six hours."

"And you calculated a transit time of what?"

"Thirteen hours," Sanjong said.

"I think we made a mistake," Evans said, biting his lip. He wasn't sure how much he should say in front of Henry. And indeed, Sanjong was shaking his head, indicating *not now*.

But they *had* made a mistake. There was no doubt about it. Assuming that Drake wanted the tidal wave to hit on the last day of the conference, he would surely want it to happen during the morning. That would provide the most visible disaster. And it would allow the whole afternoon for discussion and media interviews afterward. Every television camera in America would be at that conference, talking to the scientists who just happened to be there. It would create a gigantic media event.

So, Evans thought, assume the wave was to hit Los Angeles no later than noon tomorrow.

Subtract thirteen hours for the wave front to cross the Pacific.

That meant the wave had to be propagated at eleven P.M. Los Angeles time. Which meant that the local time in Gareda would be . . . five P.M.

Five P.M. *today.*

They didn't have a day to stop this thing from happening.

They had just eight hours.

So that was the reason for Kenner's urgency. That was why he was going ahead with his plan, despite the new problem. He had no choice, and he knew it. He had to land on the coast somewhere very near Resolution. There wasn't enough time to do anything else.

Even though it was possible they were heading right into a trap.

Leaving the forest behind, the helicopter burst out over blue water and turned around, going east. Evans saw a narrow sandy beach with patches of ragged lava rock, and mangrove swamps clinging to the water's edge. The helicopter swung low and followed the beach, heading east.

"How far from Resolution are we?" Kenner said.

"Five, six kilometers," Henry said.

"And how far from Pavutu?"

"Maybe ten kilometers, on a mud track."

"Okay," Kenner said. "Let's find a place to put down."

"There's a good place I know maybe one kilometer ahead."

"Fine. Go there."

Evans was thinking. Five kilometers walking on a beach, that was about three miles, should take them an hour and a half at most. They could make it to Resolution Bay well before noon. That would give them—

"This the spot," Henry said. A finger of rugged lava protruded into the ocean. Centuries of waves had smoothed it enough to make a landing possible.

"Do it," Kenner said.

The helicopter circled, prepared to descend. Evans was looking out over at the dense wall of jungle, where it met the beach. He saw tire tracks in the sand and a sort of gap in the trees that was probably a road. And those tire tracks—

"Say listen," Evans said. "I think—"

Sanjong jabbed him in the ribs. Hard.

Evans grunted.

"What is it, Peter?" Kenner said.

"Uh, nothing."

"We're going down," Henry said. The helicopter descended smoothly, slowly settling onto the lava. Waves lapped at the edge of the rock pad. It was peaceful. Kenner looked out the bubble canopy, scanning the area.

"Okay? This good spot?" Henry said. He seemed nervous now that they were down. "I don't want to stay so long, Jon. Because maybe they come soon . . ."

"Yeah, I understand."

Kenner cracked open the door, then paused.

"So, alla okay. Jon?"

"Just fine, Henry. Very nice spot. Get out and open this back door for us, will you?"

"Yeah, Jon, I think you can get it—"

"*Get out!*" And with astonishing swiftness there was a gun jammed against Henry's head. Henry sputtered and moaned in fear as he fumbled with his door. "But Jon, I need to stay inside, Jon—"

"You've been a bad boy, Henry," Kenner said.

"You going to shoot me now, Jon?"

"Not now," Kenner said, and abruptly he shoved him out. Henry tumbled onto the sharp lava, howling in pain. Kenner slid over to the pilot's seat and shut the door. Immediately Henry was up, pounding on the canopy, his eyes wild. He was terrified.

"Jon! Jon! Please, Jon!"

"Sorry, Henry." Kenner pushed the stick, and the helicopter began to rise into the air. They had not climbed twenty feet before a dozen men emerged from the jungle all along the beach and began firing at them with rifles. Kenner swung out over the ocean, going north, away from the island. Looking back, they could see Henry standing forlorn on the lava. Some of the men were running toward him. He threw up his hands.

"Little shit," Bradley said. "He would have gotten us killed."

"He may still," Kenner said.

They flew due north, over open water.

"So what do we do now," Sarah said, "land on the other side of the bay? Walk in from the other side?"

"No," Kenner said. "That's what they'll expect us to do."

"So, then . . ."

"We wait a few minutes and go back to the western side, same as before."

"They won't be expecting that?"

"They may. We'll go to a different spot."

"Farther away from the bay?"

"No. Closer."

"Won't ELF hear us?"

"Doesn't matter. By now, they know we're coming."

In the back, Sanjong was breaking open the wooden cases and reaching for the guns. He stopped abruptly.

"Bad news," he said.

"What?"

"No guns." He pushed a lid higher. "These crates contain ammunition. But no guns."

"That little bastard," Bradley said.

"What do we do now?" Sarah said.

"We go in anyway," Kenner said.

He turned the helicopter and, skimming the water, headed back to Gareda.

RESOLUTION
THURSDAY, OCTOBER 14
9:48 A.M.

The western arc of Resolution Bay consisted of a hilly, jungle-covered spine that jutted out into the water, terminating in a rocky point. The outer side of the spine flattened into a rocky plateau, some fifty feet above the beach, which curved off to the west. The plateau was protected by high overhanging trees.

That was where the helicopter now stood, covered in a camouflage tarp, overlooking the beach below. Evans glanced back at it, hoping that it would blend into the landscape, but instead it was only too obviously visible, especially when seen from above. The group was now already fifty feet above it, as they scrambled and clawed up the jungle slope that rose steeply from the beach. It was surprisingly tough going. They were climbing single file, and had to be careful because the ground underfoot was muddy. Bradley had already slipped, and slid some ten yards down. His whole left side was covered in black mud. And Evans could see that there was a fat leech on the back of his neck, but he decided not to point it out just then.

No one spoke. The team of six climbed in silence, trying to make as little noise as possible. Despite their best efforts, they were fairly noisy, the undergrowth crackling beneath their feet, small branches snapping as they reached to pull themselves up.

Kenner was somewhere farther ahead, leading the way. Evans couldn't see him. Sanjong was bringing up the rear. He had a rifle slung over his shoulder; he had brought it with him and assembled it from a small briefcase in the copter. Kenner carried a pistol. The rest of them were unarmed.

The air was still, wet, and stupefyingly hot. The jungle buzzed, an incessant background drone of insects. Halfway up the slope, it began to rain, lightly at first and then a stupendous tropical downpour. In a moment they were drenched. Water streamed down the hillside. It was slipperier than ever.

Now they were two hundred feet above the beach, and the prospect of losing footing was clearly nervous-making. Peter looked up at Sarah, who was just ahead of him. She moved with her usual agility and grace. She seemed to be dancing up the hillside.

There were times, he thought, huffing his way along, when he really resented her.

And Jennifer, who was ahead of Sarah, was climbing with equal ease. She hardly reached for the tree limbs, though Evans was grabbing for them constantly, feeling panic as his fingers slipped on the fungus-covered bark. Watching Jennifer, he had the sense that she was almost too good at this, too skilled. Going up this treacherous jungle hill, she radiated a kind of indifference, as if it were all to be expected. It was the attitude of an Army Ranger, or the member of some elite force, tough, experienced, conditioned. Unusual, he thought, for a lawyer. More than unusual. But then, she was Kenner's niece.

And farther up was Bradley, with the leech on his neck. He was muttering and cursing and grunting with every step. Finally Jennifer punched him, then held a finger to her lips: be quiet. Bradley nodded, and though he clearly disliked taking advice from her, he was silent from then on.

At around three hundred feet they felt the stirring of a breeze, and soon after, they climbed onto the crest of the ridge. The foliage was so thick they could not see down into Resolution Bay below, but they could hear the shouts of working men and the intermittent rumble of machinery.

Briefly, there was a kind of electronic hum, a sound that started softly, then built quickly until in a few moments it seemed literally to fill the air, and to make Evans's eardrums ache.

Then the sound was gone.

Evans looked at Kenner.

Kenner just nodded.

Sanjong climbed a tree, scaling it quickly. From his vantage point, he could look down on the valley. He came back down, and pointed to a hill leading down to the bay. He shook his head: too steep at this point. He indicated they should circle around, and descend on a more gentle slope.

So they started out, following the ridge around the bay. Most of the time they could see nothing but the six-foot-tall ferns dripping with water. After half an hour, there was a sudden break in the foliage, and they had a panoramic view of Resolution Bay spread out below them.

The bay was about a mile wide, and had structures set at intervals on the sand. The largest one was to the far right, at the eastern edge of the bay. Three others of equal size were arranged at intervals, making a sort of triangle in the western section of the bay.

Evans could see there was something funny about the houses, though. Something odd about the wood that was used. He squinted.

Sanjong nudged him. He wiggled his hand in the air.

Evans looked. Yes, it was true. The wooden structures were moving, fluttering in the air.

They were tents.

Tents made to look like wooden structures. And pretty good ones, too. It was no wonder they had fooled the aerial survey, Evans thought.

As they watched, men emerged from one or another of the tents and shouted to others down the beach. They were speaking English, but it was difficult to make out what they were saying at this distance. Most of it seemed to be technical.

Sanjong nudged Evans again. Evans saw him make a kind of pyramid with three fingers. Then he began to wiggle the fingers.

So, apparently they were tuning the generators in the tent. Or something like that.

The others in the group did not seem to be interested in the details. They were breathing hard, catching their breaths in the soft breeze, and staring down at the bay. And probably thinking, as Evans was, that there were a lot of men down there. At least eight or ten. All in jeans and work shirts.

"Christ, there's a lot of those bastards," Bradley muttered.

Jennifer nudged him hard in the ribs.

He mouthed: Oh, sorry.

She shook her head. She mouthed: You'll get us killed.

Bradley made a face. He clearly thought she was being melodramatic.

Then, from the jungle below them, they heard a cough.

They froze.

They waited in silence. They heard the buzz of cicadas, the occasional call of distant birds.

It came again, the same soft cough. As if the person was trying not to make noise.

Sanjong crouched down, listening hard. The cough came a third time, and to Evans there was the strangest sensation of familiarity about it. It reminded him of his grandfather, who had had heart failure when Evans was a kid. His grandfather used to cough like that, in the hospital. Weakly. Little coughs.

Now there was silence. They had not heard the cougher move away—if he had, he was truly noiseless—but the sound stopped.

Kenner looked at his watch. They waited five minutes, then he signaled for them to continue moving east, curving around the bay.

Just as they were leaving, they heard the cough once more. This time, there were three, in succession: *uh uh uh*. Then nothing.

Kenner signaled. Move out.

They had not gone a hundred yards when they came upon a path. It was a clear trail, even though the overhanging branches hung low. It must be an animal trail, Evans thought, wondering vaguely what kind of animals they might be. There were probably feral pigs here. There were pigs everywhere. He vaguely remembered stories of people being surprised by pigs, gored by the tusks of an aggressive boar that charged out of the underbrush—

The first thing he heard, however, was a mechanical *click*. He knew instantly what it was: the sound of a gun being cocked.

The entire group froze, strung out in single file. Nobody moved.

Another *click*.

And another. *Click!*

Evans looked around quickly. He saw nobody. It seemed they were alone in the jungle.

Then he heard a voice: *"Dai. Nogot sok, waitman. Indai. Stopim!"*

Evans had no idea what it meant, but the meaning was clear enough to them all. Nobody moved.

From the bushes ahead, a young boy emerged. He was wearing boots without socks, green shorts, a "Madonna World Tour" T-shirt, and a baseball cap that said "Perth Glory." A half-smoked cigarette stub hung from his lips. He had an ammunition belt over one shoulder and a machine gun slung over the other shoulder. He was five feet tall and could not have been more than ten or eleven. He pointed his gun with casual insolence. *"Okay, waitman. You prisner biulong me, savve? Bookim dano!"* And he jerked his thumb, indicating they should move forward. *"Gohet!"*

For a moment, they were all too astonished to move. Then, from the jungle on both sides of the path, other boys emerged.

Bradley said, "What is this, the lost boys?"

Without expression, one of the kids slammed the butt of his rifle into Bradley's stomach. Bradley gasped and went down.

"Stopim waitman bilong toktok."

"Oh, Jesus," Bradley said, rolling on the ground.

The kid hit him again, this time in the head, and kicked him hard. Bradley moaned.

"Antap! Antap!" the kid said, gesturing for him to get up. When Bradley didn't respond, the kid kicked him again. *"Antap!"*

Sarah went over and helped Bradley to his feet. Bradley was coughing. Sarah was smart enough not to say anything.

"*Oh, nais mari,*" the kid said. Then he pushed her away from Bradley. "*Antap!*"

But as they trudged forward, one of the kids went over to Bradley, and squeezed the back of his arm, the triceps. He laughed. "*Taiis gut!*"

Evans felt a chill, as the words sank in. These boys were speaking a version of English. He could decipher it, if he thought about it a little, and played the words back in his head. *Nais mari* was "Nice Mary." Maybe Mary was a word for woman. *Antap* was "And up."

And *taiis gut* was "Taste good."

They walked single file through the jungle, the kids at their side. Kenner was in the lead, then Ted, who was bleeding from his head, and Sarah, and Jennifer. Then Evans.

Evans glanced over his shoulder.

Sanjong was not behind him.

All he saw was another ragged kid with a rifle. "*Antap! Antap!*"

The kid made a threatening gesture with his rifle.

Evans turned, and hurried forward.

There was something chilling about being herded by children. Except these weren't children. He was only too aware of the cold look in their eyes. They had seen a lot in their lives. They lived in another world. It was not Evans's world.

But he was now in theirs.

Up ahead, he saw a pair of jeeps at the side of a muddy road.

He looked at his watch. It was ten o'clock.

Seven hours to go.

But somehow it didn't seem important anymore.

The kids pushed them into the jeeps, and then they drove off, down a muddy track, into the dark and trackless interior of the jungle.

There were times, Sarah thought, when she really did not want to be a woman. That was how she felt as she was driven into the muddy village of Pavutu, the rebel stronghold, in the back of an open jeep. The village seemed to be populated almost entirely by men, who came yelling into the clearing to see who had arrived. But there were women, too, including older women who stared at her height and her hair, and then came up and poked at her, as if she might not be real.

Jennifer, who was shorter and darker, stood beside her and attracted no attention at all. Nevertheless, they were herded together into one of the huge thatch houses. Inside the house was a large open space, a kind of central room, three stories high. There was a ladder made of wood leading up to a series of landings, going all the way to the top, where there was a kind of catwalk and a viewing area. In the center of the room was a fire, and at the fire sat a heavyset man with pale skin and a dark beard. He wore sunglasses and had a sort of beret with the Jamaican flag on it.

This, it seemed, was Sambuca. They were shoved in front of him, and he leered at them, but it was clear to Sarah—she had an instinct for these things—that he was not interested in them. He was interested in Ted, and in Peter. Kenner he inspected briefly, then looked away.

"*Killim.*"

They pushed Kenner out the door, poking him with the butts of their rifles. They were clearly excited at the prospect of executing him.

"*No nau,*" Sambuca said, in a growl. "*Behain.*"

It took Sarah a moment to translate in her head. Not now. Behind. Which must mean later on, she thought. So Kenner had a reprieve, at least for a while.

Sambuca turned and stared at the others in the room.

"*Meris,*" he said, with a dismissive wave. "*Goapim meri behain.*"

Sarah had the distinct impression, from the grins on the faces of the boys, that they were being given the freedom to do with the two women what they wanted. Go up 'em. She and Jennifer were led off to a back room.

Sarah remained calm. Of course she knew things were bad. But they were not bad yet. She was noticing that Jennifer did not appear to be shaken in the least. She had the same flat, uninterested expression that she might have if she was walking toward a company cocktail party.

The boys took the two women into a thatched room at the back of the larger building. There were two posts sunk in the earthen floor. One of the kids took out a pair of handcuffs and cuffed Jennifer to one post, her hands behind her back. Then he cuffed Sarah to the other post in the same way. Then another kid reached up and squeezed Sarah's tit, smiled knowingly, and walked out of the room.

"Charming," Jennifer said, when they were alone. "You all right?"

"So far, yes." There were drums starting to beat from somewhere outside, in the courtyard between the thatch buildings.

"Good," Jennifer said. "It's not over yet."

"Sanjong is—"

"Right. He is."

"But we came a long way in the jeeps."

"Yes. At least two or three miles. I tried to see the odometer, but it was spattered with mud. But on foot, even running, it'll take him a while."

"He had a rifle."

"Yes."

"Can you get free?"

Jennifer shook her head. "It's too tight."

Through the open door, they saw Bradley and Evans being led away to another room. They glimpsed the two men only for a moment. Not long after, Kenner followed. He glanced into their room, giving what seemed to Sarah a meaningful look.

But she couldn't be sure.

Jennifer sat down on the bare earth, leaning back against the pole. She said, "Might as well sit down. It could be a long night." Sarah sat down, too.

A moment later, a young boy looked in and saw that they were sitting. He came into the room, looked at their handcuffs, and then walked out again.

Outside, the drums were louder. People must have been starting to gather, because the women could hear shouts and murmurs.

"Going to be a ceremony," Jennifer said. "And I'm afraid I know what it is."

In the next room, Evans and Kenner were also handcuffed around two posts. Because there was not a third post, Ted Bradley was handcuffed and left seated on the ground. His head was no longer bleeding, but he had a huge bruise over his left eye. And he looked distinctly frightened. But his eyelids were drooping, as if he might fall asleep.

"What's your impression of village life so far, Ted?" Kenner said. "Still think it's the best way to live?"

"This isn't village life. This is savagery."

"It's all part of it."

"No, it's not. These young kids, that fat creepy guy . . . this is lunacy. This is everything gone wrong."

"You just don't get it, do you?" Kenner said. "You think civilization is some horrible, polluting human invention that separates us from the state of nature. But civilization doesn't separate us from nature, Ted. Civilization *protects* us from nature. Because what you see right now, all around you—this *is* nature."

"Oh no. No, no. Humans are kind, cooperative . . ."

"Horseshit, Ted."

"There are genes for altruism."

"Wishful thinking, Ted."

"All cruelty springs from weakness."

"Some people *like* cruelty, Ted."

"Leave him alone," Evans said.

"Why should I? Come on, Ted. Aren't you going to answer me?"

"Oh, fuck you," Ted said. "Maybe we're all going to get killed here by these juvenile delinquent creeps, but I want you to know, if it's the last fucking thing I say in my life, that you are a major and unrelenting asshole, Kenner. You bring out the worst in everybody. You're a pessimist, you're an obstructionist, you're against all progress, against everything that is good and noble. You are a right-wing pig in . . . in . . . in whatever the fuck you are wearing. Whatever those clothes are. Where's your gun?"

"I dropped it."

"Where?"

"Back in the jungle."

"You think Sanjong has it?"

"I hope so."

"Is he coming to get us?"

Kenner shook his head. "He's doing the job we came to do."

"You mean he's going to the bay."

"Yes."

"So nobody is coming to get us?"

"No, Ted. Nobody."

"We're fucked," he said. "We're fucking *fucked*. I can't believe it." And he started to cry.

Two boys entered the room, carrying two heavy hemp ropes. They attached one rope to each of Bradley's wrists, tying them firmly. Then they walked out again.

The drums beat louder.

Out in the center of the village, people took up a rhythmic chant.

Jennifer said, "Can you see out the door from where you are?"

"Yes."

"Keep an eye out. Tell me if someone is coming."

"All right," Sarah said.

She glanced back and saw that Jennifer had arched her back and was gripping the pole between her hands. She had also bent her legs so her soles touched the wood, and proceeded to shimmy up the pole at a remarkable speed, like an acrobat. She got to the top, raised her cuffed hands clear of the top of the pole, and then jumped lightly to the ground.

"Anybody?" she said.

"No . . . How'd you learn to do that?"

"Keep looking out the door."

Jennifer slid back against her pole again, as if she were still hand-cuffed to it.

"Anybody yet?"

"No, not yet."

Jennifer sighed. "We need one of those kids to come in," she said. "Soon."

Outside, Sambuca was giving a speech, screaming brief phrases that were each answered by a shout from the crowd. Their leader was building them up, working them into a frenzy. Even in Ted's room, they could feel it building.

Bradley was curled in fetal position, crying softly.

Two men came in, much older than the boys. They unlocked his handcuffs. They lifted him to his feet. Each man took a rope. Together they led him outside.

A moment later, the crowd roared.

"Hey, cutie pie," Jennifer said, when a boy stuck his head in the door. She grinned. "You like what you see, cutie pie?" She shifted her pelvis suggestively.

The boy looked suspicious at first, but he came deeper into the room. He was older than the others, maybe fourteen or fifteen, and he was bigger. He was carrying a rifle and wore a knife on his belt.

"You want to have some fun? Want to let me go?" Jennifer said, smiling with a little pout. "You understand me? My arms hurt, baby. Want to have fun?"

He gave a laugh, sort of a gurgle from deep in his throat. He moved toward her and pushed her legs open, then crouched down in front of her.

"Oh, let me go first, please . . ."

"*No meri,*" he said, laughing and shaking his head. He knew he could have her while she remained cuffed to the pole. He was kneeling between her legs, fumbling with his shorts, but it was clumsy holding the gun, so he set the gun down.

What happened next was very fast. Jennifer arched her back and kicked her legs up, clipping the kid under the chin, snapping his head back. She continued the motion, crunching into a ball, swinging her arms under her hips and butt and then up her legs, so now her hands were in front of her instead of behind. As the kid staggered to his feet, she slammed him in the side of the head with both hands. He went down on his knees. She dove on him, knocking him over, and pounded his head into the ground. Then she pulled the knife off his belt and cut his throat.

She sat on his body while he shivered and spasmed and the blood poured from his throat and onto the bare earth. It seemed to take a long time. When the body was finally motionless, she got off him, and rifled through his pockets.

Sarah watched the whole thing, her mouth open.

"Damn it," Jennifer said. "Damn it."

"What's the matter?"

"He doesn't have the key!"

She rolled the body over, grunting with the effort. She got blood on her arms from the flowing throat. She paid no attention to it.

"Where are the damn keys?"

"Maybe the other kid has it."

"Which one cuffed us?"

"I don't remember," Sarah said. "I was confused." She was staring at the body, looking at all the blood.

"Hey," Jennifer said, "get over it. You know what these guys are going to do? They're going to beat us up, gang-bang us, and then kill us. Fuck 'em. We kill as many as we can and try to get out of here alive. But *I need the damn key!*"

Sarah struggled to her feet.

"Good idea," Jennifer said. She came over and crouched down in front of Sarah.

"What?"

"Stand on my back and shimmy up. Get yourself off the pole. And hurry."

Outside, the crowd was screaming and roaring, a constant and ugly sound.

Ted Bradley blinked in the bright sunlight. He was disoriented by pain and fear and by the sight that greeted his eyes: two lines of old women, forming a corridor for him to walk down, all applauding him wildly. In fact, beyond the old women was a sea of faces—dark-skinned men and young girls and kids hardly waist high. And they were all yelling and cheering. Dozens of people, crowded together.

They were cheering him!

Despite himself, Ted smiled. It was a weak smile, sort of a half-smile, because he was tired and hurt, but he knew from experience that it would convey just the right hint of subtle pleasure at their response. As he was carried forward by the two men, he nodded and smiled. He allowed his smile to become broader.

At the far end of the women was Sambuca himself—but he, too, was applauding wildly, his hands high in the air, a broad smile on his face.

Ted didn't know what was happening here, but obviously he had misunderstood the meaning of the whole thing. Either that or they had figured out who he was and now thought better of their original plan. It wouldn't be the first time. The women were cheering so loudly as he was carried forward, their mouths gaping with excitement, that he tried to shake off the men who were holding him, he tried to walk unaided. And he did!

But now that he was closer he noticed that the applauding women had heavy sticks resting against their hips as they cheered. Some had baseball bats and some lengths of metal pipe. And as he came closer they continued to shout, but they picked up their bats and sticks and began to strike him, heavy blows on the face and shoulders and body. The pain was instant and incredible, and he sank down to the ground, but immediately the men with the ropes hauled him up again, and dragged him while the women beat him and screamed and beat him. And the pain streaked through his body and he felt a vague detachment, an emptiness, but still the blows came, merciless, again and again.

And finally, barely conscious, he came to the end of the line of women and saw a pair of poles. The men quickly tied his arms to the two poles in a way that kept him upright. And now the crowd fell silent. His head was bowed, he saw blood dripping from his head onto the ground.

And he saw two naked feet appear in his line of vision, and the blood spattered on the feet, and someone lifted his head.

It was Sambuca, though Bradley could barely focus on his face. The world was gray and faint. But he saw that Sambuca was grinning at him, revealing a row of yellow pointed teeth. And then Sambuca held up a knife so Ted could see it, and smiled again, and with two fingers grabbed the flesh of Ted's cheek and sliced it off with the knife.

There was no pain, surprisingly no pain but it made him dizzy to see Sambuca hold up the bloody chunk of his cheek and, grinning, open his mouth and take a bite. The blood ran down Sambuca's chin as he chewed, grinning all the while. Bradley's head was spinning now. He was nauseated and terrified and revolted, and he felt a pain at his chest. He looked down to see a young boy of eight or nine cutting flesh from his underarm with a pocket knife. And a woman raced forward, screaming for the others to get out of the way, and she hacked a slice from the back of his forearm. And then the whole crowd was upon him, and the knives were everywhere, and they were cutting and yelling and cutting and yelling and he saw one knife move toward his eyes, and felt his trousers tugged down, and he knew nothing more.

PAVUTU
THURSDAY, OCTOBER 14
12:22 P.M.

Evans listened to the crowd cheering and yelling. Somehow he knew what was happening. He looked at Kenner. But Kenner just shook his head.

There was nothing to do. No help was coming. There was no way out.

The door opened, and two boys appeared. They carried two heavy hemp ropes, now visibly soaked in blood. They walked up to Evans and carefully knotted the ropes to his hands. Evans felt his heart start to pound.

The boys finished and left the room.

Outside, the crowd was roaring.

"Don't worry," Kenner said. "They'll let you wait a while. There's still hope."

"Hope for *what?*" Evans said in a burst of anger.

Kenner shook his head. "Just . . . hope."

Jennifer was waiting for the next kid to come in the room. He did, finally, and took one look at the fallen boy and began to bolt, but Jennifer had her arms around his neck. She yanked him back into the room with her hands over his mouth so he couldn't scream and she made a sudden, quick twist and let him fall to the ground. He wasn't dead, but he would be there a while.

But in that moment when she had looked outside, she had seen the keys. They were out in the thatch passageway, on a bench across the hall.

There were two guns in the room now, but there was no point in firing them. It would just bring everybody on them. Jennifer didn't want to look outside again. She heard murmuring voices. She couldn't be sure whether they were coming from the next room or from the hallway. She couldn't make a mistake.

She leaned back against the wall by the door and moaned. Softly at first, and then louder, because the crowd was still very noisy. She moaned and moaned.

Nobody came.

Did she dare to look out?

She took a breath and waited.

Evans was trembling. The blood-soaked ropes were cold on his wrists. He couldn't stand the waiting. He felt like he was going to pass out. Outside the crowd was slowly becoming quieter. They were settling down. He knew what that meant. Soon it would be time for the next victim.

Then he heard a quiet sound.

It was a man coughing. Softly, insistently.

Kenner understood first. "In here," he said loudly.

There was a whacking sound as a machete blade poked through the thatched wall. Evans turned. He saw the slash in the wall widen, and a thick, brown hand reached in to pull the slash wider open still. A heavily bearded face peered through the gash at them.

For a moment Evans did not recognize him, but then the man put his finger to his lips, and there was something in the gesture that was familiar, and Evans suddenly saw past the beard.

"George!"

It was George Morton.

Alive.

Morton stepped through into the room. "Keep it down," he hissed.

"You took your sweet time," Kenner said, turning so Morton could unlock his cuffs. Morton gave Kenner a pistol. Then it was Evans's turn. With a click, his hands were free. Evans tugged at the hemp ropes, trying to get them off his wrists. But they were securely tied.

Morton whispered, "Where are the others?"

Kenner pointed to the room next door. He took the machete from Morton. "You take Peter. I'll get the girls."

With the machete, Kenner stepped out into the hallway.

Morton grabbed Evans by the arm. Evans jerked his head.

"Let's go."

"But—"

"Do as he says, kid."

They stepped through the slash in the wall, and into the jungle beyond.

Kenner moved down the empty hallway. There were openings at both ends. He could be surprised at any moment. If the alarm went up, they were all dead. He saw the keys on the bench, picked them up, and went to the door of the women's room. Looking into the room, he saw that the poles were abandoned. He didn't see either of the women.

Staying outside, he tossed the keys into the room.

"It's me," he whispered.

A moment later, he saw Jennifer scramble from her hiding place behind the door to grab the keys. In a few seconds she and Sarah had both unlocked each other. They grabbed the boys' guns and started for the door.

Too late. From around the corner three heavyset young men were coming toward Kenner. They all carried machine guns. They were talking and laughing, not paying attention.

Kenner slipped into the women's room. He pressed back against the wall, gestured for the two women to go back to the poles. They made it just in time as the men entered the room. Jennifer said, "Hi, guys," with a big smile. At that moment, the men registered the two fallen boys and the blood-soaked earth, but it was too late. Kenner took one; Jennifer got the second with her knife. The third was almost out the door when Kenner hit him with the butt of the gun. There was the crack of skull. He went down hard.

It was time to go.

Out in the courtyard, the crowd was growing restless. Sambuca squinted. The first *waitman* was long dead, the body cooling at his feet, no longer as appetizing as he was before. And those in the crowd who had not tasted glory were clamoring for their piece, for the next opportunity. The women were resting their bats and pipes on their shoulders, talking in small clusters, waiting for the game to continue.

Where was the next man?

Sambuca barked an order, and three men ran toward the thatch building.

It was a long, muddy slide down the steep hill, but Evans didn't mind. He was following Morton, who seemed to know his way around the jungle very well. They fell to the bottom, landing in a shallow running stream, the water pale brown with peat. Morton signaled for him to follow, and ran splashing down the streambed. Morton had lost a lot of weight; his body was trim and fit, his face tight, hard looking.

Evans said, "We thought you were dead."

"Don't talk. Just go. They'll be after us in a minute."

And even as he spoke, Evans could hear someone sliding down the hillside after them. He turned and ran down the stream, slipping over wet rocks, falling, getting up and running again.

Kenner came down the hillside with the two women right behind him. They banged against gnarled roots and protruding brambles as they slid down, but it was still the fastest way to get away from the village. He could see from the streaks in the mud ahead of him that Morton had gone that way, too. And he was sure that he had no more than a minute's head start before the alarm was sounded.

They came crashing down through the last of the undergrowth to the streambed. They heard gunshots from the village above. So their escape had already been discovered.

The bay, Kenner knew, was off to the left. He told the others to go ahead, running in the streambed.

"What about you?" Evans said.

"I'll be with you in a minute."

The women headed off, moving surprisingly quickly. Kenner eased back to the muddy track, raised his gun, and waited. It was only a few seconds before the first of the rebels came down the slope. He fired three quick bursts. The bodies caught in the gnarled branches. One tumbled all the way to the streambed.

Kenner waited.

The men above would expect him to run now. So he waited. Sure enough, in a couple of minutes he heard them starting down again. They were noisy—frightened kids. He fired again, and heard screams. But he didn't think he'd hit anything. They were just screams of fear.

But from now on, he was sure they would take a different route down. And it would be slower.

Kenner turned and ran.

Sarah and Jennifer were moving fast through the water when a bullet whined past Sarah's ear. "Hey," she shouted. "It's us!"

"Oh, sorry," Morton said, as they caught up to him.

"Which way?" Jennifer said.

Morton pointed downstream.

They ran.

• • •

Evans looked for his watch, but one of the kids had taken it from him. His wrist was bare. But Morton had a watch. "What time is it?" Evans asked him.

"Three-fifteen."

They had less than two hours remaining.

"How far to the bay?"

"Maybe another hour," Morton said, "if we go cross jungle. And we must. Those boys are fearsome trackers. Many times they've almost gotten me. They know I'm here, but so far I've eluded them."

"How long have you been here?"

"Nine days. Seems like nine years."

Running down a streambed, they crouched low beneath overhanging branches. Evans's thighs burned. His knees ached. But somehow it didn't matter to him. For some reason, the pain felt like an affirmation. He didn't care about the heat or the bugs or the leeches that he knew were all over his ankles and legs. He was just glad to be alive.

"We turn here," Morton said. He left the streambed, dashing off to the right, scrambling over big boulders, and then crashing into dense, waist-high ferns.

"Any snakes in here?" Sarah said.

"Yeah, plenty," Morton said. "But I don't worry about them."

"What do you worry about?"

"*Plenti pukpuk.*"

"And they are?"

"Crocodiles."

And he plunged onward, vanishing into dense foliage.

"Great," Evans said.

Kenner stopped in the middle of the river. Something was wrong. Until now, he had seen signs of previous runners in the stream. Bits of mud on rocks, wet finger marks or shoe prints, or disturbed algae. But for the last few minutes, nothing.

The others had left the stream.

He'd missed where.

Morton would make sure of that, he thought. Morton would know a good place to leave the river where their exit wouldn't be noticed. Probably somewhere with ferns and swampy, marshy grass between boulders on riverbanks—grass that would be spongy underfoot and would spring back at once.

Kenner had missed it.

He turned around and headed upstream, moving slowly. He knew that if he didn't find their tracks, he couldn't leave the river. He would be sure to get lost. And if he stayed in the river too long, the kids would find him. And they'd kill him.

RESOLUTION
THURSDAY, OCTOBER 14
4:02 P.M.

There was one hour left, now. Morton crouched among the mangroves and rocks near the center of Resolution Bay. The others were clustered around him. The water lapped softly against the sand, a few feet away.

"This is what I know," he said, speaking low. "The submarine tender is hidden under a camouflage tarp at the east end of the bay. You can't see it from here. They have been sending the submarine down every day for a week. The sub has limited battery power, so it can stay at depth for only an hour at a time. But it seems pretty clear they are placing a kind of cone-shaped explosive that depends on accurately timed detonation—"

"They had them in Antarctica," Sarah said.

"All right, then you know. Here, they're intended to trigger an underwater avalanche. Judging how long the sub stays down, I figure they are placing them at about the ninety-meter level, which happens to be the most efficient level for tsunami-causing avalanches."

"What about the tents up here?" Evans said.

"It seems they're taking no chances. Either they don't have enough cone explosives or they don't trust them to do the job, because they have placed something called hypersonic cavitation generators in the tents. They're big pieces of equipment about the size of a small truck. Diesel powered, make a lot of noise when they fire them up to test them, which they've been doing for days. They moved the tents several times, just a foot or two each time, so I assume there's some critical issue about placement. Maybe they're focusing the beams, or whatever it is those things generate. I'm not entirely clear about what they do. But apparently they're important for creating the landslide."

Sarah said, "And what do we do?"

"There's no way we can stop them," Morton said. "We are only four—five, if Kenner makes it, which he doesn't seem to be doing. There are thirteen of them. Seven on the ship and six on shore. All armed with automatic weapons."

"But we have Sanjong," Evans said. "Don't forget him."

"That Nepali guy? I'm sure the rebels got him. There were gunshots about an hour ago along the ridge where they first found you. I was a few yards below, just before they picked you up. I tried to signal you by coughing, but . . ." He shrugged, turned back to the beach. "Anyway. Assuming the three cavitation generators are meant to work together to create some effect on the underwater slope, I figure our best chance is to take one of the generators out—or maybe two of them. That would disrupt their plan or at least weaken the effect."

Jennifer said, "Can we cut the power supply?"

Morton shook his head. "They're self-powered. Diesel attached to the main units."

"Battery ignition?"

"No. Solar panels. They're autonomous."

"Then we have to take out the guys running the units."

"Yes. And they've been alerted to our presence. As you can see, there's one standing outside each tent, guarding it, and they've got a sentry somewhere up on that ridge." He pointed to the western slope. "We can't see where he is, but I assume he is watching the whole bay."

"So? Big deal. Let him watch," Jennifer said. "I say we just take out all these guys in the tents, and trash the machines. We've got enough weapons here to do the job, and—" She paused. She had removed the magazine from her rifle; it was empty. "Better check your loads."

There was a moment of fumbling. They were all shaking their heads.

Evans had four rounds. Sarah had two. Morton's rifle had none. "Those guys had practically no ammo . . ."

"And we don't either." Jennifer took a long breath. "This is going to be a little tougher without weapons." She edged forward and looked out on the beach, squinting in the bright light. "There's ten yards between the jungle and those tents. Open beach, no cover. If we charge the tents we'll never make it."

"What about a distraction?"

"I don't know what it could be. There's one guy outside each tent and one guy inside. They both armed?"

Morton nodded. "Automatic weapons."

"Not good," she said. "Not good at all."

Kenner splashed down the river, looking hard left and right. He had not gone more than a hundred yards when he saw the faint imprint of a wet hand on a boulder. The damp print had almost dried. He looked more closely. He saw the grass at the edge of the stream had been trampled.

This was where they had left the stream.

He set out, heading toward the bay. Morton obviously knew his way around. This was another streambed, but much smaller. Kenner noticed with some unease that it sloped downward fairly steeply. That was a bad sign. But it was a passable route through the jungle. Somewhere up ahead, he heard the barking of a dog. It sounded like the dog was hoarse, or sick, or something.

Kenner hurried ahead, ducking beneath the branches.

He had to get to the others, before it was too late.

Morton heard the barking and frowned.

"What's the matter?" Jennifer said. "The rebels chasing us with dogs?"

"No. That's not a dog."

"It didn't really sound like a dog."

"It's not. They've learned a trick in this part of the world. They bark like a dog, and then when the dogs come out, they eat them."

"Who does?"

"Crocs. That's a crocodile you hear. Somewhere behind us."

Out on the beach, they heard the sudden rumbling of automobile engines. Peering forward through the mangroves, they saw three jeeps coming from the east side of the bay, rumbling across the sand toward them.

"What's this?" Evans said.

"They've been practicing this," Morton said. "All week. Watch. One stops at each tent. See? Tent one . . . tent two . . . tent three. They all stop. They all keep the motors running. All pointed west."

"What's west?"

"There's a dirt track, goes up the hill about a hundred yards and then dead-ends."

"Something used to be up there?"

"No. They cut the road themselves. First thing they did when they got here." Morton looked toward the eastern curve of the bay. "Usually by this time, the ship has pulled out, and moved into deep water. But it's not doing it yet."

"Uh-oh," Evans said.

"What is it?"

"I think we've forgotten something."

"What's that?"

"We've been worried about this tsunami wave heading toward the California coast. But a landslide would suck water downward, right? And then it would rise back up again. But that's kind of like dropping this pebble into this ditch." He dropped a pebble into a muddy puddle at their feet. "And the wave the pebble generates . . . is circular."

"It goes in all directions . . ."

"Oh no," Sarah said.

"Oh yes. All directions, including back to this coast. The tsunami will hit here, too. And fast. How far offshore is the Solomon Trench?"

Morton shrugged. "I don't know. Maybe two miles. I really don't know, Peter."

"If these waves travel five hundred miles an hour," Evans said, "then that means it gets to this coast in . . ."

"Twenty-four seconds," Sarah said.

"Right. That's how much time we have to get out of here, once the undersea landslide begins. Twenty-four seconds."

With a sudden chugging rumble, they heard the first diesel generator come to life. Then the second, then the third. All three were running.

Morton glanced at his watch. "This is it," he said. "They've started."

And now they heard an electronic whine, faint at first but rapidly building to a deep electronic hum. It filled the air.

"Those're the cavitators," Morton said. "Kicking in."

Jennifer slung her rifle over her shoulder. "Let's get ready."

Sanjong slid silently from the branches of the overhanging tree, onto the deck of the *AV Scorpion*. The forty-foot ship must have a very shallow draft, because it was pulled up close to the peninsula on the eastern side, so that the huge jungle trees overhung it. The ship couldn't really be seen from the beach; Sanjong had only realized that it was there when he heard the crackle of radios coming from the jungle.

He crouched in the stern, hiding behind the winch that raised the submarine, listening. He heard voices from all sides, it seemed like. He guessed that there were six or seven men onboard. But what he wanted was to find the timing detonators. He guessed that they were in the pilothouse, but he couldn't be sure. And between his hiding place and the pilothouse was a long expanse of open deck.

He looked at the mini-sub hanging above him. It was bright blue, about seven feet long, with a bubble canopy, now raised. The sub was raised and lowered into the water by the winch.

And the winch . . .

He looked for the control panel. He knew it had to be nearby because the operator would have to be able to see the submarine as it was lowered. Finally he saw it: a closed metal box on the other side of the ship. He crept over, opened the box, and looked at the buttons. There were six, marked with arrows in all directions. Like a big keypad.

He pressed the down arrow.

With a rumble, the winch began to lower the submarine into the water.

An alarm began to sound.

He heard running feet.

He ducked back into a doorway and waited.

From the beach, they faintly heard the sound of an alarm over the rumble of the generators and the cavitation hum. Evans looked around. "Where's it coming from?"

"It must be from the ship, over there."

Out on the beach, the men heard it, too. They were standing in pairs by the entrance to the tents, pointing. Wondering what to do.

And then, from the jungle behind them, a sudden burst of machine-gun fire opened up. The men on the beach were alarmed now, swinging their guns, looking this way and that.

"Screw it," Jennifer said, taking Evans's rifle. "This is it. It won't get any better."

And firing, she ran out onto the beach.

The crocodile had charged Kenner with frightening speed. He had little more than a glimpse of huge white jaws open wide and thrashing water before he fired with his machine gun. The jaw smashed down, just missing his leg; the animal writhed, twisted, and attacked again, jaws closing on a low-hanging branch.

The bullets hadn't done anything. Kenner turned and ran, sprinting down the streambed.

The croc roared behind him.

Jennifer was running across the sand, heading for the nearest tent. She went about ten yards before two bullets struck her left leg and knocked her down. She fell onto hot sand, still firing as she fell. She saw the guard at the entrance to the tent drop. She knew he was dead.

Evans came up behind her and started to crouch down. She shouted, "Keep going! Go!" Evans ran forward, toward the tent.

On the ship, the men halted the descent of the submarine, stopping the winch. Now they could hear the gunshots coming from the beach. They had all rushed to the starboard side of the ship, and now they were looking over the railing, trying to see what was going on.

Sanjong went down the deck on the port side. No one was there. He came to the cabin. There was a big board there, dense with electronics. A man in shorts and a T-shirt was crouched over it, making adjustments. At the top of the board were three rows of lights, marked with numerals.

The timing board.

For the undersea detonations.

Sarah and Morton were sprinting along the edge of the beach, staying close to the jungle, as they headed for the second tent. The man outside the tent saw them almost at once and was firing bursts of machine-gun fire at them, but he must have been very nervous, Sarah thought, because he wasn't hitting them. Branches and leaves snapped all around them from the bullets. And with every step, they were getting close enough for Sarah to fire back. She was carrying Morton's pistol. At twenty yards, she stopped and leaned against the nearest tree trunk. She held her arm stiffly and aimed. The first shot missed. The second one hit the man outside the tent in the right shoulder, and he dropped his gun in the sand. Morton saw it, and left the forest, running across the sand toward the tent. The man was struggling to get up. Sarah shot again.

And then Morton disappeared inside the tent. And she heard two quick gunshots and a scream of pain.

She ran.

Evans was inside the tent. He faced a wall of chugging machinery, a huge complex of twisting pipes and vents, ending in a flat, round plate eight feet wide, set about two feet above the surface of the sand. The generator was about seven feet high; all the metal was hot to the touch. The noise was deafening. He didn't see anybody there. Holding his rifle ready—painfully aware that the magazine was empty—he swung around the first corner, then the second.

And then he saw him.

It was Bolden. The guy from the Antarctic. He was working at a control panel, adjusting big knobs while he looked at a shaded LCD screen and a row of dials. He was so preoccupied, he didn't even notice Evans at first.

Evans felt a burst of pure rage. If his gun had been loaded he would have shot him. Bolden's gun was leaning against the wall of the tent. He needed both hands to adjust the controls.

Evans shouted. Bolden turned. Evans gestured for him to put up his hands.

Bolden charged.

Morton had just stepped into the tent when the first bullet struck his ear and the second hit his shoulder. He screamed in pain and fell to his knees. The movement saved his life because the next bullet whined past his forehead, ripping through the tent cloth. He was lying on the ground next to the chugging machinery when the gunman came around, holding his rifle ready. He was a twentyish man, bearded, grim, all business. He aimed at Morton.

And then he fell against the machine, blood hissing as it splattered on hot metal. Sarah was standing inside the tent, firing her pistol once, twice, three times, lowering her arm each time as the man fell. She turned to Morton.

"I forgot you were a good shot," he said.

"You okay?" she said. He nodded. "Then how do I turn this thing off?"

Evans grunted as Bolden smashed into his body. The two men stumbled back against the tent fabric, then forward again. Evans brought the butt of his gun down on Bolden's back, but it had no effect. He kept trying to hit him in the head, but only connected with his back. Bolden, for his part, seemed to be trying to drive Evans out of the tent.

The two men fell to the ground. The machinery was thumping above them. And now Evans realized what Bolden was trying to do.

He was trying to push Evans under the plate. Even by being near the edge, Evans could feel the air vibrating intensely. The air was much hotter here.

Bolden hit Evans in the head, and his sunglasses went flying across the ground, beneath the flat plate. Instantly, they shattered. Then the frames crumpled.

Then they pulverized.

Vanished into nothing.

Evans watched with horror. And little by little, Bolden was pushing him closer to the edge, closer, closer . . .

Evans struggled, with the sudden strength of desperation. Abruptly, he kicked up.

Bolden's face mashed against hot metal. He howled. His cheek was smoking and black. Evans kicked again, and got out from beneath him. Got to his feet. Standing over Bolden, he kicked him hard in the ribs, as hard as he could. He tried to kill him.

That's for Antarctica.

Bolden grabbed Evans's leg on the next kick, and Evans went down. But he kicked once more as he fell, hitting Bolden in the head, and with the impact, Bolden rolled once.

And rolled under the plate.

His body was half under, half out. It began to shake, to vibrate. Bolden opened his mouth to scream but there was no sound. Evans kicked him a final time, and the body went entirely under.

By the time Evans had dropped to his hands and knees, to look under the plate, nothing was there. Just a haze of acrid smoke.

He got to his feet, and went outside.

Glancing over her shoulder, Jennifer ripped her blouse with her teeth and tore a strip of cloth for a tourniquet. She didn't think an artery had been hit, but there was a lot of blood on one leg and a lot of blood in the sand, and she was feeling a little dizzy.

She had to keep watching because there was one more tent, and if the guys from that tent showed up . . .

She spun, raising her gun as a figure emerged from the forest.

It was John Kenner. She lowered the gun.

He ran toward her.

Sanjong fired into the glass in front of the control deck, but nothing happened. The glass didn't even shatter. Bulletproof glass, he thought in surprise. The technician inside looked up in shock. By then Sanjong was moving toward the door.

The technician reached for the control switches. Sanjong fired twice, once hitting the technician, once aiming for the control panel.

But it was too late. Across the top of the panel, red lights flashed, one after another. The undersea detonations were taking place.

Automatically, a loud alarm began to sound, like a submarine claxon. The men on the other side of the ship were shouting, terror in their voices, and with good reason, Sanjong thought.

The tsunami had been generated.

It was only a matter of seconds now before it would hit them.

The air was filled with sound.

Evans ran from the tent. Directly ahead he saw Kenner lifting Jennifer in his arms. Kenner was shouting something, but Evans couldn't hear. He could vaguely see that Jennifer was soaked in blood. Evans ran for the jeep, jumped in, and drove it over to Kenner.

Kenner put Jennifer in the back. She was breathing shallowly. Directly ahead, they saw Sarah helping Morton into the other jeep. Kenner had to shout over the noise. For a minute Evans couldn't understand.

Then he realized what Kenner was saying. "Sanjong! Where is Sanjong!"

Evans shook his head. "Morton says he's dead! Rebels!"

"Do you know for sure?"

"No!"

Kenner looked back down the beach.

"Drive!"

Sarah was in the car, trying to hold Morton upright and drive at the same time. But she had to let go of him to shift gears, and as soon as she did he'd flop over against her shoulder. He was wheezing, breathing with difficulty. She suspected that his lung was punctured. She was distracted, trying to count in her head. She thought it was already ten seconds since the landslide.

Which meant they had fifteen seconds to get up the hill.

Sanjong leapt from the ship to the trees on the shore. He grabbed a handful of leaves and branches. He scrambled down to the ground and began to climb the hill frantically. On the ship, the men saw him, and they jumped, too, trying to follow him.

Sanjong guessed that they all had half a minute before the first wave struck. It would be the smallest wave, but it would still probably be five meters high. The runup—the splash on the hillside—could be another five meters. That meant he had to scramble at least thirty feet up the muddy slope in the next thirty seconds.

He knew he would never make it.

He couldn't do it.

He climbed anyway.

Sarah drove up the muddy track, the jeep slipping precariously on the incline. Beside her, Morton was not saying anything and his skin had turned an ugly blue gray. She yelled, "Hold on, George! Hold on! Just a little!" The jeep fishtailed in the mud, and Sarah howled in panic. She downshifted, grinding gears, got control, and continued up. In the rearview mirror, she saw Evans behind her.

In her mind, she was counting:

Eighteen.

Nineteen.

Twenty.

From the third tent on the beach, two men with machine guns jumped into the last remaining jeep. They drove up the hill after Evans, firing at him as they drove. Kenner was firing back. The bullets shattered Evans's windshield. Evans slowed.

"Keep driving!" Kenner yelled. "Go!"

Evans couldn't really see. Where the windshield wasn't shattered it was spattered with mud. He kept moving his head, trying to see the route ahead.

"Go!" Kenner yelled.

The bullets were whizzing around them.

Kenner was shooting at the tires of the jeep behind them. He hit them, and the jeep lurched over onto its side. The two men fell out into the mud. They scrambled to their feet, limping. They were only about fifteen feet above the beach.

Not high enough.

Kenner looked back at the ocean.

He saw the wave coming toward the shore.

It was enormous, as wide as the eye could see, a foaming line of surf, a white arc spreading as it came toward the beach. It was not a very high wave, but it grew as it came ashore, rising up, rising higher . . .

The jeep lurched to a halt.

"Why did you stop?" Kenner yelled.

"It's the end of the damn road!" Evans shouted.

The wave was now about fifteen feet high.

With a roar of surf, the wave struck the beach and raced inland toward them.

To Evans, it seemed as if everything was happening in slow motion—the big wave churning white, boiling over the sand, and somehow keeping its crest all the way across the beach, and into the jungle, completely covering the green landscape in white as the water boiled up the slope toward them.

He couldn't take his eyes off it, because it seemed never to lose its power, but just kept coming. Farther down the muddy track the two men were scrambling away from their fallen jeep, and then they were covered in white water and gone from sight.

The wave rushed up the slope another four or five feet, then suddenly slowed, receded, sweeping back. It left behind no trace of the men or their jeep. The jungle trees were ragged, many uprooted.

The wave slid back into the ocean, farther and farther away, exposing the beach far out to sea, before it finally died away, and the ocean was gentle again.

"That's the first," Kenner said. "The next ones will be bigger."

Sarah was holding Morton upright, trying to keep him comfortable. His lips were a terrible blue color and his skin was cold, but he seemed to be alert. He wasn't talking, but he was watching the water.

"Hang on, George," she said.

He nodded. He was mouthing something.

"What is it? What are you saying?"

She read his lips. A weak grin.

Wouldn't miss it if it was the last thing I did.

The next wave came in.

From a distance, it looked exactly like the first, but as it neared the shore they could see that it was noticeably bigger, half again as large as the first, and the roar as it smashed into the beach was like an explosion. A vast sheet of water raced up the hill toward them, coming much higher than before.

They were almost a hundred feet away. The wave had come a good sixty feet up the slope.

"The next one will be bigger," Kenner said.

· · ·

The sea was quiet for several minutes. Evans turned to Jennifer. "Listen," he said, "do you want me to—"

She wasn't there. For a moment he thought she had fallen out of the jeep. Then he saw she had fallen on the floor, where she lay curled in pain. Her face and shoulder were soaked in blood.

"Jennifer?"

Kenner grabbed Evans's hand, pushed it back gently. He shook his head. "Those guys in the jeep," he said. "She was okay until then." Evans was stunned. He felt dizzy. He looked at her. "Jennifer?"

Her eyes were closed. She was hardly breathing.

"Turn away," Kenner said. "She'll make it or she won't."

The next wave was coming in.

There was nowhere they could go. They had reached the end of the track. They were surrounded by jungle. They just waited, and watched the water rush up in a hissing, terrifying wall toward them. The wave had already broken. This was just surge rushing up the hillside, but it was still a wall of water nine or ten feet high.

Sarah was sure it was going to take them all, but the wave lost energy just a few yards away, thinning and slowing, and then sliding back down to the ocean.

Kenner looked at his watch. "We have a few minutes," he said. "Let's do what we can."

"What do you mean?" Sarah said.

"I mean, climb as high as we can."

"There's another wave?"

"At least."

"Bigger?"

"Yes."

• • •

Five minutes passed. They scrambled up the hillside another twenty yards. Kenner was carrying Jennifer's bleeding body. By now she had lost consciousness. Evans and Sarah were helping Morton, who was moving with great difficulty. Finally, Evans picked Morton up and carried him piggyback style.

"Glad you lost some weight," Evans said.

Morton, not speaking, just patted him on the shoulder.

Evans staggered up the hill.

The next wave came in.

When it receded, their jeeps had vanished. The spot where they had been parked was littered with the trunks of uprooted trees. They stared, very tired. They argued: Was that the fourth wave or the fifth? No one could remember. They decided it must have been the fourth.

"What do we do?" Sarah said to Kenner.

"We climb."

Eight minutes later, the next wave came in. It was smaller than the one before. Evans was too tired to do anything but stare at it. Kenner was trying to stop Jennifer's bleeding, but her skin was an ugly pale gray and her lips were blue. Down at the beach, there was no sign of human activity at all. The tents were gone. The generators were gone. There was nothing but piled-up debris, tree branches, pieces of wood, seaweed, foam.

"What's that?" Sarah said.

"What?"

"Someone is shouting."

They looked across to the opposite side of the bay. Someone was waving to them.

"It's Sanjong," Kenner said. "Son of a bitch." He grinned. "I hope he's smart enough to stay where he is. It'll take him a couple of hours to get across the debris. Let's go see if our helicopter is still there or if the wave took it. Then we'll go pick him up."

PACIFIC BASIN
FRIDAY, OCTOBER 15
5:04 P.M.

Eight thousand miles to the east, it was the middle of the night in Golden, Colorado, when the computers of the National Earthquake Information Center registered an atypical seismic disturbance originating from the Pacific basin, just north of the Solomon Islands, and measuring 6.3 Richter. That was a strong quake, but not unusually strong. The peculiar characteristics of the disturbance led the computer to categorize it as an "anomalous event," a fairly common designation for seismic events in that part of the world, where three tectonic plates met in strange overlapping patterns.

The NEIC computers assessed the earthquake as lacking the relatively slow movement associated with tsunamis, and thus did not classify it as a "tsunami-generating event." However, in the South Pacific, this designation was being reexamined, following the devastating New Guinea earthquake of 1998—the single most destructive tsunami of the century—which also did not have the classic slow tsunami profile. Thus, as a precaution, the computers flagged the earthquake to the sensors of the MORN, the Mid-Ocean Relay Network, operating out of Hilo, Hawaii.

Six hours later, mid-ocean buoys detected a nine-inch rise in the ocean level consistent with a tsunami wave train. Because of the great depth of the mid-ocean, tsunamis often raised the sea level only a few inches. On this particular evening, ships in the area felt nothing at all as the big wave front passed beneath them. Nevertheless, the buoys felt it, and triggered an alarm.

It was the middle of the night in Hawaii when the computers pinged and the screens came up. The network manager, Joe Ohiri, had been dozing. He got up, poured himself a cup of coffee and inspected the data. It was clearly a tsunami profile, though one that appeared to be losing force in its ocean passage. Hawaii was of course in its path, but this wave would strike the south shore of the islands, a relative rarity. Ohiri made a quick wave-force calculation, was unimpressed with the results, and so sent a routine notification to civil defense units on all the inhabited islands. It began "This is an information message . . ." and finished with the usual boilerplate about the alert being based on preliminary information. Ohiri knew that nobody would pay much attention to it. Ohiri also notified the West Coast and Alaska Warning Centers, because the wave train was due to strike the coast in early mid-morning of the following day.

Five hours later, the DART buoys off the coast of California and Alaska detected the passage of a tsunami train, now further weakened. Computers calculated the velocity and wave force and recommended no action. This meant that the message went out to the local stations as a tsunami information bulletin, not an alert:

BASED ON LOCATION AND MAGNITUDE THE EARTHQUAKE WAS NOT SUFFICIENT TO GENERATE A TSUNAMI DAMAGING TO CALIFORNIA–OREGON–WASHINGTON–BRITISH COLUMBIA OR ALASKA. SOME AREAS MAY EXPERIENCE SMALL SEA LEVEL CHANGES.

Kenner, who was monitoring the messages on his computer, shook his head when he saw this. "Nick Drake is not going to be a happy man today." It was Kenner's hypothesis that they had needed the cavitation generators to extend the effect of the underwater detonations, and to create the relatively long-lasting landslide that would have produced a truly powerful ocean-crossing tsunami. That had been thwarted.

Ninety minutes later, the much-weakened tsunami train struck the beaches of California. It consisted of a set of five waves averaging six feet in height that excited surfers briefly, but passed unnoticed by everyone else.

Belatedly, Kenner was notified that the FBI had been attempting to reach him for the past twelve hours. It turned out that V. Allen Willy had vacated his beach house at two A.M. local time. This was less than an hour after the events in Resolution Bay had taken place, and more than ten hours prior to the tsunami notification.

Kenner suspected that Willy had gotten cold feet, and had been unwilling to wait. But it was an important and telling mistake. Kenner called the agent and started proceedings to subpoena Willy's phone records.

None of them was allowed to leave the island for the next three days. There were formalities, forms, interrogations. There were problems with emergency care for Morton's collapsed lung and Jennifer's massive blood loss. Morton wanted to be taken to Sydney for surgery, but he was not allowed to leave because he had been reported as a missing person in America. Although he complained bitterly about witch doctors, a very good surgeon trained in Melbourne took care of his lung in Gareda Town. But Jennifer had not been able to wait for that surgeon; she had needed three transfusions during five hours of surgery to remove the bullets in her upper body, and then she was on a respirator, near death for the next forty-eight hours. But at the end of the second day she opened her eyes, pulled off her oxygen mask, and said to Evans, sitting at her bedside, "Stop looking so gloomy. I'm here, for God's sake." Her voice was weak, but she was smiling.

Then there were problems about their contact with the rebels. There were problems about the fact that one of their party had disappeared, the famous actor Ted Bradley. They all told the story of what had happened to Bradley, but there was no way to corroborate it. So the police made them tell it again.

And suddenly, abruptly, unaccountably, they were allowed to leave. Their papers were in order. Their passports were returned. There was no difficulty. They could leave whenever they wanted.

Evans slept most of the way to Honolulu. After the plane refueled and took off again, he sat up and talked to Morton and the others. Morton was explaining what had happened on the night of his car crash.

"There was obviously a problem with Nick and what he was doing with his money. NERF was not doing good things. Nick was very angry—dangerously angry. He threatened me, and I took him at his word. I had established the link between his organization and ELF, and he was threatened, to put it mildly. Kenner and I thought he would try to kill me. Well, he did try. With that girl at the coffee shop, that morning in Beverly Hills."

"Oh yes." Evans remembered. "But how did you stage that car crash? It was so incredibly dangerous—"

"What, do you think I'm crazy?" Morton said. "I never crashed."

"What do you mean?"

"I kept right on driving, that night."

"But." Evans fell silent, shaking his head. "I don't get it."

"Yes, you do," Sarah said. "Because I let it slip to you, by accident. Before George called me and told me to keep my mouth shut about it."

It came back to him then. The conversation from days ago. He hadn't paid much attention at the time. Sarah had said:

He told me to buy a new Ferrari from a guy in Monterey and have it shipped to San Francisco.

When Evans expressed surprise that George was buying another Ferrari:

I know. How many Ferraris can one man use? And this one doesn't seem up to his usual standard. From the e-mail pictures it looks kind of beat up.

And then she said:

The Ferrari he bought is a 1972 365 GTS Daytona Spyder. He already has one, Peter. It's like he doesn't know . . .

"Oh, I knew all right," Morton said. "What a waste of money. The car was a piece of crap. And then I had to fly a couple of Hollywood prop guys up to Sonoma to beat the hell out of it and make it look like a crash. Then they flat-bedded it out that night, set it on the road, fired up the smoke pots . . ."

"And you drove right past a wreck that was already in place," Evans said.

"Yes," Morton said, nodding. "Drove right around the corner. Pulled off the road, climbed up the hill, and watched you guys."

"You son of a bitch."

"I'm sorry," Morton said, "but we needed real emotion to distract the police from the problems."

"What problems?"

"Ice-cold engine block, for one," Kenner said. "That engine hadn't run for days. One of the cops noticed it was cold while the car was being put on the truck. He came back and asked you the time of the accident, all of that. I was concerned they would figure it out."

"But they didn't," Morton said.

"No. They knew something was wrong. But I don't think they ever guessed identical Ferraris."

"No one in his right mind," Morton said, "would intentionally destroy a 1972 365 GTS. Even a crappy one."

Morton was smiling, but Evans was angry. "Somebody could have told me—"

"No," Kenner said. "We needed you to work Drake. Like the cell phone."

"What about it?"

"The cell phone was a very low-quality bug. We needed Drake to suspect that you were part of the investigation. We needed him pressured."

"Well, it worked. That's why I got poisoned in my apartment, isn't it?" Evans said. "You guys were willing to take a lot of risks with my life."

"It turned out all right," Kenner said.

"You did this car crash to pressure Drake?"

"And to get me free," Morton said. "I needed to go down to the Solomons and find out what they were doing. I knew Nick would save the best for last. Although if they had been able to modify that hurricane—that was the third stunt they planned—so that it hit Miami, that would have been spectacular."

"Fuck you, George," Evans said.

"I'm sorry it had to be this way," Kenner said.

"And fuck you, too."

Then Evans got up and went to the front of the plane. Sarah was sitting alone. He was so angry he refused to speak to her. He spent the next hour staring out the window. Finally, she began talking quietly to him, and at the end of half an hour, they embraced.

Evans slept for a while, restless, his body sore. He couldn't find a comfortable position to rest. Intermittently, he would wake up, groggy. One time he thought he heard Kenner talking to Sarah.

Let's remember where we live, Kenner was saying. We live on the third planet from a medium-size sun. Our planet is five billion years old, and it has been changing constantly all during that time. The Earth is now on its third atmosphere.

The first atmosphere was helium and hydrogen. It dissipated early on, because the planet was so hot. Then, as the planet cooled, volcanic eruptions produced a second atmosphere of steam and carbon dioxide. Later the water vapor condensed, forming the oceans that cover most of the planet. Then, around three billion years ago, some bacteria evolved to consume carbon dioxide and excrete a highly toxic gas, oxygen. Other bacteria released nitrogen. The atmospheric concentration of these gases slowly increased. Organisms that could not adapt died out.

Meanwhile, the planet's land masses, floating on huge tectonic plates, eventually came together in a configuration that interfered with the circulation of ocean currents. It began to get cold for the first time. The first ice appeared two billion years ago.

And for the last seven hundred thousand years, our planet has been in a geological ice age, characterized by advancing and retreating glacial ice. No one is entirely sure why, but ice now covers the planet every hundred thousand years, with smaller advances every twenty thousand or so. The last advance was twenty thousand years ago, so we're due for the next one.

And even today, after five billion years, our planet remains amazingly active. We have five hundred volcanoes, and an eruption every two weeks. Earthquakes are continuous: a million and a half a year, a moderate Richter 5 quake every six hours, a big earthquake every ten days. Tsunamis race across the Pacific Ocean every three months.

Our atmosphere is as violent as the land beneath it. At any moment there are one thousand five hundred electrical storms across the planet. Eleven lightning bolts strike the ground each second. A tornado tears across the surface every six hours. And every four days, a giant cyclonic storm, hundreds of miles in diameter, spins over the ocean and wreaks havoc on the land.

The nasty little apes that call themselves human beings can do nothing except run and hide. For these same apes to imagine they can stabilize this atmosphere is arrogant beyond belief. They can't control the climate.

The reality is, they run from the storms.

"What do we do now?"

"I'll tell you what we do," Morton said. "You work for me. I'm starting a new environmental organization. I have to think of a name. I don't want one of these pretentious names with the words *world* and *resource* and *defense* and *wildlife* and *fund* and *preservation* and *wilderness* in them. You can string those words together in any combination. World Wildlife Preservation Fund. Wilderness Resource Defense Fund. Fund for the Defense of World Resources. Anyway, those fake names are all taken. I need something plain and new. Something honest. I was thinking of 'Study the Problem And Fix It.' Except the acronym doesn't work. But maybe that's a plus. We will have scientists and field researchers and economists and engineers—and one lawyer."

"What would this organization do?"

"There is so much to do! For example: Nobody knows how to manage wilderness. We would set aside a wide variety of wilderness tracts and run them under different management strategies. Then we'd ask outside teams to assess how we are doing, and modify the strategies. And then do it again. A true iterative process, externally assessed. Nobody's ever done that. And in the end we'll have a body of knowledge about how to manage different terrains. Not preserve them. You can't preserve them. They're going to change all the time, no matter what. But you could manage them—if you knew how to do it. Which nobody does. That's one big area. Management of complex environmental systems."

"Okay . . ."

"Then we'd do developing-world problems. The biggest cause of environmental destruction is poverty. Starving people can't worry about pollution. They worry about food. Half a billion people are starving in the world right now. More than half a billion without clean water. We need to design delivery systems that really work, test them, have them verified by outsiders, and once we know they work, replicate them."

"It sounds difficult."

"It's difficult if you are a government agency or an ideologue. But if you just want to study the problem and fix it, you can. And this would be entirely private. Private funding, private land. No bureaucrats. Administration is five percent of staff and resources. Everybody is out working. We'd run environmental research as a business. And cut the crap."

"Why hasn't somebody done it?"

"Are you kidding? Because it's radical. Face the facts, all these environmental organizations are thirty, forty, fifty years old. They have big buildings, big obligations, big staffs. They may trade on their youthful dreams, but the truth is, they're now part of the establishment. And the establishment works to preserve the status quo. It just does."

"Okay. What else?"

"Technology assessment. Third world countries can leapfrog. They skip telephone lines and go right to cellular. But nobody is doing decent technology assessment in terms of what works and how to balance the inevitable drawbacks. Wind power's great, unless you're a bird. Those things are giant bird guillotines. Maybe we should build them anyway. But people don't know how to think about this stuff. They just posture and pontificate. Nobody tests. Nobody does field research. Nobody dares to solve the problems—because the solution might contradict your philosophy, and for most people clinging to beliefs is more important than succeeding in the world."

"Really?"

"Trust me. When you're my age, you'll know it is true. Next, how about recreational land use—multipurpose land use. It's a rat's nest. Nobody has figured out how to do it, and it's so hot, so fierce that good people just give up and quit, or vanish in a blizzard of lawsuits. But that doesn't help. The answer probably lies in a range of solutions. It may be necessary to designate certain areas for one or another use. But everybody lives on the same planet. Some people like opera, some people like Vegas. And there's a lot of people that like Vegas."

"Anything else?"

"Yes. We need a new mechanism to fund research. Right now, scientists are in exactly the same position as Renaissance painters, commissioned to make the portrait the patron wants done. And if they are smart, they'll make sure their work subtly flatters the patron. Not overtly. Subtly. This is not a good system for research into those areas of science that affect policy. Even worse, the system works against problem solving. Because if you solve a problem, your funding ends. All that's got to change."

"How?"

"I have some ideas. Make scientists blind to their funding. Make assessment of research blind. We can have major policy-oriented research carried out by multiple teams doing the same work. Why not, if it's really important? We'll push to change how journals report research. Publish the article *and* the peer reviews in the same issue. That'll clean up everybody's act real fast. Get the journals out of politics. Their editors openly take sides on certain issues. Bad dogs."

Evans said, "Anything else?"

"New labels. If you read some authors who say, 'We find that anthropogenic greenhouse gases and sulphates have had a detectable influence on sea-level pressure' it sounds like they went into the world and measured something. Actually, they just ran a simulation. They talk as if simulations were real-world data. They're not. That's a problem that has to be fixed. I favor a stamp: WARNING: COMPUTER SIMULATION—MAY BE ERRONEOUS and UNVERIFIABLE. Like on cigarettes. Put the same stamp on newspaper articles, and in the corner of newscasts. WARNING: SPECULATION—MAY BE FACT-FREE. Can you see that peppered all over the front pages?"

"Anything else?" Evans was smiling now.

"There are a few more things," Morton said, "but those are the major points. It's going to be very difficult. It's going to be uphill all the way. We'll be opposed, sabotaged, denigrated. We'll be called terrible names. The establishment will not like it. Newspapers will sneer. But, eventually, money will start to flow to us because we'll show results. And then everybody will shut up. And then we will get lionized, which is the most dangerous time of all."

"And?"

"By then, I'm long dead. You and Sarah will have run the organization for twenty years. And your final job will be to disband it, before it becomes another tired old environmental organization spouting outmoded wisdom, wasting resources, and doing more harm than good."

"I see," Evans said. "And when it's disbanded?"

"You'll find a bright young person and try to excite him or her to do what really needs to be done in the next generation."

Evans looked at Sarah.

She shrugged. "Unless you have a better idea," she said.

Half an hour before they reached the California coast, they saw the spreading brown haze hanging over the ocean. It grew thicker and darker as they approached land. Soon they saw the lights of the city, stretching away for miles. It was blurred by the atmosphere above.

"It looks a bit like hell, doesn't it," Sarah said. "Hard to think we're going to land in that."

"We have a lot of work to do," Morton said.

The plane descended smoothly toward Los Angeles.

AUTHOR'S MESSAGE

A novel such as *State of Fear*, in which so many divergent views are expressed, may lead the reader to wonder where, exactly, the author stands on these issues. I have been reading environmental texts for three years, in itself a hazardous undertaking. But I have had an opportunity to look at a lot of data, and to consider many points of view. I conclude:

- We know astonishingly little about every aspect of the environment, from its past history, to its present state, to how to conserve and protect it. In every debate, all sides overstate the extent of existing knowledge and its degree of certainty.

- Atmospheric carbon dioxide is increasing, and human activity is the probable cause.

- We are also in the midst of a natural warming trend that began about 1850, as we emerged from a four-hundred-year cold spell known as the "Little Ice Age."

- Nobody knows how much of the present warming trend might be a natural phenomenon.

- Nobody knows how much of the present warming trend might be man-made.

- Nobody knows how much warming will occur in the next century. The computer models vary by 400 percent, de facto proof that nobody knows. But if I had to guess—the only thing anyone is doing, really—I would guess the increase will be 0.812436 degrees C. There is no evidence that my guess about the state of the world one hundred years from now is any better or worse than anyone else's. (We can't "assess" the future, nor can we "predict" it. These are euphemisms. We can only guess. An informed guess is just a guess.)

- I suspect that part of the observed surface warming will ultimately be attributable to human activity. I suspect that the principal human effect will come from land use, and that the atmospheric component will be minor.

- Before making expensive policy decisions on the basis of climate models, I think it is reasonable to require that those models predict future temperatures accurately for a period of ten years. Twenty would be better.

- I think for anyone to believe in impending resource scarcity, after two hundred years of such false alarms, is kind of weird. I don't know whether such a belief today is best ascribed to ignorance of history, sclerotic dogmatism, unhealthy love of Malthus, or simple pigheadedness, but it is evidently a hardy perennial in human calculation.

- There are many reasons to shift away from fossil fuels, and we will do so in the next century without legislation, financial incentives, carbon-conservation programs, or the interminable yammering of fearmongers. So far as I know, nobody had to ban horse transport in the early twentieth century.

- I suspect the people of 2100 will be much richer than we are, consume more energy, have a smaller global population, and enjoy more wilderness than we have today. I don't think we have to worry about them.

- The current near-hysterical preoccupation with safety is at best a waste of resources and a crimp on the human spirit, and at worst an invitation to totalitarianism. Public education is desperately needed.

- I conclude that most environmental "principles" (such as sustainable development or the precautionary principle) have the effect of preserving the economic advantages of the West and thus constitute modern imperialism toward the developing world. It is a nice way of saying, "We got ours and we don't want you to get yours, because you'll cause too much pollution."

- The "precautionary principle," properly applied, forbids the precautionary principle. It is self-contradictory. The precautionary principle therefore cannot be spoken of in terms that are too harsh.

- I believe people are well intentioned. But I have great respect for the corrosive influence of bias, systematic distortions of thought, the power of rationalization, the guises of self-interest, and the inevitability of unintended consequences.

- I have more respect for people who change their views after acquiring new information than for those who cling to views they held thirty years ago. The world changes. Ideologues and zealots don't.

- In the thirty-five-odd years since the environmental movement came into existence, science has undergone a major revolution. This revolution has brought new understanding of nonlinear dynamics, complex systems, chaos theory, catastrophe theory. It has transformed the way we think about evolution and ecology. Yet these no-longer-new ideas have hardly penetrated the thinking of environmental activists, which seems oddly fixed in the concepts and rhetoric of the 1970s.

- We haven't the foggiest notion how to preserve what we term "wilderness," and we had better study it in the field and learn how to do so. I see no evidence that we are conducting such research in a humble, rational, and systematic way. I therefore hold little hope for wilderness management in the twenty-first century. I blame environmental organizations every bit as much as developers and strip miners. There is no difference in outcomes between greed and incompetence.

- We need a new environmental movement, with new goals and new organizations. We need more people working in the field, in the actual environment, and fewer people behind computer screens. We need more scientists and many fewer lawyers.

- We cannot hope to manage a complex system such as the environment through litigation. We can only change its state temporarily— usually by preventing something—with eventual results that we cannot predict and ultimately cannot control.

- Nothing is more inherently political than our shared physical environment, and nothing is more ill served by allegiance to a single political party. Precisely because the environment is shared it cannot be managed by one faction according to its own economic or aesthetic preferences. Sooner or later, the opposing faction will take power, and previous policies will be reversed. Stable management of the environment requires recognition that all preferences have their place: snowmobilers and fly fishermen, dirt bikers and hikers, developers and preservationists. These preferences are at odds, and their incompatibility cannot be avoided. But resolving incompatible goals is a true function of politics.

- We desperately need a nonpartisan, blinded funding mechanism to conduct research to determine appropriate policy. Scientists are only too aware whom they are working for. Those who fund research— whether a drug company, a government agency, or an environmental organization—always have a particular outcome in mind. Research funding is almost never open-ended or open-minded.

Scientists know that continued funding depends on delivering the results the funders desire. As a result, environmental organization "studies" are every bit as biased and suspect as industry "studies." Government "studies" are similarly biased according to who is running the department or administration at the time. No faction should be given a free pass.

- I am certain there is too much certainty in the world.

- I personally experience a profound pleasure being in nature. My happiest days each year are those I spend in wilderness. I wish natural environments to be preserved for future generations. I am not satisfied they will be preserved in sufficient quantities, or with sufficient skill. I conclude that the "exploiters of the environment" include environmental organizations, government organizations, and big business. All have equally dismal track records.

- Everybody has an agenda. Except me.

APPENDIX I
Why Politicized Science Is Dangerous

Imagine that there is a new scientific theory that warns of an impending crisis, and points to a way out.

This theory quickly draws support from leading scientists, politicians, and celebrities around the world. Research is funded by distinguished philanthropies, and carried out at prestigious universities. The crisis is reported frequently in the media. The science is taught in college and high school classrooms.

I don't mean global warming. I'm talking about another theory, which rose to prominence a century ago.

Its supporters included Theodore Roosevelt, Woodrow Wilson, and Winston Churchill. It was approved by Supreme Court justices Oliver Wendell Holmes and Louis Brandeis, who ruled in its favor. The famous names who supported it included Alexander Graham Bell, inventor of the telephone; activist Margaret Sanger; botanist Luther Burbank; Leland Stanford, founder of Stanford University; the novelist H. G. Wells; the playwright George Bernard Shaw; and hundreds of others. Nobel Prize winners gave support. Research was backed by the Carnegie and Rockefeller Foundations. The Cold Springs Harbor Institute was built to carry out this research, but important work was also done at Harvard, Yale, Princeton, Stanford, and Johns Hopkins. Legislation to address the crisis was passed in states from New York to California.

These efforts had the support of the National Academy of Sciences, the American Medical Association, and the National Research Council. It was said that if Jesus were alive, he would have supported this effort.

All in all, the research, legislation, and molding of public opinion surrounding the theory went on for almost half a century. Those who opposed the theory were shouted down and called reactionary, blind to reality, or just plain ignorant. But in hindsight, what is surprising is that so few people objected.

Today, we know that this famous theory that gained so much support was actually pseudoscience. The crisis it claimed was nonexistent. And the actions taken in the name of this theory were morally and criminally wrong. Ultimately, they led to the deaths of millions of people.

The theory was eugenics, and its history is so dreadful—and, to those who were caught up in it, so embarrassing—that it is now rarely discussed. But it is a story that should be well known to every citizen, so that its horrors are not repeated.

The theory of eugenics postulated a crisis of the gene pool leading to the deterioration of the human race. The best human beings were not breeding as rapidly as the inferior ones—the foreigners, immigrants, Jews, degenerates, the unfit, and the "feeble minded." Francis Galton, a respected British scientist, first speculated about this area, but his ideas were taken far beyond anything he intended. They were adopted by science-minded Americans, as well as those who had no interest in science but who were worried about the immigration of inferior races early in the twentieth century—"dangerous human pests" who represented "the rising tide of imbeciles" and who were polluting the best of the human race.

The eugenicists and the immigrationists joined forces to put a stop to this. The plan was to identify individuals who were feeble-minded—Jews were agreed to be largely feeble-minded, but so were many foreigners, as well as blacks—and stop them from breeding by isolation in institutions or by sterilization.

As Margaret Sanger said, "Fostering the good-for-nothing at the expense of the good is an extreme cruelty . . . there is no greater curse to posterity than that of bequeathing them an increasing population of imbeciles." She spoke of the burden of caring for "this dead weight of human waste."

Such views were widely shared. H. G. Wells spoke against "ill-trained swarms of inferior citizens." Theodore Roosevelt said that "Society has no business to permit degenerates to reproduce their kind." Luther Burbank: "Stop permitting criminals and weaklings to reproduce." George Bernard Shaw said that only eugenics could save mankind.

There was overt racism in this movement, exemplified by texts such as

The Rising Tide of Color Against White World Supremacy, by American author Lothrop Stoddard. But, at the time, racism was considered an unremarkable aspect of the effort to attain a marvelous goal—the improvement of humankind in the future. It was this avant-garde notion that attracted the most liberal and progressive minds of a generation. California was one of twenty-nine American states to pass laws allowing sterilization, but it proved the most forward-looking and enthusiastic—more sterilizations were carried out in California than anywhere else in America.

Eugenics research was funded by the Carnegie Foundation, and later by the Rockefeller Foundation. The latter was so enthusiastic that even after the center of the eugenics effort moved to Germany, and involved the gassing of individuals from mental institutions, the Rockefeller Foundation continued to finance German researchers at a very high level. (The foundation was quiet about it, but they were still funding research in 1939, only months before the onset of World War II.)

Since the 1920s, American eugenicists had been jealous because the Germans had taken leadership of the movement away from them. The Germans were admirably progressive. They set up ordinary-looking houses where "mental defectives" were brought and interviewed one at a time, before being led into a back room, which was, in fact, a gas chamber. There, they were gassed with carbon monoxide, and their bodies disposed of in a crematorium located on the property.

Eventually, this program was expanded into a vast network of concentration camps located near railroad lines, enabling the efficient transport and killing of ten million undesirables.

After World War II, nobody was a eugenicist, and nobody had ever been a eugenicist. Biographers of the celebrated and the powerful did not dwell on the attractions of this philosophy to their subjects, and sometimes did not mention it at all. Eugenics ceased to be a subject for college classrooms, although some argue that its ideas continue to have currency in disguised form.

But in retrospect, three points stand out. First, despite the construction of Cold Springs Harbor Laboratory, despite the efforts at universities and the pleadings of lawyers, there was no scientific basis for eugenics. In fact, nobody at that time knew what a gene really was. The movement was able to proceed because it employed vague terms never rigorously defined. "Feeble-mindedness" could mean anything from poverty and illiteracy to epilepsy. Similarly, there was no clear definition of "degenerate" or "unfit."

Second, the eugenics movement was really a social program masquerading as a scientific one. What drove it was concern about immigration and racism and undesirable people moving into one's neighborhood or country. Once again, vague terminology helped conceal what was really going on.

Third, and most distressing, the scientific establishment in both the United States and Germany did not mount any sustained protest. Quite the contrary. In Germany scientists quickly fell into line with the program. Modern German researchers have gone back to review Nazi documents from the 1930s. They expected to find directives telling scientists what research should be done. But none were necessary. In the words of Ute Deichman, "Scientists, including those who were not members of the [Nazi] party, helped to get funding for their work through their modified behavior and direct cooperation with the state." Deichman speaks of the "active role of scientists themselves in regard to Nazi race policy . . . where [research] was aimed at confirming the racial doctrine . . . no external pressure can be documented." German scientists adjusted their research interests to the new policies. And those few who did not adjust disappeared.

A second example of politicized science is quite different in character, but it exemplifies the hazards of government ideology controlling the work of science, and of uncritical media promoting false concepts. Trofim Denisovich Lysenko was a self-promoting peasant who, it was said, "solved the problem of fertilizing the fields without fertilizers and minerals." In 1928 he claimed to have invented a procedure called vernalization, by which seeds were moistened and chilled to enhance the later growth of crops.

Lysenko's methods never faced a rigorous test, but his claim that his treated seeds passed on their characteristics to the next generation represented a revival of Lamarckian ideas at a time when the rest of the world was embracing Mendelian genetics. Josef Stalin was drawn to Lamarckian ideas, which implied a future unbounded by hereditary constraints; he also wanted improved agricultural production. Lysenko promised both, and became the darling of a Soviet media that was on the lookout for stories about clever peasants who had developed revolutionary procedures.

Lysenko was portrayed as a genius, and he milked his celebrity for all it was worth. He was especially skillful at denouncing his opponents. He used questionnaires from farmers to prove that vernalization increased crop yields, and thus avoided any direct tests. Carried on a wave of state-sponsored enthusiasm, his rise was rapid. By 1937, he was a member of the Supreme Soviet.

By then, Lysenko and his theories dominated Russian biology. The result was famines that killed millions, and purges that sent hundreds of dissenting Soviet scientists to the gulags or the firing squads. Lysenko was aggressive in attacking genetics, which was finally banned as "bourgeois pseudo-science" in 1948. There was never any basis for Lysenko's ideas, yet he controlled Soviet research for thirty years. Lysenkoism ended in the 1960s, but Russian biology still has not entirely recovered from that era.

Now we are engaged in a great new theory, that once again has drawn the support of politicians, scientists, and celebrities around the world. Once again, the theory is promoted by major foundations. Once again, the research is carried out at prestigious universities. Once again, legislation is passed and social programs are urged in its name. Once again, critics are few and harshly dealt with.

Once again, the measures being urged have little basis in fact or science. Once again, groups with other agendas are hiding behind a movement that appears high-minded. Once again, claims of moral superiority are used to justify extreme actions. Once again, the fact that some people are hurt is shrugged off because an abstract cause is said to be greater than any human consequences. Once again, vague terms like *sustainability* and *generational justice*—terms that have no agreed definition—are employed in the service of a new crisis.

I am not arguing that global warming is the same as eugenics. But the similarities are not superficial. And I do claim that open and frank discussion of the data, and of the issues, is being suppressed. Leading scientific journals have taken strong editorial positions on the side of global warming, which, I argue, they have no business doing. Under the circumstances, any scientist who has doubts understands clearly that they will be wise to mute their expression.

One proof of this suppression is the fact that so many of the outspoken critics of global warming are retired professors. These individuals are no longer seeking grants, and no longer have to face colleagues whose grant applications and career advancement may be jeopardized by their criticisms.

In science, the old men are usually wrong. But in politics, the old men are wise, counsel caution, and in the end are often right.

The past history of human belief is a cautionary tale. We have killed thousands of our fellow human beings because we believed they had signed a contract with the devil, and had become witches. We still kill more than a thousand people each year for witchcraft. In my view, there is only one hope for humankind to emerge from what Carl Sagan called "the demon-haunted world" of our past. That hope is science.

But as Alston Chase put it, "when the search for truth is confused with political advocacy, the pursuit of knowledge is reduced to the quest for power."

That is the danger we now face. And that is why the intermixing of science and politics is a bad combination, with a bad history. We must remember the history, and be certain that what we present to the world as knowledge is disinterested and honest.

APPENDIX II
Sources of Data for Graphs

World temperature data has been taken from the Goddard Institute for Space Studies, Columbia University, New York (GISS); the Jones, et al. data set from the Climate Research Unit, University of East Anglia, Norwich, UK (CRU); and the Global Historical Climatology Network (GHCN) maintained by the National Climatic Data Center (NCDC) and the Carbon Dioxide Information and Analysis Center (CDIAC) of Oak Ridge National Laboratory, Oak Ridge, Tennessee.

The GISS station page is not easy to find from their home page, but it is found at http://www.giss.nasa.gov/data/update/gistemp/station data/.

The Jones data set reference is P. D. Jones, D. E. Parker, T. J. Osborn, and K. R. Briffa, 1999. Global and hemispheric temperature anomolies—land and marine instrument records. In *Trends: A Compendium of Data on Global Change*. Carbon Dioxide Information Analysis Center, Oak Ridge National Laboratory, US Department of Energy, Oak Ridge, Tennessee.

Global Historical Climatology Network is maintained at NCDC and CDIAC of Oak Ridge National Laboratory. The home page is http://cdiac.esd.ornl.gov/ghcn/ghcn.html.

Temperature data for the United States comes from the United States Historical Climatology Network (USHCN) maintained at NCDC and CDIAC of Oak Ridge National Laboratory, which states: "We recommend using USHCN whenever possible for long-term climate analyses. . . ."

The USHCN home page is http://www.ncdc.noaa.gov/oa/climate/research/ushcn/ushcn.html.

The reference is D. R. Easterling, T. R. Karl, E. H. Mason, P. Y. Hughes, D. P. Bowman, R. C. Daniels, and T. A. Boden (eds.). 1996. *United States Historical Climatology Network (US HCN) Monthly Temperature and Precipitation Data*. ORNL/CDIAC-87, NDP-019/R3. Carbon Dioxide Information Analysis Center, Oak Ridge National Laboratory, Oak Ridge, Tennessee.

Graphs are generated in Microsoft Excel from tabular data provided on the websites.

The satellite images are from NASA (http://datasystem.earthkam.ucsd.edu). The rendering of the globe image on the title page and part-opener pages is adapted from NASA (http://earthobservatory.nasa.gov/Observatory/Datasets/tsurf.tovs.html).

BIBLIOGRAPHY

What follows is a list of books and journal articles I found most useful in preparing this novel. I found the texts by Beckerman, Chase, Huber, Lomborg, and Wildavsky to be particularly revealing.

Environmental science is a contentious and intensely politicized field. No reader should assume that any author listed below agrees with the views I express in this book. Quite the contrary: many of them disagree strongly. I am presenting these references to assist those readers who would like to review my thinking and arrive at their own conclusions.

Aber, John D., and Jerry M. Melillo. *Terrestrial Ecosystems*. San Francisco: Harcourt Academic Press, 2001. A standard textbook.

Abrupt Climate Change: Inevitable Surprises (Report of the Committee on Abrupt Climate Change, National Research Council). Washington, DC: National Academy Press, 2002. The text concludes that abrupt climate change might occur sometime in the future, triggered by mechanisms not yet understood, and that in the meantime more research is needed. Surely no one could object.

Adam, Barbara, Ulrich Beck, and Jost Van Loon. *The Risk Society and Beyond*. London: Sage Publications, 2000.

Altheide, David L. *Creating Fear, News and the Construction of Crisis*. New York: Aldine de Gruyter, 2002. A book about fear and its expanding place in public life. Overlong and repetitive, but addressing a highly significant subject. Some of the statistical analyses are quite amazing.

Anderson, J. B. and J. T. Andrews. "Radiocarbon Constraints on Ice Sheet Advance and Retreat in the Weddell Sea, Antarctica." *Geology* 27 (1999): 179–82.

Anderson, Terry L., and Donald R. Leal. *Free Market Environmentalism*. New York: Palgrave (St. Martin's Press), 2001. The authors argue government

management of environmental resources has a poor track record in the former Soviet Union, and in the Western democracies as well. They make the
case for the superiority of private and market-based management of environmental resources. Their case histories are particularly interesting.

Arens, William. *The Man-Eating Myth*. New York: Oxford, 1979.

Arquilla, John, and David Ronfeldt, eds. *In Athena's Camp: Preparing for Conflict
in the Information Age*. Santa Monica, Calif.: RAND National Defense
Research Institute, 1997. See particularly part III on the advent of netwar and
its implications.

Aunger, Robert, ed. *Darwinizing Culture*. New York: Oxford University Press,
2000. See especially the last three chapters, which devastate the trendy concept of memes. There is no better example of the way that trendy quasi-
scientific ideas can gain currency even in the face of preexisting evidence that
they are baseless. And the text serves as a model for the expression of brisk
disagreement without ad hominem characterization.

Beck, Ulrich. *Risk Society: Towards a New Modernity*. Trans. Mark Ritter. London:
Sage, 1992. This highly influential text by a German sociologist presents a
fascinating redefinition of the modern state as protector against industrial
society, instead of merely the ground upon which it is built.

Beckerman, Wilfred. *A Poverty of Reason: Sustainable Development and Economic
Growth*. Oakland, Calif.: Independent Institute, 2003. A short, witty, sting-
ing review of sustainability, climate change, and the precautionary principle
by an Oxford economist and former member of the Royal Commission on
Environmental Pollution who cares more about the poor of the world than
he does the elitist egos of Western environmentalists. Clearly argued and fun
to read.

Bennett, W. Lance. *News: The Politics of Illusion*. New York: Addison-Wesley,
2003.

Black, Edwin. *War Against the Weak: Eugenics and America's Campaign to Create
a Master Race*. New York: Four Walls, 2003. The history of the eugenics
movement in America and Germany is an unpleasant story, and perhaps for
that reason, most texts present it confusingly. This book is an admirably clear
narrative.

Bohm, R. "Urban bias in temperature time series—a case study for the city of
Vienna, Austria." *Climatic Change* 38 (1998): 113–28.

Braithwaite, Roger J. "Glacier mass balance: The first 50 years of international
monitoring." *Progress in Physical Geography* 26, no. 1 (2002): 76–95.

Braithwaite, R. J., and Y. Zhang. "Relationships between interannual variability
of glacier mass balance and climate." *Journal of Glaciology* 45 (2000): 456–62.

Briggs, Robin. *Witches and Neighbors: The Social and Cultural Context of European Witchcraft*. New York: HarperCollins, 1996.

Brint, Steven. "Professionals and the Knowledge Economy: Rethinking the Theory of the Postindustrial Society." *Current Sociology* 49, no. 1 (July 2001): 101–32.

Brower, Michael, and Warren Leon. *The Consumer's Guide to Effective Environmental Choices: Practical Advice from the Union of Concerned Scientists*. New York: Three Rivers Press, 1999. Of particular interest for its advice on mundane decisions: paper vs. plastic shopping bags (plastic), cloth vs. disposable diapers (disposable). On broader issues, the analysis is extremely vague and exemplifies the difficulties of determining "sustainable development" that are pointed out by Wilfred Beckerman.

Carson, Rachel. *Silent Spring*. Boston: Houghton Mifflin, 1962. I am old enough to remember reading this poetic persuasive text with alarm and excitement when it was first published; it was clear even then that it would change the world. With the passage of time Carson's text appears more flawed and more overtly polemical. It is, to be blunt, about one-third right and two-thirds wrong. Carson is particularly to be faulted for her specious promotion of the idea that most cancer is caused by the environment. This fear remains in general circulation decades later.

Castle, Terry. "Contagious Folly." In Chandler, Davidson, and Harootunian, *Questions of Evidence*.

Chandler, James, Arnold I. Davidson, and Harry Harootunian. *Questions of Evidence: Proof, Practice and Persuasion Across the Disciplines*. Chicago: University of Chicago Press, 1993.

Changnon, Stanley A. "Impacts of 1997–98 El Niño-Generated Weather in the United States." *Bulletin of the American Meteorological Society* 80, no. 9, (1999): 1819–28.

Chapin, F. Stuart, Pamela A. Matson, and Harold A. Mooney. *Principles of Terrestrial Ecosystems Ecology*. New York: Springer-Verlag, 2002. Clearer and with more technical detail than most ecology texts.

Chase, Alston. *In a Dark Wood: The Fight over Forests and the Myths of Nature*. New Brunswick, N.J.: Transaction Publishers, 2001. Essential reading. This book is a history of the conflict over the forests of the Northwest, a cheerless and distressing story. As a former professor of philosophy, the author is one of the few writers in the environmental field who shows the slightest interest in ideas—where they come from, what consequences have flowed from them in the historical past, and therefore what consequences are likely to flow from them now. Chase discusses such notions as the mystic vision of wilderness and the balance of nature from the standpoint of both science and philosophy. He is contemptuous of much conventional wisdom and the muddle-headed attitudes he calls "California cosmology." The book is long and sometimes rambling, but extremely rewarding.

————. *Playing God in Yellowstone: The Destruction of America's First National Park.* New York: Atlantic, 1986. Essential reading. Arguably the first and clearest critique of ever-changing environmental beliefs and their practical consequences. Anyone who assumes we know how to manage wilderness areas needs to read this sobering history of the century-long mismanagement of Yellowstone, the first national park. Chase's text has been reviled in some quarters, but to my knowledge, never seriously disputed.

Chen, L., W. Zhu, X. Zhou, and Z. Zhou, "Characteristics of the heat island effect in Shanghai and its possible mechanism." *Advances in Atmospheric Sciences* 20 (2003): 991-1001.

Choi, Y., H.-S. Jung, K.-Y. Nam, and W.-T. Kwon, "Adjusting urban bias in the regional mean surface temperature series of South Korea, 1968–99." *International Journal of Climatology* 23 (2003): 577–91.

Christianson, Gale E. *Greenhouse: The 200-Year Story of Global Warming.* New York: Penguin, 1999.

Chylek, P., J. E. Box, and G. Lesins. "Global Warming and the Greenland Ice Sheet." *Climatic Change* 63 (2004): 201–21.

Comiso, J. C. "Variability and Trends in Antarctic Surface Temperatures From *in situ* and Satellite Infrared Measurements." *Journal of Climate* 13 (2000): 1674–96.

Cook, Timothy E. *Governing with the News: The News Media as a Political Institution.* Chicago: University of Chicago Press, 1998.

Cooke, Roger M. *Experts in Uncertainty.* New York: Oxford University Press, 1991.

Davis, Ray Jay, and Lewis Grant. *Weather Modification Technology and Law.* AAAS Selected Symposium. Boulder, Col.: Westview Press, Inc., 1978. Of historical interest only.

Deichmann, Ute. *Biologist Under Hitler,* tr. Thomas Dunlap. Cambridge, Mass.: Harvard University Press, 1996. Difficult in structure, disturbing in content.

Doran, P. T., J. C. Priscu, W. B. Lyons, J. E. Walsh, A. G. Fountain, D. M. McKnight, D. L. Moorhead, R. A. Virginia, D. H. Wall, G. D. Clow, C. H. Fritsen, C. P. McKay, and A. N. Parsons. "Antarctic Climate Cooling and Terrestrial Ecosystem Response." *Nature* 415 (2002): 517–20.

Dörner, Dietrich. *The Logic of Failure: Recognizing and Avoiding Error in Complex Situations.* Cambridge, Mass.: Perseus, 1998. What prevents human beings from successfully managing the natural environment and other complex systems? Dozens of pundits have weighed in with their unsubstantiated opinions. Dörner, a cognitive psychologist, performed experiments and found out. Using computer simulations of complex environments, he invited intellectuals to improve the situation. They often made it worse. Those who did well gathered information before acting, thought systemically, reviewed progress, and corrected their course often. Those who did badly clung to their theories, acted too quickly, did not correct course, and blamed others when things went wrong. Dörner concludes that our failures in managing complex systems do not represent any inherent lack of human capability. Rather they reflect bad habits of thought and lazy procedures.

Dowie, Mark. *Losing Ground: American Environmentalism at the Close of the Twentieth Century.* Cambridge, Mass.: MIT Press, 1995. A former editor of *Mother Jones* concludes that the American environmental movement has lost relevance through compromise and capitulation. Well written, but weakly documented, the book is most interesting for the frame of mind it conveys—an uncompromising posture that rarely specifies what solutions would be satisfactory. This makes the text essentially nonscientific in its outlook and its implications, and all the more interesting for that.

Drake, Frances. *Global Warming: The Science of Climate Change.* New York: Oxford University Press, 2000. This well-written overview for college students can be read by any interested reader.

Drucker, Peter. *Post-Capitalist Society.* New York: Harper Business, 1993.

Eagleton, Terry. *Ideology: An Introduction.* New York: Verso, 1991.

Edgerton, Robert B. *Sick Societies: Challenging the Myth of Primitive Harmony.* New York: Free Press, 1992. An excellent summary of the evidence disputing the notion of the noble savage that goes on to consider whether cultures adopt maladaptive beliefs and practices. The author concludes that all cultures do so. The text also attacks the currently trendy academic notion of "unconscious" problem-solving, in which primitive cultures are assumed to be acting in an ecologically sound fashion, even when they appear wasteful and destructive. Edgerton argues they aren't doing anything of the sort—they *are* wasteful and destructive.

Edwards, Paul. N., and Stephen Schneider. "The 1995 IPCC Report: Broad Consensus or 'Scientific Cleansing'?" *EcoFable/Ecoscience* 1, no. 1 (1997): 3–9. A spirited argument in defense of changes to the 1995 IPCC report by Ben Santer. However, the article focuses on the controversy that resulted and does not review in detail the changes to the text that were made. Thus the paper talks about the controversy without examining its substance.

Einarsson, Þorleifur. *Geology of Iceland.* Trans. Georg Douglas. Reykjavík: Mal og menning, 1999. Surely one of the clearest geology textbooks ever written. The author is professor of geology at the University of Iceland.

Etheridge, D. M., et al. "Natural and anthropogenic changes in atmospheric CO_2 over the last 1000 years from air in Antarctic ice and firn." *Journal of Geophysical Research* 101 (1996): 4115–28.

Fagan, Brian. *The Little Ice Age: How Climate Made History 1300–1850.* New York: Basic Books, 2000. Our experience of climate is limited to the span of our lives. The degree to which climate has varied in the past, and even in historical times, is hard for anyone to conceive. This book, by an archaeologist who writes extremely well, makes clear through historical detail how much warmer—and colder—it has been during the last thousand years.

Feynman, Richard. *The Character of Physical Law.* Cambridge, Mass.: MIT Press, 1965. Feynman exemplifies the crispness of thought in physics as compared with the mushy subjectivity of fields such as ecology or climate research.

Finlayson-Pitts, Barbara J., and James N. Pitts, Jr. *Chemistry of the Upper and Lower Atmosphere: Theory, Experiments, and Applications.* New York: Academic Press, 2000. A clear text that can be read by anyone with a good general science background.

Fisher, Andy. *Radical Ecopsychology: Psychology in the Service of Life.* Albany, N.Y.: State University of New York Press, 2002. An astonishing text by a psychotherapist. In my opinion, the greatest problem for all observers of the world is to determine whether their perceptions are genuine and verifiable or whether they are merely the projections of inner feelings. This book says it doesn't matter. The text consists almost entirely of unsubstantiated opinions about human nature and our interaction with the natural world. Anecdotal, egotistical, and wholly tautological, it is a dazzling example of unbridled fantasy. It can stand in for a whole literature of related texts in which feeling-expression masquerades as fact.

Flecker, H., and B. C. Cotton. "Fatal bite from octopus." *Medical Journal of Australia* 2 (1955): 329–31.

Forrester, Jay W. *Principles of Systems.* Waltham, Mass.: Wright-Allen Press, 1971. Some day Forrester will be acknowledged as one of the most important scientists of the twentieth century. He is one of the first, and surely the most influential, researcher to model complex systems on the computer. He did groundbreaking studies of everything from high-tech corporate behavior to urban renewal, and he was the first to get any inkling of how difficult it is to manage complex systems. His work was an early inspiration for the attempts to model the world that ultimately became the Club of Rome's

Limits of Growth. But the Club didn't understand the most fundamental principles behind Forrester's work.

Forsyth, Tim. *Critical Political Ecology: The Politics of Environmental Science*. New York: Routledge, 2003. A careful but often critical examination of environmental orthodoxy by a lecturer in environment and development at the London School of Economics. The text contains many important insights I have not seen elsewhere, including the consequences of the IPCC emphasis on computer models (as opposed to other forms of data) and the question of how many environmental effects are usefully regarded as "global." However, the author adopts much of the postmodernist critique of science, and thus refers to certain "laws" of science, when few scientists would grant them such status.

Freeze, R. Allan. *The Environmental Pendulum: A Quest for the Truth about Toxic Chemicals, Human Health, and Environmental Protection*. Berkeley, Calif.: University of California Press, 2000. A university professor with on-the-ground experience dealing with toxic waste sites has written a cranky and highly informative book detailing his experiences and views. One of the few books by a person who is not only academically qualified but experienced in the field. His opinions are complex and sometimes seemingly contradictory. But that's reality.

Furedi, Frank. *Culture of Fear: Risk-taking and the Morality of Low Expectation*. New York: Continuum, 2002. As Western societies become more affluent and safer, as life expectancy has steadily increased, one might expect the populations to become relaxed and secure. The opposite has happened: Western societies have become panic-stricken and hysterically risk averse. The pattern is evident in everything from environmental issues to the vastly increased supervision of children. This text by a British sociologist discusses why.

Gelbspan, Ross. *The Heat Is On: The Climate Crisis, the Cover-Up, the Prescription*. Cambridge, Mass.: Perseus, 1998. A reporter who has written extensively on environmental matters presents the classic doomsday scenarios well. Penn and Teller characterize him in scatological terms.

Gilovitch, Thomas, Dale Griffin, and Daniel Kahneman, eds. *Heuristics and Biases: The Psychology of Intuitive Judgment*. Cambridge, UK: Cambridge University Press, 2002. Psychologists have created a substantial body of experimental data on human decision making since the 1950s. It has been well replicated and makes essential reading for anyone who wants to understand how people make decisions and how they think about the decisions that others make. The entire volume is compelling (though sometimes disheartening), and articles of particular interest are listed separately.

Glassner, Barry. *The Culture of Fear.* New York: Basic Books, 1999. Debunks fear-mongering with precision and calmness.

Glimcher, Paul W. *Decisions, Uncertainty, and the Brain.* Cambridge, Mass.: MIT Press, 2003.

Glynn, Kevin. *Tabloid Culture.* Durham, N.C.: Duke University Press, 2000.

Goldstein, William M., and Robin M. Hogarth, eds. *Research on Judgment and Decision Making.* Cambridge, UK: Cambridge University Press, 1997.

Gross, Paul R., and Norman Leavitt. *Higher Superstition: The Academic Left and Its Quarrels with Science.* Baltimore: Johns Hopkins University Press, 1994. See chapter 6, "The Gates of Eden" for a discussion of environmentalism in the context of current postmodern academic criticism.

Guyton, Bill. *Glaciers of California.* Berkeley, Calif.: University of California Press, 1998. An elegant gem of a book.

Hadley Center. "Climate Change, Observations and Predictions, Recent Research on Climate Change Science from the Hadley Center," December 2003. Obtainable at *www.metoffice.com.* In sixteen pages the Hadley Center presents the most important arguments relating to climate science and the predictions for future warming from computer models. Beautifully written, and illustrated with graphic sophistication, it easily surpasses other climate science websites and constitutes the best brief introduction for the interested reader.

Hansen, James E., Makiko Sato, Andrew Lacis, Reto Ruedy, Ina Tegen, and Elaine Matthews. "Climate Forcings in the Industrial Era." *Proceedings of the National Academy of Sciences* 95 (October 1998): 12753–58.

Hansen, James E. and Makiko Sato, "Trends of Measured Climate Forcing Agents." *Proceedings of the National Academy of Sciences* 98 (December 2001): 14778–83.

Hayes, Wayland Jackson. "Pesticides and Human Toxicity." *Annals of the New York Academy of Sciences* 160 (1969): 40–54.

Henderson-Sellers, et al. "Tropical cyclones and global climate change: A post-IPCC assessment." *Bulletin of the American Meteorological Society* 79 (1997): 9–38.

Hoffert, Martin, Ken Caldeira, Gregory Benford, David R. Criswell, Christopher Green, Howard Herzog, Atul K. Jain, Haroon S. Kheshgi, Klaus S. Lackner, John S. Lewis, H. Douglas Lightfoot, Wallace Manheimer, John C. Mankins, Michael E. Mauel, L. John Perkins, Michael E. Schlesinger, Tyler Volk, and Tom M. L. Wigley. "Advanced Technology Paths to Global Climate Stability: Energy for a Greenhouse Planet." *Science* 298 (1 November 2001): 981–87.

Horowitz, Daniel. *The Anxieties of Affluence.* Amherst, Mass.: University of Massachusetts Press, 2004.

Houghton, John. *Global Warming, the Complete Briefing.* Cambridge, UK: Cambridge University Press, 1997. Sir John is a leading figure in the IPCC and a world-renowned spokesperson for climate change. He presents a clear statement of the predictions of the global circulation models for future climate. He draws principally from IPCC reports, which this text summarizes and explains. Skip the first chapter, which is scattered and vague, unlike the rest of the book.

Huber, Peter, *Hard Green: Saving the Environment from the Environmentalists, a Conservative Manifesto.* New York: Basic Books, 1999. I read dozens of books on the environment, most quite similar in tone and content. This was the first one that made me sit up and pay serious attention. It's not like the others, to put it mildly. Huber holds an engineering degree from MIT and a law degree from Harvard; he has clerked for Ruth Bader Ginsburg and Sandra Day O'Connor; he is a fellow at the conservative Manhattan Institute. His book criticizes modern environmental thought in both its underlying attitudes and its scientific claims. The text is quick, funny, informed, and relentless. It can be difficult to follow and demands an informed reader. But anyone who clings to the environmental views that evolved in the 1980s and 1990s must answer the arguments of this book.

Inadvertent Climate Modification, Report of the Study of Man's Impact on Climate (SMIC). Cambridge, Mass.: MIT Press, 1971. A fascinating early attempt to model climate and predict human interaction with it.

IPCC. *Aviation and the Global Atmosphere.* Intergovernmental Panel on Climate Change. Cambridge, UK: Cambridge University Press, 1999.

———. *Climate Change 1992: The Supplementary Report to the IPCC Scientific Assessment.* Intergovernmental Panel of Climate Change. Cambridge, UK: Cambridge University Press, 1992.

———. *Climate Change 1995: Economic and Social Dimensions of Climate Change.* Intergovernmental Panel of Climate Change. Cambridge, UK: Cambridge University Press, 1996.

———. *Climate Change 1995: Impacts, Adaptation and Mitigation of Climate Change Scientific/Technical Analysis.* Contribution of Working Group II to the Second Assessment Report of the IPCC. Intergovernmental Panel of Climate Change. Cambridge, UK: Cambridge University Press, 1996.

———. *Climate Change 1995: The Science of Climate Change.* Intergovernmental Panel of Climate Change. Cambridge, UK: Cambridge University Press, 1996.

———. *Climate Change 2001: Impacts, Adaptation, and Vulnerability.* Intergovernmental Panel of Climate Change. Cambridge, UK: Cambridge University Press, 2001.

————. *Climate Change 2001: Synthesis Report.* Intergovernmental Panel of Climate Change. Cambridge, UK: Cambridge University Press, 2001.

————. *Climate Change 2001: The Scientific Basis.* Cambridge, UK: Cambridge University Press, 2001.

————. *Climate Change: The IPCC Response Strategies.* Intergovernmental Panel of Climate Change. Washington, DC: Island Press, 1991.

————. *Emissions Scenarios.* Intergovernmental Panel of Climate Change. Cambridge, UK: Cambridge University Press, 2000.

————. *Land Use, Land-Use Change, and Forestry.* Intergovernmental Panel of Climate Change. Cambridge, UK: Cambridge University Press, 2000.

————. *The Regional Impacts of Climate Change: An Assessment of Vulnerability.* Intergovernmental Panel on Climate Change. Cambridge, UK: Cambridge University Press, 1998.

Jacob, Daniel J. *Introduction to Atmospheric Chemistry.* Princeton, N.J.: Princeton University Press, 1999.

Joravsky, David. *The Lysenko Affair.* Chicago: University of Chicago Press, 1970. A readable account of this depressing episode.

Joughin, I., and S. Tulaczyk. "Positive Mass Balance of the Ross Ice Streams, West Antarctica." *Science* 295 (2002): 476–80.

Kahneman, Daniel, and Amos Tversky, eds. *Choices, Values and Frames.* Cambridge, UK: Cambridge University Press, 2000. The authors are responsible for a revolution in our understanding of the psychology behind human decision-making. The history of the environmental movement is characterized by some very positive decisions made on the basis of inadequate information, and some unfortunate decisions made despite good information that argued against the decision. This book sheds light on how such things happen.

Kalnay, Eugenia, and Ming Cai. "Impact of Urbanization and Land-Use on Climate." *Nature* 423 (29 May 2003): 528–31. "Our estimate of .27 C mean surface warming per century due to land use changes is at least twice as high as previous estimates based on urbanization alone." The authors later report a calculation error, raising their estimate [*Nature* 23 (4 September 2003): 102]. "The corrected estimate of the trend in daily mean temperture due to land use changes is .35 C per century."

Kaser, Georg, Douglas R. Hardy, Thomas Molg, Raymond S. Bradley, and Tharsis M. Hyera. "Modern Glacier Retreat on Kilimanjaro as Evidence of Climate Change: Observations and Facts." *International Journal of Climatology* 24 (2004): 329–39.

Kieffer, H., J. S. Kargel, R. Barry, R. Bindschadler, M. Bishop, D. MacKinnon, A. Ohmura, B. Raup, M. Antoninetti, J. Bamber, M. Braun, I. Brown, D.

Cohen, L. Copland, J. DueHagen, R. V. Engeset, B. Fitzharris, K. Fujita, W. Haeberli, J. O. Hagen, D. Hall, M. Hoelzle, M. Johansson, A. Kaab, M. Koenig, V. Konovalov, M. Maisch, F. Paul, F. Rau, N. Reeh, E. Rignot, A. Rivera, M. Ruyter de Wildt, T. Scambos, J. Schaper, G. Scharfen, J. Shroder, O. Solomina, D. Thompson, K. Van der Veen, T. Wohlleben, and N. Young. "New eyes in the sky measure glaciers and ice sheets." *EOS, Transactions, American Geophysical Union* 81, no. 265 (2000): 270–71.

Kline, Wendy. *Building a Better Race: Gender, Sexuality and Eugenics from the Turn of the Century to the Baby Boom.* Berkeley, Calif.: University of California Press, 2001.

Koshland, Daniel J. "Credibility in Science and the Press." *Science* 254 (1 Nov. 1991): 629. Bad science reporting takes its toll; the former head of the American Association for the Advancement of Science complains about it.

Kraus, Nancy, Trorbjorn Malmfors, and Paul Slovic. "Intuitive Toxicology: Expert and Lay Judgments of Chemical Risks." In *Slovic*, 2000. The extent to which uninformed opinion should be given a place in decision making is highlighted by the question of whether ordinary people have an intuitive sense of what in their environment is harmful—whether they are, in the words of these authors, intuitive toxicologists. As I read the data, they aren't.

Krech, Shepard. *The Ecological Indian: Myth and History.* New York: Norton, 1999. An anthropologist carefully reviews the data indicating that native Americans were not the exemplary ecologists of yore. Also reviews recent changes in ecological science.

Kuhl, Stevan. *The Nazi Connection: Eugenics, American Racism, and German National Socialism.* New York: Oxford University Press, 1994.

Kuran, Timur. *Private Truths, Public Lies: The Social Consequences of Preference Falsification.* Cambridge, Mass.: Harvard University Press, 1995.

Landsea, C., N. Nicholls, W. Gray, and L. Avila. "Downward Trend in the Frequency of Intense Atlantic Hurricanes During the Past Five Decades." *Geophysical Research Letters* 23 (1996): 527–30.

Landsea, Christopher W., and John A. Knaff. "How Much Skill Was There in Forecasting the Very Strong 1997–98 El Niño?" *Bulletin of the American Meteorological Society* 81, no. 9 (September 2000): 2017–19. Authors found the older, simpler models performed best. "The use of more complex, physically realistic dynamical models does not automatically provide more reliable forecasts. . . . [Our findings] may be surprising given the general perception that seasonal El Niño forecasts from dynamical models have been quite successful and may even be considered a solved problem." They discuss in detail that the models did not, in fact, predict well. Yet "others are using the supposed success in dynamical El Niño forecasting to support other agendas . . . one could even have less confidence in anthropogenic global studies because of the lack of skill in predicting El Niño. . . . The bottom line is that the successes in forecasting have been overstated (sometimes drastically) and misapplied in other areas."

Lave, Lester B. "Benefit-Cost Analysis: Do the Benefits Exceed the Costs?" In Robert W. Hahn, ed., *Risks, Costs, and Lives Saved: Getting Better Results from Regulation*. New York: Oxford University Press, 1996. A critical review of problems in cost-benefit analysis by an economist who supports the tool but acknowledges that opponents sometimes have a point.

Lean, Judith, and David Rind. "Climate Forcing by Changing Solar Radiation." *Journal of Climate* 11 (December 1988): 3069–94. How much does the sun affect climate? These authors suggest about half the observed surface warming since 1900 and one-third of the warming since 1970 may be attributed to the sun. But there are uncertainties here. "Present inability to adequately specify climate forcing by changing solar radiation has implications for policy making regarding anthropogenic global change, which must be detected against natural climate variability."

LeBlanc, Steven A., and Katherine E. Register. *Constant Battles*. New York: St. Martin's Press, 2003. The myth of the noble savage and the Edenic past dies hard. LeBlanc is one of the handful of archaeologists who have given close scrutiny to evidence for past warfare and has worked to revise an academic inclination to see a peaceful past. LeBlanc argues that primitive societies fought constantly and brutally.

Levack, Brian P. *The Witch-Hunt in Early Modern Europe*. Second Edition. London: Longman, 1995. In the sixteenth century, the educated elites of Europe believed that certain human beings had made contracts with the devil. They believed that witches gathered to perform horrific rites, and that they flew across the sky in the night. On the basis of these beliefs, these elites tortured countless people, and killed 50,000 to 60,000 of their countrymen, mostly old women. However, they also killed men and children, and sometimes (because it was thought unseemly to burn a child) they imprisoned the children until he or she was old enough to be executed. Most of the extensive literature on witchcraft (including the present volume) does not in my view fully come to grips with the truth of this period. The fact that so many people were executed for a fantasy—and despite the reservations of prominent skeptics—carries a lesson that we must always bear in mind. The consensus of the intelligentsia is not necessarily correct, no matter how many believe it, or for how many years the belief is held. It may still be wrong. In fact, it may be *very* wrong. And we must never forget it. Because it will happen again. And indeed it has.

Lilla, Mark. *The Reckless Mind: Intellectuals in Politics.* New York: New York Review of Books, 2001. This razor-sharp text focuses on twentieth-century philosophers but serves as a reminder of the intellectual's temptation "to succumb to the allure of an idea, to allow passion to blind us to its tyrannical potential."

Lindzen, Richard S. "Do Deep Ocean Temperature Records Verify Models?" *Geophysical Research Letters* 29, no. 0 (2002): 10.1029/2001GL014360. Changes in ocean temperature cannot be taken as a verification of GCMs, computer climate models.

———. "The Press Gets It Wrong: Our Report Doesn't Support the Kyoto Treaty." *Wall Street Journal*, 11 June 2001. This brief essay by a distinguished MIT professor summarizes one example of the way the media misinterprets scientific reports on climate. In this case, the National Academy of Sciences report on climate change, widely claimed to say what it did not. Lindzen was one of eleven authors of the report. http://opinionjournal.com/editorial/feature.html?id=95000606

Lindzen, R. S., and K. Emanuel. "The Greenhouse Effect." In *Encyclopedia of Global Change, Environmental Change and Human Society. Volume 1.* Andrew S. Goudie, ed., New York: Oxford University Press, 2002, pp. 562–66. What exactly is the greenhouse effect everybody talks about but nobody ever explains in any detail? A brief, clear summary.

Liu, J., J. A. Curry, and D. G. Martinson. "Interpretation of Recent Antarctic Sea Ice Variability." *Geophysical Research Letters* 31 (2004): 10.1029/2003 GL018732.

Lomborg, Bjorn. *The Skeptical Environmentalist.* Cambridge, UK: Cambridge University Press, 2002. By now, many people know the story behind this text: The author, a Danish statistician and Greenpeace activist, set out to disprove the views of the late Julian Simon, an economist who claimed that dire environmental fears were wrong and that the world was actually improving. To Lomborg's surprise, he found that Simon was mostly right. Lomborg's text is crisp, calm, clean, devastating to established dogma. Since publication, the author has been subjected to relentless ad hominem attacks, which can only mean his conclusions are unobjectionable in any serious scientific way. Throughout the long controversy, Lomborg has behaved in exemplary fashion. Sadly, his critics have not. Special mention must go to the *Scientific American*, which was particularly reprehensible. All in all, the treatment accorded Lomborg can be viewed as a confirmation of the postmodern critique of science as just another power struggle. A sad episode for science.

Lovins, Amory B. *Soft Energy Paths: Toward a Durable Peace.* New York: Harper and Row, 1977. Perhaps the most important advocate for alternative energy wrote this anti-nuclear energy text in the 1970s for Friends of the Earth, elaborating on an influential essay he wrote for *Foreign Affairs* the year before. The resulting text can be seen as a major link in the chain of events and thinking that set the US on a different energy path from the nations of Europe. Lovins is trained as a physicist and is a MacArthur Fellow.

McKendry, Ian G. "Applied Climatology." *Progress in Physical Geography* 27, no. 4 (2003): 597–606. "Recent studies suggest that attempts to remove the 'urban bias' from long-term climate records (and hence identify the magnitude of the enhanced greenhouse effect) may be overly simplistic. This will likely continue to be a contentious issue. . . ."

Manes, Christopher. *Green Rage: Radical Environmentalism and the Unmaking of Civilization.* Boston: Little Brown, 1990. Not to be missed.

Man's Impact on the Global Environment, Assessments and Recommendations for Action, Report of the Study of Critical Environmental Problems (SCEP). Cambridge, Mass.: MIT Press, 1970. The text predicts carbon dioxide levels of 370 ppm in the year 2000 and a surface-temperature increase of .5 C as a result. The actual figures were 360 ppm and .3 C—far more accurate than predictions made fifteen years later, using lots more computer power.

Marlar, Richard A., et al. "Biochemical evidence of cannibalism at a prehistoric Puebloan site in southwestern Colorado. *Nature* 407, 74078, 7 Sept. 2000.

Martin, Paul S. "Prehistoric Overkill: The Global Model." In *Quaternary Extinctions: A Prehistoric Revolution.* Paul S. Martin and Richard G. Klein, eds. Tucson, Ariz.: University of Arizona Press, 1984, 354–403.

Mason, Betsy. "African Ice Under Wraps." *Nature online publication,* 24 November 2003.

Matthews, Robert A. J. "Facts versus factions: The use and abuse of subjectivity in scientific research." In Morris, *Rethinking Risk,* pp. 247–82. A physicist argues "the failure of the scientific community to take decisive action over the flaws in standard statistical methods, and the resulting waste of resources spent on futile attempts to replicate claims based on them, constitute a major scientific scandal." The book also contains an impressive list of major scientific developments held back by the subjective prejudice of scientists. So much for the reliability of the "consensus" scientists.

Meadows, Donella H., Dennis L. Meadows, Jorgen Randers, and William W. Behrens III. *The Limits to Growth: A Report for the Club of Rome's Project on the Predicament of Mankind.* New York: New American Library, 1972. It is a shame this book is out of print, because it was hugely influential in its day, and it set the tone ("the predicament of mankind") for much that followed. To read it now is to be astonished at how primitive were the techniques for assessing the state of the world, and how incautious the predictions of future trends. Many of the graphs have no axes, and are therefore just pictures of technical-looking curves. In retrospect, the text is notable not so much for its errors of prediction as for its consistent tone of urgent overstatement bordering on hysteria. The conclusion: "Concerted international measures and joint long-term planning will be necessary on a scale and scope without precedent. Such an effort calls for joint endeavor by all peoples, whatever their culture, economic system, or level of development. . . . This supreme effort is . . . founded on a basic change of values and goals at individual, national and world levels." And so forth.

Medvedev, Zhores A. *The Rise and Fall of T. D. Lysenko.* New York: Columbia University Press, 1969. Extremely difficult to read.

Michaels, Patrick J., and Robert C. Balling, Jr. *The Satanic Gases: Clearing the Air about Global Warming.* Washington, DC: Cato, 2000. These skeptical authors have a sense of humor and a clear style. Use of graphs is unusually good. The Cato Institute is a pro–free market organization with libertarian overtones.

Morris, Julian, ed. *Rethinking Risk and the Precautionary Principle.* Oxford, UK: Butterworth/Heinemann, 2000. A broad-ranging critique that discusses, for example, how precautionary thinking has harmed children's development.

Nye, David E. *Consuming Power,* Cambridge, Mass.: MIT Press, 1998. America consumes more power per capita than any other country, and Nye is the most knowledgeable scholar about the history of American technology. He draws markedly different conclusions from those less informed. This text is scathing about determinist views of technology. It has clear implications for the validity of IPCC "scenarios."

Oleary, Rosemary, Robert F. Durant, Daniel J. Fiorino, and Paul S. Weiland. *Managing for the Environment: Understanding the Legal, Organizational, and Policy Challenges.* New York: Wiley and Sons, 1999. A much-needed compendium that sometimes covers too much in too little detail.

Ordover, Nancy. *American Eugenics: Race, Queer Anatomy, and the Science of Nationalism.* Minneapolis, Minn.: University of Minnesota Press, 2003. Fascinating in content, confusing in structure, difficult to read, but uncompromising. The author insists on the culpability of both the left and right in the eugenics movement, both in the past and in the present day.

Pagels, Heinz R. *The Dreams of Reason: Computers and the Rise of the Sciences of Complexity.* New York: Simon and Schuster, 1988. The study of complexity represents a true revolution in science, albeit a rather old revolution. This delightful book is sixteen years old, written when the revolution was exciting and new. One would think sixteen years would be enough time for the understanding of complexity and nonlinear dynamics to revise the thinking of environmental activists. But evidently not.

Park, Robert. *Voodoo Science: The Road from Foolishness to Fraud*. New York: Oxford University Press, 2000. The author is a professor of physics and a director of the American Physical Society. His book is especially good on the "Currents of Death" EMF/powerline/cancer controversy, in which he was involved (as a skeptic).

Parkinson, C. L. "Trends in the Length of the Southern Ocean Sea-Ice Season, 1979–99." *Annals of Glaciology* 34 (2002): 435–40.

Parsons, Michael L. *Global Warming: The Truth Behind the Myth*, New York: Plenum, 1995. A skeptical review of data by a professor of health sciences (and therefore not a climate scientist). Outsider's analysis of data.

Pearce, Fred, "Africans go back to the land as plants reclaim the desert." *New Scientist* 175 (21 September 2002): 4–5.

Penn and Teller. *Bullshit!* Showtime series. Brisk, amusing attacks on conventional wisdom and sacred cows. The episode in which a young woman signs up environmentalists to ban "dihydrogen monoxide" (better known as water) is especially funny. "Dihydrogen monoxide," she explains, "is found in lakes and rivers, it remains on fruits and vegetables after they're washed, it makes you sweat . . ." And the people sign up. Another episode on recycling is the clearest brief explanation of what is right and wrong about this practice.

Pepper, David. *Modern Environmentalism: An Introduction*. London: Routledge, 1996. A detailed account of the multiple strands of environmental philosophy by a sympathetic observer. Along with the quite different work of Douglas and Wildavsky, this book considers why mutually incompatible views of nature are held by different groups, and why compromise among them is so unlikely. It also makes clear the extent to which environmental views encompass beliefs about how human society should be structured. The author is a professor of geography and writes well.

Petit, J. R., J. Jouzel, D. Raynaud, N. I. Barkov, J.-M. Barnola, I. Basile, M. Bender, J. Chappellaz, M. Davis, G. Delaygue, M. Delmotte, V. M. Kotlyakov, M. Legrand, V. Y. Lipenkov, C. Lorius, L. Pepin, C. Ritz, E. Saltzman, and M. Stievenard. "1999. Climate and atmospheric history of the past 420,000 years from the Vostok ice core, Antarctica." *Nature* 399: 429–36.

Pielou, E. C. *After the Ice Age: The Return of Life to Glaciated North America*. Chicago: University of Chicago Press, 1991. A wonderful book, a model of its kind. Explains how life returned as the glaciers receded twenty thousand years ago, and how scientists analyze the data to arrive at their conclusions. Along the way, an excellent reminder of how dramatically our planet has changed in the geologically recent past.

Ponte, Lowell. *The Cooling*. Englewood, N.J.: Prentice-Hall, 1972. The most highly praised of the books from the 1970s that warned of an impending ice age. (The cover asks: "Has the next ice age already begun? Can we survive it?") Contains a chapter on how we might modify the global climate to prevent excessive cooling. A typical quote: "We simply cannot afford to gamble against this possibility by ignoring it. We cannot risk inaction. Those scientists who say we are entering a period of climatic instability [i.e., unpredictability] are acting irresponsibly. The indications that our climate can soon change for the worse are too strong to be reasonably ignored" (p. 237).

Pritchard, James A. *Preserving Yellowstone's Natural Conditions: Science and the Perception of Nature*. Lincoln, Neb.: University of Nebraska Press, 1999. Balance of evidence that elk have changed habitat. Also the nonequilibrium paradigm.

Pronin, Emily, Carolyn Puccio, and Lee Rosh. "Understanding Misunderstanding: Social Psychological Perspectives." In Gilovitch, et al., pp. 636–65. A cool assessment of human disagreement.

Rasool, S. I., and S. H. Schneider. "Atmospheric Carbon Dioxide and Aerosols: Effects of Large Increases on Global Climate." *Science* (11 July 1971): 138–41. An example of the research in the 1970s that suggested that human influence on climate was leading to cooling, not warming. The authors state that increasing carbon dioxide in the atmosphere will not raise temperature as much as increasing aerosols will reduce it. "An increase by only a factor of 4 in global aerosol background concentration may be sufficient to reduce the surface temperature by as much as 3.5 K . . . believed to be sufficient to trigger an ice age."

Raub, W. D., A. Post, C. S. Brown, and M. F. Meier. "Perennial ice masses of the Sierra Nevada, California." *Proceedings of the International Assoc. of Hydrological Science*, no. 126 (1980): 33–34. Cited in Guyton, 1998.

Reference Manual on Scientific Evidence, Federal Judicial Center. Washington, DC: US Government Printing Office, 1994. After years of abuse, the Federal Courts in the US established detailed guidelines for the admissibility of various kinds of scientific testimony and scientific evidence. This volume runs 634 pages.

Reiter, Paul, Christopher J. Tomas, Peter M. Atkinson, Simon I. Hay, Sarah E. Randolph, David J. Rogers, G. Dennis Shanks, Robert W. Snow, and Andrew Spielman. "Global Warming and Malaria: A Call for Accuracy." *Lancet* 4, no. 1 (June 2004).

Rice, Glen E., and Steven A. LeBlanc, eds. *Deadly Landscape*. Salt Lake City, Utah: University of Utah Press, 2001. More evidence for a strife-filled human past.

Roberts, Leslie R. "Counting on Science at EPA." *Science* 249 (10 August 1990): 616–18. An important brief report on how the EPA ranks risks. Essentially it does what the public wants, not what the EPA experts advise. This is sometimes but not always a bad thing.

Roszak, Theodore. *The Voice of the Earth*. New York: Simon and Schuster, 1992. Roszak is often at the leading edge of emerging social movements, and here he gives an early insight into a blend of ecology and psychology that has since become widespread, even though it is essentially pure feeling without objective foundation. Nevertheless, ecopsychology has become a guiding light in the minds of many people, particularly those without scientific training. My own view is that the movement projects the dissatisfactions of contemporary society onto a natural world that is so seldom experienced that it serves as a perfect projection screen. One must also recall the blunt view of Richard Feynman: "We have learned from much experience that all philosophical intuitions about what nature is going to do fail."

Russell, Jeffrey B. *A History of Witchcraft, Sorcerers, Heretics and Pagans*. London: Thames and Hudson Ltd., 1980. Lest we forget.

Salzman, Jason. *Making the News: A Guide for Activists and Non-Profits*. Boulder, Col.: Westview Press, 2003.

Santer, B. D., K. E. Taylor, T. M. L. Wigley, T. C. Johns, P. D. Jones, D. J. Karoly, J. F. B. Mitchell, A. H. Oort, J. E. Penner, V. Ramaswamy, M. D. Schwarzkopf, R. J. Stouffer, and S. Tett. "A Search for Human Influences on the Thermal Structure of the Atmosphere." *Nature* 382 (4 July 1996): 39–46. "It is likely that [temperature change in the free atmosphere] is partially due to human activities, though many uncertainties remain, particularly relating to estimates of natural variability." One year after the 1995 IPCC statement that a human effect on climate had been discerned, this article by several IPCC scientists shows considerably more caution about such a claim.

Schullery, Paul. *Searching for Yellowstone: Ecology and Wonder in the Last Wilderness*. New York: Houghton Mifflin, 1997. The author was for many years an employee of the Forest Service and takes a more benign approach to events at Yellowstone than others do.

Scott, James C. *Seeing Like a State: How Certain Schemes to Improve the Human Condition Have Failed*. New Haven, Conn.: Yale University Press, 1998. An extraordinary and original book that reminds us how seldom academic thought is genuinely fresh.

Shrader-Frechette, K. S. *Risk and Rationality: Philosophical Foundations for Populist Reforms*. Berkeley, Calif.: University of California Press, 1991.

Singer, S. Fred. *Hot Talk, Cold Science: Global Warming's Unfinished Debate*. Oakland, Calif.: Independent Institute, 1998. Singer is among the most visible of global warming skeptics. A retired professor of environmental science who has held a number of government posts, including Director of Weather Satellite Service and Director for the Center for Atmospheric and Space Sciences, he is a far more qualified advocate for his views than his critics admit. They usually attempt to portray him as a sort of eccentric nutcase. This book is only seventy-two pages long, and the reader may judge for himself.

Slovic, Paul, ed. *The Perception of Risk.* London: Earthscan, 2000. Slovic has been influential in emphasizing that the concept of "risk" entails not only expert opinion but also the feelings and fears of the population at large. In a democracy, such popular opinions must be addressed in policy making. I take a tougher stance. I believe ignorance is best addressed by education, not by unneeded or wasteful regulation. Unfortunately, the evidence is that we spend far too much soothing false or minor fears.

Stott, Philip, and Sian Sullivan, eds. *Political Ecology: Science, Myth and Power.* London: Arnold, 2000. Focused on Africa. Stott is now retired, witty, and runs an amusing skeptical blog.

Streutker, D. R. "Satellite-measured growth of the urban heat island of Houston, Texas." *Remote Sensing of Environment* 85 (2003): 282–89. "Between 1987 and 1999, the mean nighttime surface temperature heat island of Houston increased 0.82 ± 0.10 °C."

Sunstein, Cass R. *Risk and Reason: Safety, Law, and the Environment.* New York: Cambridge University Press, 2002. A law professor examines major environmental issues from the standpoint of cost-benefit analysis and concludes that new mechanisms for assessing regulations are needed if we are to break free of the current pattern of "hysteria and neglect"—in which we aggressively regulate minor risks while ignoring more significant ones. The detailed chapter on arsenic levels is particularly revealing for anyone wishing to understand the difficulties that rational regulation faces in a highly politicized world.

Sutherland, S. K., and W. R. Lane. "Toxins and mode of envenomation of the common ringed or blue-banded octopus." *Medical Journal Australia* 1 (1969): 893–98.

Tengs, Tammo O., Miriam E. Adams, Joseph S. Plitskin, Dana Gelb Safran, Joanna E. Siegel, Milton C. Weinstein, and John D. Graham. "Five hundred life-saving interventions and their cost effectiveness." *Risk Analysis* 15, no. 3 (1995): 369–90. The Harvard School of Public Health is dismissed in some quarters as a right-wing institution. But this influential and disturbing study by the Harvard Center for Risk Analysis of the costs of regulation has not been disputed. It implies that a great deal of regulatory effort is wasted, and wasteful.

Thomas, Keith. *Man and the Natural World: Changing Attitudes in England 1500–1800.* New York: Oxford University Press, 1983. Are environmental attitudes a matter of fashion? Thomas's delightful book charts changing perceptions of nature from a locus of danger, to a subject of worshipful appreciation, and finally to the beloved wilderness of elite aesthetes.

Thompson, D. W. J., and S. Solomon. "Interpretation of Recent Southern Hemisphere Climate Change." *Science* 296 (2002): 895–99.

Tommasi, Mariano, and Kathryn Lerulli, eds. *The New Economics of Human Behavior.* Cambridge, UK: Cambridge University Press, 1995.

US Congress. *Final Report of the Advisory Committee on Weather Control.* United States Congress. Hawaii: University Press of the Pacific, 2003.

Victor, David G. "Climate of Doubt: The imminent collapse of the Kyoto Protocol on global warming may be a blessing in disguise. The treaty's architecture is fatally flawed." *The Sciences* (Spring 2001): 18–23. Victor is a fellow at the Council on Foreign Relations and an advocate of carbon emission controls who argues that "prudence demands action to check the rise in greenhouse gases, but the Kyoto Protocol is a road to nowhere."

Viscusi, Kip. *Fatal Tradeoffs: Public and Private Responsibilities for Risk.* New York: Oxford University Press, 1992. Start at section III.

———. *Rational Risk Policy.* Oxford: Clarendon, 1998. The author is a professor of law and economics at Harvard.

Vyas, N. K., M. K. Dash, S. M. Bhandari, N. Khare, A. Mitra, and P. C. Pandey. "On the Secular Trends in Sea Ice Extent over the Antarctic Region Based on OCEANSAT-1 MSMR Observations." *International Journal of Remote Sensing* 24 (2003): 2277–87.

Wallack, Lawrence, Katie Woodruff, Lori Dorfman, and Iris Diaz. *News for a Change: An Advocate's Guide to Working with the Media.* London: Sage Publications, 1999.

Weart, Spencer R. *The Discovery of Global Warming.* Cambridge, Mass.: Harvard University Press, 2003.

West, Darrell M. *The Rise and Fall of the Media Establishment.* New York: Bedford/St. Martin's Press, 2001.

White, Geoffrey M. *Identity Through History: Living Stories in a Solomon Islands Society.* Cambridge, UK: Cambridge University Press, 1991.

Wigley, Tom. "Global Warming Protocol: CO_2, CH_4 and climate implications." *Geophysical Research Letters* 25, no. 13 (1 July 1998): 2285–88.

Wildavsky, Aaron. *But Is It True? A Citizen's Guide to Environmental Health and Safety Issues.* Cambridge: Harvard University Press, 1995. A professor of political science and public policy at Berkeley turned his students loose to research both the history and the scientific status of major environmental issues: DDT, Alar, Love Canal, asbestos, the ozone hole, global warming, acid rain. The book is an excellent resource for a more complete discussion of these issues than is usually provided. For example, the author devotes twenty-five pages to the history of the DDT ban, twenty pages to Alar, and so on. Wildavsky concludes that nearly all environmental claims have been either untrue or wildly overstated.

———. *Searching for Safety.* New Brunswick, N.J.: Transaction, 1988. If we want a safe society and a safe life, how should we go about getting it? A good-humored exploration of strategies for safety in industrial society. Drawing on data from a wide range of disciplines, Wildavsky argues that resilience is a better strategy than anticipation, and that anticipatory strategies (such as the precautionary principle) favor the social elite over the mass of poorer people.

Winsor, P. "Arctic Sea Ice Thickness Remained Constant During the 1990s." *Geophysical Research Letters* 28, no. 6 (March 2001): 1039–41.

MICHAEL CRICHTON was born in Chicago in 1942. His novels include *The Andromeda Strain, Jurassic Park, Timeline*, and *Prey*. He is also the creator of the television series *ER*.